Tsamma Season

Also by Rosemund J Handler

Madlands
Katy's Kid

TSAMMA SEASON

Rosemund J Handler

PENGUIN BOOKS

PENGUIN BOOKS

Published by the Penguin Group
Penguin Books (South Africa) (Pty) Ltd, 24 Sturdee Avenue, Rosebank, Johannesburg 2196, South Africa
Penguin Group (USA) Inc, 375 Hudson Street, New York, New York 10014, USA
Penguin Group (Canada), 90 Eglinton Avenue East, Suite 700, Toronto, Ontario, Canada M4P 2Y3 (a division of Pearson Penguin Canada Inc)
Penguin Books Ltd, 80 Strand, London WC2R 0RL, England
Penguin Ireland, 25 St Stephen's Green, Dublin 2, Ireland (a division of Penguin Books Ltd)
Penguin Group (Australia), 250 Camberwell Road, Camberwell, Victoria 3124, Australia (a division of Pearson Australia Group Pty Ltd)
Penguin Books India Pvt Ltd, 11 Community Centre, Panchsheel Park, New Delhi – 110 017, India
Penguin Group (NZ), 67 Apollo Drive, Mairangi Bay, Auckland 1310, New Zealand (a division of Pearson New Zealand Ltd)

Penguin Books (South Africa) (Pty) Ltd, Registered Offices:
24 Sturdee Avenue, Rosebank, Johannesburg 2196, South Africa

www.penguinbooks.co.za

First published by Penguin Books (South Africa) (Pty) Ltd 2009

Copyright © Rosemund J Handler 2009

ISBN 978 0 143 02584 9

Typeset by CJH Design in 10.5/14 pt Charter
Cover design: luckyfish
Printed and bound by Interpak Books, Pietermaritzburg

For Noa and Saul

Tsamma melon

Citrullus lanatus grows widely in Africa and Asia. A wild relative of the watermelon, in Southern Africa it grows in the Kalahari and in parts of the Karoo, where it is known as Tsamma. These wild melons were – and in remote places still are – an important source of water and food to indigenous inhabitants, particularly during times of drought. They are also eaten by animals.

I will bring you to a land
deep and wide
where red dunes surge to the sand
like the fast-rising tide

November, 1921

THERE IS A HUNGER THROUGHOUT England for stories, a hunger that has everything and nothing to do with the War that has exacted such a horrifying toll from the lives of millions, and that lingers still, a dark shadow that bedevils our every thought. Three years and more have passed since loved ones were lost, and news of the fate of large numbers of the missing has not yet reached their families. But some of the darkness has lifted at last, and people yearn to believe in the existence of a different world from the dreadful one that took possession of their lives for four long years. Among these bereaved and despairing families are those eager to read of remote lands and faraway people, where the magical is commonplace, and evil a mere strand in the intricate weave of the imagination.

Thus it is that Tsamma Season, the story of my family and our unique home, is privileged to feed this famine of the soul. The Kalahari Desert has captivated the collective fancy, and it is fitting that I have been invited to share something of its enigmatic character in a room lined with towering shelves of books at Cambridge University, among luminaries who once spurned my presence at this stronghold of tradition and erudition.

It is autumn and already very cold, but the air in the room is thick, heated with the breath of many people. As I make my way through the murmurous throng to the podium, a bobbing of heads accompanies me, each face succeeded by the next. Though I am the target of all eyes, from the moment I enter the room it is as if I myself am blind. Unseeing of many, I seek only a single face. A smooth blond head rivets my winnowing glance for an instant, the familiar contours soaring through me, only to cool in bleak disappointment.

Strangers are present to welcome me. He is not.

I reach the podium, turn and regard the room. A hush falls, so profound that my rapid breathing is loud in my ears. Rows of expectant faces gaze up at me. I search one more time. But my longing finds no expression, for it has neither right nor reason on its side. Despite the still-swelling audience eager to listen to the tale of my other great love, despite the gleaming piles of books, the room feels like my heart.

Empty.

Cape Town to Upington, 1914

SITTING IN TOTAL DARKNESS, I wonder if I am too late. The journey thus far, apart from the occasional lurch and pitch and a drawn-out hissing, has been surprisingly smooth and silent, unlike my clamorous thoughts. I have tried to sleep – I am fortunate in being alone in the carriage – but I cannot. Instead, other journeys rise up before me, turning over and over in my mind like the wheels of the train, winding on through the blackness, the festering of disquiet. Outside my window irregular sparks of light flare bravely: farms or villages, infinitesimal in the thick wilderness of night.

Looking back, I see it at last: at the heart of those beginnings the ending was coiled, waiting to strike when the time was right. Now, in the deep cushioned shadows of the railway carriage, alone for the first time in many years, it seems to me that the beginnings, the stories themselves, have shape-shifted so often in the blur of years that they are almost unfamiliar. The crammed freight of my childhood has concertinaed into a mush, unreadable, elusive; as blank as if that childhood, so painstakingly written, had somehow unwritten itself. Events that at the time bore the hallmark of finality – the ending of a chapter, the frame around a block of time – are in retrospect a staging post on another kind of journey whose destination has reinvented itself, become wayward and obscure.

My gaze meets that of the incorporeal image in the window. It draws me in, merging with the impenetrable darkness outside. Memories, limned by the dust of nostalgia, drift by, but they are unreliable, the bloodless unfinished business of a dream. Clarity is embedded in a few vivid, fleeting shards: the vibrato in a laugh; a mole punctuating a curl of lip; a body odour, yeasty, warm, its powdery presence making my head spin.

Neither parcelled up nor apportioned, the past travels untidily with me and inside me through the sooty night, bound up with what lies ahead. I am powerless to intervene; to avert outcomes. To plaster up the ripped poultice of history that approaches closer with every hiss of steam that scalds the cold black skies.

Danie, who had telegraphed me his understated urgency, is waiting for me at the station in Kimberley. I have not seen him for nearly fourteen years. He is much changed, his expression set, his brush of blond hair neatly trimmed and pasted down. I see in his startled blue eyes (the same eyes, the same spark of humour in their depths, surely?) that other than my ineluctably red, red hair the woman I have become is unrecognisable to him; an entirely different being from the girl who left with distraught promises and tears.

With a brief shake of his head in the direction of the porter, he hefts my luggage, and I follow him to a car whose sleek creamy torso graces the stony station grounds like royalty among peasants.

We will be driving to Upington alone, he says. I hope that is acceptable to you. Father wanted to come along, but he has been ill and it would have been unwise for him to travel such a long distance.

I notice at once that the heavy Afrikaans accent is almost absent from his clipped baritone. Is it the university in Cape Town that has groomed his voice and speech into those of a stranger; or is it the exigencies, the gratuitous refinements, of adulthood?

He holds open the door of the Ford. I climb onto the soft leather seat.

For brief moments he is out of my field of vision. I glance ahead, through the windscreen. Without warning, the light cannons into my eyeballs. The static of the distant desert crackles through me, a fiery thrumming in my chest, half hope, half fear.

I inhale the arid air of childhood, and pray I am not too late.

PART ONE

PART ONE

Beginnings

THESE RECORDINGS, PENNED by me between the ages of twelve to sixteen years, and amended only slightly in later readings, would not have begun if my mother had not been their catalyst. By the time I was sixteen, lonely and perplexed by the events that had overtaken us, my writing had become a task that occupied my mind and prevented too much brooding.

I had learned to write at the age of four, and soon got into the habit of writing down what interested me on whatever bits of paper I could find. Over the years, I accumulated a neat pile of notes about events in my day that had pleased or inspired me, printed in an orderly script mother described as preternaturally precise in one so young. When I grew older, eager to provide stimulation for my enquiring mind, she suggested I write a journal about our lives in the uncommon setting of our home, drawing on my notes, and adding to them when I chose.

At twelve years of age, observant, vigorous, underoccupied, I was sorely in need of a challenge. It took a while for me to pick up my quill, in part owing to laziness, in part to doubts about the project. But within a fortnight of the discussions with my parents, encouraged by their assurances that such a journal would be well sown in the fertile ground of their pioneering days, and that they would assist by providing details of choices they had made separately and together before I was born, I sat myself under a tree and began writing.

But that was before there was an after. Mother had no inkling, back then, that such a journal, its genesis a hybrid of love and sound teaching, might one day draw the public eye, and be regarded by some as a record of indictment; even of shame.

Much thought on this matter over many months has convinced me, dear reader, that the people in these writings will intrigue you, will provoke your compassion and even, perhaps, make you smile. I beg only that you withhold judgement: that you mark instead the pioneering spirit of my family, and the devotion of the parties who honoured and supported that spirit. That you note, too, that this devotion was greatly valued, and returned, for the most part, in full measure.

This story belongs to them; it is all that remains to speak for them. Thus it is their creation as much as it is my own.

Beginnings, sublime with possibility, may be beautiful; they may also be cunning, curious or challenging. My beginning is none of these, simply because it is my name: as common as 'once upon a time'. But the true motive for confiding my name – not one, but three – before all else, is to get the matter over with. I did not know at the time of writing whether any person outside my own family would ever read my journal and discover the obvious anomaly. Regardless, the case cannot be stated other than baldly: I am called Emma Jeremiah Dorothea Johannsen. You will have noted, doubtless with some confusion, the second name. Jeremiah is a bruise of protest that will never quite heal, but you need not be confused by it: in every way, in every cell of my being, I am a girl. Nothing about me, not a hair of the bristling mane on my head, could possibly be construed as being better suited to the male sex.

The names were decided with finality only a good while after my birth in 1887. The reasons for this delay will later become clear, though the name Jeremiah was always a certainty, because father believed, with some justification, that the expected child, whether girl or boy, was likely the only one he would ever have and must therefore bear the name of Jeremiah Johannsen, his father and my grandfather, who was a seaman, lost at sea when he was thirty-nine years old.

Mother disagreed with father; she felt that a boy's name, grandfather or not, would be a burden to a girl, perhaps all her life. But father was adamant, and in the end she surrendered to his wishes. When I was old enough to remonstrate with her, she sighed and informed me that Jeremiah as a *middle name instead of a first* was the true compromise!

The name Dorothea originates from my maternal grandmother, of whom I knew very little; according to mother she lived a blameless life, yet suffered from a succession of mysterious afflictions that plagued her for a large part of it. The name I consider my very own – Emma – was chosen by mother and belonged to no member of either family but was much admired by her, as it was the title of a book written by one of her favourite authors, Jane Austen.

As soon as I could write, I made a frequent practice of writing my name out in full up to thirty times, and thirty times I would cross out the name Jeremiah, and fifteen times both Jeremiah and Dorothea; then I would cross it all out and write *Emma Johannsen* in a decorative script, fervently wishing I were the proud owner of those two names alone. I complained to mother that I was probably the only girl who had ever been burdened with the name of a boy, and admitted that I despised my third name, Dorothea, as well. Being Jeremiah Dorothea made me ever vulnerable to other people's jokes. When I grew especially despondent on the subject, mother would remind me of a simple fact: How many girls do you know, Em, she would ask patiently (two: Poppie and Imp), and since we are very far afield of public opinion, what does it matter?

She was right; she usually was. The few people around me had neither the time nor the inclination to indulge in mockery, but this did not eliminate occasional savage bouts of profound self-dislike, which would spill over onto other parts of me, such as my hair.

Mother's rationality about most things, her dependable soundness and good sense, were a source of great comfort, and the part of her character that I believed would never change. A schoolteacher by training, she naturally viewed education as paramount, and taught me everything she knew of an academic nature. I think she considered me well informed for a twelve-year-old girl living in a world as remote from a city or its society as can be conceived of, and she saw in these circumstances an opportunity not to be wasted. The schoolteacher in her viewed the journal as an excellent educational project, and the mother in her was hopeful that it would keep me occupied for an extended period of time.

Mother herself loved to read and write, and greatly treasured her small hoard of books and papers, and Grandmother Dorothea's leather-bound copy of the Bible. She valued privacy and her own company highly, and I sensed many times that she was weary of my questions. But as I grew older I found that rather than acquiring complacency about my precocious learning, there were many things of which I felt myself to be ignorant. Foremost among my concerns was that the company of children other than Poppie or Imp – both of whom you will soon encounter in these pages – was unknown to me; I therefore had no conception of how advanced the learning was of other students of my age, no means of comparison and no feel for what it would be like to acquire my education in a classroom with many others, as had been mother's experience.

I had read all the books we owned, some without mother's approval. She advised me that one of the advantages of a journal was that I could confide my innermost secrets with impunity, since journals are private, written only for the benefit of the writer. After giving the matter some thought, I told her that I did not think I could write to myself, as my innermost secrets were few and probably quite dull. In the end we agreed that I would start by describing some of the more compelling events and characters that had influenced our lives, using a similar format to the books I had read.

Mother promised she would read my writings only when and if I gave her permission to do so, but confessed to curiosity, suggesting that since my journal was not to be my confidante, privacy was less of an issue, and she would be honoured if I would consider sharing with her a limited selection of my choice.

I informed her that such sharing would not take place in the foreseeable future; perhaps not until I became an adult, and she looked askance at the prospect of the long wait, raising her dark eyebrows in hopes of a reprieve.

I did not give her one. I did not then dream that the wait would not end.

Thus we shook hands on it. Mother produced a thick stack of the paper that she made herself, from dried-out dung, and presented it to me. She had the knack of creating all kinds of useful things from very little, and father, of course, was accomplished in other areas; their combined skills contributed in no small way to our survival in an environment

12

which, you will note, tolerated no half measures.

Before I go any further, it must be said that much of what you will read, especially in the earlier chapters, originates from the mouths of my parents; to some, the use of language may seem forward for a young girl. If so, permit me to enlighten you: mother had no compunction at any time during the years of my growing up in making lavish use of words and sentences that were diverse, complicated and adult in nature. By some progenitive process of osmosis, her language became mine. I enjoyed no lengthy childhood of simple sentences, but was soon steeped in the complexities, springing from a brief infancy to an adulthood of language, with almost no bridge in between.

The first meeting between Alf Johannsen and Deirdre Bolton, my parents, took place on board a ship coming out to South Africa from England. Each, armed with disparate purposes, was bound for very different destinations.

Father, half Swedish on his father's side and half German on his mother's, had spent much of his life, like his father before him, at sea. His second trip to Africa took place less than six months after he had last departed its shores; on this voyage, he was not a sailor, but a passenger, his head full of serious and carefully laid plans.

His first visit to the southern part of Africa was in 1884, after the Germans had occupied South West Africa and renamed it German West Africa. His ship docked at Walvis Bay, where he and his fellow sailors laboured, unloading and loading goods. After a fortnight, in the company of two friends weary of work and of the sea, he took some time off to explore the country. The three men hired a wagon and a team of oxen, purchased substantial supplies, and began a journey across scores of miles of countryside.

Father, who would have described himself as a seasoned seadog back then, was surprised to find he was strangely drawn to the immense skies, the aloof, arid spaces and the solitary lives he encountered. Gaunt goatherds, dwarfed by the ancient sandscape, swayed like reeds in the distance, their animals languishing about them; farmers, wizened and workworn, eked out a living farming sheep. A blister on the unbroken, heat-struck horizon became an isolated farm shack, a clump of bushes, a haphazard pile of molten rock. Every tensile creature whose head poked from a pit in the scrubby earth knew its place in its inhospitable home, possessed the secret knowledge of its own survival.

In the austere setting of this vast land, father's mind was stimulated to make pictures where he knew none existed: in the shuddering glare of noon figures of men could be seen advancing in serried, grainy ranks; at evening the flanks of beasts would bleed into the saffron dust of the sky.

In a curious mood of exaltation, father succeeded in persuading his reluctant friends to embark with him on a journey into the Kalahari Desert. They returned to the nearest habitation of some size, restocked with essential provisions, bought rifles and ammunition for the shooting of game, and lined up enormous barrels of water along the sides of the wagon.

Their journey was destined to occupy fully forty days and forty nights.

They discovered iron-oxide-coated sand, spidery scrub and wind-mown grasses, a great wasteland in which, on any given day, unpredictable weather patterns rearranged the dunes, as if a sculptor in the heavens, in a mood of violent rage, was demolishing his creation. Fierce sandstorms bullied and battered the cringing acacias and shrubs, blinding eyes, clogging ears and nostrils, and stealing whatever was not tied down. Thunderstorms fired bolts of lightning from steely clouds and volleys of cannon fire rumbled through the afternoons, emptying out the heavens. The heavy water was gulped by the parched earth, leaving its rufous crusts barely stained with moisture. Then, as if the unseen sculptor had discovered his muse, a satiny dawn would flow to the horizon, trailing ribbons of pink and gold along the unruffled slopes of the dunes.

The Kalahari, too, conjured up images that father knew could not be real. A heat haze ahead became his old home, the sea, lapping at the sand; glistening lines of blue beckoned from a distance; slim vessels seemed to glide along the mirrored surface, bearing smudged figments that dissolved into pockets of mist.

The three men shot for the pot, and for drying. Wild game was plentiful, largely visible where it stood, stark silhouettes of gemsbok atop the crests of dunes, wildebeest milling in the riverbeds, or springbok that shimmered in the dry valleys as if prancing on water. So unused to the sight of men were the animals that entire herds might gaze at them unmoving, chewing the cud, theirs for the taking.

After three weeks of roaming, father's friends were eager to leave the desert. The relentless malice of the sun and the wind that drilled grit into eyes, nostrils, tongues and teeth was driving them to madness. When moon and stars vanished in a sandstorm whose ferocity turned the night to a ghostly blizzard that entombed every tree, bush and shard of calcrete, the sailors were overcome with superstitious fear. They yearned for a sighting of foamy waves and green islands; for the corrugated sea building up to a storm; for the familiar rolling and pitching of their ship braving known perils.

But father was transformed by the Kalahari, captivated by the capricious extremes that his friends deplored. The yellow sun strewing its fire by day, the moon its cold, gouged radiance by night, filled him with wonder.

After a successful day of hunting, during which the men killed four springbok and a steenbok, they set up camp in a small glade of kameeldoring trees, the Afrikaans name for the camel thorn, a life-giving acacia that provides shade and shelter for desert animals and birds, and on whose pods, pulp and leaves browsers and many other creatures in the Kalahari depend for nourishment.

With the intention of skinning and drying the meat the next day, the three weary men draped the animals across the highest branches as best they could, and took to their blankets. As was their habit, father's friends slept in the wagon, and he beneath it.

Upon waking after dawn, they found that two of the springbok were missing. In their place, at the foot of the tree from whose branches two springbok were still suspended, were four of the biggest tsamma melons they had ever seen. Tsammas ripen during the dry winters, and are the most dependable source of moisture when they are most sorely needed. They grow naturally in patches in the desert, and are a staple source of liquid and nourishment for the clans of Kalahari Bushmen, and for birds and animals. Jackals, springbok, even lion, are adept at piercing the outer shell to get to the juice within. The melons were a treat, as the barrels of water had become depleted and the men had already begun digging in likely spots in the dry riverbed, without much success. They knew their visitors had been Bushmen, though in all the time they had been in the desert, they had not glimpsed even a single one of the little men.

Days passed in searing heat and duststorms, and they would have given much for a few more tsamma melons. They hunted springbok, warthog, and some of the smaller creatures, like ground squirrels and sandgrouse; even a meerkat, or suricate, once. Father found the meerkat families enchanting: their alert gaze, eyes rimmed with black to repel the sun, their upright stance and inquisitive bobbing heads made him laugh, and after the first killing, he vowed never to harm another one. For the change in flavour, snakes and lizards were occasionally killed, the heads of cobras, horned adders and mole snakes alike chopped off and their lengths cooked over fires that were tiny protesting sparks against the darkness and silence, split occasionally by the unnerving grunts, scuffles and squeals of predator and prey.

Many nights were chill enough to stiffen the bones, but it seemed to father that it was the most frigid which coaxed forth stars like nothing they had ever seen before: a glittering canopy of butterflies that swarmed around the moon, stained the sky silver and tossed gossamer shadows across sand glowing with an incandescence that strained the eye. The nights that frightened the men most were those when the moon had shrivelled to a slit in the sky, and the smothering blackness seemed to pose an impenetrable riddle.

Once, before dawn, they were woken by the lowing of oxen. Father, beneath the wagon, wrestled out of his blankets to be confronted by the sight of two huge black-maned lions on their hind legs, pawing and biting at the gemsbok hung with considerable difficulty from the branch of a nearby grey kameeldoring. The beautiful, bloodied brutes, tearing away at meat that did not belong to them, were disdainful of the scent and presence of men and agitated oxen alike.

Rather than angering him, the sight moved father to awe.

He spoke to me of those lions at some length; I noticed that in the excitement of reminiscence, his German accent, which rarely manifested itself by the time I was old enough to speak, became quite marked.

Zat vas it, Em; zat vas luf.

Love, father? For those lions that were stealing your gemsbok? I asked, bewildered.

He did not reply for a moment, and I knew the scene was repeating itself in his mind's eye.

My God, Em, he murmured, those animals were splendid beasts! I watched them like a small child, my heart kicking at my ribcage, the blood sizzling through my veins. I felt privileged: perhaps, for a few moments, I even understood what it was like to be them, in undisputed charge of their world. I thought of William Hazlitt, who wrote that 'men do not become by nature what they are meant to be, but what society makes them. The generous feelings and high propensity of the soul are ... shrunk up, seared, violently wrenched and amputated, to fit us for intercourse with the world ...' That is the world I wanted to leave, Em;

the world that I did not want for you.

He shook his head and sighed. At the time, he continued, those lions seemed the embodiment of life itself, a primal, forgotten way of life, as ancient as the dinosaurs. I cannot explain it properly, but they gave me the kind of insight that, until then, I had lacked: a clearer vision of the wilderness's uncompromising checks and balances, its purity; strange though this may sound, I felt a common cause between myself and those beasts. As never before, they made me aware of the swiftly passing days of my own unsettled existence.

Father's respect and affection for the oceans, his own and his family's living for decades, appeared paltry in comparison with the feelings aroused by his sojourn in the Kalahari. His discordant self-doubt, his restless imaginings quieted. When they finally left the desert behind, his two companions were exhausted and relieved. Father, burning with his newfound revelations, was profoundly reluctant to return to his ship. God and paradise, he said, were not the myths of mankind; they were to be found in the desert wilderness.

Alf Johannsen was thirty-six years old when he made his return visit to South Africa. He had visited most places in the world, had done everything a sailor can do, and much besides. With plenty of money in his pockets, unspent during his years at sea, his mind was buoyant with anticipation of the future. As soon as possible after the ship had docked in Cape Town, he was set on returning to the Kalahari Desert. Only this time, his mission was not merely to explore it, but to make his life there. The sailors on board, some of whom remembered him from other voyages, were puzzled by his decision. You have never previously strayed from the sea for any length of time, they said. How will you wrest a living from one of the most inhospitable wastelands on the planet?

Deirdre Bolton, an English schoolteacher from London, was also on board. She had lost her mother and her younger sister in an influenza epidemic in that city. From the age of fifteen she had been taking care of her parent, a widowed invalid, for many years before she died. Having long given up thoughts of marriage, Deirdre had studied at home and at a nearby teachers' college, working long hours as a tutor to provide an income for the family. After the illness and deaths of her mother and sister, she was worn out and desolate, crushed by the lonely chore of burying them. The empty phrases of the harried minister who had assisted with the burials had done little to assuage the bitter burden of her grief. She missed her young sister badly, and as the weeks passed became more and more uncertain of what lay in wait for her. Alone, the future appeared ominous and hopeless.

Some dark months later, she read an advertisement in a London newspaper, offering work in South Africa to schoolteachers. The insertion described sunny skies, wide open spaces and friendly people. To Deirdre Bolton, living in a tiny, damp room overlooking a murky alleyway running with filth, the thought of sunlight and rainless skies seemed almost impossible to envisage.

Shortly thereafter, she made up her mind that a fresh start was essential to her mental health, and resolved to leave England. She applied for a post, and was sent a free berth on a mailship from London to Cape Town.

By the time she met father on the ship, mother had come to view herself as an impoverished, independent, slightly cantankerous spinster.

I was almost thirty years old, Em, she smiled, her old-young gaze as far from spinsterish as can be imagined, her cheekbones the colour of the riverbed on a winter morning, her long neck white as the underbelly of a springbok.

Father, his plans cut and dried, neither expected nor desired another love so soon after discovering his first. As it turned out, he had no real say in the matter. He took one look at the Englishwoman, and found he urgently desired to see more.

On board ship, it was not that easy. When she was about, she was hidden under hoods and cloaks against the weather, only her bright eyes visible, occasionally amused at father's blatant curiosity. He spied on her from a porthole, or from behind the backs of other people; she appeared downcast and sad, and he wondered whether she was a widow.

On the upper deck, the wild wind and waves sprayed their dew on Deirdre Bolton's bared face. She touched her tongue to her lips and tasted, for the first time in months, the tang of being alive rather than the salt of mourning. She was leaving sadness behind her at last.

Over and over, I have witnessed the special gifts of patience and charm that father possessed: he could mesmerise almost any creature into submission, from a spider as wide as his palm to an angry cobra. He loved to tease mother by saying that the task of convincing her to entrust him with her life was not nearly as much of a challenge as persuading a thick-tailed scorpion to evacuate the outhouse.

I visualised mother gradually opening up to him over the days of the voyage, her pretty red mouth turning up, dimples forming, her smile like the sun sailing from behind a cloud and taking father by surprise.

By the end of the voyage, she had abandoned her plans to work as a schoolteacher in Cape Town in order to marry an importunate stranger; not only that, she had agreed to journey with him to a largely unexplored region in a foreign country; a region rumoured to be more isolated and hostile than any she had ever dreamed existed.

Even while accepting father's proposal of marriage, and consenting thereby to join him in his quest, mother acknowledged to herself, not without trepidation, the risk she was taking. She was no longer leaving a large city to work in a smaller, foreign one, as planned; she was committing herself, on all fronts, to the unknown.

The Kalahari Desert preceded both mother and me in father's shortlist of great loves. Mother, his second, and I, his third, teased him about who held first place in his heart. He would chuckle, insisting that his second and third loves were easily as strong as the first; that he was blessed to have three loves in his life, as different from one another as only great loves can be.

Mother professed herself content: second was good enough for her if her rivals were the Kalahari and me.

I often rose at dawn, in a hushed universe that belonged to me alone, and sat outside to watch the inferno spreading in azure and green tinted skies, straddling the rosy riverbeds and mantling the tops of the acacias with gold and rust. The thorny shrubs and grasses, the spectral shapes of the dark, took form from the growing light that whitened the chalk stone strewn about on the ground like the fragmented bones of animals. In the distance, remodelled dunes rose to crisp points, or fell away to finely chiselled eyelids, pantiled domes of sand built up or razed by the changing seasons of the night.

When mother needed to put her feet up for a while at the end of the day, we would sit together near the back door of our dwelling to witness the coming of that night. At full moon, pools of light and shadow floated in the riverbed, and the sky was a garden of warm, liquid light. In winter, swiftly sabotaging the extravagant finale of sunset, darkness would take the desert captive beneath its inky wing. Some nights, I merged so completely with the dark that I could scarcely rouse myself to follow mother indoors. Only the cold, biting at my limbs, would send me to my bed.

At first, I listened to father's earnest teachings with the strong desire to please him, but I was still very young when I found myself caught up in his enthusiasm. Soon, my appreciation of our home bore more than a little of his own passionate commitment to it. When he could spare the time, we walked together around the farm and he unveiled to me a treasure trove of secret lives, some entombed to escape the burning sun.

Regard carefully, Em, he would say, the riverbed, the shade of the kameeldoring, the branches of the shepherd's tree; observe the tremor on the dune ahead of you; always look behind you and from side to side; and never forget to watch the sky. If you are patient and diligent you will discover such a diversity of creatures that only a fool could live here and not know that God lives here too.

Apart from the intricate habits of the animals, reptiles and birds, father pointed out the delicate tracery on the sand of insects: crawlers, creepers, bouncers, pouncers, biters, stingers and sprayers. He showed me their concealed lairs, labyrinths, nests and webs. He taught me the false menace in the enormous pincers of one scorpion species and the real danger in the thick tail of another; he described the similarities and differences between venomous snakes, such as the horned viper and golden-hooded cobra, and those whose bite was painful but not poisonous, such as the mole snake.

Father shared his broad knowledge generously with me, but it went without saying between us that there was much the Kalahari would never share with any human being other than a Bushman. There were secrets that would remain forever unknowable, protected by the desert's bland, deceptive crust, its mercurial temperament, its idiosyncrasies that invariably confounded expectations.

For both of us, this only enhanced its allure.

As soon as I could write, I began a list of insects, each noted shortly after I had found and inspected it, taking careful heed of any particular features, such as eyes that moved independently of each other, an unusual length or breadth of thorax, or exceptionally long legs. From time to time, father would check my list. I knew he was gratified, but also somewhat mystified that I had never in the slightest part of myself been repelled by the brutal crunching, sucking, guerrilla hordes. Most girls, in his experience, abhorred even common bugs and beetles.

I would finish my annotations while he waited, peering up at him from under my lids, proud that I had some new earwig, caterpillar, butterfly or spider on my list to discuss with him. Sometimes, he would bend swiftly to kiss my cheek, his beard as hard as the grizzled scrub, his eyes the milky blue of the afternoon sky, the skin around them puckered and pleated from squinting into sun and distance; also, perhaps, from laughter. They laughed a lot in the early days, he and mother; I loved hearing their laughter and watching them together, even though I did not always understand the joke.

It soon became clear that father's thoughts about me were shadowed by ambivalence. I think he regarded me as overly curious, even slightly odd, and wondered about his own responsibility in what he half-jokingly described as my 'obsessive engagement' with our environment. In his previous life, young girls of his acquaintance lived in cities and spent their time with friends like themselves rather than Bushmen; dogs rather than meerkats and mongooses; tutors and needlework rather than noting the habits of predators and adding to endless lists of insects.

You have no idea, have you, Em, he remarked more than once as I scribbled, what city girls talk about, what they do; how can you, living in a world of insects?

I would shrug, and he would tell me that they discussed clothes, ate cakes and sweets, and visited shops and eating houses. On Sundays, rather than sliding down dunes, city girls went to church.

I would pull a face and reply with what I thought was commendably restrained logic: I have never seen a city, a shop, an eating house or a church, father, so how can I miss them? And why should I care what city girls do anyway? When we spoke in this way mother's dimples appeared; she would compress her lips to hide her smile.

In truth, I felt little curiosity about people's lives in such places. I was very sure of my likes and dislikes: I loved the desert and revelled in exploring it; I enjoyed reading and writing, despised needlework and scorned, in particular, the peculiar habits, depicted by father, of city girls. I informed him, repeatedly, that Poppie and Imp were the only friends I needed.

It was father who gave Poppie her name. She and Imp were toddlers when my parents first saw them. Poppie, big-eyed, with an aureole of curly hair, was easy to name. But her friend was a tiny, squirrelly child, her smiling face crinkled and folded. Mother named her for her grin, which she said instantly made one suspect mischief. When I asked about their Bushman names, she shook her head: only a Bushman could pronounce them.

I had never seen a city, or even a town or village, but mother had spent her former life in a very large city, and she deplored it. She described London as cold and hard, with buildings that were noble and beautiful, but far too many more that were miserable and hideous, bordered by filthy, busy streets and pavements crowded with rushing, rainswept people.

Even before my family died, Em, she mused one evening as we watched the onset of night together, I was becoming low. I did not know why, but I know now: Life in a big city was draining me, sucking out my very soul.

Mother had taught French, and she quoted Balzac: 'In the desert, there is all and there is nothing. God is there and man is not.'

Her doubts about her future assuaged, she experienced a contentment she had never known before, revelling in the Kalahari's limitless horizons and rugged beauty, throwing her boundless energy into the building and organising of the homestead. Though the incessant wrestling with daily challenges wore her down, and may have contributed to occasional moods of withdrawal, for a goodly time she was utterly captivated by her desert home, regarding the repose she and father shared as the reward of living their lives as they chose: in isolation from the demands and dictates of society.

My parents built their farm with their own hands, and the willing hands of our people. It was sited on ruins dating from earlier in the century, belonging to a community who, father said, judging from a few stone artifacts he found, had practised both a hunter-gatherer and a stone-age way of life.

In undertaking a similar challenge, my parents had to adopt something of the stoicism of that primitive tribe. The farm, a mere speck in the billowing immensity that surrounded us, was fourteen days by ox-wagon from the nearest town, which was Upington; and the duration of the journey depended on weather and winds.

For the longest time, our home defined who I was. The moods of the Kalahari, scorching days and freezing nights, a multitude of inhabitants and their closely held secrets, all were part of me, swirling in the river of my being, rising and dwindling, yet always finely in tune with the undertow, the ebb and flow of the desert.

To the Kalahari

SHORTLY AFTER THE SHIP docked in Cape Town, my parents were married quietly in a small church near Table Mountain, which was covered that day by an enormous cloud. Father said it felt as if the mountain was their wedding table, laid with a thick, snowy cloth and mounds of cream cakes for their guests to eat. In fact the only people at the ceremony were the pastor, who conducted the marriage ceremony, and his wife and grown daughter, who were witnesses and also provided the lunch afterwards – which mother described as somewhat meagre.

In my parents' bedroom on the farm, nailed to the wall, was their faded wedding picture, taken outside the church by the pastor's daughter. When I was three years old, I asked mother if I could look at it. She took down the thin black frame from the wall, and put it in my hands. I asked her what a church was, and she explained. She said she and father believed in God, but did not believe He needed buildings to contain Him. I gazed, frowning, at the blurred fawn figures for some time. How can God fit into such a tiny place, I asked, if He is as big as the desert?

Mother picked me up in her arms and hugged me. She told me then, and later, when I was older and could understand better, that the God in whom she and father placed their trust was everywhere: in mountains, oceans, deserts, in the stars and all of nature. No building, no matter how magnificent, could confine or define Him; nor was He trapped between the pages of the Bible. She compared their religious feelings to those of the Bushmen, and to other native peoples such as the Aborigines of Australia and the American Indians, all of whom shared a great love and respect for the natural world, believing it to be full of guiding spirits which had an influence over every aspect of life, from birth to death, and had to be propitiated accordingly.

Growing up in the Kalahari, this made sense to me. Only a great spirit like God – a kind of master magician – could have created such remarkable patterns of colour and camouflage. The lion and the sand flea filled me equally with wonder; as I became more familiar with the adaptations to both killing and survival – intricate, cunning tricks to fool the harsh seasons of life in the desert – I became convinced that the Kalahari was indeed God's home as well as mine.

My parents wanted a baby from the day they were married, but it was almost two years before I came along. I was not baptised when I was born, not because mother was against baptism, but because she was in a hurry to embark on the return journey from Upington to our farm.

We had been away twenty-two months in all. Mother ran into some trouble with bleeding not long after my birth, and the local midwife, a farmer's wife, advised her to stay in bed until she was entirely healed, as there was a danger that the bleeding could recur on the unstable journey to our home, where poor father was anxiously awaiting us.

I was strong from the start, and grew a great deal very quickly; mother attributed this to the rich milk of the Boer wet nurse rather than her own paltry drops. The nurse, who had a baby of her own to feed as well, was glad of the money mother paid for her milk.

Father could not leave the farm, and did not know precisely when I was born, because the messengers, a poor-white couple who owned two mules and a cart, and were well paid to deliver the news, never reached him. Nobody ever discovered if it was theft, wild animals or drunkenness that caused them to vanish; and they were never found.

Eventually, a message got through to father, informing him that mother and baby were well, but no mention was made of the sex of the child. Father had to wait for long months, chewing his nails and throwing stones on the ground with Brandbooi, who claimed to be able to read the sex of the child from the pattern of the stones after they struck. (The stones claimed I was a boy.)

Mother was afraid that father would be disappointed that I was not of the male sex. When, at last, he held me clumsily in his arms, tears filled his eyes and dropped onto my red curls. He inspected me in minute detail as I gazed at him, round-eyed. He told mother that I had her laughing eyes, and was as beautiful as she was.

Though unwilling to mar his joy, mother told him then that she might never be able to give him a son. The farmer's wife had said that her womb had been severely weakened by my birth, and having another baby could be very dangerous.

Which is how I became Emma *Jeremiah* Dorothea Johannsen.

I am losing the thread of my story, and must now go back a little, to Cape Town and the days following the wedding.

My parents, driven by the zeal of their mission, lost no time. Father counted out a portion of the generous savings secreted in his baggage – mother had scarcely a penny to her name – and the newly wed pair went shopping.

Over the next few days, they purchased a big, sturdy old covered wagon, a team of oxen, a host of essential supplies, and set about loading the wagon close to the store from which they had purchased the provisions. The owners were curious as to their destination. Satisfying this curiosity, it turned out, spread consternation. The ensuing buzz encouraged everyone in the environs to gather around; all offered warnings and advice. The journey was regarded as risky at best and extremely perilous at worst. Though the track was said to be fair, weather could make it very unreliable in parts. Men shook their heads and women whispered behind their hands. My parents were cautioned to take spare oxen along in case of disease, and persuaded to buy six mules to bear additional provisions.

They were assisted in the heavy work of loading and harnessing by a Hottentot from the harbour area, clumsy from imbibing too much Cape wine. The storeowner, professing himself eager to hear further details of their plans, stood with his hands on his hips and issued instructions to the labourer and to my beleaguered father, interspersed with a litany of unwanted tales of calamity suffered by predecessors on similarly lengthy journeys into the relative unknown.

Ten days after the wedding, the heavily laden wagon rolled out of Cape Town northwards, bound for Upington.

The journey was the most gruelling experience of mother's life up to that time.

Many miles from Cape Town, the wagon wheels grinding along the track in vast open veld, father was sleepily driving the oxen when a dirt-seamed face and loping body hove before his half-closed eyes. Streaming along below him, arms pumping at a great rate, this apparition almost caused him to lose his seat. For a few seconds, jerked rudely from his doze, scared witless, he thought he was having a nightmare.

The apparition was only too real: it was the Hottentot labourer who had assisted in the loading of the wagon. While my parents were otherwise occupied, he had stolen into the wagon and concealed himself beneath sacks of flour and other supplies. Terrified of discovery, he had passed the night watchfully, in spite of his inebriated state. But once the journey had begun, he had believed himself safe from eviction and succumbed to his exhaustion, unhindered by the ceaseless jolting. On a steep rise in one of the bleakest parts of the journey, the wheels creaking alarmingly, the stowaway tumbled off the wagon and found himself on the stony track, in close proximity to a gigantic puff adder engaged in sunning itself.

The Hottentot picked himself up and took off like a bird. Barefoot on the uneven ground, he only reduced speed once he had caught up with the wagon and was alongside father – evidently the lesser peril.

Father, travel-weary and irate, was tempted to leave the man to the mercies of puff adders and other hungry creatures to be encountered in such desolation. But mother saw that he was starving and parched with thirst, and persuaded her new husband to take the stowaway along, claiming that he might even be useful.

The Hottentot's given name, which mother had requested, was not easy to pronounce or recall. Observing their difficulty, he offered the name Kobie, which he said had been conferred on him by his sundry employers in the Cape. Kobie could not or would not explain his motives for stowing away in their wagon, and in the end, my parents did not press him. Unable to lay his hands on any grog, he turned out to be a good wagon driver, more than capable of relieving father of that duty along the way.

Later, on the farm, Kobie became an excellent worker who could turn his hand to most things. Strong, dexterous and quick to learn, he was largely incommunicative, being morose by nature, and spent much of his time taking care of the sheep – a challenging job in itself, even with the dogs to assist him.

Unfortunately, the Bushman Brandbooi and the Hottentot Kobie detested each other on sight, ingrained with ancient tribal hatreds that no outsider could fully comprehend, let alone influence. Kobie was often the butt of the Bushwomen's jokes. They regarded him as the ugliest man they had ever seen, and he maintained his dignity in the face of their giggles only by ignoring their existence – unless otherwise instructed by father.

Even with Kobie's help, the journey was dogged by a combination of difficult terrain, poor weather and bad luck. Rather than the seven weeks father had been hoping for, they were more than three months on the road, losing two mules on the way. The animals simply lay down, impervious to Kobie's curses and kicks, and would not get up. Finally, mother persuaded father to leave them rather than shoot them in front of her.

Father and I agreed that she did not do them any favours.

The only real highlight of their journey was when they reached the great Orange River, where they diverted from the track to visit the mighty waterfall known as Augrabies, from the Nama word Aukoerebis, which means Place of Great Noise. Here, rather than just overnight, they outspanned for some days of much needed rest.

Mother revived rapidly. She found the constant boom of the falls soothing and melodious to the ear, and the spray cooled her face like the softest rain. Each day, she sat on a rock some distance from the wagon, regarding the thickly foaming waters in awe. Once, greatly daring, she walked close to the great main waterfall. Spray rained down upon her and the rocks were wet and slippery; one false step would have tossed her into the thrashing torrents below. At a point closer to the edge than caution dictated, between two smooth wet boulders, she came upon a small wooden cross with a sinister message carved crookedly into the wood: *Here fell Johnno, 1875.*

Heart pounding at her own temerity, mother turned with exaggerated care and retreated to the safety of the wagon.

Later that afternoon, they received a visit from a troop of baboons.

Fearful at first, the creatures kept a watchful distance. Then two huge males observed mother peeling an orange picked earlier from trees growing near the river, and began plaguing her mercilessly, ignoring father's shouts and the stones Kobie threw. Eventually father took his rifle and shot into the air, and the greedy creatures fled in terror.

At sunset, the three of them sat beside the river, the colours a glorious palette of its name, reflected in fast-moving water and brilliantly glowing rocks. One evening, as they smiled at the antics of a herd of springbok on the opposite cliff, Kobie broke his silence. He spoke for longer than he was ever to do at one time again, mostly in Afrikaans, with some English thrown in that he had picked up in the Cape.

He said he was born in the north of the country, many miles from the closest settlement, a place called Keimoes. His father, a sheep herder, was a drunkard who concocted his own potent brew, and his mother's subsistence farming barely fed her family. Kobie was the eldest. From an early age, he had begun wandering great distances from the family hut, living off what he could kill or steal. He covered a broad swathe of the unforgiving terrain, and had visited the Augrabies Falls before, hunting springbok and klipspringer along the banks of the Orange River, and fishing in its waters.

On his return home from one of these adventures he found that his mother was expecting yet another baby, to add to the nine she already could not feed. A few days later, he left and made his way, with difficulty, to Cape Town to find work. Once there, he had only limited success, at times starving amid the plenty he saw around him.

Judging from their first encounter, father guessed that a good portion of the Hottentot's tiny income had been spent on cheap liquor. When father asked if he had stowed away in order to return to his family in the north, Kobie laughed.

Nooit, baas. I work for you now.

Father, who was very good at languages, translated Kobie's story for mother. Not only did father speak Dutch, one of the official languages of South Africa, but during his first visit to the country he had rapidly picked up Afrikaans, the lingua franca of Dutch, and the languages of the indigenous peoples. German was the tongue spoken at home when he was a boy, but his Swedish was fluent, as was his English, both languages greatly enhanced by his sailing career, during which he consorted with a variety of sailors and their hangers-on from all over the globe. Mother – known to sniff disapprovingly about the company father kept in the past

– did not have his broad experience of languages, but spoke excellent French, which she passed on to me.

A secondary linguistic gift of father's was one which mother deplored: he could swear in six languages. Kobie, who worked closely with him on the farm, picked up the choicest of these. Curses in German, Swedish, Dutch, English, Arabic or Spanish tumbled freely from them both when they were under pressure, which was not infrequent. If I were in the vicinity, father resorted to words which he believed – mistakenly – I would not understand.

The next day, Kobie walked with them a little way along the river, pointing in the distance to where there were a few small islands. For many years, he said, the larger, densely overgrown islands had been strongholds for river pirates, sheep rustlers and thieves, and travellers such as themselves had been set upon and robbed, even murdered. When settlements had sprung up, and the town of Upington was founded and began to prosper, most of the bandits had been driven into the unexplored northern wilderness.

He guided my parents to a protected cove along the river, where they found three battered, lopsided tombstones mounted in the sand, each engraved with skull and crossbones, but lacking names.

River pirates, explained Kobie. When they were drunk, they would kill one another. Once, I watched from the bushes while a man used his fists and feet on his brother after they had been drinking and laughing together. He killed his own brother as easily as I would kill a rat.

The night after Kobie showed them the graves of the river pirates, it seemed to grow dark early. The moon cast a feeble glow from behind thick cloud. Mother tossed and turned in her makeshift bed, but could not sleep. In the small hours, above the roar of the waterfall, she heard rustlings and murmurings outside the wagon. She sat up, her hands on her thudding heart, and heard the escalating clamour of a savage struggle. An unearthly rattling and clashing rose up from the ground, resonating in her trembling limbs, and wild lamentations shook the tent. Mother covered her ears in superstitious dread.

The next morning, she told the two men of the terrible night she had passed. Father had slept undisturbed by her side; though sympathetic, he dismissed her experience as a nightmare.

But Kobie shivered and cast about him fearfully.

You heard the ghosts of the river pirates, madam. They are known to haunt the river on the darkest nights.

Father, concerned about mother's lingering distress from the night she had endured, had to be persuaded to translate.

On their last day at the Augrabies Falls, when the sky flushed coral and the sand sparkled with gold, mother walked across broad expanses of rock which appeared as ancient as the earth itself. An immense moonscape, some distance from the falls, glowed smooth and pale in the fading light, as if the moon had fallen to earth and left its imprint. Long white strips of guano were painted on the highest peaks. A Verreaux's eagle rose into the setting sun with a stately beating of black and white wings, like a wizard in flight. It floated above her for a moment, then swung towards the sheer precipices of red rock.

In Upington at long last – named after Sir Thomas Upington, Attorney General of the Cape – they outspanned a discreet distance away from a handful of homesteads, in the shade of trees where the proximity of the river moistened the air. The spot was shown to them by a wizened, almost naked Bushman, who asked them for spirits while keeping a sharp eye out for Kobie, aggressive towards Bushmen on principle.

In this peaceful spot, my parents rested for several days. Then, feeling somewhat restored from the rigours of their journey, they walked past the buildings of the old Olyvenhoutsdrift mission to the largest district store, an elongated white-washed edifice with a corrugated-iron roof, owned by a dour man who showed little interest in them, though they were quite obviously strangers and new in town. To one of father's questions, posed in German-accented Afrikaans, as to the ownership of the land thereabouts, the storekeeper replied in heavily accented English that it was mostly owned by Boers. A few Uitlanders, too, owned huge tracts of sheep-farming land, specifically the 'verdomde' British. He gave father, clearly another unwanted Uitlander, the evil eye, but was glad enough to take his money, muttering as he did so about the rights of people who had been in the area since before the time of the river bandits.

Father, who missed neither the words nor their implications, had also read something of the history of Upington. He remarked rather mischievously that he had indeed heard that descendants of a notorious bandit known as Captain Afrikaner still lived in the area. Not content with earning himself a ferocious glare, he further increased the man's ire by remarking that the town's closeness to the river would surely soon be exploited through the building of irrigation canals, which would attract many more settlers and Uitlanders, thus ensuring its prosperity and growth.

The first irrigation canal was in fact dug in 1890, not many years after father's prediction.

The interior of the Upington store was high-roofed, the store itself rambling and cluttered. It was also high-smelling, which to father's chagrin did not in the least deter mother. Instead, the place gave her a profusion of bright ideas, selling as it did everything from castor oil to boots, medicines, firewood and fertiliser, as well as bolts of gingham and calico, and a few dusty bottles of ink and paper, which mother pounced on with delight, as she had brought a good supply of quills with her from England. There was a selection of old pistols and rifles, there were saddles, bridles, hides, gunpowder, choppers, spades, knives large and small, fish hooks and fish lines, twine, wool blankets, mouldy coffee beans, sweetly scented tea leaves, huge rounds of smelly sheep's milk cheeses, black cooking pots of all sizes, even some delicate English china. An ancient piano was perched precariously on boxes, and a battered old banjo lay in a corner. A surprisingly large selection of expensive liquor, as well as row upon row of cheap spirits and some dusty bottles of Cape wine, lined the uppermost shelves.

To the far side of the store's interior there was a splintered and broken counter which appeared to have the dual purpose of barring dark-skinned people while selling cheap spirits to them from behind it. Beyond the store, at a respectable distance from the paying customers, evidence of the consumption of the cheapest spirits was splayed in the persons of various dozing Griqua, Hottentots, Bushmen and assorted Kaffirs, clad in the bleached, tattered rags of beggary and surrounded by heaps of empty bottles. There were a few poor whites in little better condition. Three Uitlanders – two filthy Germans and an Englishman with a bristling red moustache – sat on the crumbling wall at the side of the store, consuming a bottle of brandy and eyeing mother in a brazen manner that made her extremely uncomfortable.

My parents replenished their stocks carefully, as prices were high. They purchased a quantity of solid planks of different lengths for the flooring of the home they planned to build, they chose a few gemsbok and hartebeest hides for the walls and floor (until they could shoot and dry their own), additional wax candles, thick as a man's wrist, and a large iron pot that stood on bow legs and could be placed directly onto a fire. Chunks of oven-baked and hardened bread – known as *boerbeskuit* in Afrikaans – bottles of fruits and preserves, and dried fruit made by farmers' wives were irresistible to mother, as were a few bottles of ink and a good quantity of paper. A flagon of spirits for treating cuts and infections was added to the list, and plenty of the dried game meat known locally as biltong. (On the farm, father soon learned to make his own succulent biltong.)

Mother, who owned three dresses including her bridal gown, succeeded in persuading father to buy her some pretty material, cream-coloured with tiny red roses, she came upon in a hidden corner of the store; from this, she sewed herself a new dress which she wore for many years. Finally, since they knew visits to the town would be rare, they threw in everything else they thought might be useful, from extra needles to a sunhat like a wheel that mother insisted would better protect her complexion from the harsh sun. A tiny, spotted mirror with a crack in the corner cost very little. Mother tucked it away in her trunk, and it became one of her greatest treasures. But that fracture of metallic light was guilty of showing me my own face, and I held no affection for the thing, even less for what I saw reflected in its heartless depths: unruly rust-coloured curls, a freckled nose as flat as a button and eyes that were neither green nor blue.

A last-minute purchase, which mother said engendered fierce whispering between herself and father, gladdened her heart as none other had: two books to add to her small collection. Stained and creased, but with all the pages readable, they were Gulliver's Travels and a thick old Oxford dictionary with a dull red leather cover. The grumpy store owner agreed with alacrity to accept good money for them. Inside the dictionary, a name was penned in faded black ink: *GW Marlowe*. Though lacking any evidence of the provenance of the books, he thought they might have belonged to a deceased missionary, who had pawned them years before to buy food.

At a safe distance from the fetid environs of the imbibers, the store, not surprisingly, was a meeting place and social centre. The people my parents encountered there were mostly Boer farmers, self-reliant, preoccupied and taciturn. Two old men, observed on several occasions, lived in the town; themselves observant of my parents, they finally made an approach. They turned out to be both inquisitive and talkative.

Mother understood very little of the conversation, and was pleased to look elsewhere for entertainment. The two locals, speaking in guttural Afrikaans, advised father that he was not only misinformed but deluded to believe he could survive in the Kalahari, let alone farm sheep or anything else. They took it upon themselves to urge him in the name of good sense to reconsider, and listed, one echoing the other, some of the trials: scalding heat, freezing cold, sandstorms, thunder and lightning, flooding; added to those climatic perils was the presence of dangerous wild animals and reptiles. Did father know that the only humans in the Kalahari were Bushmen? Of course he could not know this, father was an Uitlander, how could he know that Bushies were like animals themselves; they had always lived in the Kalahari and knew how to survive there, but they were ignorant savages, nomads wandering about in the desert with no single place they called home.

Why, asked one of these doomsayers, genuinely perplexed, would a white man possessed of all his faculties want to live in a desert? Unless, hinted the other in a sly manner, there had been some trouble with the law? But of course not, responded the first man, indignant on father's behalf. It was clear to any right-thinking person that father was no scoundrel, but a man of means. Yet, if this man of means admired a godforsaken, stony sinkhole of sheep droppings so much, why did he not buy some land and farm in the region of Upington? There was good land for fifty miles in every direction! At least the town had the river, the company of townsfolk and other farmers, the comfort of the church!

Father shrugged off this inquisitorial barrage of opinion, innuendo and judgement. Have you then visited the Kalahari, he asked quietly.

The old men looked surprised. Both shook their heads.

I have been, said father. And it is there that I can print my own footstep.

The men looked down at his shoes, then back to his face. That is where God's footstep belongs; no white man has trodden there, declared the older of the two forbiddingly.

Presies, replied father.

The men, who assumed both my parents were English, shook their heads at each other: they were talking to an *Engelsman,* and everybody knew those people were *mal.*

Father bought a large box trailer from a farmer and hitched it to the wagon. He then chose an enormous ram and a goodly number of young ewes from a second farmer to put in the trailer. Finally he bought two strong geldings, one black, one golden brown, from a third farmer.

The sheep farmer strongly cautioned father that the animals might not survive the journey to the Auob River, father's destination. On his first visit to the Kalahari, he had camped for a time above the Auob (the bitter river), and while exploring the area had come upon an old stone kraal. The place had remained in his mind, and with the passing of time, he had fixed on it as the chosen site for his new home.

Mother, standing dreamily beside father, understood almost nothing of the farmer's urgent words, and paid no attention until she noticed that the man's eyes had fixed on her.

What about this little woman, said the farmer, still in Afrikaans, his stare unwavering. She doesn't have the build, she is soft and delicate; an indoor woman. She will not make a good farmer's wife. Perhaps here, by the river, but not where you are going.

His gaze travelled from mother to the sheep father had just purchased from him, and he shook his head for the second time.

There is a chance the sheep might survive the journey, and this poor woman – your wife – also. But what about the hardships that await her? Where will she find the society of her own kind?

When you get to know mother in these pages, you will realise that the Boer was not a good judge of women – though he may have been of sheep. When I was growing up my goal was to become as clever and useful as mother, who proved to be as tough as Meisie in tackling those hardships, and just as resourceful. As to his misguided though well-intentioned concern about the absence of society of her own kind, mother claimed not to miss it in the least, having had more than her fair share of such company in the past.

Father's last purchase was two English sheepdogs from a man who bred them. They were mixed with another breed, something wilder. Chummy, the male, two years old with watchful golden eyes, was already an experienced sheep herder. In accordance with his name, he was good-natured and friendly. May, a female, was smaller and a little younger, though fast and keen. The Boer described her as an excellent leader who guarded her sheep better than his wife did her newborn babe. Father intended to whelp her once they had settled above the Auob.

May was the month of mother's birthday and father regarded the name as a good omen. Sailors, said mother, are notoriously superstitious. Darling May was with us for a long time, and we loved her dearly. The story of Chummy, also beloved, merits its own chapter in this journal.

It was my parents' last night in Upington. The purchases were stowed securely in the wagon; the sheep milled around in a rough pen of branches and stones under the close supervision of the two loosely tied dogs; Kobie was already dozing beneath a tree. They settled to supper around the fire, enjoying the cooler breath of evening and looking forward to the final leg of the long journey to their new home.

From out of the deepening shadows, a woman walked up to the fire and stood looking down at mother, seated beside it. Mother stared back up at her, caught by surprise. She and father rose quickly to their feet as the woman greeted them in Afrikaans.

Mother saw at once that their visitor, wearing the Boer bonnet, or kappie, was a farmer's wife. Her chunky body was held stiffly, hands hanging loose by her sides; her light eyes, from shyness or habit, were gazing beyond mother into the growing dusk. Bare toes, half-buried in the rapidly cooling sand, peeped between the folds of the rough calico gown she wore. Declining with a brusque shake of her head the beautiful crystal glass half full of water that mother offered, she began speaking in halting English, her voice pitched high and cracking slightly, as if unaccustomed not only to the language but to speech itself.

It turned out that she was the wife of the farmer who had sold father the dogs. Mother recalled that he had mentioned a newborn babe, yet there was little evidence of youth in the woman's face and figure. From her husband, she knew of my parents' destination, and had apparently come with the express purpose of urging mother to reconsider the journey she was about to undertake.

Her point of view was somewhat different from the male doomsayers:

Your delicate complexion will wither in that heartless desert, mevrouw, it will dry up and become the bark of an old log, a tanned hide. *In one month it will be near the colour of a kaffir's skin.*

In the silence that fell after this impassioned statement, the visitor reached out and brushed the other woman's soft doomed cheek, shutting her eyes tightly, as if she were in pain; or perhaps to expel an appalling vision of deterioration.

The palm on mother's face was like the fall of a crisp autumn leaf.

Smiling, embarrassed, mother took a step back, begging her visitor to take some refreshment. Again, this was refused.

I will pray for you, mevrouw. *Ek sal voor jou bijd,* the woman repeated in Afrikaans.

Mother thanked her warmly for her trouble, pondering the true

35

reason for the visit as she watched the sad, stooped back merge with the encroaching darkness. Perhaps, spying from behind a curtain during the purchase of the dogs, the uncommon sight of a fresh English complexion had caused the Boer woman to revisit the anguish of her bargain: her beauty sacrificed to marriage, a hard climate, endless work, too many children.

A languid moon was rising in the sloe-coloured sky, flattened on one side like the entrance to a sorcerer's cave, its lustrous rocky shelves and inlets stocked with spells and secrets.

Mother wondered, then, what trials lay ahead. A chill, the finger of the sorcerer in the sky, trailed down her spine.

The sheep survived, except for a single ewe that lambed after a week's travelling, and then died of it. Father cut out the liver and whatever he thought they could consume before the heat got to the meat, then threw the rest to the dogs and the crows. He killed the lamb, which could not survive without its mother, and skewered most of it on a shaved branch.

They cooked it on the fire that night, the three of them gnawing it to the bone in less than the time it had taken to coax the fire to burn fiercely.

In spite of the scalding days that drank mother's sweat like blotting paper, she had never before experienced such appetite, her stomach clamouring to be filled like a voracious predator of the night. Exhausted, her flesh bruised and bones aching from the jolting of the wagon on the rough track, her longing for sleep and solid earth beneath her wracked body almost a sickness, her desire for food was yet greater: the scent and crackle of cooking meat flooded her mouth with the saliva of greed.

Father and Kobie shared the night watch, three hours at a time, the dogs beside the watchperson, heads on front paws, eyes open as often as not, nostrils scouring the raw air for hints of incursions by prowlers skulking in the shadows. Some nights, said mother, the moon was a smudged fissure in the sky and the darkness so intense that it seemed itself a presence – a massive, observant, melancholic power, capable of beneficence or perfidy both.

Each afternoon, when the sun was low in the sky, they outspanned. Kobie tethered the horses, and untied Chummy and May. The dogs travelled most of the way in the back of the wagon. They slept a good part of the day away until the time came for father to shoot for the pot, at which point, as if born to the job, they raced out onto the sand in great excitement alongside the big brown gelding, and retrieved whatever the killed animal was. They brought it to father between their jaws, and seemed to take turns, never once fighting each other over which of the two of them brought him the spoils of the hunt.

The oxen were fed, and the sheep released from the big box trailer to munch on the scrub under the watchful eyes of Chummy and May. Later father fed them, usually bones and leftovers, which he threw at them by turn and which never once hit the ground, so accomplished were both dogs at catching their dinner and instantly devouring it. Kobie built the evening fire, doling out precious sticks of firewood and using any dried dung he could find. When the flames had subsided, the meat was put on a grid to cook; sometimes, if they had found a suitable spot and outspanned earlier, they stewed the food in the big black pot they had bought in Upington.

The three of them ate their evening meal together, as had become their custom. My parents entertained no notions of their higher status as Europeans when it came to dining on their journey, and for much of living too; they have passed these values on to me. However, Kobie, as he had done at Augrabies and Upington, ate his meal turned away from them. The European cultures consider this impolite, and when taxed by father about his habit, Kobie explained that turning away from watching employers eat was a custom of his people and a mark of respect.

The meal consisted in large part of whatever father had managed to shoot for the pot. If he had not shot a springbok, steenbok or hare that day, it was biltong, leftovers, and what father called fire cakes, a kind of griddle scone, and a little dried fruit to finish.

Owls hooted on and off through the hours of darkness, and there was much caterwauling of jackals. In between the patter and pidgin of creatures of the night, the silence had a quality of expectancy, as of an empty bowl waiting to be filled. Once, a spotted eagle owl passed so close to the open end of the wagon, where mother lay gazing at the star-cloudy indigo sky, that she heard the rustle of its wings. An exploring brown hyena was on several occasions easily dispatched by Chummy who, surprisingly, slept through the visits of shy, curious families of bat-eared foxes, the latter merely causing May's ears to twitch as her head rested on her front paws. These beautiful insectivores did not know to be afraid of humans or even of dogs; their encounters with both species were so rare. Though ever alert, May did not destroy their innocence, studying the gambolling young ones as if amused by them. She was a dog born with good sense and intelligence, qualities which would serve her well among the diverse wild inhabitants of the Kalahari.

Thus the long days and nights passed, in heat and cold and fierce, stinging winds, but otherwise uneventful.

One hot afternoon, dozing away the heat of the day in the wagon, mother awoke to hear father shouting. She gathered herself, put on her wheel of a hat, and climbed down. To her astonishment, father was turning somersaults like a child.

When he caught sight of her, he whooped, scrambled to his feet and ran past her to the wagon. He emerged with his rifle.

What is it, what's wrong, asked mother, bewildered, still half-asleep, sighting no dangerous predator, nothing at all except a pale spreading sky and a riverbed as dry as the inside of her mouth.

Father did not reply. Instead, he shot the rifle into the air. The oxen lowed, the horses neighed in fear; birds exploded from trees, squirrels and mongooses vanished into their holes; gemsbok, spooked blemishes in the distance, began galloping wildly. From a nearby kameeldoring an enormous martial eagle, sheltering among the branches while spying out for prey, took to the skies, its mighty wingspan stirring up the dead air.

Mother thought the heat had got to father. Before she could say a word, he dropped the rifle and scooped her into his arms, kissing her cheek.

Your new home, he said proudly, pointing to a low rise above the riverbed.

Where? she asked. There is nothing there. I see nothing at all.

Father, smiling broadly, did not seem to hear her.

Mother looked up at the low hills and grew afraid. She had known to expect little, but what loomed above her was less than a bump in the sand, no more marked than a termite mound. She looked around her at the washed-out sky, the heat-glazed wilderness, and a sense of powerlessness brought weakness to her limbs. Abruptly, she understood the Bushman belief in a fanged serpent god of monstrous size that could encircle and consume them. The desert drew her like a living thing. She felt its choking grit in her throat, a shifting, sliding force with the breath of a furnace.

The shrilling of cicadas buzzed in her head, weighing on the still, scorched air. Her desolation joined with the distant, seamed horizons.

How can a place like this, she thought despairingly, *become my home?*

From Ruins to Rafters

WITH BACK-BREAKING WORK, that is how. And a good deal of help from our friends.

Mother climbed the crest of the hill, which was much further than it had looked from the wagon, and looked around her. She saw nothing but a poor rock-strewn ruin, long abandoned, and a view of scrub and dunes so arid that it seemed no living thing could possibly survive there. The wind blew ceaselessly; she had to clutch onto her hat with one hand while pinning down her skirts with the other.

Meanwhile, father was capering around her, jubilantly pointing out the advantages of the site. There were kameeldorings and shepherd's trees, there were three thorns and black thorns, even acacia karroo, a sweet thorn, in the distance; there were hornbills and shrikes, goshawks and rollers. The site, exulted father, was even better than he remembered, elevated above the surrounding area and above the high-water mark of flash flooding of the Auob. It sloped gently, and there were flat areas where they could grow mealies and a few vegetables. Best of all, there was plenty of room for spacious, well-drained kraals for the sheep.

Mother's heart was not comforted. Where will we build our home, she asked, looking around despondently.

Father led her by the hand to the top of the rise.

Here, he said. Look at the view from your window.

And indeed, the view was endless, but where was she to find a window to look through? Water, she pleaded, what of water? Father took her hand again and led her some way down the scrubby hillside, to a flat area surrounded by stones.

This is a well, a borehole, long abandoned. But I am convinced we will quickly find water here again.

He looked up at the sky. We will not need it yet. We must put out the barrels; a storm is coming.

It broke before Kobie and father could get the wagon up the hill. The sheep clustered together as rain lashed down, drenching everything within minutes.

Mother, her hat streaming water, a mini waterfall in itself, wondered if her husband had lost his mind. She sat on a chunk of chalk stone in the mud, stung by drops of rain the size of pebbles, and thought about the words of the Boer woman. She decided she had never been more miserable in her life.

That night, they slept on damp bedding as even the strong canvas covering of the wagon became weighed down beneath torrents of rain, and wetness seeped unpleasantly into every dry thing inside it. Kobie, who usually slept beneath the wagon or beside the fire, was almost swept away by a mudslide, and was forced to take shelter inside.

All night the wagon groaned beneath the brutal beating of the rain.

The interior, said mother, smelt as if the entire flock of wet sheep had bedded down with them. The only one who slept the night through was Kobie.

Father was up at dawn, and a wondrous dawn it was, the rain gone and the riverbed still awash with pools of receding floodwaters. It was a sight he never thought to see after such a downpour: the dunes blushing beneath the enormous golden eye of the rising sun, and a rainbow of such radiance climbing the sky that he viewed it as a blessing from the desert gods on the home they would begin building that very day.

He attacked the work with vigour before he had even breakfasted, laying out the calcrete, or chalk stone, to mark the site of the dwelling. There were rocks strewn about which father thought to be of a great age, perhaps borne to the spot from some distance away, by what means he could not imagine; he and Kobie used some of them to mark out the first kraal, on a gentle slope some distance from the site selected for the dwelling.

The sun was swiftly sucking up the moisture, and Kobie succeeded in getting a fire going. Mother prepared the porridge, the damp of the night still in her bones, though the sky by then was brilliantly blue and the sand glowing in sunlight.

Barely halting their labours to eat, the two men completed the foundation of the dwelling that very day. In the afternoon, father dispatched Kobie with an axe to cut branches of kameeldoring trees alongside the riverbed to form the rafters of the roof. While Kobie was busy, father and mother walked down to the pools in the riverbed. Keeping a sharp eye out for snakes, and muddy to well above the ankles, they began collecting dune reed for thatching.

In the days following, they worked from first light until the heat forced them to seek shade beneath a kameeldoring, where all three of them slept as if dead. The sheep, roughly penned behind branches in their new kraal, were left in the care of the dogs.

Gradually the pile of branches, neatly chopped to various lengths, grew. The dune reeds dried out and were bound in sheaves with string; this was mother's particular job, for which she wore old leather gloves that soon became dirty and torn, but protected her hands and fingers from deep lacerations. Each day, Kobie gathered dung of wildebeest and gemsbok in the riverbed and surrounds, and spread it in the sun to dry. He dug for mud, and stacked it in piles with calcrete stone and any other stones he could find for reinforcement of the walls.

They had purchased hides of gemsbok and red hartebeest in Upington, but they soon found that there were not nearly enough to line the walls and ceilings and for the floorboards, neatly laid by father above blocks of dried-out dung. More hides were needed to be cut into strips for binding, and to make extra saddles for the two horses.

The day came at last when the floor was laid, the mud and daub walls were smooth and dry, and the rafters prepared for roofing. The fireplace in the kitchen, and the chimney of stone above it, were built painstakingly by Kobie; in the fireplace, he piled up stones in a neat square, with a hole at the top for a grid or a pot. Thick cakes of dung made a good hearth.

Though the rain barrels were still fairly full from the downpour, a priority was to dig the well; after that, the tan-pit. When the tan-pit was ready, father would hunt gemsbok and hartebeest, and the process of tanning the essential hides could begin.

Meanwhile the wind blew, the rafters of the dwelling shook, and morning dew dampened the dune reeds which, without hides to line them, sagged limp as wet rags.

On a night when the moon seemed the width of an eyelash above a black eyeball of sky, Chummy and May began barking frantically. The tone was different from any my parents had heard from them before. They started up, thinking a predator, a lion or a hyena, was in the vicinity of the sheep pen.

Kobie was already outside. Father lit two flares and gave one to Kobie. He hefted the rifle and the two made for the main kraal, built at an angle some way below the home for good drainage. A bright moon discourages predators, as they are easily seen by their prey. That night, the faint sickle of moon made it dark enough to be a perfect opportunity for lions to hunt, and dangerous for men, with their inferior night vision, to be hunting them.

Father and Kobie cast their flares about in all directions. The sheep stirred, yet seemed free of agitation. The dogs had not calmed, and Kobie was worried. May, usually so sensible, had vanished into the night and did not respond to father's repeated calls.

Chummy, who had been standing beside father, barking incessantly, stopped and began growling instead. The growls grew in volume.

May exploded from the blackness. She crouched down on her front legs in front of father, barking furiously. Kobie cast his flare in the direction of the branches of two large kameeldorings not far ahead of them, thinking to surprise a leopard. May bounded towards the trees, still barking, her nose pointing up at the larger tree, a dense clump against the sky.

Father strained to see what the dog clearly could; but try though he might, he could not discern even a single branch.

Brandbooi

May by the scruff of her neck to silence her. Kobie raised the flare. Something moved in the lower limbs of the tree: knobbly and dark, it seemed part of it, a node of a branch trembling in the wind. Kobie raised the flare still higher. Crouching behind a large branch in a desperate bid to evade the light was their intruder.

In the thick dark, father was almost convinced it was a baboon, even though he knew there were no baboons in the Kalahari. Kobie's loud click of disgust told him otherwise. In Kobie's mind, there was little enough difference between a baboon and a Bushman.

Father's first thought was for the sheep. His only experience of Bushmen in the Kalahari had been the single incident on his first visit to the desert, when an honest if unsolicited barter had taken place, the Bushmen helping themselves to two springbok and leaving tsamma melons in exchange. But the farmers in Upington had warned him that Bushmen are notorious thieves who will steal a sheep as easily as a drink of water, and have legendary appetites: two Bushmen can devour an entire carcass in a night of gorging. From his reading, father knew the true motive for this gorging. It is not merely owing to greed, or because the little men seldom had enough food to fill their bellies: as nomads, they are simply not equipped to carry quantities of food with them, and thus are in the habit of devouring their kills on the spot.

While father debated what to do with the Bushman, Kobie, in no such dilemma, prattled away at him. He shrank back beneath the onslaught of the Hottentot's aggressive gobbledegook: Woza jou***///*#****voetsek!**#!!** brak hond!

Listening to Kobie's abuse, two thoughts came to father: first, that neither white nor black man was friend to the Bushmen; and second, they are renowned also for their ability to vanish into thin air. Finding this individual could only mean that he wanted to be found: in spite of his shy, fearful behaviour, the Bushman had turned up for a reason.

Father wondered what that reason could be. He put out a hand and Kobie stopped talking. In the ensuing silence, the little man in the tree unfolded his small quaking form and shimmied down the trunk. Had not Kobie reached out and grabbed him by the torn hide that girded his loins, he might yet have melted into the night.

With the light of the flare full on him, the two men inspected the Bushman. Slight, with sinewy arms and shapely, powerful legs, in height he barely reached father's chest. Without looking up, he turned his head away from the flare, mumbling to himself; father thought he might have been gibbering in fear. Kobie, less ignorant, explained that the man was speaking in his own language. The sounds were a variety of clicks: a sucking action of the tongue, a 'tsk, tsk', soft and sharp pops of the tongue against the palate; then a click that resembled the clucking sound Kobie used with the sheep, or father for urging on his horse.

After listening for a moment, Kobie, holding tightly to the captive's arm, addressed him again. His head still bent, the Bushman answered in a firmer voice. To father's astonishment, he understood something of the communication, since a few of the words were in Afrikaans. As the little man's voice rose slightly in volume, he shook off Kobie's grip and began using both hands freely. There was much pointing of fingers, which went into his mouth and prodded repeatedly at his lean hard stomach.

Judging by that organ's flatness, it had not been filled in some days.

He is hungry, father said to Kobie, puzzled. Yet he bears a bow and arrows on his back, surely he can hunt.

Ja, replied Kobie, but he say the rain chase away the animals, even the squirrels, and he has not been able to catch and eat meat for four days; he has eaten only ants-in-the-mountain.

Termites. It is no wonder then that he is hungry.

Kobie nodded and pointed to father's rifle. It is good to shoot this baboon, baas. He will steal from you, and he will eat up all your sheep.

So why did father risk taking in a refugee of such ill-repute? The decision, he explained to me, had been practical rather than charitable: he was in dire need of extra hands on the farm, and he reasoned that if the man worked well and was given food in exchange for his labours, both parties would benefit.

The plan worked, but not quite as simply as father had envisaged.

The Bushman was, of course, our Brandbooi, the Boer name he offered when he saw that a hail of nasal, aspirated and glottal clicks – his Bushman name – made little impression on father's bewilderment. In the weeks following his arrival, Brandbooi told father his story, making copious use of an evocative patois. A significant figure in my life from the time I was a toddler, Brandbooi was a storyteller of note. Perhaps something of father's skill as a raconteur has crept in, but I have attempted as faithfully as possible to render on paper the cadence of the Bushman's picturesque speech and mannerisms.

As his story unspooled beneath my pen, I began to feel more and more confident that if he could read it, he would approve.

Though born in the Kalahari, Brandbooi was no primitive Bushman, untouched by the white man's ways. When he was still a young boy, his family and certain members of their clan had made the decision to split off from the main body and migrate to South West Africa. Once there, they were persecuted and pursued by all the peoples whose lands they traversed: white farmers, the Herero, Ovambo, Nama and other tribes. When two men of the clan were found shot to death, the remaining members sought refuge in Damaraland.

After Brandbooi's parents died in Damaraland – his father stampeded to death by an angry elephant bull, his mother of a sickness of the stomach – he decided to return with his clan to the Kalahari. There had been a drought, and survival for desert dwellers had become a struggle.

The game herds were spread thinly over hundreds of miles, wandering into the farthest wilderness in search of water.

On their way home, to stave off starvation, the clan thieved at every opportunity from white men and black in remote villages and farms, and from travellers and pedlars. Not long after returning to the Kalahari, where the drought finally broke in a series of torrential thunderstorms, something happened to Brandbooi's wife and children, and to the wives and children of other members of his clan. He described the events to father with few words, much rapid finger signing and many drawings in the sand. Human and animal figures were sketched in minute detail; around them, he strewed little mounds of broken reeds and grasses.

While Brandbooi was out hunting one day with the other men, a great flash flood boiled up from out of nowhere. His wife and two children, and six other women and their children, were foraging in the riverbed as usual, where they sought the eggs of sandgrouse, prodded under stones for scorpions, lizards and snakes, and kept a sharp eye out for centipedes and caterpillars sometimes used in the making of poison for their arrows.

When they returned from the hunt, Brandbooi and the other men found that their wives and children had vanished. The river was still high and dangerous, and it struck them that while they had been thinking only of their stomachs and a good cooking fire, their families had been stolen from them by the waters. Shocked and grieving, the men muttered in perplexity to one another for long sleepless hours, trying but failing to come up with a single one of the small clan's beliefs that had been transgressed. What dread insult had the clan committed, albeit unwittingly, against the spirits? How else to explain such a fearsome punishment?

At dawn, Brandbooi understood with a terrible finality that he would not see his children again until it was time for the spirits to take him also. His head filled up with an agonising pain and his heart swelled until it pressed against his ribs, growing larger and larger until it burst from his chest like a hawk from its nest.

Before he could snatch it back, grasp it tightly in his hands and replace it where it belonged behind his ribs, it took to the sky and flew away from him.

He knew then that he, too, must leave that place of death. In the icy dawn, his body began agitating and contorting without his volition. His shuddering limbs changed shape as he lay helpless: beak and feathers

46

sprouted; his eyes turned yellow and sharp as thorns. He rose onto horny feet with stabbing claws. Mighty wings launched him high into the cloudless sky, where he followed the clear path of his fleeing heart.

This path took him to the lands of the white man. Once there, his heart returned to its rightful place in his chest, the hawk shed its feathers, wings and claws, and Brandbooi became a Bushman again.

He found himself standing on his own strong legs in a place utterly unfamiliar to him. Looking around, he spotted a deep thick bush, from which he skilfully evicted an angry porcupine, killing it with a large stone. After erecting a neat monument of quills to its spirit in the very circle where its blood dyed the sand red, Brandbooi plucked the plump animal, cooked it on a small, carefully tended fire, and ate it in its entirety. Feeling much refreshed, he began building himself a shelter, bordered by porcupine quills, in a clearing he swept clean with his hands.

That night, for the first time since the spirits had seen fit to frown so cruelly upon him, he slept soundly on unknown sand whose soft warmth retained the heat of the day.

During the weeks that followed, Brandbooi drank from the white man's pans and ate the white man's sheep and whatever else he could catch, feasting on young warthogs, springbok, steenbok, squirrels, mongooses, snakes and lizards, all of which abounded on the white man's lands. It did not take long for his body to grow plump; and with this increase in his girth, as is often the case, his spirit grew lazy.

A day came when the wind bore him a message. This message told him that the Boer was aware that a Bushman was trespassing on his lands; that the Boer knew where that Bushman dwelt and was deeply offended by his presence. He was coming with firesticks to hunt him down: to take the life of the thief in payment for the killing and eating of sheep and game that did not belong to him and for the drinking of water from the Boer's pans.

But Brandbooi was unafraid. He felt his energy grow from a tiny flame to a conflagration and understood, with lightness in his heart, that the spirits had taken pity on him once more. Again, feathers and wings sprouted in place of his limbs, and he rose on currents of air. Faster than the flying sand, he flew above the tops of the trees, looking down at vultures' nests taking fire from the late afternoon sun.

The enraged Boer sought his trespasser in vain.

This time, when Brandbooi came back to himself, he decided he owed his safety to the intervention of the god of the wilderness, watching over him in recompense for the loss of his children. Or perhaps, he thought, it might have been his reward for the strict adherence to his clan's beliefs while he feasted on the fat of the white man's lands. He was certain he had never once violated those beliefs: never let his shadow fall upon an animal he had killed, never forgotten to leave an offering in thanksgiving to the spirit of the animal; and before he dug for water or drank it, he had propitiated the spirit of that water with a piece of dried meat if he had it, some locusts if he did not, or even, sometimes, an arrow hewn from a driedoring.

In spite of Brandbooi's diligence and vigilance, the god of the wilderness abandoned him. Even as events were overtaking him, he understood, with a fearful sinking of his heart, the reason: he had not amputated the first joint of the baby finger of the left hand of his one-year-old daughter before the waters had taken her. Had he done this in its right time, he would have secured a life of feasting and pleasure for her in the next world, and his own safety in this one. He had fully intended to perform the amputation rites on his return from that last ill-fated hunting trip, had even selected the knife-edged stone. But by then it was too late: the greedy floodwaters had swallowed her.

Owing to this violation, on a day with no cloud or redeeming breeze to temper the hot sun bleeding into a wan sky, the white man finally ran his quarry to ground.

Early that morning, a young warthog had lingered too long behind its speedy family and had fallen to one of his arrows; Brandbooi had consumed almost all of it in a single hour. In the afternoon, he woke from sleep with a great thirst. His throat felt painfully dry; he touched it gingerly, wondering if an irate porcupine, passing by, had speared it with a quill.

Later, he realised it was this thirst that made him unusually careless. He had scarcely offered up the scorpion he had killed to the spirit of the pan when an ancestral enemy, a terrifying shape-shifter in the form of a white man's dog, had erupted from behind a tree. Without a sound – a bark, even a growl – this unnatural beast, head as heavy and black as a lion's, seized Brandbooi's thigh between jaws foaming with rivers of drool.

Far worse than the lion dog was what reared above him: a serpent-shadow of monstrous size, behind which stood the white man. Brandbooi, shivering in shock, his blood spilling into the sand, saw that the length of the firestick aimed at him by the white man was almost the length of the man himself.

The Bushman recognised that the serpent-shadow was the dark spirit that guided the white man in his evil deeds, and fear ran through him like a torrent of arrows, his dread of the shadow greater by far than his fear of the Boer, his firestick or the bloody-fanged dog; the latter wrenching at his leg as if about to tear it from his body.

Pain caused Brandbooi to sweat water that he did not have to spare. The bright afternoon turned dim; he blinked a few times, but the light did not return. Instead, a voice spoke loudly in his head. This voice did not emanate from the white man's throat; it came from the shadow itself.

Brandbooi closed his eyes and waited for the crack of the firestick that would water the land with Bushman blood.

At this point in the tale, father could not refrain from interrupting. Why did you not simply turn into a hawk again and fly away from such a terrible situation?

Brandbooi ceased his rapid sketching in the sand. He hung his head in shame and repeated to father in rapid cross-lingual patois the transgression against his daughter that had brought catastrophe upon him. But the greater transgression, he admitted, was his own greed, which had ignited a fever in him for the easy meat that did not belong to him, but was there for the taking on the Boer's land.

Thus laziness and self-indulgence had clipped his wings and blunted his claws. By not returning to his own home in the Kalahari once the life force had been returned to him and the sharp edge of his grief had blunted a little, he had sacrificed the transforming magic of the hawk.

Furthermore, finished Brandbooi solemnly, owing to those same trespasses against the god of the wilderness, I, Brandbooi, will never again be granted the privilege of flying as a hawk with the other birds of the sky.

Kobie approached just then to report to father on the progress of the well, which was dug to the point where it was ready for dynamiting. As usual, Kobie ignored the Bushman, whose sketching stick was poised to continue the story, as completely as if he were a toktokkie at father's feet. Hawking up phlegm, the Hottentot held it in his mouth for a moment, then spat with devastating accuracy into the dead centre of one of Brandbooi's meticulous circles in the sand.

The Bushman looked up at him with red-streaked, angry eyes. You will not live long, he said, in quite passable Afrikaans.

Kobie did not even glance at the little man. He spat again, this time between Brandbooi's legs.

Brandbooi blows on a stick

FROM THE MOMENT Brandbooi knew father would let him stay, he worked each day tirelessly, gratefully, until darkness brought enforced rest. He explained to father that he had been found in the tree by Chummy and May because he had returned to his home and the gods of the wilderness had relented (though not to the extent of shape-changing). It was of immense importance that the spirits witness the lengths to which he was prepared to go in order to make amends for his foolishness, and to convince them that he would never trespass against them again.

The price father would pay for his generosity turned up a week after the advent of Brandbooi. In the shade of the same kameeldoring in whose branches Brandbooi had hidden, the barking dogs cornered a bedraggled group of Bushmen: two old men and three women, the youngest of them with two babies on her back.

The group, ignoring the dogs, awaited their fate apathetically. The toddlers were unnaturally still and silent, the tiny beaks of their mouths gaping, the habit of concealment instinctive, even more powerful than starvation or thirst.

When the Bushmen had been fed and the toddlers were asleep, Brandbooi told my parents the rest of the story. His urgent strokes in the sand were dramatised by acrobatic charades and exclamations in Afrikaans; he even used a few English words he had picked up in the week he had been on the farm.

Before Brandbooi's startled eyes, the immense shadow-serpent glided away into the sand. Miraculously, the Boer pulled off the dog and jerked the Bushman none too gently onto his feet.

Brandbooi could scarcely stand; his leg was bleeding heavily, bone glistening white through the torn flesh. Grasping his arm in a huge fist, the Boer dragged him along the ground. The dog, furious at the loss of its meal, began baying like a frenzied hyena, earning itself a kick that sent it squealing.

The Bushman was thrown bodily into the corner of a cart which stood in the shade of a nearby tree. The Boer climbed aboard, whipped the mules and they took off at a canter, the dog running behind. Brandbooi, burning up in agony, wondered how he had failed to hear the approach of such a noisy contraption. As each bruising jolt of the cart fed the flames in his leg, he was forced to conclude that the spirits had stopped up all his senses. The fatter he became on stolen meat, the heavier grew his limbs, the blinder his eyes, the deafer his ears.

He must have lost consciousness for a few minutes. When he opened his eyes, he looked about him and saw a long whitewashed dwelling, surrounded on all sides by large kraals containing massed clouds of white that he knew were a great many sheep. He heard the Boer's voice barking commands. Two tall, slightly blurred figures lifted him from the cart, carried him a short distance and threw him to the ground. Free with their fists, they tied his limp trunk with a length of thick rope to a post in one of the kraals, then bound his wrists around the post. The fire in his leg roared in his head, disguising the roughness with which they manhandled him.

Even in his semi-conscious state, Brandbooi could smell the bitter hatred on the breath of the men, and knew they were Hottentots. Dizzy and faint, he thought there was a good chance they would finish him off while the farmer ate his evening meal. Sprawled against the post on stony ground, surrounded by incurious sheep, he observed the blood draining from his wound through half-closed eyes and felt certain that soon there would be none left in his veins. Rousing himself by scratching his lower back with the hard rope around his wrists, he tried desperately to fight off a growing sleepiness, knowing that if he did not succeed, he was in serious danger of falling into the long sleep from which he would not waken in this world.

Despite his efforts, his eyelids fluttered and closed. Later, when his eyes opened, he did not know whether minutes or hours or even days had passed.

Above him, another pair of eyes hovered anxiously. They were the colour of the sky in the late afternoon before the sun begins its journey to the home of the spirits in order to make way for its young sister, the moon.

Brandbooi had never before seen anyone like the strange-eyed creature gazing down at him. He feared he had slept too long, and had entered that spirit world himself. Perhaps, he thought dazedly, she was a spirit of the sun, since her long hair was the colour of a hartebeest when the sun stood straight above it; or perhaps she belonged to the moon, since her skin shimmered with the radiance of a full moon.

The spirit spoke words that Brandbooi did not understand. She crouched on her haunches beside him and inspected his horrible wound. Her hair, weightless as a spiderweb, tickled his arm; her little nose dilated, quivering like that of a newborn springbok inhaling the bloody smells of the afterbirth and the new world outside the womb of its mother.

Abruptly, a voice boomed in Brandbooi's ears and something struck his leg. He felt a pain so ghastly it was as if he had been shot with a firestick. He heard the scream of a jackal pelted with a stone, and knew with deep shame that the jackal was himself.

Another cry echoed his. Through the mist before his eyes, Brandbooi tried to see the creature with eyes of the sky. But the day had darkened to night.

The Hottentots roused him by bearing him to a shelter, where they threw an old blanket over him. By that time, the blood that had drained from Brandbooi's veins left his body feeling like grass trampled beneath the hooves of a herd of wildebeest.

He awoke in the freezing night, he knew not how much later, to hear the soft clicks of his own tongue. He knew at once that he had not embarked on the long sleep he had so dreaded. Gentle hands brushed his leg. Before pain drove him back into the arms of sleep, he felt his heart throbbing lightly in his chest.

Brandbooi told father that the Boer who had captured him had a well-organised slave labour force working on his extensive farm. The workers were mostly Hottentots, Griquas and Kaffirs, but there were also a few Bushmen: two men and two women past middle age, and a younger woman the Boer called Meisie, who spoke the Bushman dialect but whose height and milky skin spoke of mixed blood.

There were also two baby girls, just beginning to walk. Both were in the care of Meisie, who fed them a little porridge and sheep's milk each morning and evening. In reply to Brandbooi's question, she said that she was not their mother, nor was there a father standing up for either of the two children. Meisie said she had found the smaller of the two babies when she was but a few days old; she had been left to die like a baby rat, on a heap of rubbish behind the outhouse. Though she did not believe the child would survive, she fed her drops of sheep's milk with her (unmutilated) baby finger. Imp – for Imp it was – must have had strong spirits watching over her, because after a brief struggle with death, she gained strength and thrived.

The little sky-eyed spirit girl with the gentle heart loved the babies. When her mother was not watching and the Hottentot nursemaid was gossiping with the other servants behind the outhouse, she would sneak off to the shelters and find the old Bushwoman who cared for the babies while Meisie worked. The little girl picked them up one by one, and kissed and fondled them until they giggled and the old woman begged her to leave, fearing punishment to herself.

Meisie and one of the other Bushwomen, whom the Boer mockingly called Dokter, tended Brandbooi's wound. In spite of the Boer's derision, Dokter was respected as a healer; she had successfully treated his wife's insomnia and the painful stomach of his daughter, administering minute doses of the Bushman poison bulb, which is also used in arrow poison. Her beer, brewed from the fruits of the witgat, or shepherd's tree, was known to be favoured by the Boer, who sometimes chose to drink it above his white man's spirits.

Dokter treated Brandbooi's wound with poultices made of insect larvae

54

and stings, powdered leaves, roots and pods, and other secret ingredients and combinations. She also coaxed him to swallow a small quantity of a potion so vile that he would have preferred to eat dirt. Within a week, he was able to stand, and shortly after that to begin working, which is what saved his life. The Boer who threw the serpent-shadow was greedy for workers who could do the heaviest work with the least nourishment.

Brandbooi dragged rocks around for kraal walls, cut down trees and chopped wood until he thought his arm would fall off; after that he lifted rocks onto the wagon until its groans disguised the groans of his exertions. So hard was the work that he would fall into his cold shelter at night and sleep dreamlessly until dawn.

This dreamlessness was unusual and deeply troubling to Brandbooi, because one of the best entertainments in life until his difficulties began were his dreams. They were of the moon and stars and good spirits, of rain and springs of cool water and ostrich eggs bigger than his head; of mounds of roasting meat and tsamma melons brimming with sweet juice. The wonders of the desert were revealed to him all night long; every night a new and inspiring dream presenting itself for his enjoyment.

All day as he toiled after the empty night before, he missed the dreams which had held him in the dark as a mother holds her young child; which had fed him his daily thoughts as a mother's milk sustains that child at her breast. He longed for his dreams almost as much as he had once longed for a sight of his drowned family, none of whom had as yet returned to honour him in a dream.

Brandbooi had been working for the Boer for some time – he flashed father the fingers of both hands twice – when he overheard the Boer instructing a skinny Kaffir to find the Hottentot nursemaid, promising him meat if he located her speedily. The others told Brandbooi that their master's unsmiling, silent wife had spied on the maid and discovered her resting while her charge played with the two Bushman girls; instead of punishing the nursemaid herself, she had told her husband what she had seen.

The woman was found in the place Brandbooi had often seen her, sitting in the sun behind the outhouse, snoring against its rear wall. This time, though her eyes were closed, her mouth was full. The Kaffir escorted her, unsuspecting, to her master; then he brought the Boer the plate of food she had stolen.

From behind the woodshed, Brandbooi watched his master strip the nursemaid to the waist and tie her to a pole. While she squealed like a dassie in the talons of an eagle, he beat the poor woman almost to death with a sjambok.

The punishment meted out was by no means the worst that could happen. Brandbooi was told of a neighbouring farmer who had hunted down a small clan of Bushmen on his land, pursuing them with dogs, horses and guns as one would a leopard that preyed on one's sheep. When the farmer ran the exhausted, starving group to ground, he found two old men, four women and three sick children. The farmer shot them all, one after another, as they sat in the dust beneath a kameeldoring. The children were left for last.

Like shooting squirrels. Less than that, said Brandbooi, because you can eat a squirrel but you cannot eat a Bushman, even a Bushman child. Only the hyenas and jackals can do that, and the vultures and crows.

Food was occasionally stolen because the Boer kept his labour force hungry; he believed people with an empty stomach worked harder and would do anything he asked to get their rations – and, if possible, the rations of the next man as well. Brandbooi was nervous and watchful at all times: the hungrier the labourers became, the greater the danger they presented to the Bushmen, whom they despised and abused at every opportunity. Lean, listless and foul-tempered, the men were ready to inflict injury or even kill for the smallest piece of meat or an extra dollop of mealie meal.

Dokter made sure that the Bushmen suffered less than the others. She ground a special powder from the Hoodia succulent, a recipe passed down from her ancestors that suppressed appetite as it sustained energy, and ensured that they swallowed it.

One hot morning, the white man went off on horseback to shoot on his lands for the pot, taking with him two Hottentot slaves on mules, and two extra mules to carry the carcasses. Meisie said the Boer liked to camp out on his lands and would sometimes stay away for three days. This did not help Brandbooi: a sullen Kaffir was delegated to supervise his labours and to assist when necessary, but this assistance was viewed by the Kaffir as an opportunity to slouch against whatever wall there was and shout at the Bushman. As the sun rose higher in the sky, the heat beat down and cooked every creature that had not taken shelter. The man fell asleep at last, jerking awake now and then in confusion and fear, only to shout and curse until his tongue grew heavy.

As Brandbooi was pondering how many more rocks he would have to haul in his life before he dropped dead from all the water he was losing from his body and the tiny portion of porridge he was feeding it, a soft voice spoke to him in Afrikaans.

He whirled around, dropping the rock he was carrying.

Behind him stood the little spirit girl. Her hair in the sun was red and gold, and so shiny that it made his eyeballs burn with tears to look upon her. But her face was pale and sad, and he thought he could see the white bird bones beneath the skin.

Just then, the Kaffir again shuddered into wakefulness. Sunspots danced across his face, his expression that of a startled giraffe. Brandbooi felt laughter rising from the depths of his belly. The Kaffir dipped his head to the little girl, then stared at the Bushman with feverish, angry eyes and bellowed at him to get to work.

Brandbooi turned back to the rocks he was sorting by size and weight, but not before he had crinkled his cheeks in a friendly manner in the direction of the girl.

The Kaffir, afraid to sleep in case the child reported him to her father, got on to his haunches, waiting for the replacement nursemaid, a Griqua woman, to appear. But nobody came for the little girl; the Griqua maid was nowhere to be seen. Fearing the consequences if the child was seen in their company, the Kaffir rose reluctantly to his feet. Cursing under his breath, he stalked off to find the nursemaid.

The spirit girl came closer, smiling. She seemed relieved that the Kaffir had left them. Brandbooi had picked up a few words of Afrikaans, and when the girl pointed to his leg and said something, he thought he understood.

Before he could move away, she reached out with her tiny fingers and gently touched the hard carapace which had grown across the lumpy flesh of the wound. *Goed,* she said.

Honoured by the little white spirit's kind attention, Brandbooi felt a strong urge to express his appreciation in some way. The only thing he could think of was to give her a demonstration of what he had regarded as the best sorcery he had ever seen when he himself was a young child, the sorcery that had given him his Bushman name – Brandbooi being an approximation in the Afrikaans tongue.

He looked about him, and found two slim but solid sticks of wood of uneven lengths. Glancing up at the dwelling and its surrounds, he saw there was nobody in sight, only the bleached sky and a pallid, thirsty sun, and the wind which blew the spirit child's hair behind her like a red hartebeest in flight.

Brandbooi took the two sticks and, as he had done countless times since he was a small child, rubbed them against each other; then he blew on them lightly. The spirit child watched, fascinated. This was Brandbooi's magic, and it did not take him long. A small flame burst from between his palms and the child exclaimed in wonder, reaching out a hand to touch it. Brandbooi laughed, holding the burning sticks out of the reach of her questing fingers.

Which was when it happened.

Among all seasons and weathers, Brandbooi trusted the wind least. Full of trickery and mischief, quick to lose its temper and slow to relent, it loved to make trouble. When it lost control it could rage ceaselessly, as if possessed by the most vengeful of spirits, and stampede all in its path.

As the Bushman pulled the crackling sticks away from the spirit girl, the wind saw them together and became jealous. It raised its voice, and dust and sand began flying. Soon it was shrieking and tugging at the sticks.

At first, the flames seemed to shrivel. Then, pounded by a vicious gust, the sticks flared up. Seizing the opportunity, the wind sucked them up and spat them directly onto the woodshed. Not content with the roar of burning wood and the great spume of smoke rapidly climbing the sky, it snatched up the fire and tossed it onto the stables, and from there to the outhouses.

Before a single bucket of water could be filled, towering flames flew through the air and landed on the roof of the Boer's whitewashed dwelling.

The Naming

AS THE FIRE RAGED around them, Brandbooi realised two things: one, his own foolish, boastful actions had provoked the wind and two, he had sentenced his own people to death. Owing to this carelessness, their lives now belonged to him, and could only be saved by him.

He immediately took to his heels and ran almost as fast as the flames themselves, leaving behind the spirit girl, who seemed already to have vanished in the smoke. He was not worried about her, knowing that her powers would be strong enough to prevent her from being consumed.

In spite of the infernal heat of the fire and the victorious wind, in spite of the acrid smoke hurled in his face, quenching its thirst on fluids in his eyes, nostrils and mouth, Brandbooi gathered up his people. The small group seized their few possessions, including some useful items that did not belong to them but were conveniently to hand, and took whatever food and water they could find.

Then they fled from the fire and what remained of the farmstead as fast as they could go, Meisie bearing the two babies, bunched together, on her back.

When Bushmen, especially those with some water and a morsel in their stomachs, are forced by an extreme circumstance to vanish, there is no white man, no rifle, no dog, no power on this earth that will ever find them, boasted Brandbooi. Father brought up the matter of the lion dog that had found him, but the Bushman was dismissive: the Boer's dog was an exception, no ordinary dog but a creature possessed of supernatural powers which enabled it to think with greater cunning than its master and to become the half-man, half-beast that had hunted Brandbooi down.

Father laughed. It seemed to have slipped the Bushman's agile mind that, by his own admission, carelessness and greed had roused the anger of the spirits, and the Boer and his dog had been the instruments selected to inflict the punishment.

Brandbooi's people did not turn up at the farm empty-handed. They brought a pile of gifts which my parents sorely needed just then: eland and red hartebeest hides, well dried and tanned, gleaming richly in the sunlight. Though father realised that they were almost certainly filched from the Boer, he did not concern himself with the morality of the thing. He and Kobie immediately put them to good use.

In spite of Kobie's gloomy resistance, the newcomers were permitted to build shelters not far from the main sheep kraal, and were soon put to work, fashioning a soak-tub and building the tan-pit for treating hides. These labours, closely supervised by father, followed careful written instructions given him by one of the most successful game hunters in the Upington region.

My parents' attitude to the people working on the farm was vastly different from the Boer's: to them a well-fed worker was a productive worker, a hungry one sleepy and lacking in initiative. Rations and treats were issued weekly. The people were given meal, sheep's milk, buttermilk, cheese and even butter, which the women taught mother how to churn after Dokter pounded a portion of root from the shepherd's tree to a powder, and explained its use as an excellent preservative for milk and butter. When father hunted successfully, there were extra rations of meat. Mother sewed calico garments for the women to cover themselves, and

Meisie showed mother how to make a kind of coffee, called gaat – also from the roots of the useful shepherd's tree.

A vegetable patch, fed carefully with cups of precious well water and fertilised with dung, produced dwarfish mealies, shrivelled onions, teeny turnips, and yellowish, shrunken carrots; mother insisted they were delicious in a soup or stew.

One of the old women lacked her right hand. Brandbooi, whose repertoire of English words grew like weeds, explained to mother how this loss had come about.

It happened that the favoured Kaffir of the Boer was a burly bully, who fattened himself by stealing food from the others at every opportunity. His standard method was to hold a rock above his chosen victim's head with one hand while extending the other for the rations. This man had stolen meat from the Boer one day, and when the theft was discovered, he had accused Dokter, the powerful medicine woman.

The Boer had not bothered to investigate further, choosing to believe that a Bushman was guilty. But he was superstitious about Dokter, and in need of her skills. Thus he craftily substituted her with another Bush-woman. She was older than Dokter and, unlike the others, had not even merited a Boer name, for until the theft she had been all but invisible to her master.

After accusing the frightened woman of the theft, the Boer instructed his chief Kaffir to assemble all the slaves in the front yard of his dwelling. His wife stood in the doorway and watched as her husband and another Kaffir placed a large block of wood on the ground in front of the trembling Bushwoman. The Boer then instructed her to kneel and place her right hand on the wood. He tied the hand to the block with a strip of leather. Then he picked up an axe lying on the ground nearby and chopped off the hand at the wrist – as cleanly as if it were a length of kindling.

After this appalling act, he forbade the slaves to take the poor woman into her shelter and went in to his dinner, leaving her to bleed to death. But as soon as her master had entered his dwelling, the woman's clan sister, Dokter, came silently and swiftly to her side and immediately seared the wound with fire, then covered it with a poultice tied on with the strip of leather used in the amputation.

In this way, the nameless woman's life was saved.

Evil incarnate, mother exclaimed indignantly to father after examining the woman's stump. A sheep for slaughter receives better treatment: at least it dies quickly. She is probably not nearly as old as she looks; it is just that their lives have been so hard, and that hardship is written on their faces and bodies. Slavery is barbaric, and such inhumane acts should be severely punished!

Grinding her teeth, mother cursed the Boer in her own way: I wish that terrible man a long life of pain, bereavement and remorse.

A curse which, in time, she would have cause to remember.

Meisie, the youngest of the Bushwomen, had carried the toddlers on her back for the many miles of wilderness they had traversed to get to the farm. Energetic and feisty by nature, she began working as soon as she had settled. From the first day, she and mother connected intuitively. Mother found her to be a true treasure, quick to learn and able to complete speedily and deftly the many tasks she was set, sometimes assisted by the woman whose hand had been chopped off.

The vegetable patches, under attack from birds and rodents and all manner of insect pests, were given into the special care of Poppie and Imp, who toddled about in the planted areas and made life difficult for the pests. The care of the little girls was shared among the Bushwomen.

Mother visited the vegetable patch daily, partly because she loved to play with the children. Her attentions, and the treats she brought with her, first received with habitual shyness and caution, became a daily event eagerly anticipated by all three of them. While enjoying the toddlers romping around her, mother was dogged by anxiety and disappointment that she had not yet conceived. She began to wonder if there was something wrong with her, or if she was simply too old. Father had no such doubts. She would have his child, and it would not be long. Meanwhile, to cheer her up, he suggested they have a party. The dwelling, the shelters for Kobie and the Bushmen, the kraals, well, tan-pit, the little dairy and the vegetable and mealie patch were in place; the time had come to celebrate, and to name their homestead.

You, my love, said father, must choose the name.

The day before the party, Kobie dug a deep rectangular pit. Father had shot and skinned four springbok, and would be roasting them on fine metal skewers and a griddle he had brought from the Cape. He intended starting the fire at dawn on the day of the party, so that the meat would be slow-cooked, crisp on the outside and juicy within. In the big black potje, mother and Meisie stewed mutton, lamb and vegetables all day over a low fire.

On the day of the party, work stopped at noon. When the shadows grew longer, the heat softened, and the sand glittered like gold dust. The Bushmen gathered at the roasting pit, clad in their finest strips of hide, with ostrich-shell jewellery in their ears and feathers adorning their heads; around their necks and waists kameeldoring pods, springbok horns and beads were strung with sinew. Mother wore her best dress, which was her lacy white wedding dress. Even Kobie was neatly dressed in an old blue shirt and trousers father had given him, both garments carefully laundered for the occasion.

The air, scented with the juices of roasting meat and the anticipation of festivity, caused nostrils to dilate and eyes to glisten. Father brought out two bottles of his precious store of Cape wines and distributed a little in mother's pretty glasses. Everybody became quite jolly, especially Kobie, who had not touched a drop in many months.

Brandbooi came forward and suggested that his people dance a spirit dance of their ancestors to celebrate the joyous occasion and to offer up respect and gratitude for the meat they would consume that day. Father willingly agreed; a Bushman dance was a privilege outsiders seldom had the opportunity to enjoy.

Mother held the babies in her arms as Brandbooi began dancing and the other Bushmen followed, forming a circle. Slowly at first, then faster, the people gyrated, the older men and women as nimble on their feet as the younger. Then the circle tightened and Brandbooi and Meisie were suddenly in the centre, leaping into the air like two young springboks in a mating dance. They capered and sprang, throwing their limbs about with reckless abandon, then reverted to tiny mincing steps in an ever-tightening circle with the others. Finally, the two whirled and pranced in mesmerising mimicry of antelope leaping over bushes and reeds in a desperate bid to escape a predator. At one point, the excitement was so high that the air seemed to spark and turn fiery. Even Kobie was transfixed: sullen and jealous to begin with, after imbibing a further portion of wine he had become quite merry.

Without warning, the medicine woman, Dokter, fell to the ground. Her eyes disappeared into her head; the whites gleamed like tarnished pearls in her face. Blood began pouring from her nostrils. Mother ran to assist, but Brandbooi detained her by standing in her path, his head respectfully bent. He informed her with word and gesture that her intervention was not required; that the bleeding was of great significance since it meant the old woman's trance had successfully expelled an evil spirit.

What evil spirit? asked mother, puzzled. This is a party, a celebration!

Meisie, who seemed to have shed not a drop of perspiration in the exertions of the dance, smiled and touched mother's arm reassuringly; then she knelt to assist the old woman, stemming the flow of blood with a rag.

After all had eaten their fill – faces shining with grease, bellies so round they resembled overripe tsamma melons – father asked mother to say a few words, and to announce the name she had selected for the farm. The people already knew some words of English, but on this occasion, to ensure that mother's crisp British diction was clearly understood, father translated, in a cross-cultural patois that he had rapidly adopted – and adapted.

When we first reached this part of the Auob River, said mother, my husband shot his rifle into the air below this very site on which we now stand. This was to mark the end of our journey, and to express the joy he felt that we had arrived safely at last. But I was filled with uncertainty as to what lay ahead, and wondered if I would be brave enough to confront the difficulties of living in this lonely place. I saw nothing but barren sand and scrub and I could not visualise, no matter how hard I tried, transforming it into the home it has become. That is partly because I did not dream of people with hearts as generous and good as yours, or of the hard labour you willingly gave to build our farm. It is you who have transformed it into the haven it is; a haven shared by us all.

Mother paused for a moment, and the listening silence of the desert took over, the only sound the soughing of a breeze too feeble even to stir the sand. Looking into the upturned faces around her, she pointed to their various accomplishments.

I cannot thank you enough for all this; for what you have achieved. Until this very moment, I had been unsure of the name. Now, looking into my own heart, I have decided to name our home *Rêve Perdu*. Lost Dream.

The people murmured among themselves, slightly confused. Mother asked father to pour more wine, and urged the people to refill their plates with roasted meat, which still perfumed the air in a way that made the saliva flow all over again.

The next morning, beneath a tree not thirty yards from our dwelling, Chummy and May discovered the carcass of a huge male lion.

He lay on his side, his black mane mangy and tattered, thick ribs visible through the tawny hide. His eyes were wide open, large and golden, with flies lingering in them as if they were pools of honey. Enormous yellow fangs in shiny blackened gums were frozen in a snarl; formidable claws splayed out from paws as big as dinner plates. From mere feet away, he seemed to be reclining lazily in the heat of the day.

Brandbooi, prodding the mane with his toe, was unsurprised. That old medicine woman is much too strong for this evil spirit, he announced to father. She has the power to expel at one time – he held up four fingers – this many, equally as strong as this one.

Later events caused me to wonder about the name mother gave our homestead: did she foresee, at the moment of the naming, a future that caused her choice to be more sombre than father would have preferred?

I asked her the reason for this choice one evening as we sat together outside the back door. Despite the annoyance of sand fleas, I was cross-legged in the sand at her feet.

I like the dream part of the name, mother, but why lost?

Her mood that evening was strangely restless, hard to define. Her eyes had a flat, grainy look to them that obscured their lovely hazel colour. She watched the sun bronze the tops of the kameeldorings for a moment, looking thoughtful.

The meaning of the name has metamorphosed over the years, Em. It seemed a good name back then for such a tiny speck in the universe: lost, meaning isolated, lonely; dream, as in enchantment. A fantasy in a remote, enchanted place.

She turned away, and I saw by the set of her mouth that I was again Em of the endless questions, some of them tricky and discomfiting.

At the time of the naming, I think I was trying to describe our lives here, lost to civilisation, to society; in a sense lost in time and space. We had chosen to settle in a place where our own existence counted for nought to anybody; a world unknown, therefore non-existent to most people.

I shook my head and rebuked her gently. This is our world, mother, but it is the real world too. We count here; that should be enough. You have said yourself that we live every day rather than merely endure, that our lives are challenging but also creative. As for society, what of our people? What of the creatures that live here? The Kalahari has educated me as no other place could; and you are part of that; you and father. You have shown me the way.

Her hand reached down and caressed my cheek.

Perhaps I am not explaining myself clearly, Em. I will try harder. I think the 'lost dream' part has something to do with our way of life here: we live outside the constraints and refinements of normal society. You have little knowledge or understanding, naturally, of such socialisation.

I think it is the very absence of such 'socialisation' that gives meaning to our lives, I continued stubbornly. Here nobody tells us what to do or how to do it, how to think or behave; we make all those decisions for ourselves. That is not lost; if anything, that is found. A found dream.

It was as if she did not hear me.

I believed at first, she said sadly, that if I made a great effort to be part of this wilderness respectfully, gratefully, like the Bushmen, if I created a good home for my family within it, it would open up, share some of its secrets. I hoped, foolishly, to bend it to my will in certain ways. Instead of which it has brought me to submission while excluding me absolutely. More than that: it has changed me beyond recognition.

She murmured something else I did not catch. I waited, feeling the chill of night already closing in.

There is no vernal whiff here, no green autumnal chill, she sighed. Those nuances belong to other worlds. There is only sun-dazed scrub and scouring sand, and nights – nights that grip every living thing in fists of ice.

Shivering slightly, she looked up at the darkening sky. Yet these extremes have also been an important lesson to me. They have taught me that all our endeavours in the Kalahari are as nothing to it; that we ourselves are nothing more than a grain or two of sand in the wind. No city could have taught me half so well the insignificance of our place in the universe.

Rising to her feet, she took my hand and we walked inside.

The name I gave our farm that day was the work of a seer, Em. I am no seer. But when one lives one's dream, one sacrifices a substantial part of it – and of oneself. Just as your father had before me, I fell in love with this place, and over the years it has crept inside me. Now it owns us both. It is our only dream. We have, in some sense, *merged* with it, sacrificed part of ourselves; yet we remain excluded. We will never be part of the Kalahari, as a Bushman is.

She tied on her apron to help Meisie with dinner. The Kalahari must not be permitted to take you as well, Em.

I was not certain that I understood all mother's words that day – or even the mood that freed her to speak so to me – but my own mood was infected by hers. I peered out into the shadows, and saw a spotted eagle owl huddled beside a thick bush. It did not move a feather, as still as the cold night that grew rapidly colder; I wondered if it was sitting on an egg. As I watched, one yellow eye closed in a slow wink.

The strange tension mother had aroused seeped into the darkness outside.

A week after the celebration, mother discovered she was pregnant with me. In truth it was not she who observed the change, but Meisie. Mother had been far too busy to note the significance of her curbed flow, which had apparently been absent for months when Meisie, pointing to the growing mound of her mistress's stomach, spread the five fingers of her right hand to indicate how far along she thought mother was.

Suki, Dot and the Lions

SLANG AND UIL WERE the names the Boer had given to the two old Bushmen, and they were content to keep them. Their Bushman names had been discarded for so long that they themselves seemed to have half-forgotten them. Father found the names oddly appropriate: Slang, deceptively wizened, was as swift and as stealthy as a snake, and Uil's orange-tinted eyes saw further and clearer than anyone else's, especially at night. The woman who lacked a hand had lived for many years ignored and nameless, her Bushman name seldom used even by her own people. Mother, in consultation with Meisie, called her Doekie; the reason for this choice was that the woman had taken a sharp stone, cut a striped skirt mother had given her into strips, and bound a different-coloured strip around her head each day.

Doekie was so thrilled with her name that for a few weeks she referred to herself almost exclusively in the third person: Doekie will make pap; Doekie will fetch water.

Dokter, healer and smeller-out of spirits, approached mother and implored her to select a new name; she hated the Boer and wanted his memory banished. So Dokter became Tam, an abbreviation of a tree mother loved that does not grow in the Kalahari. The tamarisk has tiny scale-like leaves and slender branches and is rather small, almost a shrub rather than a tree. Tam too was small, even for a Bushwoman, but her powers were such as to render her height inconsequential.

When the time came for mother to leave the farm to give birth to me in Upington, father gave careful thought as to who was to accompany her. He himself could not leave the farm, and he needed either Brandbooi or Kobie to remain with him. Meisie could not go as she would be performing a good many of mother's tasks as well as her own. Kobie and Slang had developed a particular antipathy for each other, which grew worse as each day passed. Kobie claimed the old man gave him the evil eye and wanted him dead; Slang complained Kobie stank worse than any white man and he could not bear to be near him.

In the end father decided to send Kobie; he knew the way and could drive the wagon better than Brandbooi could. And he himself needed a break from Kobie's persistent rancour towards the Bushmen, which translated into whining about them at every opportunity. Instead of sending a second man, father chose Doekie to go along as well. She seemed to antagonise Kobie least, and she could take care of mother who, despite her immense tummy, was fortunately in excellent health for the fourteen-day journey.

About five weeks before the baby was due, they left, fully provisioned, at dawn. Though the journey was uneventful, the bickering of Kobie and Doekie was almost as much of an irritation as the discomfort of riding in the wagon on the little-used track. Often, mother simply got out and walked, especially in the early morning when the sun barely tipped the horizon and shrubs still bore the sheen of dew. When mother was not in the immediate vicinity, Kobie and Doekie fell silent, as if she were a provocateur in their disagreements. The peace that descended was a blessing, the only sounds the wagon wheels grinding along the track and the occasional calling of a bird.

On one of these early morning ambles mother saw a full-grown bateleur eagle on the track in front of her. To her surprise, it did not take to the sky as she approached, but pinned a fierce gaze on her until she came quite close; then it turned its beautiful black head away in disdain and flew up to a dead tree. From its perch, the eagle gazed at her expectantly; then, as if in greeting, it barked – *kow-wah*. The sound resonated in the cool morning air.

Uplifted by the encounter, mother was sure it was a good omen. Less than two days later, they reached Upington. Not a moment too soon, as her pains had begun.

She was put to bed in the birthing room in the home of a local midwife whose husband owned the farmland for miles around their homestead. Pains, arrows dragged slowly through mother's innards, came with little or no remission between them, but no baby butted its way into the hot little room. The midwife, chattering away to mother in a quaint, oddly reassuring mix of English and Afrikaans, was not worried: most first babies took their time about entering the world. And who could blame them, she asked, for delaying such an ordeal and remaining for as long as possible where they were safe and comfortable?

Mother had ceased to listen. She had not expected such prolonged agony and was tiring rapidly, at times wandering inside her mind, greeting the black and red bateleur which she saw still perched, waiting for her, on the branch of the dead tree.

After a few brief, shattering moments of clarity, when she was certain she would have to go under the knife if only there was a surgeon within a hundred miles of the town to cut the baby out of her, the midwife delivered me.

Thirty hours had passed; the night was dark and the hour late. In spite of her exhaustion, mother said the most thrilling moment of her life was the sight of my round face in the candlelight, my perfect limbs, the almost instantaneous pinkness of my cheeks. But best of all was my plume of hair, already the strong Titian colour it was (sadly) destined to remain.

The next morning, mother awoke to the slimy embrace of blood-drenched nightclothes and soaked bedding. The reek was of a slaughterhouse. Lying at her side, I was bathed in blood, every part of me wet and red as a fresh-killed lamb. She screamed in horror, thinking, at first, that I was bleeding to death in her bed.

The midwife fought for many hours to save mother's life, and it was her skill and devotion that somehow succeeded in keeping mother's heart beating in spite of the great loss of blood. Three days after her ordeal, she regained full consciousness, and asked for me. Only then did the midwife know for certain that her patient would regain her health. Later, the midwife told her she had lost two birth mothers who had shed less blood.

While mother's life was in danger, I was growing plump on the milk of a wet nurse who had her own baby to feed and sufficient milk to feed a dozen babies.

Mother cradled me joyfully, barely attending as the midwife advised that she have no more children. She could not give a reason for the haemorrhage, but thought that mother's advanced age for a first child (thirty-two) might have had something to do with it. Mother immediately enquired how long the delay would be before they could return to the Auob. The woman shook her head: It would be many months before it would be safe to undertake such an arduous journey.

Twenty-two months after I was born, mother was strong enough to go home. By that time I was toddling about, the pet of the farmers' wives. I was especially favoured by the Boer woman who had come to warn mother of the hazards of the desert to her complexion. This kind lady was distressed to see that some, if not all, of her predictions had come to pass: mother's skin had hardened and turned nut brown, her lips were cracked and flecked with dry skin; broken nails, for the first time in many months, had had time to repair, but her beautiful auburn hair, streaked with gold from the sun, displayed also a sprinkling of white – perhaps from the struggle to regain her health and strength.

Kobie, waiting idly for the command to prepare the wagon to return to the farm, was finally told by mother that there would be a lengthy delay owing to her ill-health and enforced recuperation. He declined to offer his labour to the farmers thereabouts – mother's suggestion – and succumbed instead to disappointment and boredom, falling back into his old ways and spending his time pursuing mischief and imbibing cheap spirits. Doekie gleefully reported to mother that during his long periods of absence he was reputed to be sharing the ill-gotten gains of acquaintances who were layabouts and thieves.

Doekie, on the other hand, only too pleased to be rid of Kobie, served mother faithfully. The midwife claimed she did more work with one hand than her own servants did with two. When she had the time, Doekie was also an attentive and loving nanny who called me Suki, an affectionate name whose provenance was obscure.

In the matter of names, mother decided to wait until she and father could choose a name together; she thought Doekie's choice, until such time, as pretty as any. She herself, however, called me Dot, after her mother.

As the months passed and no message arrived from father, mother became concerned, wondering if word of my birth and her own frail health, conveyed by an itinerant couple who owned a wagon and mules and were known to the midwife (and well paid for their mission) had fallen prey to one of the hazards of the journey and failed to reach him. Deprived of news, she knew father would be exceedingly anxious about our well-being.

One morning, without a word to anyone, mother left the homestead after breakfast and walked the short distance to the general store, which had grown a great deal in size and in the variety of stock since her last visit. After some investigation of the surrounding area, she located Kobie. Clad in rags, he lay on his back on the stony ground, snoring loudly, fully exposed to the already cruel sunlight of the morning.

Rank garbage and heaps of empty bottles and bottle tops were strewn in every direction. Close to Kobie's loose fingers, a bottle stood upright, still half-full of spirits, a reek of fermentation in the arid air.

Mother bent to retrieve the bottle. Holding it at arm's length, she emptied the contents over Kobie's head, careful to avoid his open mouth with its few stumps of teeth. This heinous act, one which mother had never thought to perform in her life, elicited only a prolonged, fetid eruption and a kicking out of the right foot.

Her action had caught the fascinated if inebriated attention of other layabouts, who drew closer to witness this unprecedented, eccentric behaviour of a white woman in their midst. Undeterred, mother got a good grip on the empty bottle, bent down and, precisely as one would knock on a door, tapped none too gently on Kobie's forehead. To her consternation, the taps had to escalate considerably in number and intensity before Kobie finally started up to a sitting position.

Casting about him wildly, his rheumy eye alighted on the bottle clutched in mother's hand. Noting its emptiness, his mouth gaped in shock.

Glowering, holding the bottle aloft like a flag or a sjambok, a single staccato command flew from mother's mouth, the tone regrettably high-pitched: Kobie had but two days to prepare himself for his duties on the long journey home.

For the homeward journey, the wagon was laden with provisions: flour, candles, great bundles of potatoes and onions, even oranges grown on the banks of the Orange River; and of course me, a small, excited animal on Doekie's lap. It was very early, but the chill of the night had lost its grip and the penumbra of the horizon was beginning to catch fire. Bouncing up and down, I would not settle for hours, even though the day began, soon enough, to show its true red-hot colours.

The first twelve days on the furrowed, choppy track, though scorching and bone-breaking by day and very cold by night, passed peacefully. Kobie, driving the oxen, was stoop-shouldered and morose, but carried out his duties – driving, outspanning, shooting a steenbokkie or a springbok if one presented itself, preparing the fire and such – efficiently enough. There was little evidence of his quick temper; Doekie, fuelled by boredom and mischief, tried more than once to provoke him, but he merely stooped even lower to the ground as he went about his work.

Unable to hide her satisfaction, Doekie informed mother in Kobie's hearing that he was low because he thirsted for spirits. Mother retorted that if father had any say in the matter, Kobie would be parched for the rest of his life – and much the healthier for it.

I thrived on the journey, to mother's delight, eating whatever I was given, and stimulated equally by the sight of a lilac-breasted roller, a wildflower or a star in the sweeping dome of the sky. I walked about energetically whenever we outspanned and had to be watched, for I had a tendency to wander. To Doekie's annoyance, Kobie became quite a favourite with me, and the few words he spoke on that journey were apparently spoken to me. He even began taking me for short walks in the late afternoons, borne aloft on his shoulders, both of us gazing at the sky as we waited for the appearance of the evening star.

On a night when the moon was a lemony sliver that barely tinted the sky, mother retired with a smile on her face. The journey was almost over; she permitted herself to look forward to the reunion with her husband, and the expression on his face at the sight of his small, busy daughter.

I slept beside mother, with Doekie lying not far from us, across the partially open entrance to the wagon; a position she favoured for the freshness of the night air. When the moon was brighter and the night not so cold, Doekie preferred to sleep outside, beside the dying fire. As a young Bushwoman on the move with her clan, she had often slept on the sand outside the shelters.

Kobie, as he always did, bedded down beneath the wagon.

Mother awoke in the night. Usually a sound sleeper, she listened for a moment, her eyes wide, but heard nothing. Sitting up, she gazed across Doekie's sleeping figure into the dense, almost moonless darkness, wondering what had disturbed her.

There was an odour in the air, feral and thick. Alarmed, mother pushed her blankets aside.

A hand stilled her; a voice whispered a single word in her ear: *Stilte*.

Kobie. Inside the wagon. He never slept inside!

What is it? whispered mother, wondering why she was whispering.

Kobie's hand gripped her wrist. A snuffling and grunting from outside the wagon told her why.

Lions.

God, what about the oxen, she murmured. Why are they not bawling and bellowing?

A whiff of sleep-stale breath reached her even through the pungent stench of the lions.

Four, whispered Kobie. Young males. They have killed one of the oxen and pulled it beneath the wagon. They are eating it beside the very spot where I sleep. The other animals are where I have tethered them, beside the kameeldoring. They are safe.

How could this happen, whispered mother. How is it that we did not hear the oxen?

Spirit lions. Swift, silent killers like these can only be spirit lions.

Kobie's sibilant hiss was so full of primal terror that chills shook mother from head to foot. He pointed to Doekie's still sleeping form.

Even she has not yet woken, and she is Bushman.

Doekie, as if knowing that he was talking of her, called out something in her sleep. Abruptly the wagon began shaking. Kobie left mother's side and peered out through a slit in the closed canvas.

What he saw made him step backwards in such a hurry that he fell over Doekie, who awoke and sat up. At sight of him, she clicked away angrily in the Bushman tongue.

An ear-shattering roar, close enough to shake every piece of timber that held the wagon together, roused me. I began to cry. Mother held me, placing her trembling palm gently over my mouth; I inhaled the musky, unfamiliar scent of her fear and cried the louder.

Kobie spoke firmly into the darkness.

They are not hungry for us, but we must remain still and quiet. If we move, they will come to kill us.

Mother held me tightly.

Doekie cringed against the side of the wagon. Spirit lions, she said, emitting a few frightened clicks. Tam can kill them. Tam has the power to kill them all.

But Tam was not there.

The eeriest aspect of the night's drama was the riddle of the silent oxen: they had been known to be disturbed by the proximity of a brown hyena – why had they not raised the alarm when they sniffed hunting lions? Even jackals could sometimes rouse them to a communal lowing and snorting of protest. That the lions were spirits was as good an explanation as any, but did not diminish the trauma of four lions in their prime feasting on an ox beneath the very spot where mother lay with her child in her arms.

To make matters worse, I would not settle. I was not troubled by the lions, of whose ferocity and imminent threat I was ignorant, but by tremors that made mother twitch uncontrollably as she bit back the impulse to scream, run, anything but sit still and listen, her head filling with snuffling and growling, with the tearing of flesh and crunching of bones.

For the remainder of the night, the feeding lions kept them awake. Every move the beasts made shook the wagon, and every half-hour a cacophony of protracted, ferocious snarling erupted as they scrapped.

The panic this din caused was almost comical, said mother, if you were not caught up in it. To Kobie's irritation, Doekie clawed him painfully with her uncut nails in a desperate bid for reassurance. Cutting her loose led to a silent tussle between them, interrupted by the wagon listing to one side as the lions shoved violently from beneath it.

At the height of the bloodthirsty battles royal, mother was convinced that the wagon would overturn, plunging us all into the jaws of the warring animals.

At first light, mother stirred to a welcome silence.

Kobie and Doekie were not in the wagon. She peered out and saw them standing in the wintry air of dawn by a breakfast fire.

Kobie walked over.

The lions have gone, madam, he said.

Then why have you lighted the fire? We must leave immediately and eat our breakfast elsewhere, replied mother, alarmed. They will be back for the rest of the meat.

Kobie glanced behind him, then back at her. Mother noticed that his eyes were clearer in the grey light than they had been for days.

His shoulders straightened. The lions will not be back, madam. There is nothing left.

Mother climbed down from the wagon and stared underneath it.

The sand was churned up, and there was a noxious whiff of death and decay. But not a single drop of blood, not a shred of flesh nor a splinter of bone marred the previous night's battleground.

Meisie

FATHER WAS WAITING at the point where the dry riverbed of the Auob met the track. Kobie stopped the wagon and mother dismounted, holding me in her arms. She walked towards her husband, and could not tell if it was laughter or tears she saw in his expression; perhaps it was both.

As mother had suspected, he had been anxious about us for a very long time, as he had received no communication from the itinerant couple dispatched for this purpose, or from anyone else. Latterly, he had taken to waiting at that same place in the Auob every afternoon for an hour, in hopes that our wagon would crest the horizon. At times he imagined he heard the creaking of wheels and the lowing of oxen, but it was only the wind in the kameeldorings and his own longing.

Just the day before, he had finally come to a decision: he would wait no longer but come alone to seek us out, leaving the farm in the hands of the Bushmen. When the wagon rolled into his vision, a reality at last, father was too overcome, at first, to do anything but gaze in disbelief. It had been a long separation.

Mother offered him his daughter, but I shrank back and hid my face in her neck, shy of the perspiring, muscled stranger with teary eyes. Father embraced us both, weeping. Mother was at a loss to comfort him, but he took me from her and lifted me into the air, from where I eyed him in astonishment.

His smile wide, he told mother that I was beautiful; that we were both beautiful.

Of this reunion, I remember almost nothing. Mother's long convalescence had caused father to miss most of my first two years. The memory I choose to believe I retained from that first meeting, likely reinforced by proximity, was father's characteristic odour: smoky, dusty, gritty in the nostrils. Unchanging as the years went by, unchangeable by any circumstance of hard labour or emotional distress, that odour was a part of him I held very dear.

That first day, mother introduced me to him as Dot or, she laughed, Suki. Father scoffed at both names, examining my every feature carefully and extolling the rust-red hair of his father, Jeremiah, on my head. Had I been a boy, Jeremiah would have been my first name, and mother would not have disputed this; but when she heard the names he had in mind she laughed the harder at first, then plucked four letters decisively from the air: my first name, she informed him, would be Emma; the title of her favourite Jane Austen novel.

Later that week, my parents used well water in a simple ceremony and anointed me with several drops, which I attempted to catch on my tongue, for each of my forenames and my surname: Emma Jeremiah Dorothea Johannsen.

Within days, I became Em – though Doekie continued to call me Suki.

Meisie was overjoyed to see mother again, and immediately took me from Doekie, whom I had grown to love and who loved me fiercely in return. Mother did not feel she could intervene and hoped matters between them would resolve themselves. I quickly grew fond of Meisie, and often pottered about after both women while they worked. As mother had hoped, the two soon came to a pragmatic accommodation as far as my guardianship was concerned at those times when mother was otherwise occupied.

Poppie and Imp were my playmates from the first moment we saw one another. Though younger than them by almost two years, I was firm in character, and easily assumed command. Delighted with the novelty of my company, my two new friends vied with each other to comply with my every wish.

Several weeks later, it dawned on mother that Brandbooi and Meisie were sharing a shelter as Doekie and Tam shared a shelter, and Slang and Uil theirs. Poppie and Imp lived in a small lean-to beside Brandbooi and Meisie. Kobie lived alone, in a hut that he built with more care than the Bushmen who, he scoffed, built their homes as if they were leaving them the following day: the first strong wind would blow them away, and good riddance.

Mother broached the subject of the shared shelter to Meisie as they were preparing firecakes and porridge for breakfast.

Has Brandbooi taken you to wife, Meisie?

Meisie was silent, looking down, her fingers busy.

What is it? Are you going to have a child? That would be fine; more company for Em, and for Poppie and Imp.

Meisie's hands stilled. She did not look up. Mother thought her hesitation understandable. How to find the courage to trust a white woman when whites have abused and betrayed your people, and every instinct urges discretion?

When Meisie spoke, her voice trembled.

Brandbooi asked me to be his woman on the Boer's farm almost as soon as he was well enough, madam. I refused him then. I told him it was because I could not have children. He said he didn't care; he still wanted me for his wife. But I had many thoughts about his wife and children, about the big water that had taken them to the spirit world. I knew that I could not be a proper wife to him, the wife that every Bushman must have.

She looked at mother at last, her eyes brimming with sadness.

To a Bushman, madam, children are like his faith in the spirits. He must have them both. There is no other way. Brandbooi needs a wife who can give him children to replace those he lost. But he would not listen when I told him this, many times. He kept asking to take me to wife and I kept refusing him, until one day he brought me Poppie and Imp and said that they would be our family, and the spirits would rejoice.

I told him I would like to ask madam's opinion on the matter, but the months went by, and you did not return. And Brandbooi is very strong in his spirit; stronger than me.

It is good to be with him, Meisie?

It is good to be with him, madam.

Then I agree with Brandbooi: the spirits must indeed rejoice that Poppie and Imp have a mother and a father.

Mother hesitated. How do you know for certain that you cannot conceive a child?

Meisie told her how she knew. Later, mother obtained Meisie's permission to tell me part of the story for my journal. I do not know it all because mother said at twelve and a half, I was too young. But she did not believe I was too young to learn a significant lesson about the nature of mankind.

The women on the Boer's farm, married or not, belonged to him, and were his for the taking. Other than Meisie's story, mother did not confide the details of the multiple atrocities which the Boer committed against the farm women, and against all his workers; but she told me that his animosity towards Bushmen in general was expressed in particular in acts of extreme cruelty towards the poor Bushwomen.

Both Poppie and Imp were the white man's seed. Unnamed by the Bushmen because of the disgrace of their half-caste parentage, both were rescued from infanticide – openly encouraged in such cases – by Meisie's uncommonly merciful heart.

Imp's mother was herself half Bushman, half Hottentot, and this unfortunate mix caused her to be spurned by both peoples on the farm. For years she laboured alone, ignored and excluded by all but Meisie who, feeling compassion for the woman's isolation, tried to be kind to her.

To the Boer, her master, the half-caste woman was a plaything. The curse of her mixed blood rendered her even more powerless than the other workers, and more vulnerable to the Boer's abuse. One of his previous victims, in the final month of her pregnancy and well aware of the Boer's unnatural predilections and the danger to her unborn child had, in desperation, run away. But there was nowhere to run, and the Boer had caught her. When they returned together to the farm, the woman's hands were bound and there was no baby accompanying them.

Only days after Imp's mother had given birth to her baby girl, her master came to her, and forced himself upon her.

Meisie, whose shelter was not far away, knew what was happening;

all the women knew. They trembled and blocked their ears to the Boer's grunts and his victim's moans, and were guiltily thankful that they themselves were spared. Meisie lay on her pallet, listening to the woman's voice pleading with the Boer, and felt deeply ashamed that she was not brave enough to help her.

The Boer's voice carried in the empty night: he was asking for the child.

In fear for her life and unable to raise such an accursed child on her own, the woman had abandoned it on the waste dump behind the outhouse. In the listening darkness, her voice rose in anguish as she entreated her master to rescue his child.

Meisie heard nothing more from the Boer, but the woman screamed once, a sound that made sweat break out all over Meisie's body. Minutes later, the tense hush was broken by the woman's voice: *If you do not leave me, I will tell your wife that my child is your seed.*

The Boer must have driven the poor woman out of her senses, thought Meisie, her sweat turning to drops of ice beneath her gemsbok hide cover. Tears she had not shed in many months rolled freely down her cheeks.

She resolved to rescue the baby from the dump. She got up and stealthily made her way there. Stumbling about in rubbish in the dark, she heard a cry. The baby was alive – tiny and slippery as a newborn hare. She concealed Imp beneath her arm and took her to Dokter.

Later that same night, beneath a sky roiling with storm clouds, the Boer returned and took Imp's mother from her shelter. Meisie, peeping dangerously from her own shelter, saw the woman emerging, tightly bound and gagged. The Boer tied her to the back of his mule cart, and drove slowly away from the farm, the lion dog loping behind.

Meisie got up and followed. The dog knew her scent and ignored her presence. Not far away, the Boer stopped the cart, untied the woman's hands, took out his rifle and killed her with a single shot to the head. The night echoed with the report.

Meisie found herself sitting under a tree. She wiped her wet face. How would the master explain the sound to his wife? she thought dazedly.

She watched him light a flare and place it in the cart. Then he dragged the body of the woman he had murdered close to the burning flare, and began chopping at her with an axe.

In the dim light, Meisie saw him offer the flesh to his dog.

It was very late. The Boer and his dog had long since left the place of the killing.

Meisie could not find the strength to return to her shelter. She sat on under the tree, thinking about the spirits for a while, then forced herself painfully to her feet and began covering up the poor torn-up remains with sand, stones and dead branches. When she could see nothing of the corpse, she began tramping back through the cold night to the farm. Each step she took on the hard ground caused a spasm in her chest, as if the lion dog that had devoured the dead woman's organs and licked up her blood was now attacking Meisie's heart.

She made no sound as she walked, but the clamour of her soul-spirit was deafening. Why had she not done something, no matter the sacrifice? But what could she do, she was nothing! Where was the God of the K'ang? Where were the spirits hiding when deeds of the devil were being perpetrated? Why was it that the white man went unpunished, time after time? Why did he feel no remorse? What evil god was on his side that gave him the freedom and the power to commit the next atrocity?

The questions tumbled about in her head, but no answers came to her. She turned her face up to the sullen sky and spoke in anger and confusion and grief: Why have you abandoned this woman who could expect help from no other? What trespass had she committed in her short life to bring upon herself such a terrible end?

The lion dog reared up before her like the visitation of a deadly spirit she had conjured up with her fierce, impious questions.

Behind the dog sat the Boer on his horse.

As her master climbed down, Meisie saw his teeth like little white flares in the dark.

Stupid, he said to her quietly. *Dom.* Did you think I would not check the shelters before retiring?

When he had finished, the Boer stood up and strapped on the belt with his guns. Then he pulled her by one arm onto her feet and tossed her into the bushes.

Meisie could scarcely feel the thorns in her flesh. Every breath was a fistful of thorns in her lungs. She was only too well aware that she had brought her fate upon herself, she had virtually begged for it by following them even though she had known her quest, whatever it was, was hopeless. In spite of this knowledge, she had ignored the Boer's legendary cunning and chosen to take a terrible risk for reasons that were obscure.

Perhaps to record, if only in her own mind, what her master was capable of.

As the Boer picked up his rifle and climbed onto his horse, she silently willed him to kill her as he had Imp's mother.

He did not do so. Having killed once that night, it seemed he had lost the appetite for murder, or more likely could not be bothered to spend the extra bullet. He probably thought all the blood he had spilt would surely attract hyenas, which would do the second killing for him.

As the Boer rode away, the dog, which had sat throughout with its head on its front paws, its liquid eyes in the dark like the scales of a serpent, rose to its feet. It loped over to the Driedoring bush and sniffed her, its nose cold on her naked bleeding thigh.

Turning its enormous head away, the dog sped into the darkness after its master.

Meisie lay, she did not know for how long, in the bush. After a while she tried to raise herself, to sit; but could not. The slightest move tore through her like a hail of sharpened stones. She could smell fresh blood on the air, her body reeked of it; all around her was the scent of death. She wondered hazily where the hyenas and vultures were, but felt no fear of the dark and its lurking hazards. None compared with the master and the torments he was so expert at inflicting.

But the hyenas did not find her that night. When the sky lightened, she stirred. A burr of sound escaped from deep in her throat. Her eyes were glued shut. Ignoring her throbbing limbs and the lashing of her wounds, she rose, inch by inch, to her feet, her protesting body submitting, finally, to the power of her will.

Taking one tiny step at a time, she hobbled back to the farm.

Dokter, familiar with the ways of her younger friend, had been anxiously searching for Meisie since before dawn. When she stumbled upon her at last Meisie had fallen in a grassy patch close to the farm. She was floundering on her knees, as helpless as a bee without its sting. Dokter clicked in her ear, and gently guided her to the shade of a tree. Then she hurried back to fetch Slang and Uil, who bore the injured woman to the nearest shelter.

The next morning, the Boer walked into the shelter, shoving Dokter to one side as if she were a reed in his path. His hair was neatly brushed and he smelt of frying bacon.

Meisie lay on a pallet which, in spite of Dokter's efforts, was stained with blood.

The Boer touched her leg with his boot. When he spoke his deep voice, accustomed to shouting, was soft.

If I see any one of you near my wife, I will shoot you where you stand and cut you up for biltong like a springbok. I will do this even though your meat is not tasty enough for biltong; it is hyena meat. Hyenas eat cockroaches like you. You are all cockroaches, Hotnots and Kaffirs too; but you Bushmen are the worst cockroaches of all. My wife does not like cockroaches. It would be best for you to remember that. And to remember also that the dog, unlike my wife, is very fond of cockroaches. He crunches them between his teeth before he swallows them.

Yet the Boer himself, Meisie calmly informed mother, continued to favour the taste of cockroaches. Just like his dog. At least once a week.

Some months later, Dokter's poultices and medicaments had gone a long way to healing Meisie's wounds, but her rancour had grown until she carried the weight of it inside her like a rock. Poppie's mother, meanwhile, had given birth to a second child, a son. Though they tried to hide the birth and the baby, somebody, perhaps one of the Kaffirs who hated them, glimpsed the boy and told the Boer.

Poppie and Imp (unnamed back then), were taller than the average Bushman child, and pale-skinned with greenish eyes; but at a rapid glance, they were not markedly different in appearance from the other Bushmen; as a result, the Boer paid them no attention, and neither did anybody else.

But this new child, full brother to Poppie, was beautiful, and perilously white: a blanched, blue-eyed flower of a baby.

He was eight days old when the Boer came. It was dusk, the end of the working day. Poppie's mother sobbed and pleaded, following her master as he kicked the straw around in all the shelters, then searched the woodpile behind them. He found the infant, wrapped in rags, between two logs.

He bent and picked up the bundle in one fist and regarded it for a moment. There was an expression of confusion on his face, as if he had picked up the wrong bundle. Then he touched his son's downy head with a calloused forefinger.

Meisie saw that the eyes of the baby were identical to those of the Boer, blue as wildflowers after a storm. The infant was gazing up at his father. Poppie's mother, wailing, ran to take her son.

It was too late. Huge thumbs on his tiny neck had cut off the air. The Boer shoved the baby's mother aside and put the tiny corpse under his shirt. If any one of you approaches the compost heap, he said, you will join this little dead animal inside it. There will be no mercy.

He buried his son in manure.

He knew we were watching, Meisie told mother bitterly, and he did not care. His own wife had not borne him a son. And Dokter's curses ensured that she never would. After we retired to our shelters that night, Poppie's mother swallowed the poison put out for the rats. We found her at dawn, lying on the compost heap where her son was buried.

The Language of Growing

LANGUAGE, EM, DECLARED FATHER, resembles the weather. Words, whether in the European, Hottentot or Bushman tongue, are like storms, winds, droughts, floods. Learn their origins, observe their formation, listen to them well and they will guide you. If you do not manage them – and, in the case of words, master them – they will turn on you and take charge; they will mock, confuse and imperil you. Worst of all, they will remain forever beyond your reach or understanding.

My parents firmly believed in the importance of language, not merely for communication, but for the window it offered into culture, customs and the more intricate patterns of thought and behaviour. All our people were schooled in spoken English and some Afrikaans. They picked up English, in particular, with notable alacrity – although I could not say we returned the favour in any way as regards their own tongues.

Mother believed this facility for language on the part of our people owed much to a desire to please father, whom they loved and respected. Father thought differently: he claimed native peoples from different tribes and cultures, speaking diverse tongues and dialects, were forced to live in close proximity to one another owing to their livelihoods – on farms, for example – and become accustomed to the foreign tongues of their employers. From necessity, they also develop a facility for communicating with one another. Europeans, on the other hand, are distinctly lacking in will or the required skills.

Father was chagrined at his own lack of success in gaining even a working competence in the Bushman tongue, in spite of the fact that he spoke a variety of European languages well. But you, Em, he said, as the daughter of an accomplished linguist in your father and a disciplined teacher in your mother, have good exposure to the languages of both Bushman and Hottentot. It is nothing less than a rare opportunity to excel.

Father's humour, as always, was half serious.

The ideas of my parents, until I turned three, had not yet become a fully formed reality for me, merely a slight but persistent nuisance. As firm believers in the sentence well spoken and written, they were firmly convinced that reading and writing in my first language should be acquired by me as soon as possible. Thus, almost from the day I turned three, my carefree mornings were largely behind me and lessons were begun. Poppie and Imp, near five years old by then, were instructed to sit beside me in the classroom, a small area adjoining the kitchen. The idea was that they should learn alongside me. But as regards them at least, mother found to her disappointment that she could not enforce her regime for long. After an hour, sometimes a little more, she would turn her back to inscribe something on her paper board, only to find that Poppie and Imp had fled and I was alone.

Mother complained to Meisie, who explained that a Bushman learns all his important lessons from nature and the spirits that dwell in nature. The world was full of guiding spirits, and wisdom emanated from sun, moon and stars, from seasons and animals, and from the insects and plants that adapted to them. The Bushman people lived their lessons. For Poppie and Imp, said Meisie, and for all Bushmen, song, dance and play will supersede any lesson in the world.

From time to time, in the cool of the evening, the Bushmen would do a spirit dance, usually beneath the biggest kameeldoring tree on the farm.

We were not always invited but when we were, I would watch in delight as even Doekie capered like a young girl. I longed to spring up and join in, but mother said the dances had a serious side and children were not always welcome. When Poppie and Imp danced, I was permitted to dance along with them – though my clumsiness was an annoyance when it came to certain movements that my friends executed with natural grace.

Tam, though the oldest of the Bushwomen, was the leader of the dance. Watching her I would feel a chill, in spite of the fading warmth of the day. In those early days, I loved Meisie and Doekie without thought, and I was fond of Tam, but I was also a little afraid of her. The spirit dances seemed to remove her to another plane: to my child's eyes she changed from a little Bushwoman into something unfamiliar and frightening, her springing shadow expanding in her communion with the spirits until it overshadowed everyone else's, and the Tam we knew was, for a time, outside herself and beyond our reach.

Some mornings, after a dance, a dead creature would be found near a tree: a mongoose, a yellow hornbill, a pale chanting goshawk; once a hyena cub, another time a honey badger. But never again did we find a lion – or any other cat, for that matter. When the dead animals were discovered, Brandbooi, Meisie and the others were filled with awe, and immediately performed certain rituals of gratitude to mollify the spirits of the animals, which had died to save us from lurking evil. This evil came out of nowhere, but was smelt out by Tam, and evicted with her uncanny powers.

Privately, father shrugged this off. He confided to mother that Tam had her reasons for the strategic location of dead creatures after a dance, but mother said she was only too happy to have such a powerful soul on our side.

I felt envious of Tam and the respect she received from the others. At four years old, I too wanted to be a shape-shifter, a conqueror of evil spirits, and above all, the leader of the dance.

I want to grow up to be like Tam, mother, I said. I do so want to be a Bushwoman. I will learn the Bushman tongue so I can chant with them and dance as well as Poppie. But to do this, I need to practise, and I can only practise if you allow me to keep my mornings of play with my friends.

Mother smiled, genuinely amused, but impervious to my pleas.

Fortunately, before the hours of lessons became too strictly enforced, I managed to have an adventure or two. One of my last adventures before the advent of the classroom probably thrust me even sooner into mother's hands than had been her intention.

Chummy and May were patient, responsible and good-natured dogs, putting up well with three little girls who pestered them at every opportunity. They permitted us to climb on their backs, and to ride and jump off at will; Chummy even bore Poppie and me on his back together, and managed by his own skill to keep us there until Doekie, tongue clicking at a furious rate, removed us.

Early one hot summer morning, even our childish high spirits had succumbed to lethargy. The three of us were at the rear of our dwelling, sketching in the sand with the sharp end of stones and small sticks. With the heat, our progress had slowed and the sketches had deteriorated to mere slashes. Behind us, the stone wall glinted in the pitiless sun. Even a toe ventured from the shade caused our feet to burn through the soles of our shoes. The shoes were made out of gemsbok hide by Slang, who turned out to be a good shoemaker though he never wore shoes himself; the soles of his feet were so calloused and encrusted that even scalding sand or a sharp thorn did not penetrate.

The pale yellow ball of the sun rested heavily upon my head. The skies, drained of colour, were cloudless; not even a raptor circled. Every living thing in the Kalahari had gone to ground. The bare horizons flashed like a sliver of mother's cracked mirror; dots sprang in front of my eyes. The chalk stone was clumsy in my slippery fingers, and the magnificent gemsbok that only the day before had surveyed me curiously from a nearby dune, refused to come to life in the sand.

Doekie, a short distance away beneath a shepherd's tree, was doing the laundry in a basin, using scented soap mother had brought with her from Upington, a gift of the midwife. The odour was oppressive in the breathless air.

The drooping eyelids of my friends were contagious. We would often sleep the hot afternoons away in the shade of a kameeldoring, with the dogs resting beside us, but sleepiness was uncommon in the morning, when we were much too busy even to think about rest. A stone held loosely between my sweaty fingers, my lids heavy, I watched Imp's head loll to her chest. My eyes snapped open: I was not going to allow the heat to sabotage our morning. A walk, I thought dizzily, a walk will wake us up – although a single step in any direction took us into the teeth of the relentless sun.

Acting on this took some willpower on my part, but at four years old my child's logic (or lack of it) told me that the shade must be sacrificed to prevent a wasted morning. I staggered to my feet and prodded Poppie, who was barely awake, with my toe.

She shook herself like a sandgrouse in a riverbed. She saw I was on my feet, and her mouth dropped open.

Where are you going, Em?

(Poppie had mastered English with a rapidity that astounded mother and superseded Imp's facility with the language by far.)

For a walk, Pop.

But it is too hot, she whined, nodding her head, which she had learned to do from me and did not always apply appropriately.

Well, I would rather walk than sleep, I replied crossly, and stepped out of the shade. I was immediately drenched in perspiration which trickled down my neck, chest and back like worms crawling along my skin. Wondering where I was going, I walked away from the homestead, from the shelter of the acacias and shrubs and shade. The burning of my feet spurred me to greater speed, even as a hot blanket of weariness slumped across me.

Even in those early days, mother often accused me of stubbornness; father called it willpower. Poppie was dragging her heels behind me, but I was well acquainted with her inquisitive nature and knew she would follow. Not many minutes later, we found ourselves well below the homestead and a fair distance away from it, close to a clump of broken reeds in the riverbed.

To put the situation in perspective: the riverbed without adult supervision was forbidden terrain. The reasons were obvious; I knew them well and, up until that day, had been obedient to their sound good sense.

For the first time that morning, a faint breeze rustled through the dune reeds. Poppie's breathing was audible behind me, but she did not speak and I knew, like me, she had no breath to spare. I walked among the reeds, relishing their listless stirring and sparing no thought for poor Doekie who, when the laundry was rinsed, would discover that Imp was alone, fast asleep in the shade, and Poppie and I were missing.

A springbok in the riverbed eyed us from the distance, its body wavering in the haze. The mongooses were sensibly concealed in their dark caverns beneath the cracked sand; not even a playful squirrel peeped from its burrow.

But one creature was abroad. Its movement was so infinitesimal that I missed it entirely. It rose from the sand towards me in a slow, shimmering motion. Thicker than father's wrist, the scales were intricately braided, glistening in the sun's glare. I heard Poppie's cry behind me as if from a distance.

I had seen snakes before and, thanks to father, knew something about them. Only weeks before, I had watched from a safe distance as he and Brandbooi removed a Cape cobra – a glorious rich gold in colour, its hood dangerously spread – from the outhouse. The previous summer, Imp had come too close to a mole snake in her attempt to sketch it. Though not venomous, it had struck a painful gash in her thigh.

As still as the heat-struck landscape all about me, I gazed my fill at the huge serpent, mesmerised by its broad sinuous upper length, rapidly inflating as I watched. How, I thought stupidly, could I retain the image well enough to sketch it in the sand? I wished Brandbooi were there: the creature seemed the epitome of the supernatural serpent in his stories. Or was this the kind of snake that had brought such trouble to Adam and Eve?

In retrospect, there was a strange beauty to that frozen moment, a mutual fascinated recognition that made what happened after seem less significant – even though it stayed with me for a long time.

A sound finally penetrated my trance: a protracted hiss. Abruptly, I realised the appalling danger I was in.

Then the dogs were there: Chummy first, barking hysterically, May streaking behind him.

Blinded by my senseless mission, I had not given a thought to them either. Watching us walking away from the farm, they were forced into a dilemma, for they were trained, as we were, never to leave the farm without the company of father, Brandbooi or Kobie.

The puff adder shuddered; the hissing expanded to a buzz, a drone, a roar in my ears. My throat closed.

Chummy attacked. The puff adder, striking with horrifying speed, sank its memorable fangs into Chummy's smooth black nose.

Before I could draw breath, the serpent had vanished into the great burning maw of the sun. But the strike – the blur of speed and power, the bullseye of its aim – remained etched in my mind, repeating itself through many fretful nights of dreaming.

Neighbours

OUR BELOVED CHUMMY survived, but only just, owing to the miraculous properties of the medicaments and unguents concocted by Tam and assiduously administered by her and father thrice daily. A full three weeks after he was bitten, Chummy finally stood on his four legs unaided. Sadly, he was a changed dog, felled by the power of the giant snake's toxin, fought off with less than total success. His darling face was damaged, its topography unfamiliar and, though still beloved, scarred and ugly. His nose, once a wet, shining black beacon, had healed brownish and dull, resembling nothing so much as a pocked and blighted potato.

More wounding to me was the change to his gentle nature. From a spirited, smiling, courageous leader-of-the-pack kind of dog, he became a slow-moving, timid follower of May, who had given birth to three healthy pups the summer before, two males and a beguiling little female. I missed the old Chummy more than anyone, as he would no longer tolerate my affection, let alone Poppie or me on his back, and would bare his teeth at the slightest provocation.

A rumour on the wind, signs in the sand, perhaps Tam's finely honed senses, brought news that sent a wave of speculation and excitement through our small community. Neighbours! Our very first!

Brandbooi, ostensibly on a foray for tsamma melons, slipped away to investigate. He reported a wisp of smoke some miles away, to the south of our homestead. He dared not venture closer for fear of being shot on sight. Father said his fears were justified; he had heard talk of Bushmen, desperate for food in difficult times, approaching the homestead of a farm only to be shot dead before they could plead their case.

He and mother conferred, and decided a visit would be appropriate to welcome the new neighbours; and, of course, to satisfy our curiosity. They packed a selection of gifts which might be useful to newcomers, among them – despite my vociferous protests – one of the two male pups. The people, whoever they were, would farm sheep, said father – what else? – and a good sheep dog would be invaluable to them. The advent of neighbours was unprecedented, and my parents gave in to my pleas to accompany them, with Poppie and Imp in tow. Father drove the mule cart he and Kobie had recently built, and we rode away one fine, colourful dawn, Poppie, Imp and me chattering in excitement despite the earliness of the hour.

The ride turned out to be longer and rougher than we expected. For much of the time father drove the little cart in the riverbed, where we stopped from time to time to watch squirrels and mongooses at play and allow the pup a few minutes of exercise, chasing the flocks of sandgrouse cheeping and rustling in the grasses. Father estimated the location of our neighbour's farm – if such it could be described – to be about ten miles distant from ours, on one of the gentle inclines above the Auob.

After some hours of a bumpy ride, the three of us, Poppie, Imp and I, became unruly. Mother, clutching onto her big wheel of a hat, ignored our squabbles until the noise became too much; then she issued a sharp reprimand, which was heeded, though not for long.

Fortunately, there were distractions: we soon passed a family of giraffes, scattered all about us and across the rise. There were so many that we stopped to count them while they gazed inquisitively back at us, their large, liquid eyes unblinking, their jaws momentarily still. One of them, a dark-spotted male, came up to the wagon to inspect us at close quarters, his long, scarred neck bent towards us as if he were about to browse. Father claimed the giraffe coveted mother's hat as a tasty morsel; better still, set upon his twitching ears and thick horns, it would go a long way to protecting him from the sun. Mother clutched her hat as if it was at risk, and we all laughed so much the giraffe turned away in disdain.

The baby giraffes were also curious, and quite unafraid. I longed to venture among them and engage them in play, but father said if I were to do such a thing the mothers would use their powerful hindquarters and kick me as they would an attacking lion.

A few miles further on, we spotted the dwelling above us. Father pulled up close by and we dismounted.

Is this where they live, I asked, looking around in dismay.

The dwelling consisted of four uneven walls of dune reeds, and a flat, sloping roof, also of reeds, with stones holding down the corners. There were some trees nearby, and the shelter itself was built in the shade of a large acacia. An enormous sociable weaver nest, suspended precariously from a branch, threatened to tumble to the scraggy roof below it.

A young man emerged from the hut, his lower lip gaping. As unkempt as the dwelling in appearance, his trousers were filthy and his large feet unshod. A bushy dark beard brushed his bare chest.

A girl peeped over his shoulder. Even I could not mistake the expression on her face. As father and mother approached, smiling in an attempt to put the couple at ease, the girl trembled and cast wildly about, as if expecting others to emerge from behind us.

Plainly terrified, she backed into the dwelling.

My parents had expected the new neighbours to be surprised by the visit; they had hoped it would be a pleasant surprise. Why, they asked themselves, should our presence in the middle of nowhere in the Kalahari Desert provoke such fear?

The man goggled at us, seemingly at a loss for words. Barely out of his teens, he was tall and well made, his skin the polished ochre of the dunes. Father quietly introduced us and explained where we lived. He said we had come in the hopes of assisting them in their new home in any way we could. We unloaded the gifts from the mule cart as the man, hands loose at his sides, stared, dumbfounded, at the growing pile.

He found his voice at last and called the girl by name: Frances.

Frances emerged from the hut, clutching a baby in her bony arms. She was fair-skinned, her hair wispy and so light it appeared colourless. Mother smiled at her and presented her with a small basket of her best onions and carrots (shrunken but tasty). The girl's blue eyes swam with tears, and she bade mother and father enter the poor dwelling. Poppie, Imp and I crowded in behind them.

On the badly laid dung floor were two pallets, and a wooden box in which Frances gently placed her tiny, limp, silent infant.

The couple seemed overcome by our presence and the gifts. When told that the pup, scampering about in the sand outside, was his, the man's eyes, dark and sombre, opened wide. He found his tongue, and spoke a few words in Afrikaans. His name was Izak Smit, he said; his wife Frances was English and spoke only a little Afrikaans.

He took father to see his wagon and four mules tethered nearby, the animals lacking the sense to stand in the shade the man had found for them. When Frances was feeling more settled and could manage on her own with the baby, perhaps in a fortnight, he told father, he planned to leave for Upington to buy the sheep he intended to farm.

A glance at the frail girl and the pitiful hut was sufficient for mother to judge that two weeks was a vain hope. Frances and her baby daughter could not be left alone in such a place. Mother lifted the sleeping baby gently from her box and inspected her. Frances said she was six months old, but in size and weight she appeared far younger. Mother wondered how the little thing had survived the journey from wherever her parents had come. The paucity of provisions, the inadequate dwelling clumsily erected, indicated that they had left with the minimum and in a hurry. Why had they taken such a risk?

Poppie, Imp and I removed ourselves to play a game of catch in the nearby scrub – after first scouting it for any concealed menace, of course. While we were outside, my parents conversed with the couple in English. Upon hearing mother's pristine British accent, Frances, confused at first, was delighted, as if she found herself on familiar ground at last in the bewildering expanse of wilderness.

For mother, the immediate concern was the health of the baby.

Father addressed Izak. I have no wish to pry, but your baby seems in need of special care. It is difficult to begin afresh in any new home, but the desert environment is a great challenge, and makes excessive physical demands upon one. It might be best, while you are in Upington, if we took your wife and baby back with us to our homestead. There my wife and Tam, our skilled medicine woman, can take good care of them both.

The couple seemed dazed at first by the offer, but father's quiet conviction and mother's tenderness with the baby soon dispelled the suspicion and fear with which our appearance had been greeted. Izak and Frances followed as mother took the blankets we had sat upon in the wagon and spread them in the generous shade of a nearby tree. She fetched the basket, woven by Doekie, containing the picnic we had brought to share with our new neighbours. There were firecakes, cheese and preserves, thick slices of lamb and springbok, and cold boiled potatoes, carrots, onions, turnips and a few of mother's precious hand-reared tomatoes.

All from our farm, said mother proudly, except the preserves; and was gratified to see the relief on the young couple's faces.

My parents nibbled at the food, and we children raced around between bites; but Frances and Izak ate ravenously. When every scrap was gone, the couple, unasked, explained why they had come to the Kalahari.

Frances's small, freckled hand, the veins prominent in the pinkish skin, was lost in Izak's huge brown one. They took turns, Izak speaking in Afrikaans and Frances in English, and glanced at each other often for reassurance. They did not interrupt each other's speech, as I was wont to do with my parents, but waited politely until the other had finished before resuming.

They came from Kimberley, hundreds of miles away.

Frances's father had come out from England with his wife and young daughter (thirteen at the time) to be a foreman in the diamond mine. Izak, born in Kimberley, was the son of a farmer who owned vast stretches of land in the region.

Izak's story, however, was not straightforward.

The man who became his father had a wife whose obesity had rendered her incapable of bearing children. The farmer loved his land, and desperately desired a son who would inherit the farm and in turn pass it on to his own seed. It was not to be. Though fond of her husband, this woman loved eating above all things; she was an excellent cook who ate her own cooking all day, yet she often rose at night with hunger pangs and raided the pantry.

Aware of her husband's profound disappointment, she felt helpless and guilty.

One night, when he was long since asleep, she heaved her enormous bulk out of bed and roused her maidservant, Rita. Rita, wiry and energetic, was mystified when her mistress sat her down in the dark, spotless kitchen scented with potatoes and oranges. She was not kept in suspense long: her mistress took both her hands in her own plump ones, and implored her to bear her master a child.

Rita, of mixed race – Hottentot, Kaffir and white blood ran in her veins – lacked a husband or kin of her own; she loved her kind mistress and had devoted her life to serving her.

She gave her consent. The following night she entered the master bedroom, as arranged. Her mistress was waiting: she rose from the enormous creaking four-poster bed, pulled back the covers for her servant, and left the room.

Izak Jacobus Petrus Pretorius Smit was raised as the son of a wealthy landowner, much loved and spoiled by both his biological mother and her mistress (whom he also called mother) and worshipped by his father. He grew tall, robust and handsome, and enjoyed nothing better than to play, and later to work, alongside the servants and farm workers who, like his family, adored and indulged him.

The first time it struck him that the world might not feel the same way about him was when he was ten years old. His mother had finally prevailed upon her husband to employ a tutor from Cape Town to educate the boy, since his father would not consent to part with him for even a day, and sending him to town for his schooling was out of the question for reasons obvious to his three parents – but not, until the advent of the tutor, to the boy himself.

An English schoolmaster recently arrived from London, this man had a strong accent and weak bluish eyes set far back in a bony bespectacled head which, though he was yet young, bore only a few wisps of hair, repeatedly combed with his fingers as he waited in the parlour to meet his pupil.

At first sight of Izak, his pale face grew impossibly white. But where is my pupil, he asked Izak's mother in high-pitched tones. *Who* is this?

Izak's mother responded politely in her best English, though her plump cheeks had darkened to the colour of apoplexy. This is he, sir. This is my son.

The tutor took a step back. I was employed to educate a white farmer's son. This is a black child.

He is not black! He is my son, and you are employed to have a civil tongue in your head and to do as you are told, retorted Izak's mother angrily.

The man turned his back on her. I would speak with the master of this establishment, he declared stiffly.

After a brief but heated exchange in the privacy of that master's study, one of the servants was dispatched in the mule cart to drive the tutor back to Kimberley.

After he had left, Izak's father called the bewildered ten-year-old boy into his study. He spoke with great sadness.

Nobody could love you, my son, more than I do. But there are things that you do not yet know, that this man's behaviour compels me to tell you.

Izak waited, his heart filled with dread, as his father's jowls sagged.

What I must tell you is this, my son: other families, as you may have observed among the servants on the farm, have only one mother and one father, and they are of the same race. But you have two mothers and one father, and you are of mixed blood. We love you more than we love ourselves, but it is because of this mingling of brown and white that your own life will be more difficult. The world is a cruel place: one who enters it with mixed blood may be subjected to the worst cruelty and bigotry. Therefore it is best that you live out your days on our property, and venture seldom to town.

He sighed heavily. Your life on the farm will be a good and busy one, and the time will come when we will find a white woman who will consent to marry you and bear my grandchildren.

From that day, Izak's world changed in ways he could never have imagined. He began seeing the people on the farm through different eyes, and observed things he had never heeded before: he noticed that some were darker than others and that the darker ones did the lowliest work; that the lighter-skinned men sought lighter-skinned wives and favoured their lighter-skinned offspring. He looked in the mirror many times a day, which he had never done before, and saw reflected there not the sturdy, well-favoured boy he had always seen as he combed his hair in the morning. Instead, he saw a stranger with thick dark brows, eyes the colour of the river and skin the reddish brown of an ox's flank. At the dining table he placed his arm beside that of his mother and saw that he was inferior to her, though she patted his arm and his face lovingly and told him he was the most splendid boy in the world.

He did not believe her. He did not believe any of them.

When he was seventeen years of age, Izak went with his father into town. It was the first time he had left the farm since he was ten years old. His father had stepped into a concealed burrow dug by a porcupine and had twisted his ankle; in trying to save himself from a bad fall, he had also damaged his wrist. He asked Izak to drive him into town to visit the doctor, and Izak – who, as he grew older and taller, became increasingly taciturn and withdrawn – could not refuse him.

Frances was a shy, friendless schoolgirl who had come late to the school. The other pupils, even the few English among them, shunned her. Most of the pupils spoke Afrikaans, and her refined English accent was not popular even among the teachers, who were themselves Boers and none too fond of the English. But her father had done very well in the mines from the beginning, and they soon moved from the centre of town to a large, attractive home on the outskirts, with a generous garden carefully tended by her mother and two gardeners. Frances grew older in the care of Kaffir maids whom she came to love as she had never loved her straight-backed, remote mother, who was far more interested in her flowers and in her piano – which she played constantly, with consummate skill – than in her daughter.

Her father was a hard-fisted, driven man whose cold gaze frightened his daughter, though he seldom addressed her and seemed scarcely to acknowledge her existence. He learned to speak Afrikaans well, and in three years rose rapidly in the ranks of the diamond mine. He frequently hobnobbed with the top management, and was away from home for most evenings, dining in their homes and participating in high-level meetings in which his opinions seemed much valued.

Frances saw Izak for the first time one afternoon when school was over. She was walking through town to her home. The day was hot and she was considering purchasing a cool drink from a store on the corner when she happened to glance up. Her eyes met those of a boy seated above her, in a wagon.

He was watching her with a curious expression on his face. She noticed that he was dark and handsome, and her hand crept up to smooth her untidy hair. Abruptly conscious of how lonely she was, she found herself doing something she never did with strangers: she smiled up at him.

Izak began coming into town regularly, waiting for Frances in the shadow of an enormous oak not far from the school. She smiled to herself when she saw him, and looked around; if nobody was in sight she climbed swiftly into the covered back of the wagon, and Izak drove her out to the farm for the afternoon.

Her mother rarely noticed her absence; but the maidservants did. One afternoon, her favourite maid, curious and concerned, hid behind an outer wall of the school. She watched her mistress leave the school grounds alone and followed her; shocked, she witnessed Frances climbing nimbly into the back of Izak's wagon.

That evening, before she went off duty, the maidservant took Frances aside and told her what she had seen, warning her that she was still a schoolgirl and too young to understand the consequences of consorting with a coloured man.

It is dangerous, what you are doing, said the maid anxiously. You are playing with a fire that will turn on you and consume you.

Frances shook her head. Mesmerised by the handsome boy whose love convinced her, as nothing had before him, that she was beautiful and desirable, she told the maidservant that she was deeply in love, and that Izak Smit would know what to do. She implored the woman to keep their secret.

Though afraid for her own safety, the maidservant loved her young mistress, and agreed. Thus the liaison continued, with the active encouragement of Izak's mother and father, who viewed Frances as their son's future wife – the fulfilment of their dream of grandchildren to inherit the lands.

Izak's real mother, Rita, was alarmed by the presence of the diminutive white girl on the farm. She told her son that what he was doing was wrong; that one day he would deeply regret it. And by that time, it would be too late.

Some months after the young couple met, Izak's father and mother swept aside Rita's timid protests, and a pastor, sworn to silence, was brought in from the coloured community to marry the young couple. The small, solemn ceremony was attended only by the family, with two workers as witnesses, also sworn to silence, and well compensated for it. Frances was not yet sixteen.

As a married woman, she continued to live at home and to attend school, and most afternoons were spent on the farm. Well before sunset, a farmhand would drive her into town, where she would be met by her maidservant, who waited for her beneath the oak tree near the school. The two would arrive at her home together.

If her mother enquired as to her whereabouts, which she seldom did, Frances would say she had spent the afternoon with a friend or at the school library. If the maidservant was asked, she corroborated her charge's story.

Six months after the little marriage ceremony, Izak's father, feeling his age, decided that the time had come for him to inform Frances's family of the situation. Further concealment was undignified and unjust; Frances was now sixteen years old, and he was certain that once her parents were convinced of the young couple's love for each other, sanctified by marriage, they would consent to her living on the farm permanently with her husband. Perhaps, he speculated to his wife privately, Frances's family might even be gratified: after all, as the son of one of the wealthiest farmers in the district Izak was hardly a pauper!

Frances was horrified. She tried desperately to dissuade her father-in-law from embarking on his foolhardy mission. Familiar with her father's politics and under no illusions about his ruthless character, she knew instinctively what he was capable of. He habitually described people of colour in the most virulently derogatory terms and, though he did not love his daughter and never had, she was part of his family: a white British girl. Izak would be nothing more than a worthless black boy to him, and he would do anything to destroy what he would regard as a degrading and disgusting union.

Izak's father, accustomed to being his own master, was a stubborn man. He would not listen to Frances's tearful pleas and dismissed his son's doubts. It was time that his beloved Izak – worth ten of any man he knew – was accorded the recognition he deserved!

A few afternoons later, he instructed Frances to remain with her husband. For the first time ever, she would spend the night at the farm.

After a hard day of sheep shearing side by side with his son and the workers, Mr Smit bathed and dressed himself formally in the shiny black suit used only for weddings and funerals. He waved away his driver, climbed onto the wagon and drove alone into town.

He did not return to the farm that night, though they waited into the small hours.

Izak knew what had happened, felt in his bones the simple and dreadful reason that his beloved father would never come home: he had been murdered by the Englishman and his cronies. And it was his, Izak's, fault.

Towards dawn, as they all sat around the kitchen table, exhausted but sleepless, Frances's maidservant arrived at the farm, driving a borrowed cart. She was shaking and perspiring. She said a group of white men from the town, among them Frances's father, was coming to the farm to fetch Frances and take her home. When asked about Izak's father, she shook her head; she did not know what had happened to him. She urged the couple to make haste and flee, repeating the exact words she had overheard her master use: *'we will have to kill the blighted seed before it fattens the bird'*.

Izak and Frances left that same night in a mule cart, with few possessions aside from the bag of money given them by Izak's distraught mother and the food prepared by the equally stricken Rita.

Frances was already pregnant.

Weeks later, they received a message from Izak's mother, informing them that her husband was still missing and exhorting her son in the strongest terms to stay away from the farm, as he was in great danger.

They were on the run for months, shunning people, towns and farms, sleeping rough under blankets on the ground, concealing themselves and the wagon in thickets a good distance away from any tracks. When they needed food and provisions they bought them from remote farms, and were hasty and watchful in all their dealings. Frances posed as an imperious young mistress, returning from town to the family farm, driven by her silent, submissive servant.

No matter how hard she tried, she knew her constant fear infected the masquerade, made it unconvincing. As her time drew near, she was told by a farm worker of a shack on a farm near Upington, where a coloured midwife lived. They located the woman, and she took them into her small dwelling for the birth of the child.

One month after the birth of their daughter, word reached the midwife that there were strange white men in the vicinity, offering a reward for information as to the whereabouts of a mixed race boy and a white girl of Frances's description. Even though Frances's health was poor and the baby was not thriving, they were forced to move on.

Eliza and the Spirit Dance

WHEN THE TIME came for us to leave for home, mother insisted that for the baby's sake, Frances should accompany us. The tiny infant had not woken to feed during the long hours of our visit, and mother was worried. She chucked her under the chin repeatedly, and though she stirred and opened her eyes – the dark eyes of her father – she closed them shortly thereafter, and refused to suck.

Izak, relieved and grateful, urged his wife to pack; he said he would leave for Upington the next morning. Frances handed the baby to mother and began gathering her few belongings together.

When the time came to part, Frances wept.

When will I see you again, Izak? When will you be back? I fear it is not safe in Upington, my darling; perhaps you should wait a while longer, until my father has returned to Kimberley. I know for certain that he cannot leave his work for long.

I will not wait any longer upon a murderer or his accomplices, replied Izak curtly. I will buy the sheep, because sheep are what I know and I can farm them and make a life for us here, as far as possible from those who hate us.

He kissed her cheek, and she clung to him. I love you and our daughter above all things in this world, he said, and I will not tarry in town for him to take my life as he has my father's.

Father said nothing in front of the women, but he was seriously concerned about Izak's safety in an inhabited area. It seemed Frances's father had both the resources and the determination to trace his daughter to the ends of the earth, should he so desire. If word reached him of his mixed blood granddaughter (an infant whiter than the river sand), there was no telling what he might do.

They bade Izak a safe journey and the cart, fully loaded, rolled away from the melancholy dwelling. Mother held the baby while Frances, beside her, caressed the puppy with trembling fingers. Tears falling freely, she gazed back at her husband, waving and blowing kisses until the wagon reached a bend in the riverbed and his tall, still figure was swallowed up by the desert.

The following day, in the cool kitchen, the baby nestled in the crook of Meisie's arm as mother watched Tam mix minute portions of what resembled grass seeds and a gluey substance the colour of sheep's milk, more pungent than the most aged cheese.

Frances, after her initial astonishment at the sight of our well set up homestead in such a wilderness, had fallen into a deep sleep on the cushiony bed in my small room. Looking down at her tear-stained face, mother remarked softly to me, standing beside her – peeved that my room had been purloined and shamefaced about being peeved – that the poor young woman had probably not enjoyed a decent rest in many days.

Tam parted the sleeping baby's lips with a sliver of reed. She put a speck of the mixture on the end of the reed and brushed it on to the infant's tongue. Though her eyes were still tightly closed, the baby's bluish lips pursed, and to mother's surprise, she swallowed. Tam put a second, slightly larger dot of the mixture, this time on the tip of her unmutilated left baby finger, and inserted it into the corner of the infant's mouth. She sucked, albeit feebly. Then she opened her midnight eyes, gazed up at

Tam and began to cry, a weak but persistent mewling that mother knew would pierce the thick veil of slumber that still encased her mother.

Go and wake Frances, mother instructed me. I did not have to: instantly roused, she was sitting bolt upright on my bed, looking about her distractedly.

Tam, asked mother, watching the baby suck, what on earth is in that potion? She slept far too much, sucked poorly and hardly ever cried, and now it is as if the little thing has come alive. She is hungry at last!

The question was a good one. Within a day of imbibing Tam's potion, Eliza – for that was her name – had left behind her long sickly sleep and become very interested in sucking. Not only that, as the days passed she slept far less and became quite lively and active, kicking her legs and spinning her arms, turning over and even, to mother's astonishment, attempting to sit up.

Frances, whose milk was now flowing in abundance, was overjoyed; she thanked Tam over and over, and promised that when her husband returned she would be given a special gift. Unmoved by the gratitude, Tam pointed upwards.

K'ang and the spirits tell me what to do. I cannot tell you how they do what they do, madam, she replied to mother. They will not allow it. But I will dance for them, and give thanks for this baby's good health.

She did. A week after the baby awoke and began thriving, all the Bushmen danced, a wild capering, ululating and chanting that seemed to reach the stars. Frances, holding her sleeping baby, watched in admiration and amazement. When, at last, Tam fell to the ground, her nose bleeding copiously, her wide eyes showing only the whites, Frances sprang to her feet.

Good God, what is happening to her, you must help, she enjoined mother.

Mother bade her young visitor sit quietly. The dance has been successful, she said calmly. Tam has triumphed again.

Poppie went to Tam and wiped away the blood streaming from her nose with a clean rag. Then she gently roused the old medicine woman and sat her up against the trunk of a kameeldoring.

Turning to the spectators, Poppie's small pug face was solemn. A great evil spirit has been felled tonight, she announced.

The next morning we searched vigorously among the shrubs and grasses for the dead animal that had housed the evil spirit. It was imperative that we locate the carcass after a spirit dance and, after certain rituals were performed, bury it. That day, we found not the smallest sign of any creature, not even a footprint; there was nothing, living or dead, in the environs of the dance, besides sheep.

Poppie ran to report this disturbing intelligence to Tam, who was resting in her shelter. Tam instructed her to seek further out.

This spirit is especially cunning, she said, and lies in the riverbed below, at the edge of the thickest clump of reeds.

Poppie, Imp and I set forth, this time accompanied by Brandbooi and an excited May. Well ahead of the rest of us, the dog was the first to sniff out the felled spirit. She looked back at us, barking urgently to encourage us to make haste. She was standing, hackles raised, at the edge of a reed-filled dip in the riverbed, precisely where Tam had said the spirit would be found. By the time we reached the spot, May had stopped barking and was gazing at the thing in perplexity, growling deep in her throat, her head to one side and a front paw lifted.

At the sight of the evil spirit, even Brandbooi began to tremble. The old woman's magic is too strong! he exclaimed.

I agreed. Many months separated the events, yet an unchildish sense of the intangible, of the macabre, crept icily to the tips of my fingers and toes. The malign presence, the unforgettable patchwork of colours poised at my feet, reared up as if to strike.

It was the puff adder that had stolen Chummy's indomitable spirit. If anything, it was more bloated than before, the glinting, half-open slits of its eyes appearing animated in spite of the fact that it was, without question, quite dead.

Visitors

THE WEEKS PASSED peacefully and baby Eliza grew, her beguiling smiles and chuckles defeating even the unforgiving heat of the sun, which occasionally submitted to her playful spirit by concealing its face behind a cloud. Frances, though her brow furrowed with anxiety as the days slid by and the horizon remained bare of any sign of Izak's return, was nonetheless easily distracted by her plump, happy baby, whose eyes became darker as her skin grew whiter, carefully shielded from the sun's malice by the pretty dresses and hats sewn by mother.

On a morning that brought the first chill breath of the impending winter, father, Brandbooi and Kobie went hunting in the far north for eland, gemsbok and red hartebeest, as our supplies of dried meat were low, and the hides would come in useful during the cold nights to come.

The day after their departure, everybody was hard at work, shouldering in addition to their usual tasks the burden of the many duties carried out by the hunting men. Slang and Uil were with the sheep, Doekie and Meisie at the tan-pit; Tam was in the vegetable patch. Frances was playing with Eliza in my bedroom.

Poppie, Imp and I, as every morning, were caged dispiritedly in the classroom with mother, who was drilling us on the basics of arithmetic, which I detested. Poppie and Imp were pretending to listen, as usual, but no sooner was mother's attention elsewhere than their quills were still. Though they did not fidget as I did, I could see in their eyes that they were dreaming of games and dances, of songs and mythical beasts. Not a single word mother said was penetrating those busy dreams.

How does such gross inattention escape her vigilance – so acute when it comes to me? I reflected irritably. Then I thought of the day before, when mother read us a poem by a poet called William Wordsworth, who, while wandering lonely as a cloud, found a crowd of daffodils. Poppie and Imp for once were full of questions: how did a man walk like a cloud, and what were daffodils? Mother, pleased that they were showing interest, drew a daffodil on a piece of paper. The girls looked dubious. In England, explained mother, where I come from, these flowers can grow in clumps, like tsamma melons.

Ah, tsamma melons, said Imp, and quickly drew a tsamma melon wearing a daffodil like a hat. Mother shook her head and laughed.

My musings were abruptly interrupted when, without permission, my friends sprang to their feet.

I sniffed the air. Dust, oil, a sharpness of fresh dung.

Sit down, said mother crossly, ignorant of anything unusual afoot.

Mother, I exclaimed excitedly, can you not smell it?

Enough of your foolish pranks, Em. Just do as you are ...

She did not complete the sentence. Meisie walked uninvited into the classroom.

Madam, there are people. Many white people. You must come quickly.

Where is Frances? asked mother calmly.

She is with Eliza in Em's room, replied Meisie. She is putting her down to sleep.

Go to her immediately and tell her to stay there.

Mother rose to her feet, patted her hair, and walked from the dwelling into the sunlight with the three of us at her heels. She cast us an anxious, admonishing look, to which we paid no heed.

I had never before seen so many men in one place, white men with tall hats on their heads. Ox-wagons were parked in a circle in the riverbed below us. Visitors were extremely rare, given that it took a fortnight of hard travel to get to our homestead. This visitation was unprecedented.

What was surprising – nay, frightening – was that even from above the riverbed, we could see rifles below us, gleaming in every man's hand. As we stared, the men began to climb the rise. I counted as they marched in a rapid, disciplined line to where we stood waiting.

There were fourteen of them in all.

Fourteen men for a single young girl and a babe, murmured mother. Thank God your father is not at home.

I admired mother as never before on that day.

We hung back with our people, who had abandoned their labours as news of the visitors flew from the dwelling and reached the outermost kraal. She stood alone among the men, undaunted by their guns, nostrils flaring slightly from the sour, viscid reek of their long journey.

The men removed their hats, but did not speak.

Who among you is your spokesman? asked mother.

We do not do business with women, replied one of the men in a brusque voice, clearly used to command. Though the shortest of them all, he was stocky and powerful, with the appearance of a fighter. His blue eyes were lightless and cold.

Well, then, you have no business to do here, responded mother politely. For my husband is not on the property today.

You speak English, madam, said the man, sounding impressed. You are from England. We should therefore understand each other without difficulty and conclude our business quickly, since I too am English.

He hesitated. May I enquire as to the whereabouts of your husband, madam?

He has ridden north and will not return for some days. I am not aware of the business to which you refer. Please state your purpose here, and then we will be happy to provide you with fresh water from our well for your journey.

The blue eyes faded in colour. Do not play games with me, madam. You have my daughter. I am here to reclaim her and take her to her rightful home.

He turned to a tall blond man standing behind him, a little apart from the rest.

Mr du Plessis here is a policeman and a lawyer; he is authorised to arrest my daughter's kidnappers should I so instruct him.

I heard mother's low, musical laugh. I knew she was not amused. Her voice, when it came, was that of a woman I did not know, steely and steady; her slight figure and pretty face contrasted sharply with her brave words.

I am no kidnapper, sir. Your threats do not intimidate me.

Nobody could have predicted the short man's next move: the speed of it, the contained ferocity.

In two strides he had me behind him, my arm pinned in a grip that might as well have been the teeth of a lion for the acuteness of the pain. I yelped, and mother winced in response, her hand extended towards me in reflex.

Fetch my daughter Frances, madam, the man said softly, and I will return this child to you. *Your child for mine.* Until you give my daughter up to me, your own daughter – given the company among which we stand, I am certain that she is your daughter – will remain captive with my men.

He glanced behind him and gave a brief shake of his head. As for her being in that company, it would be a difficulty on my part to guarantee her safety.

The travel-stained men brayed their amusement; I saw wide mouths and rotted teeth, and I squirmed in Frances's father's bruising fist. The grinning men were so hideous to me that they seemed barely human.

Although I tried to hold it in, a frightened cry escaped me.

Mother had turned very pale. I saw in her face that she would not yield, and I stopped struggling.

You will have to shoot me with your rifle, sir, for I will not deliver up one child in barter for another.

The man jerked his head in the direction of our dwelling.

Meisie was suddenly at the entrance. Shaking, she stood her ground, her small figure stretched across the doorway, one arm on each doorpost. There was a shuffling of boots in the dust as the men competed to be first to enter the dwelling.

Before I could draw breath Meisie lay on the ground, thrust aside and trampled as one would a tussock of grass, her cheek scraped and bleeding from her fall.

Frances's father loosened his grip slightly as we waited. It was not long.

Through the narrow doorway two men emerged sideways. Frances was between them, screaming and struggling. Her face was bright scarlet, her arms and legs thrashing; her eyes, the blue of her father's, started from her head. I was unpleasantly reminded of a young wildebeest I had seen in the jaws of two hyenas, the poor creature torn to pieces as I watched.

Her father's grip on me loosened. I ran to mother, who embraced me. An odd silence fell when Frances saw her father.

He lifted a hand, and the men let her go. Father and daughter stared at each other, neither, for the moment, finding words. There was the sound of a bird – a pale chanting goshawk, I think it was. Frances put her face in her hands and moaned.

A third man appeared in the doorway. In his arms was Eliza, gurgling and smiling, her plump limbs kicking.

The father spoke at last. Daughter, whose child is this?

Frances began shrieking, the veins standing out like wire in her neck. Where is he? Where is Izak? *What have you done to my husband?*

He did not reply.

Frances turned so white that mother took a step towards her.

Frances's father pushed her aside. He held out his arms to the man who had Eliza. The baby's dark eyes gazed up at him, her tiny fingers reaching out to grip his beard.

He gave his men an order. Take my daughter down to my wagon and ensure that she stays there until we leave, which will be as soon as you – he indicated three of the men – have fetched the water we require for the return journey.

The three men sprang to obey. Frances began wailing and lunging against her captors in a desperate bid to reach the baby, but her father held Eliza under one arm and would not permit his daughter to approach one step closer.

My parents made various enquiries as to the fate of Frances and Eliza. By this time, our home had existed for some years, and once or twice a year, a visitor – a traveller or explorer, even an enterprising smous, or pedlar – would turn up at the farm. The novelty of the company was most welcome, and in exchange for our hospitality, these visitors would entertain us with news and events from afar.

Mysteriously, the enquiries my parents made bore no fruit: not a soul in Upington admitted to having seen Frances and Eliza, let alone the posse of thirteen men led by her father. It was as if an army of phantoms had passed through with invisible captives.

To all intents and purposes, it was as if Izak, Frances and Eliza had never lived, and the pleasant, all-too-brief sojourn on our farm of mother and baby had been a mere figment of fantasy.

Many months later, father and Kobie travelled to Upington to sell our beautiful game hides and excellent biltong, and to replenish our supplies. It was about this time that my eavesdropping career began, and on father's return, I heard him talking to mother.

It seems in the bar adjacent to the big supply store, there was talk of the discovery of a man's body. Father enquired further, and was told it was found in scorched scrub near a rubbish dump, about the time of the events described in this chapter. The corpse was naked, said father's informer, and impossible to identify, as the facial features were burned beyond recognition. He added that the police said it did not matter; nobody would miss him as he was just a drunk Kaffir.

Are you missing a Kaffir? the man asked inquisitively. You know, whoever killed this Kaffir castrated him and cut into his flesh with a knife. The police thought the killer was trying to send – to write – a message.

The man laughed. He must have been a very bad Kaffir.

I understood the purpose of castration, but thought it applied only to farm animals. My curiosity was so intense that, one day before lesson time, I confessed to mother that I had overheard their conversation, and entreated her to explain.

Mother shook her head, exasperated. No good comes of eavesdropping, Em. Some things are not meant for your ears.

Was it Izak, mother?

Who knows, sighed mother. They said even the crows disdained to feed on what was left of the poor man.

Lost and Found

THE VEGETABLE PATCH had to be closely guarded at all times, a duty usually assumed by Poppie, Imp or me after lessons. Small antelope such as steenbok were occasional visitors, as were jackals, but the more common thieves were squirrels, suricates (my favourites), hares, lizards, rodents, many varieties of birds and of course, insects.

My spell of duty was fairly regular: it was when I had eaten my lunch and everybody else was having theirs. I liked being there on my own, sitting beneath the only acacia karroo, or sweet thorn, we had on the farm, and happily chewing the delicious sweet gum it produced while keeping an eye out for a beady-eyed crimson-breasted shrike. I had got into the habit of taking with me a piece of mother's handmade paper and sketching the creatures that seemed to materialise out of nowhere. If I was perfectly still they would venture quite close, in hopes of sneaking a taste of whatever seasonal vegetable mother or Meisie had so lovingly planted.

Sometimes, if the wind direction was in my favour, I escaped detection. This gave me the opportunity to observe and capture something of a creature's essential nature in the sketch, though I confess Imp had much greater ability than I when it came to sketching. To encourage us, mother had begun supplying us with larger sheets of paper and Imp, with admirable economy of circles and strokes, produced gemsbok, hartebeest, springbok and giraffe with startling accuracy, vividly capturing their habits and mannerisms: a giraffe would be bending its long graceful neck to drink, or stretching it to browse on the topmost branches of a kameeldoring; a gemsbok was heraldic on a dune, its tail seeming to swish; a springbok would be caught in mid-prance. I knew that I would never be able to sketch as well as Imp, but I liked the special feel of mother's paper beneath my fingers and hoped that if I practised hard, my artistic ability would improve.

At the end of a particularly hot summer, a cooler day finally dawned. Sitting in the shade after lunch was most pleasant, and no animal tested my vigilance by appearing too near mother's tempting patch of cabbages and carrots.

I put my paper aside and my head back against the tree. I must have dozed, because when I opened my eyes, a dainty visitor I had never before had the opportunity to evict was sniffing appreciatively at a cabbage (or was it a lettuce?).

The young gemsbok was a beautiful creature. He took a tentative nibble, then looked up and caught my eye. He was a splendid male, his beige coat sleek and glowing, the already impressive length of his horns presaging a noble pair when he reached adulthood. Though considerably larger in height and girth than a springbok, I knew at once that the young antelope was not old enough to be separated from his mother.

I looked about for her, but there was no other animal in the vicinity. I was puzzled. Where was she? Why had she permitted him to stray? Had she been hunted and killed by a lion, or merely distracted long enough to lose sight of her offspring?

Rising to my feet as unobtrusively as possible, I decided I would find father and ask his advice. Left to his own devices, the gemsbok was easy prey for hyenas, which were frequent night visitors to the farm, or other predators; and if by some chance he escaped their clutches, how would he feed himself properly? I anticipated father's pragmatic answers to

114

these questions, for I had heard them many times before: It is nature's way, Em. It is foolish to become sentimental. These things happen every day. Rescuing an animal will make no difference, other than to deprive others of nourishment.

I concurred with him in theory, but continued doggedly to save the lives of baby birds, squirrels, beetles, spiders, even, once, a baby mongoose. Appealing to Meisie or Brandbooi on these matters was not a good idea. Brandbooi would smile and wave me away, then take out his bow and arrow and shoot the gemsbok. Afterwards he would capture a locust in his fist, or some other hopper or crawler rooted out from under a stone, and sacrifice it in thanksgiving to the spirits for the gift of meat.

Eyeing the gemsbok, I decided that father would find him irresistible, just as I did, and I could persuade him to help me devise a plan to rescue the poor creature from certain death. I had made not the faintest crackle underfoot; but the gemsbok turned away from the cabbage and stood very still, watching me watching him.

We stood frozen for a minute or two while I worried that the dogs – other than Chummy, who slept far more than he worked – would join me at the patch, as they sometimes did. I took a careful, half-crouching step towards the gemsbok, feeling like a stalking cat. He shook his noble head and moved off. I followed at a discreet distance. He was not in any hurry; it seemed the graceful creature did not object to my presence. Perhaps, I thought happily, he even welcomed the company. This last did not strike me as absurd: he was very young, and though my scent made him wary, I did not appear to be a threat.

So the young gemsbok led, and I followed. The day remained re-markably cool and tranquil. In the excitement of my quest to keep him close, the vegetable patch was forgotten. The sand crunched as I ambled after him, and a pygmy falcon, no larger than a shrike, perched on a sociable weaver nest and watched our progress with head-swivelling interest. Another bird, a large raptor, circled in ever-widening arcs above my head, then descended in a long dive towards us. I glimpsed its pink jowls and knew it was a lappet-faced vulture.

Discouraged by our animated progress, it climbed the rising breeze and swiftly became a speck in the sky, which had become hazy, with smudges of cloud on the horizon.

The gemsbok, walking steadily northwards, stopped and sniffed the air. I wondered if he was seeking the familiar scent of his mother. I gazed hopefully about me at broad grassy stretches and russet dunes, but they were bare of any living thing. Even the smoke from our homestead could no longer be seen curling into the soft sky.

I had done it again. My breath quickened; I heard my heart thudding in my ears. I was not four years old this time, and knew I must turn back. I felt a strong impulse to call to the young gemsbok as I would to May or one of the pups and order him to follow me home. He had moved on, and I shrugged to myself: another hundred yards could not make matters any worse; perhaps his mother waited for him on the next dune.

I padded after him. His speed had increased considerably, and I realised he must have sniffed something in the air that urged him on. I longed to follow him, but it was time to turn back.

Intent on his retreating rump, I did not feel the slight sting of sand against my legs, or the rising tempo of the breeze. The young gemsbok disappeared. In his place a dark, expanding blemish, bobbing and twirling eccentrically, advanced speedily towards me.

I stood irresolute for a moment, wondering how the gemsbok could have vanished so quickly. Then, spurred by the knowledge that I was guilty of disobedience and dereliction of duty, I turned for home.

Home, like the gemsbok, had gone.

I had not taken a step forward when I was attacked: something snatched me up, whirled me in my tracks, and shook me between its teeth. Slapping brazenly at my face, biting through my tightly closed lids, whipping with needles and daggers at my bare limbs, this monster, hooting and howling in my ears with lunatic mirth, spun me in helpless circles.

I staggered as if rifle-shot. Sand clogged my nostrils, mouth and ears; my head was a leaden weight. A roar rose up the scale to a blood-chilling, triumphant falsetto. I was drowning in sand.

Unable to draw breath, ground down to grains of sand, I subsided into the bowels of the maelstrom. Was this what mother meant, I thought hazily, when she said the Kalahari must not take me as well?

My lids opened with an audible click. A delicate trail passed close to my eye, as if my eyelashes had brushed across the sand. I coughed and spat out sand. In the corner of my eye, I spotted the trailmaker: his tail had risen into the air and was quivering. He was big for his species, with enormous pincers; the spitting had disturbed him.

I scraped my gritty tongue across my gritty teeth and sat up slowly. Sand fell from me in clouds. It cascaded from my hair, my eyebrows, from the fissures, folds and crevices of every feature and every garment. It was as if I was made of sand. A sand maiden of the Kalahari.

The scorpion, whose pincers were intimidating but whose sting was not dangerous, scuttled off. I simply was not worth the trouble of a confrontation.

I saw I was in the lee of a kameeldoring, and thought there were far worse places the storm could have tumbled and tossed me. The silence was so intense it was frightening. I looked about me for signs of life.

The dunes lay pristine and glowing, reshaped into precise ripples of line and light. I had no idea how long the sandstorm had lasted, no clue how much time had passed since I had been half-smothered; but the complexion of the sky was bluish and pale, and from the position of the sun I knew it was late afternoon.

I had been missing from the farm for hours, and would be in real trouble when I got back. Shaking sand from my hair, I rose to my feet. I gazed in every direction until my eyes watered. Which would take me home? There was nothing I recognised: not the rise of the dune opposite me, not a single tree, shrub or chunk of chalk stone looked familiar. For all I knew, the entire homestead could have been buried in sand.

I swallowed, my throat as dry as mother's paper. Grains of sand fell from my mouth and nostrils as I breathed. I had to do something, so I began walking. From the sun, now low in the sky, I chose a westerly direction, which I calculated was better than northerly but by no means certain to be the direction of home.

Strangely, I felt no fear, even though it was likely I was lost. The Kalahari had unleashed one of its most ferocious moods on me and I had endured. I had been tested, and not found wanting. I trudged along, feeling that home was everywhere: in the skies and all about me. Shrubs, dunes, grasses, the smooth bar of the horizon. All of it was home. My home had not harmed me and it never would.

Sky and desert bled into each other. Brownish stains leached the light from the day; the pale dry lip of the sun touched the horizon. Still I walked. When I swallowed, my throat crackled and my tongue was so thick it blocked the air. I passed inquisitive squirrels and yellow mongooses that smiled at me and invited me into their burrows. I wished I could take shelter there, but my legs kept walking. At times, I was certain I was walking above the sand, on air, then chalk stone jabbed through the soles of my hartebeest hide shoes. The pain was remote, an ache that kept me going until I found myself in the sand of a floating riverbed, legs splayed in front of me.

River. Bed. I lay in its arms. It held me gently.

A gemsbok stood over me, her superb horns piercing the sky like a pair of spears thrown by a great warrior. She bent her exquisite head, touched me with her wet nose and spoke softly. Though I could not understand what she said, I knew instantly that she was the one: the mother of my beautiful young gemsbok.

Your son is seeking you, I told her earnestly. He is lost, and longs to be found. Take me with you, I urged. I will bring you to him.

I was borne aloft, onto her broad back. We rode towards the spot where her young son had come to me and enticed me to follow him.

Together we would find him, and mother and son would be a family once more.

Mother found me missing soon after the sandstorm began. Anxious and fearful, they had no choice but to wait until the worst of it was over before beginning to search for me. The shape-shifting powers of such a colossal sandstorm would have obliterated familiar landmarks on the banks of the riverbed and redrawn the topography of the entire area. Our people, concerned for my well-being, urged father to begin the search; but father knew how easy it was to get lost after a storm: well-known markers would have disappeared and one dune would look much like another. Thus, he wisely decided, once the sandstorm had abated, that everybody would wait at the homestead while Brandbooi alone ventured forth to find me. Brandbooi knew the desert best, well enough to smell out its secrets; his intuitive powers would take him unerringly to me through the resculpted dunes – though Tam later claimed that she was the one who had pointed him in the right direction!

Thus Brandbooi it was who spoke softly to me, put water to my lips and then lifted me on to his powerful back and carried me three miles along the riverbed to my waiting parents. At some point on our homeward journey, he placed me gently under a tree.

He saw an opportunity he could not resist.

With great care, he took out his bow and arrow (he was never without them) and shot a young gemsbok that was watching him with some curiosity from a nearby dune. He killed it instantly. Then he took a millipede and swiftly sacrificed it in thanksgiving.

The Smous

POPPIE, WHO KNEW very well that mother disliked unexpected eruptions of energy from us, catapulted into the classroom. As mother's admonishing gaze fell upon her, she lowered her head and spoke quietly:

Sorry I am late, madam, but there are visitors.

Ignoring mother's raised eyebrows, I leaped to my feet. Poppie's excitement could only mean that the smous had finally arrived.

I felt a spurt of joy. I had a birthday coming soon, and mother had promised that if he came, I could choose 'some frippery' as my gift.

The advent of a smous, an indispensable feature of the countryside to people who lived in tiny communities or on lonely farms, was a rare treat for us. A smous brought with him not only the excitement of goods for purchase but also news and gossip from villages and towns near and far. The first smous ever to have visited the farm had been a disappointment:

humourless, disgruntled with the sales he had made and continuously hungry, he ate far more than his fair share and with less delicacy than mother could have wished. He seemed less inclined to adventure and rather more to gain, and mother had expressed surprise that such a gloomy individual had taken the trouble to journey so many miles out of his way to trade with a single farm.

Indeed, our farm was difficult of access and too unprofitable to attract the interest of most individuals who peddled goods for a living along the roads and tracks, but the last visit of the smous I was hoping to see again had brought me much pleasure and amusement, which was shared by my parents.

Father agreed that a smous's business is much promoted by the nature of his temperament: a cheerful character who revels in laughter and conversation is much more likely to do good business than a man of a more morose and self-contained bent; yet since much of a smous's life is spent alone, rumbling along the tracks of the open country and outspanning at times in the middle of nowhere, he should, ideally, also take pleasure in the natural world, adapt to all weathers with equanimity, and be accustomed to – nay, even enjoy – a goodly measure of his own company.

Mother was unable to resist the opportunity for a lesson.

A smous is a good example of a man for all seasons – in both the literal and the figurative sense, Em. His work obliges him to subject himself to frequent discomfort and uncertain conditions. He must find pleasure in solitude, since it is with himself alone that he spends many of his days and nights, yet he must also welcome the society of his fellow man.

Though the goods that our very first smous bore on his wagon were only part of his inventory – the bulk he had left in storage in Upington – those trinkets he brought, described by mother as 'frills and furbelows', thrilled everybody aside from my parents. We exclaimed over brightly hued cloths and shiny beads, and were intrigued by the range of ointments, cough medicines and other medicaments which the smous claimed had miraculous powers. Tam sneered as only a Bushwoman can when told about the contents of bottles that cured anything from headaches to an ingrown toenail; mother 'humphed' under her breath but bought a large bottle of medicinal alcohol to serve as a disinfectant while instructing father to keep an eye out for Kobie's purchases, whose own eye, mother claimed, shone much too brightly at the sight of such luxuries as cough mixture and disinfectant.

Goods were paid for mostly by barter: biltong, mutton, hides or fresh vegetables for cloth, ointments, trinkets, tools and the like. The smous seemed quite taken with the intricate ostrich-egg necklaces and bracelets that were Doekie's speciality, and she acquired in exchange some enviably fine cloth for her doekies and skirts.

The smous we favoured came a year or more after the first, and he stayed for four days. His company turned out to be an unexpected pleasure, providing us with the novelty of entertainment and, in retrospect, the bonus of a holiday. When he left on his ramshackle wagon, or rather when we reluctantly permitted him to depart, he promised a return visit; but father said we should not get our hopes up since our paltry purchases could not possibly justify the many arduous miles of travel it took to reach our homestead.

Nonetheless, I earnestly desired to see Solomon Cohen again. A tiny, sunburned, cheerful man, he spoke excellent but oddly accented English, containing in the plosive consonants, said mother, the harsh music of dialect; a little like father's English pronunciation before her own impeccable use of the language succeeded in vanquishing much of his sing-song Bavarian with its dash of lilting Swedish.

Mr Cohen was a versatile conversationalist, willing to embark on enthusiastic discussions about all manner of things. He seemed to know everything there was to know in the world, and never appeared to weary of what mother termed my endless questions; rather he encouraged them, and his answers frequently provoked further questions.

Mother told him early on in the visit that he was in the wrong business.

You would have made a gifted teacher, sir. That much is obvious.

To her surprise, Mr Cohen looked grave.

In the 'old country', madam – from which I was forced to flee – my father was a respected rabbi and teacher.

He shrugged. It did him no good. It cost him his life, as the first persons the Cossacks murdered in the pogrom of our town were my father and grandfather, the latter a highly revered elder.

Before I could ask him the meaning of the words 'pogrom' and 'Cossacks', his shrewd glance brushed each eager face in his audience and he smiled a smile I will never forget. It spread slowly across his whiskery cheeks and seemed to take root there.

Strangely, it did not make me want to smile back. Instead it made me feel sad, and this sadness confused me. Then he spoke his next words.

My dears, we will not speak of these things now – we will not – of doors kicked in, of innocent faces twisted in terror before their chests are bayoneted; of gashes gaping like open mouths beseeching mercy, of screams urging flight on children and babes already impaled and dead.

His eyes sparking like the embers of a fire, Mr Cohen murmured: nay, we dare not speak of such things on a night when the bright face of the moon is dimmed by these animated young faces before me.

I looked from his fixed smile to my parents' faces, and I saw they were dismayed and distressed.

Mother, pale-faced, probed gently: Do you not have a wife and children of your own, Mr Cohen?

No family left, my dear lady, not a single soul, replied Mr Cohen, rubbing his hands together as if he were cold. The air is mild, tonight, is it not? He sighed. It makes me long for something sweet to drink.

Mr Cohen wore gloves which had long since become the colour of dirt, and a tall black hat that he did not remove for an instant for the duration of his stay, even when he slept (I peeked). Mother said she admired Mr Cohen very much. He was a clever and interesting man who had endured great tragedy – but she dreaded to think what was nesting beneath that hat!

Father explained that he wore the hat because he was a Jew. I was unclear what wearing a hat had to do with being a Jew, or even what made a Jew different from anybody else. Was the difference so terrible that the Cossacks, whoever they were, decided to murder his family? There were many questions I planned to ask Mr Cohen on his next visit; I wanted to hear how he himself had escaped the dreadful fate of his father and grandfather, for one. He did not look or act like the kind of hero I had read about in books, but there was something about him that made me wonder.

Many white people, said father, were Christians. Jews, whose beliefs differed from theirs, were often viewed with suspicion because they did not believe in Jesus Christ and the Immaculate Conception, in spite of the fact that Jesus Christ was himself Jewish. I asked father if he believed in the Immaculate Conception, and he rolled his eyes in a way that made me laugh.

Mother told me a little about the Cossacks, but refused to answer any more of my questions. She claimed she was not educated enough on the matter and, furthermore, only one who had survived such horrors should be accorded the privilege of speaking of them.

Mr Cohen *was* rather smelly, but I did not care; none of us did, because as well as being almost as wise as father, he told wonderful stories.

The one that I will remember always was his story about sexing the hyena.

Gender differences and the act of procreation hold few mysteries for one who grows up surrounded by sheep and other animals. A single central question continued to perplex me: would any creature willingly engage in such a foolish, clumsy, peculiar act if not biologically driven to do so? In mitigation of this, at lambing time the results seemed well worth the trouble. I often watched father and Kobie, and while I found the birth part unpleasantly messy, once free of blood and slime, the lambs were pure joy.

Of all the predators eager to devour our lambs, probably my least favourite was the spotted hyena. This ungainly looking beast is unusual in the animal world in that the female appears to have both male and female sex organs; the word, said mother, is hermaphrodite. Father was certain hyenas were not hermaphrodites: the female appears to have a male organ, but this does not, he claimed, do the work of a male organ. Like every other species, the female bears the young, but unlike predators such as lions – where the male is distinctively maned, and much bigger, heavier and also dominant – the female hyena is substantially larger than its male counterpart; and a single alpha female is invariably the leader of the pack.

Mr Cohen, erudite on many subjects, knew something about hyenas as well. He agreed with father.

Hyenas are decidedly not hermaphrodites, sir; though my knowledge, I confess, draws on observation and personal experience rather than on science.

He paused. Sitting at his feet, I knew a story was coming.

The reason I know that a female hyena can only be a female and not a male as well is that I have proof – for which I paid a substantial price.

He lit his pipe with care and obvious enjoyment. Though its pungency made my eyes water, I drew closer.

Early one evening in the Northern Cape, a good distance from the nearest habitation and well before the onset of darkness, I outspanned under some trees. The day had been hot and business on the two farms I had visited most satisfactory. As always when business was profitable, my appetite was keen, in spite of the excellent farmer's fare I had partaken of that noon.

Usually, owing to strict dietary laws, I prepare all my food with my own hands.

(Does he take his gloves off?)

But I am not above frequent improvisation when circumstances demand it, such as when distances between habitations are long and food scarce. As for cooking like yours, Mrs Johannsen, I consider it a privilege to make an exception, since it is obvious that your hygiene is beyond question and I would not dream of imposing my own rules.

I interrupted him, as I did often during the four days of his stay, to enquire as to the nature of those special dietary laws.

Mr Cohen replied in a manner which led me to believe that he had summed me up quite well. Do you want a lecture, Em, or a story?

A story, I replied hastily.

Then we shall leave the lecture for another day.

I soon had a fire going to cook my potjie of lamb stew, which was on that occasion enhanced by some new potatoes and carrots, a gift from the farmer's wife. Minutes after the cooking was scenting the air in a way that made my mouth water, I became aware of another mouth, slavering away not far from my own.

This belonged to a giant spotted hyena. Drool spiralled from its massive jaws to the ground, and its head was bouncing up and down as it advanced and then, evidently startled by my vociferous objection, withdrew. Now it was not the first time I had had pests in the form of jackals, hyenas and assorted rodents bent on a share of my supper; but this was without doubt the largest animal of its kind that had ever ventured so close.

I stirred the stew, and found the potatoes not sufficiently cooked. As it was not yet too dark to read, I pulled from my pack a book I was enjoying – Nicholas Nickleby, by Charles Dickens, as it so happens – opened it and began reading aloud to myself, something I indulge in frequently when alone in the bush.

The stench – a fetid miasma of death and decay – warned me that the hyena was back. This time the creature had ventured even closer, its huge round liquid eyes brimming with appeal for a morsel; not only of my potjie food which, though delectable, could not withstand the odour of the beast – but of me.

Any part would do, those moist eyes implored: an arm, a leg, what about your head with all those brains inside it?

No, not my head, you foolish animal, I replied crossly. I recalled a friend, a fellow smous, who had kicked out at a persistent hyena in exasperation and almost lost an ankle for his trouble, not to mention near dying from the poisons in the hideous wound.

This recollection propelled me to my feet. I took a threatening step toward the creature and shouted once more. Raising and lowering its head several times, drool pooling on the ground beneath its bared fangs, the famished hyena retreated into the growing shadows. But soon enough it was back, and I knew then that my uninvited guest was not going to leave without some powerful inducement to do so.

I picked up a stout length of wood, and menaced the leering beast with it. It lowered its enormous spotted head, twitched its ears, swished its tail, and reversed its curved back into the bush behind it.

Now a smous may not be genius, but he has to be a quick thinker, my young ones, because trouble lurks around every corner, waiting eagerly to ensnare him. And trouble is the last thing a businessman needs.

We gazed back at him, hanging onto his every word. He was silent for a moment, and then he winked.

Well, what did you do? I asked anxiously. How did you get rid of it?

Not *it*, my dear girl! *Her.* For the beast was without question a female. And I will tell you how I know this. I had removed the potjie and thrown more wood on the fire to assist me in keeping her at bay. But when she returned fearlessly to the roaring fire, I knew drastic measures were called for. So I tapped my head and put on my business thinking cap.

(Did he remove his hat first, or sit the cap atop it?)

As always, my dear ones, it supplied me with a solution. What do you think it was, Em?

I shook my head. Did you shoot her?

He looked pained. Dear child, I am a Jew. I carry the Old Testament, not a rifle.

He placed his forefinger to the side of his nose, whose tip, I noticed, had reddened and was quivering slightly.

Father chuckled. I hope you resisted donating to her the holy book to gnaw on instead of yourself, Mr Cohen.

I did not part with my precious copy, my good fellow. My tactics were the following: I permitted the large lady to come a little closer; then, just as she was about to snap her drool in my direction, I threw her something which I was certain *she* would be unable to resist.

He paused for dramatic effect, and the hush in the room was high praise indeed.

May I say without fear of immodesty, my dear ones, that my intuition in this case was infallible?

He nodded. I see by your rapt faces that I may.

Well, the lady caught the object I had thrown her between those steely jaws with a grace and elegance that was quite untypical of her kind; then, to my delight, she positively curtsied her appreciation, bobbing up and down with my gift delicately clenched between teeth that could crush it with one false move.

What was it, we chimed in unison, what did you throw her?

The smous smiled and shook his head sagely.

As I watched, she tossed my gift from her jaws; to my delight, it landed unerringly around her shaggy neck. Holding her head high, she padded proudly into the bush, and never again returned to plague me.

And that is how I knew she was a female, do you see? For only a lady, my dears, would value her appetite for a bauble – albeit a *dazzling* bead necklace – above her appetite for me!

The Investigation

TO MY DISMAY, the visitors Poppie had interrupted the lesson to announce had nothing to do with Mr Cohen or any other smous. As any visitor spelt release from the classroom and news from the outside world, I quickly recovered from my disappointment and walked behind mother with what I prided myself was unrushed dignity to the door to greet them.

Father was there before us. I noted that the conversation with the visitors was being conducted in lowered tones. To my surprise, when father observed us, he indicated to mother that we children were not invited to join them.

Before reluctantly turning back to the classroom in response to her instruction, I took a good look at the three visitors. Two of them were big men with blond moustaches and heavy beards; the third was smaller and grim-faced, with limp black curls. They were all dressed in uniforms darkly patched with perspiration. I stared, knowing they were policemen. Their joined gaze seemed to fasten on me.

Then, with a tremor of fear, I realised that it was not me they were glowering at. It was Poppie and Imp.

Listening from the nearest spot safely out of sight, I heard every word. Two of the officers – the bearded men – explained in Afrikaans that they had come all the way from Kimberley; from this father must have known immediately that the matter was extremely serious. One of the men asked about the people who worked for us, and father informed him that our workers had been with us for many years. They asked if there were any strangers or visitors on the farm at present; father said there were not. A second man asked if any of our people had been away for a time, visiting family, that kind of thing. None, father responded, had ever ventured further than a two-day hunting trip to the north in all the time they had worked for him; and those forays had been in his company.

The policemen were nonetheless adamant that everybody who worked on the farm must be assembled for interrogation. Father enquired about the crime that was being investigated. The small dark policeman, a sergeant from Upington whose distinctive voice was pleasantly low-pitched, replied that they were seeking a murderer or murderers and their accomplices. He added that he had been told by certain people in Upington that there were Bushmen on our farm. Bushmen labourers were among the suspects on the farm where the murders had taken place.

There was more than one murder victim then? asked father.

Two, replied one of the Kimberley policemen tersely. The farmer and his wife.

The sergeant from Upington interjected. All the Bushmen in the area of the Kalahari and its surrounds belong to certain related clans. It is well known that they will assist their people in escaping when a crime has been committed.

He paused. Bushmen have a very long memory; that too is well known.

Father did not reply to this mystifying observation. He enquired instead as to the name of the slain couple, and was given it: Mynheer and Mevrouw W. Later, when it was all over, he said he had guessed their identity before the officer responded to his question.

When did these killings take place, mother asked the sergeant, and was told two weeks earlier. Since then, he added, the countryside had been scoured for information that would lead to the killers, but without notable success.

He declined to divulge how the couple was murdered for fear of jeopardising the interrogation to come, and warned father that they had a witness with them who had seen one of the perpetrators of the heinous crime.

This person was waiting in the wagon in the riverbed below.

Between the main kraal and the shelters there was an open space, and it was there that our people gathered. The women stood to one side, the men some yards distant from them, the policemen in between. Minutes after we were excluded, Poppie, Imp and I were summoned back: the police had requested our presence during the interrogation.

Mother protested. What possible contribution could children of eight and ten years old make? Why should they be subjected to what promised to be an unpleasant ordeal for all concerned?

The appeal was in vain: the sergeant brusquely repeated his request.

Thus, burning with curiosity, the three of us joined Doekie, Meisie and Tam. Mother stood in front of us, as if to shield us all from harm.

Fortunately, the day was overcast; thick reddish cloud blocked the scorching heat of the sun. Father stood between Brandbooi and Kobie, Slang and Uil next to Brandbooi. The sergeant from Upington ignored Kobie and questioned Slang and Uil in Afrikaans, which they pretended not to understand.

Father answered for them. The policeman did not seem to mind, perhaps because the focus of his interest was clearly Brandbooi.

Naming the murdered couple, the sergeant asked him, again in Afrikaans, if he had worked for them.

Brandbooi replied, Ja, baas.

For some reason, the policeman switched to English.

How long is it since you left the Boer's farm?

Brandbooi seemed at a loss for an answer.

Father intervened. The Bushmen have been working for us for many years. They came to my farm before my daughter was born. She is now nearly nine years old.

I realise it has been a long time, sir, but when these people turned up at your farm out of nowhere, pursued the sergeant, his light eyes thoughtful, did you not wonder where they came from? Did you not consider the possibility that they were running away from something?

There is a reason I ask this question: after these murders were found and reported to us, I remembered that many years ago Mynheer W had reported a fire on his farm. By some strange coincidence, I was the policeman on duty and I wrote the report that day; I was not even a corporal back then. A few days ago, I reread that report and noticed that Mynheer W said that all his Bushmen had fled the farm; he claimed that the fire had been set by them in revenge for some imagined offence.

I have no knowledge or recollection of such a fire, replied father calmly and untruthfully. Mynheer W's farm is many miles away. At the time the Bushmen came, I desperately needed people to help me on my farm. I did not care where they came from.

He paused. My decision was a good one. My people work well, and thanks to them my farm flourishes.

All three policemen stared at father, distrust in their hard eyes and tight lips, and something else, perhaps a touch of bewilderment.

Why are you lying for this vermin, Mynheer? What kind of white man are you?

The outburst came from the younger of the two policemen from Kimberley, a powerful man whose sloping forehead was deeply dented on both sides. His small red mouth was embedded in whiskers, and his veined cheeks seemed to swell, as if filling up with angry words as yet unreleased.

Mother released a few of her own, her voice as smooth as a bird in flight. These people are our employees, sir, not vermin, and it offends me to hear you speak so.

The older policeman from Kimberley was a captain. Tall and well made, until now he had kept his counsel, merely listening and observing. In contrast to his shaggy moustache and beard, his blond hair, turning grey, was very short. His eyes worried me: they scraped mother like barbed wire, though he spoke politely enough.

My men are angry, madam; you must excuse them. These murders were particularly savage, and they were committed by a Bushman. Unfortunately we have reason to believe that it was your Bushman.

He pointed at Brandbooi with a thick forefinger that almost touched Brandbooi's quivering forehead.

Mother looked startled. How do you know the killer was a Bushman? And if it was, it certainly was not Brandbooi! He has not left our farm for longer than two days since my daughter was born!

Are we to assume you have evidence of some sort that could

incriminate my employee? enquired father. Surely, then, you are obliged to tell us how Mynheer and Mevrouw W died?

The older policeman nodded bleakly. They were both shot through the heart with a bow and arrow. It happened as they slept, and the shooting was from extremely close quarters. He hesitated. It took the doctor a long time to take out the arrows. They were Bushmen arrows, with poisoned tips. If they had not died from the arrows in their hearts, the poison would have done the job.

Father shrugged. I am sorry they died in such a terrible way. But what makes you suspect that Brandbooi was their murderer?

I had never seen Brandbooi frightened before, not even when we climbed a dune looking for tsamma melons and found instead, sitting in the shade of a shepherd's tree not twenty yards from us, a pride of lions: two huge black-maned males, three lionesses and four cubs. Though I knew not to, I turned instinctively to run. Brandbooi held my arm firmly and whispered: *Do not move.*

I obeyed, trembling. The lions sat up, tails flicking, and watched us. The cubs stopped their play and stared inquisitively, heads to one side. One large female, probably the mother of the cubs, stood. Without warning she went into a crouch, ears flat, snarling ferociously, the sound juddering through every muscle and bone in my chilled body. As she charged, Brandbooi gave vent to a long, low hiss.

The lioness backed off, her tail still bristling, her golden eyes menacing; with a few cuffs of encouragement, she hustled the four cubs in front of her. The other lions rose to their feet, one after the other. Within seconds, all we saw were swaying sandy backs that soon merged with the dunes.

I told Brandbooi he was the bravest person I had ever known, braver even than father. He smiled at me and gave that long, low hiss again.

The tsamma melons we gathered that day tasted sweeter on my tongue than ever before.

Now Brandbooi's polished cinnamon cheeks turned the colour of river sand after a long drought; pearls of sweat rolled down his cheeks and dripped off the end of his nose. I willed him to think of the lions, to remember that policemen were human, and could not tear him to pieces.

Why was he so terrified, I wondered, when he had committed no crime, and was under the protection of father?

There were sound reasons for my childish ignorance: I had never before seen a man in uniform, and while I understood that this was the garb of authority, at the time I completely lacked understanding of the dread that a white policeman, nay, any white man, could put into the heart of the most courageous Bushman; even one innocent of any crime other than being himself.

The captain's hard gaze seemed to find Brandbooi's obvious terror curious. Still, he kept further questioning of him for last. First, he walked past the women and inspected each of them carefully, ignoring mother and me but evidently captivated by something about Poppie and Imp. He glared at them until they shrank back against mother; then he lifted Poppie's chin and stared into her large, frightened green eyes, which rapidly brimmed with tears. Muttering something to himself, he finally turned his attention to Brandbooi.

Where are your bow and arrows, boy?

Brandbooi turned around: there they were, slung in their hartebeest hide pouch across his back, as they always were. The policeman picked out an arrow, examined it, and touched its blackened, sticky tip gently with his forefinger.

Did you come after dark, he enquired conversationally. Did you climb through a window and find them sleeping?

He did not, replied father.

The captain whirled on him. His blue eyes sparked fiercely.

Please do not interrupt my interrogation, mynheer!

He turned back to Brandbooi, who seemed about to sink to the ground like a shoulder-shot springbok.

We know you hated him, *booi,* because he liked your women; he was very sick in that way. Did he take your woman and give her this child?

The captain's chin pointed at Poppie.

She is his; anyone who knew him can see that. She has his eyes.

He nudged Imp's bare foot with the toe of his boot. Not this one, he said disdainfully. She is too bushy. She must be yours.

Brandbooi's voice was less than a whisper. Not my woman, baas. Not my child.

The captain shook his head. You people, you are like elephants, you take a long time but you never forget, ja? What about the fire? I do not think you have forgotten that fire. Perhaps it was not vengeance enough, even though that baas you stuck with your arrow told me it took many months and cost much money to rebuild his farm after your fire.

He paused, then bent and spoke in Brandbooi's wan face.

Did you know, *booi,* when we wanted to find you and put you in jail for a long time, that baas you killed, he said to us, no, leave it, I never want to look on the face of another Bushman again.

He touched Brandbooi's chest with the tip of the arrow he was still holding, pressed it lightly against the taut flesh.

Why do you think he did not want us to find you and punish you for setting his farm alight, *booi?*

Brandbooi said nothing.

I took a step forward, felt mother's hand firm on my shoulder.

One small push of that arrow and even Tam might not be able to help him, I reflected nervously.

Now I think I understand why that baas did not want us to find you, continued the captain, eyeing Poppie.

Surprisingly, Brandbooi spoke, his voice hoarse and shaky.

He was a bad baas. He killed his own son.

The policeman sprang like a leopard.

And *that* is why you took your bow and your arrows and you shot them both through the heart; and then you fled in fear without even pulling out the arrows and taking them with you! That baas gave your woman a son, then he killed his own child! All these years you waited for vengeance like a serpent buried in the sand; you lay in wait until the time was right and then you struck. *That, booi,* is what you did.

Brandbooi shook his head hopelessly, gazing down at the sand.

None of this fits! exclaimed father angrily. It is all nonsense! It has been many years since the fire; why would he do such a thing? And it takes at least ten or twelve days to get to Mynheer W's farm. I tell you again, man, he has not left this place for longer than two days since he first came here to work!

The captain turned on father savagely. And *you* – you are a white man with the heart of a Bushman. *You are worse than he is.*

Captain, said mother crisply, you say you have a witness who saw the murderer. Bring him from the wagon and let us make an end of this appalling business.

Father's face was suffused with rage; her timing was excellent.

The policeman turned to his deputies. Ja, the Englishwoman is right; it is time. Go to the wagon.

He turned back to Brandbooi and spat on the ground at his feet.

And then we can take you, *booi,* to the jail in Kimberley and quickly find a judge, who will order you to be hanged from the nearest tree.

He rubbed his eyes. Unless something bad happens before that, on the way to Kimberley: perhaps a lion will catch you and tear you to pieces, then devour what is left.

The two policemen on their way down to the wagon in the riverbed heard this and roared with laughter.

Flanked by the policemen, the witness appeared at the top of the rise.

I sensed Meisie shivering on my right side and Poppie on my left. I felt like a leaf blown by the wind before a wild storm.

The witness's hair was itself like the wind. It streamed behind her, its gold and auburn lights almost blinding. Tall and graceful, she blended into the background with the natural delicacy of an antelope. As she glided closer, I saw that her eyes were violet and her cheeks brushed with bronze. Not quite nine years old myself at the time, I guessed her age to be about fifteen or sixteen years.

A sigh seemed to percolate through our assembled group. I found myself touching my own carroty hair with a despair that had little to do with the events which were unfolding.

Brandbooi uttered a startling whoop of joy. Disregarding the glare of the captain, he leaped into the air as if performing an exuberant spirit dance.

The sergeant from Upington pulled his gun from his belt.

Staan stil, jou, he shouted.

The girl was staring at Brandbooi, her eyes brimming with wonder. She ran to him, bent down, and placed her arms around his neck; she hugged him and rubbed her cheek against his.

I *knew* I would see you again, she exclaimed in Afrikaans. I dreamed of you on so many nights. I longed for you. *The man who showed me how to make fire.*

Brandbooi turned to father. It is she, he said simply. She has come back. The little white spirit girl.

The spirit girl's name was Sonja. We tried to persuade her to remain with us for a while, but she shook her glorious hair and said that her father's farm now belonged to her, and all the people who worked there depended on her. Not only did she have an obligation to them to keep the farm going, she also had the more onerous duty of compensating them for the long years of abuse they had suffered at the hands of her father.

They stayed one night: the policemen in their wagon below, and

Sonja in my bed.

The three policemen, stunned by the affectionate greeting between the girl and the Bushman, were bitterly disappointed when Sonja turned from Brandbooi and smilingly informed them that he was not the murderer; furthermore, she said, none of the people present was involved.

Shocked and confused about Sonja's relationship with Brandbooi, the policemen remained unenlightened. Nobody cared any longer what they believed.

I longed for the spirit girl to stay: I wanted her to give me the recipe for her extraordinary beauty – or at the very least advise me how to turn red hair to gold. Yet, when she bade us farewell, I was secretly relieved. I had been afraid, from the first moment they had greeted, that Brandbooi would leave us. Though Sonja did not say much, I sensed that taking him back with her to her farm was what her heart most desired.

But Brandbooi, though he loved the spirit girl for the magic of her presence when he was brought low, now loved us more. Fortunately for me – for us all – he was a man whom long experience had taught to trust above all things the simple truths of his own heart.

PART TWO

Water in the Desert

I WAS CONVINCED THAT getting lost in a sandstorm was the worst experience I could have in the desert. Nobody in my family contradicted me and, for a time, neither did the weather. Four seasons of summer and winter passed, and it was late summer again when I woke to the sound of gushing water and drumming on the rafters above my ceiling. I did not have far to look for the cause.

Sitting up in bed, I pulled aside the hide covering the aperture to the outside.

I saw a world quite changed from the day before: sky and sand merged as one, dull and heavy with rain which drove through the gap, bent on drenching every dry spot in the room. In the dim light, I saw little pools glistening on the hides covering the dung floor. I put my feet down gingerly, feeling for my shoes; I found one of them, sodden and cold.

Mother came into my room, frowning. Have your breakfast quickly, Em; the river is rising.

What river? I asked, bemused. A few isolated pools in the riverbed were all that was usually left behind after a storm.

A flare of light blossomed suddenly in the gloom of the day.

Will lessons be postponed today because of the rain, mother?

Get dressed, Em, replied mother irritably.

After I had eaten, I peered out, but there was a dense haze, and the kameeldoring beside our front door blocked what was left of the view. My shoes were already wet. I heard mother's and Meisie's voices in the kitchen, and ventured outside.

The riverbed was buried in a watery mist. I took a squelchy step and heard, very close by, a soft growl. Dripping water, I looked up and saw a spotted tail, stiff as a stick, protruding from a branch of the kameeldoring. As I hastily retreated indoors, it whisked about like an angry snake. A growl tore through the thick air and settled icily inside my head.

I shouted for father, but it was mother who came from the kitchen, wiping her hands on a cloth.

Father is with Brandbooi and Kobie, they are taking the sheep to the kraal furthest from the river. Why must you shout so?

I did not think you would hear me. The river is coming. The water is rising by the minute! And there is a leopard in the tree outside our front door!

A leopard? She stared in alarm at the closed door behind me.

Poor thing, I exclaimed. It must be terrified to have climbed that tree. Perhaps the rain has washed away our scent.

Through the deafening noise of the water, we heard barking. We ran to the front entrance and peered out through a crack in the door.

Rain cascaded onto us. Chummy, water running from his ragged coat, was at the foot of the tree, barking furiously up at the leopard, whose magnificent spotted head was now visible, his ears flattened, fangs bared in a snarl. The dog whose days now passed mostly in sleep seemed to have forgotten his advanced years, his stiff body and his lame leg. Alerted, somehow, by smells of the hunt, fuelled by the proximity of an enemy, he was deaf to my call. Youth and vigour were miraculously restored to him, and he was going to make the most of them while he could.

Mother's firm grip prevented me from racing to rescue him. I called his name again, frantically, but to no avail. Chummy had found his leopard, and though he had not treed her, she was his. A gift of the rain, a nose thumbed to the indignities of old age.

I breathed deeply, feeling my lungs invaded by thick, slimy air, as if the swampy breath of a monster oozed from an ancient grave in the depths of the earth and reduced the dry air to mulch.

Trickles and puddles of water joined and became a stream.

Meisie, emerging from the kitchen to find out what all the fuss was about, pointed in horror to the bottom of the door.

Madam, she wailed, the river is inside.

There was a splash, a rumble, a tortured groan; then nothing. Chummy's barking had stopped; it seemed that even the rain had fallen silent. We stood tensely, listening and waiting. There came a creaking and a rending sound, a violent crack, as of a branch felled by a terrible blow. The ground began shaking, and a howling cacophony fell upon the dwelling, which shook helplessly beneath the battering.

Seconds later, the water was upon us.

I felt mother tugging urgently at my arm; then all three of us were under the solid oak dining table, built by father and Kobie from wood hauled all the way from Cape Town.

Not a moment too soon. The roof above us caved in beneath the impact of the kameeldoring, itself uprooted by the mighty fist of the water. We crouched under the table like moles in a burrow. I tried to pray, but found I could not. I heard only the frenzied baying of the elements, and the slurp and suck of the river all around me.

Water swirled around us, gurgling greedily, murky and thick with leaves and pods and sticks. Protected by the table, which seemed astonishingly intact, none of us was seriously hurt, though Meisie had a deep bleeding scratch on her arm from a reed or a branch. We crawled out from underneath, pawing at the water like clumsy water birds, into a tangle of tree trunk, broken branches and dune reeds layered in haphazard piles. An enormous sociable weaver nest was waterlogged in a corner, empty of life. Chunks of furniture floated by, and pieces of mother's treasured ornaments drifted on the rising waters like brightly coloured petals. A large monitor lizard was draped across the table top. I knew it had drowned, though it seemed merely to be sleeping through the chaos that surrounded it.

I stood in the water, pushing aside all kinds of debris. A small polished egg bobbed by intact. It made me think of my pygmy falcon. Where had all the birds gone? Mother clicked impatiently in my ear, and she and Meisie hauled me through the mess to the back door; the front was completely blocked by the collapsed roof and the tree. I was reluctant and anxious. What had become of Chummy and the leopard?

We walked out of our wrecked home soaking and barefoot. I thought I saw tears on mother's face, but perhaps it was rainwater.

From the direction of the kraals, father, Kobie and Brandbooi came running. Father was shouting, Thank God! You are safe!

I had never heard him use the name of the Lord, but then I had never seen him so distraught. He lifted me and hugged me; he embraced mother and Meisie, then held me again. I struggled in his enclosing arms and began to weep.

Where is Chummy, father? Where is the leopard?

He took my hand and hurried us all to the highest ground, where we found the others gathered in an agitated circle. Poppie ran to me. I pushed her away.

May came up to be petted, and tears welled up again. I wanted Chummy.

Mother, wringing her hair out and shivering, was listening to father.

The sheep are safe, other than two ewes. They were too slow, the water took them and we could not get to them in time. We had our hands full. The dogs worked harder than any of us, and all in all, we have been fortunate.

Mother shook her head, and I knew she was thinking of our poor drowned home.

Father warned everybody that the river was still rising and we should stay away from the vicinity of the dwelling. The wagon was safe, and most of the shelters had not been breached by the water. He, mother and I would spend the night in the wagon, and if the river subsided, we would begin repairs in the morning.

We sat in Brandbooi's shelter and watched the rising water. For much of the rest of that day it rained, and the water rose and gushed and roared. Trees, branches, reeds, grasses and shrubs spun helplessly in its grasp. The corpse of a springbok churned past below us, legs kicking, eyes rolling as if appealing for help. A horn protruded from the water momentarily, then it was gone. I sought Chummy through a haze of misery, desperately hoping that he would limp up to me from out of nowhere and lick away the tears that – like the rain – would not stop flowing.

Later, the water began lapping at the edges of the lowest sheep kraal, and I was filled with resentment of its terrible power. Streaming down from the sky, flashing across a riverbed that could not absorb it, it had colonised broad swathes of land that did not belong to it. You were nothing, I muttered to the river. You were not even a dribble. You were a bed of sand with many living things that depended on you. Now, without warning, you have grown into a monster with a voracious appetite, and you have devoured your own children.

I thought of the hundreds of creatures that, unlike some of the birds, could not outrun the raging torrents, could not fly or flee fast enough: the antelope, squirrels, mongooses, snakes, lizards and all the crawling creeping things on which the river would glut itself. I looked up at the dull sky, still bloated with water. Why would God – if He lived up there – punish helpless creatures that lived by instinct and sinned against nobody? Had our presence brought this disaster upon all the rest? After all, we were the ones who did not fit. By demonstrating an extreme of its desolate nature, by destroying our home, was the desert giving us an unsubtle message?

Mother would have said that as usual I was being fanciful. Seasonal flash floods, though seldom as excessive as this, did occur in the Kalahari.

In case there was any doubt, I spoke defiantly into the wet air: I am staying. I will never leave you.

Father turned to me in surprise and nodded. I know that, Em, he said. You are a good, brave girl.

Towards evening, the rain stopped and father instructed Brandbooi to light a fire in the pit near the wagon, which was less waterlogged than our other pit, but still a challenge to anybody but a maker of fire. Brandbooi's relationship with fire was almost mythical – he could get wet dung to ignite, and chunks of damp wood that would sizzle out in seconds if I tried to fire them would flare up obediently at the lightest touch from him.

He fetched a springbok carcass that had been skinned the day before and was hanging in the drying shed; we would eat it together. Father ordered us to keep a wary eye out. If the water level rose to the lowest kraal, we would need to take prompt action.

Surrounded by familiar faces, I felt their warmth reach out to me in place of the sun that had been missing for the entire day. Yet I could take no comfort, my mind gnawing away at Chummy's continued absence.

Had he attacked the leopard? Had it killed him? Had the floods taken them both?

As I gazed dispiritedly around the tight circle, something else struck me: a face I loved was missing.

Where is Imp? I cried.

Brandbooi looked up from where he was attending to the fire in the pit.

The big water make her frightened. She go to her shelter.

I rose to my feet for the first time in hours. The shelter which Imp shared with Poppie, beside Brandbooi's and Meisie's, was some distance away, on high ground.

She must have fallen asleep. I will go and wake her. She must come and eat with us.

I knew I would have to reassure her, even if I was as yet unconvinced myself, that she would be safe from the floodwaters, because the only thing Imp liked about water was drinking it. To my surprise, her shelter was empty, as were the others I inspected. I even ventured into Kobie's dark hut.

For the first time that day, I forgot about Chummy. Imp must surely be hungry by now, I said to Poppie, who had come up to meet me. I am starving. Where can she be? Could she be sketching the flood from a tree somewhere?

We looked around, puzzled. There was nothing to be seen but the dripping skies.

Poppie's green eyes narrowed. She was asking about you, many hours ago. Brandbooi told her that the baas had gone to fetch you, but she said she was afraid that the waters had found you. I told her you were too strong, but she was still worried.

Then what did she do?

She said she was going to lie down for a while in her shelter.

Poppie's face twisted in fear as a thought struck her. Perhaps she did not go to the shelter. Perhaps she went to look for you.

Father, I shouted, certainty striking me like a bolt of lightning. I think Imp went to the dwelling.

Father, Kobie, Brandbooi, Slang and Uil searched everywhere they could reach in safety, but in vain. They could not approach the dwelling, as the floodwaters had reached the level of the roof.

The rain had stopped at last, but the water had not yet begun to subside. Night was falling fast and the darkness felt like a cumbersome black mantle, the hide of some immense evil beast. I could not eat – even the Bushmen who could eat meat all night ate poorly – and I could not sleep. I would not hear of Poppie sleeping in her shelter alone, so she put her pallet in the wagon beside mine. While father and mother slept, the two of us lay awake for a long time, holding hands and gazing out at the night without exchanging so much as a whisper. Finally, when the skies seemed to be lightening from all the water they had dropped and my eyelids had become pockets of sand scraping against my eyes, I fell into a dreamless sleep.

I woke to find myself alone. I sat up and sprang from the wagon in what felt like a single movement. It was later than my usual waking time, and the world was much changed since the day before. The round warm friendly face of the sun seemed to be smiling down from skies that were a radiant blue, and the water that had deluged us had run off, leaving, like a naughty child, chaotic piles of scrub and debris in its wake.

I saw mother walking towards me and ran to meet her.

Have you found Imp?

Mother did not answer. Her eyes were swollen and red. With an unpleasant shock, I realised that I had never actually seen her cry.

Is it Chummy? Is he dead? My voice sounded shrill yet hollow, as if from inside a cave.

Mother shook her head. I do not know, Em. But we have found Imp.

Oh, thank God! Where was she? I must see her. Poor thing, she must be starving!

She was in your room, my love. On your bed.

But –.

How very stupid I am. How very bad. Imp was taken by the river and still I slept. Even though it was my fault.

That same day, the Bushmen took the little body of my friend away. Though I sobbed and implored, mother would not allow me to see her; and I was not invited to the rituals that preceded her burial.

Two days later, at dawn, the land was almost as dry as if the floodwaters had never been. We rose, and began work to repair the damage. As the day wore on, the heat tore into us with its vulturine beak, but we laboured until sucked dry of every drop of perspiration and tears.

Father, in the firm belief that the practice was barbaric, had forbidden Tam to amputate the last joint of both Poppie's and Imp's baby fingers. Brandbooi blamed this omission for the tragedy, claiming that such a transgression had provoked the gods to take Imp as compensation. For him, the new sorrow had called up the old. Imp's drowning had revived painful memories of the drowning of his own two children, and father did not decry Brandbooi's explanation as he believed it would assist him, after a period of time had elapsed, to recover his peace of mind.

I was the one who understood what had really happened, and I knew full well who was to blame. Imp was not fond of water, and I could not begin to imagine how terrified of the floodwaters she must have been. Yet her love and concern for me had been greater by far than that fear. Though still a child, I knew such friendship to be a rare privilege, and my grief at her death was compounded by guilt that I had been the cause.

For days, my appetite did not return. I slept a great deal, with Poppie by my side, our tears soaking the pillows. In this, my first experience of loss, my parents were patient and comforting, but nothing they could say softened the blow.

Brandbooi, himself inconsolable, told Poppie and me that the desert has its own mysterious ways. Sometimes, he said mournfully, for reasons that are beyond our understanding, the Kalahari chooses to possess those who love it best.

With the permission of the Bushmen, I fetched from Imp's shelter two of her beautiful drawings, one of a hartebeest mother and her calf at a pan, and one of a giraffe browsing on a kameeldoring. They remain my greatest treasures.

Chummy never returned to the farm. In an attempt to comfort me in my comfortless state, father told me that being taken by the river while challenging a treed leopard meant Chummy had died as he had lived when we first knew him as a young dog, before the puff adder had bitten him: with zest and courage.

The floodwaters had also robbed me of something else: my journal – piles of pages of neat handwriting – had been washed away. It was mother who first observed that they were gone. I did not care. I was no longer writing; it seemed an insignificant, even foolish, activity.

Observing my recurrent low moods with growing concern, mother became insistent. Hard as it was, she said, the rewriting of the journal was essential: it would be greatly enhanced by recent events, and writing about the tragedy would serve to lift my spirits.

The second version, she suggested, should be dedicated to my lost friend Imp.

John Henry

YOU GOT A BIT FAT, madam. Meisie's voice was puzzled.

I did not hear mother's reply. It was one of our few lesson-free days, and since it was one week from my twelfth birthday, I had managed to persuade father that he could spare Brandbooi from his work to keep an eye on us for a couple of hours. Poppie and I could not wait to leave the farm. We had things to do that were as remote from lessons as possible, among them dune sliding on old animal hides along towering dunes about a mile away from the farm.

That night we retired early, exhilarated but weary from the day's activities. Many months had passed since Imp's death, and Poppie had gone back to sleeping in her old shelter. I missed her at first, but I liked having my bed to myself again.

A hum of conversation woke me from a deep sleep. Judging by the pearly light of the moon shadow outside my room, it was far later than my parents' usual bedtime. I lay with my eyes wide open, frowning as the hum rose in volume, easily penetrating chinks in the mud and stone wall. Though it occurred to me that I was eavesdropping on an altercation of sorts, which was in itself unusual, rather than listening I found myself dreamily recalling the dune sliding, the pinch of fear that was part of the fun as I pitched myself down the precipitous slopes of the dunes, and Poppie's cry, half fright, half pleasure, as she plummeted down beside me. Imp had loved dune sliding even more than Poppie and I. At the thought of her, my heart slowed; I felt the pain of missing her. Staring into the dark, I wondered if she would permit me to sleep for the remainder of the night.

The ground stirred and shifted beneath me. Eddies of sand blew against my legs. The darkness was pierced by a brilliant light. The earth heaved, and a gaping pit appeared. From this pit, my parents reared up like scarecrows, entwined in a stiff embrace. Grubs coiled from their mouths and nostrils, and their eyes were filled with sand. Fat dripped off them in dollops, as if they were melting from fires burning below them. I screamed and reached out to touch them, but they split apart as a tree is sundered by lightning, and were swallowed by the sand. A stream of water flowed where they had stood. It was stippled with fat.

I sat up in bed, the horror of the dream vivid in my mind. The sheets were damp with perspiration, and my breath was coming fast. I heard raised voices. I wondered what the hour was and how long my parents had been quarrelling. I rarely heard their voices at night; their disagreements were few, and hardly ever deteriorated into acrimony. When I eavesdropped, which I did regularly, their conversations were almost always conducted in low tones and therefore irritatingly inaccessible; to pick up the gist, I was forced to press my ear against the wall separating our rooms.

But now their words were clearly audible. I felt a tremor of alarm as I listened. I knew instantly that my twelfth birthday – a birthday mother regarded as a milestone – would be forgotten.

As it turned out, nobody except mother felt in a celebratory mood.

You are forty-four years old, Deirdre! How could something like this happen?

Alf, we have been over this: I do not know. The way it usually does,

I suppose. How could I have guessed? I never gave pregnancy a thought after Em's birth. I knew it would not happen, and until now, I was right.

Until now? But what are we to do about now? Having a child at your age could kill you. Having a child at any age, as you well know, could have killed you!

You speak as though this pregnancy were my fault alone. It is not, is it? Has it ever occurred to you that perhaps there is a God? And that this pregnancy – this child in my belly – is His will? Have you ever thought of that?

If it is His *will,* as you describe it, does He mean for you to die in childbirth?

I will not die. I am a healthy woman, I have not had a lung infection for two winters, and my womb has had many years to repair itself. And Tam will be an excellent midwife.

Silence. I pressed my ear against the wall, and was deafened by father's anger.

What are you saying? That you will have the child on the farm? Have you taken leave of your senses? What does Tam know about hygiene, about modern methods that could save your life?

Mother's response was so soft I could barely hear her.

I will have the child here, Alf. I have decided. I am not mad, as you well know. What is more, you cannot stop me from doing as I wish in this matter. Do Bushwomen need Boer midwives to deliver their babies? Tam knows as much as any midwife, and as for hygiene, I will take care of that myself beforehand.

I was shocked beyond measure by the news of my mother's pregnancy: I had long taken it for granted, as they had, that I would be an only child. Uneasily, I recognised her tone of voice: it brooked no further discussion.

Father, for once, ignored her.

Christ, woman, you might bleed to death! What will Tam be able to do about that?

I cannot leave the farm, Alf. If I do, I may never return.

That is mere superstition, groaned father. And if you stay – if you stay, what then?

What was mother implying? That if she left the farm to have the baby she would die? Yet to father, it was clear that if she stayed she would die.

I was overcome by the sudden turn of events: I would not exchange mother's life for a sister or brother, yet the choice was not mine to make. Nor, it seemed, was it father's.

I was awoken by another dispute in the small hours:

Surely it is not too late for Tam to *do* something?

What are you suggesting?

You know damn well what I am suggesting.

You astonish me. You say you fear for my life, yet you wish an abortion on me – the destruction of your own seed!

I do. It seems the safer option at your age.

Safer? For whom? I thought you always wanted a son. This child could be a boy. Does that not mean anything to you? A boy who could run this place when you are too old to do it?

We have our daughter. And my people.

Your people? They are not your people. They do not belong to you.

Mother's voice was filled with scorn.

To whom, then, do they belong?

You sound like the murdered Boer, for heaven's sake. They belong to their clan. To themselves.

They will never leave me.

Who is talking of leaving, Alf?

It is just that I am afraid, Deirdre. No son is worth the sacrifice.

It is not your sacrifice. It is out of your hands. I *will* have this child.

I tried to warm myself against the chill in mother's voice, but no blanket could prevent the shivering that spread from my scalp to the tips of my toes.

Mother sang during the last three months of her pregnancy. I had never heard her sing before. Her voice was a soprano ripple of wordless melody that resonated in the desert air and surely made the meerkats and squirrels dance. I wondered why she had hidden it all these years, but when I asked her she smiled and made no answer. As the weeks passed, her hips broadened, her stomach grew round, her movements slowed. Though she was less strict about lessons, they still took place every morning until, as the time for my new brother or sister to be born drew near, she became excessively sleepy. Poppie and I had to work under our own steam, and she urged us to be disciplined: she lacked the energy to supervise us, she said, and we must make do as best we could without her.

We obediently did the work she set and attacked our chores with unaccustomed vigour, knowing that in the near future, once the baby had arrived, mother would be even less attentive, and there would be extra hours in the day for us to spend as we wished.

Tam and Meisie adopted a strict ritual of hygiene, following mother's detailed instructions, washing their hands carefully and often in a clean bucket of boiled water with plenty of soap. Tam checked mother regularly; I had no idea what was done during these examinations, but it worried me that even Tam, so sure of herself and her doctoring, would emerge each time with her expression a little grimmer. Mother, meanwhile, swelled up like a cloud full of rain: her eyes squeezed into the pouches of her cheeks, her arms and legs became uncharacteristically chubby. I wondered if the bloating was normal, or if she was perhaps eating too much – eating for two.

When mother seemed as huge as a pregnant gemsbok, her burden about to burst from her at any moment, I observed father in close consultation with Tam. Neither, upon going their separate ways, looked happy. Father had become short-tempered as never before, and I knew to burden him with my anxieties would only make things harder. Thus I spent my free time with Poppie, Meisie and Doekie, and willingly assisted with domestic tasks, fetching water from the well, folding laundry, planting and picking vegetables.

Most enjoyable was helping Doekie and mother prepare the bedroom for the birthing. A large bottle of disinfectant, a jug of boiled water and a pair of sharp scissors were made ready on a table, and spotless sheets, towels and cloths were placed at the foot of the bed in sweet-smelling piles. Tam brought in an assortment of her herbs and poultices, as well as dark liquids in ostrich-shell containers, which father eyed with suspicion.

To my distress, the larger mother became the more impatient father got and the more vehemently he berated her over the smallest thing. Mother would turn away in exasperation and weariness. It was clear to me that father held her solely responsible for the pregnancy. I thought this unfair and unreasonable: he was the planter of the seed and therefore shared the responsibility for the result. More perplexing to me was why he, who claimed to love children, and was certainly a loving father to me and a benevolent caretaker of Poppie and Imp, should remain so unreconciled to the inevitable arrival of his second child.

Finally, after witnessing a particularly hostile verbal assault, during which mother shook her head, bit her lip and spoke not a word in retaliation, I was provoked enough, as soon as mother was out of earshot, to ask father with some indignation why he continued to be so horrid to her in her delicate state.

Father replied bluntly.

Because I am driven half mad with worry, Em, and have no other way to vent it. This child may be the death of your mother! After giving birth to you, she was warned, as you know, not to have any more children. Having this baby without benefit of good medical assistance in Upington is simply madness. I regret my ill-temper, especially for your sake; but I cannot find it in my heart to forgive her for endangering herself.

But father, more than twelve years have passed since my birth, and mother's health is excellent. Since the decision to remain on the farm was made some months back, why do you not relent? Surely at this late stage it would be far too hazardous even to contemplate travelling to Upington?

Father's brow darkened. You are too young to speak to me thus. The facts are that your mother is too old to birth a baby; not only is she too old to have one, she is too old to raise one.

He turned away abruptly. The back of his neck was an angry red, the tendons stretched tight. I knew he loved mother and feared for her life, but it occurred to me to wonder whether something else – I could not think what – lay at the core of his simmering temper.

Unlike father, I was certain mother would not die. I lacked the ancestral and intuitive wisdom of Tam, Doekie or Meisie and the experience of both my parents, yet my certainty had little to do with wishing or hoping. I knew that mother would live.

Perspiration broke out on her brow and rolled down her nose and cheeks. Huge damp patches blossomed on her dress, hastily sewn from an old sheet when her increased size outgrew her narrow garments. She held tight to her massive belly, as if trying to calm the baby within it.

Even I understood that she was in pain. With Meisie on one side and me on the other, she rose to her feet with difficulty. I felt as if I were a puny craft manoeuvring a floundering ship on turbulent waters. Tam, enveloped in a fragrant soapy cloud, waited beside the birthing bed in my parents' bedroom. Wizened and dwarfish, her face was grave, her mouth compressed to a thin line.

To my surprise, I found that my lips were moving. I was praying to whoever was out there and prepared to listen: to the spirit god of Brandbooi and Tam, to the Christian god, to the Jewish god of Mr Cohen the smous.

Father and Brandbooi were away hunting, and I was relieved that father would be spared the distress of witnessing mother's travail.

Tam clicked something to Meisie, who ushered me out of the room. I turned away reluctantly as they put mother gently to bed. She sat in an upright position with her English duck down pillows behind her back and gave me a little wave.

Do not look so apprehensive, my love. You must not worry; it will soon be over and you will have a little sister or brother. Think on that, and nothing else. Father will be back before nightfall and I will see you both then.

Promise you will ask Meisie to call me as soon as the baby has arrived, I entreated.

She nodded, trying unsuccessfully to smile.

Before the door closed behind me I heard her grunt. The sound was of a wildebeest brought down by a lion.

Doekie was manning the kitchen, boiling vats of water. Distracted, her brow deeply furrowed, she dispatched Poppie and me to the vegetable garden to pick whatever was ripe. I was only too happy to be occupied rather than to sit idle, visualising the birth that would soon, in a mess of blood and fluids, tear my mother's misshapen body apart.

The day wore on, and there was no news. Doekie brought our meals to Poppie's shelter and would not allow us into the dwelling. Once, I heard an appalling shriek. We were out of earshot of the dwelling, and I wondered if it was the voice of my own dread imagination.

Again and again, I pleaded with Doekie to permit me to accompany her; to enter the birthing room for only a moment to reassure myself that mother was all right. But Doekie was firm.

Your mother needs all her strength. She wants you to stay strong also. She says I must tell you that all is well with her.

Father had not yet returned. As the hours stretched into late afternoon and then evening, I felt disappointment turn to resentment. Where was he when his own child – my brother or sister – was about to be born? Did he not know that mother needed him? I glowered at the horizon until my eyes stung, longing to see father and Brandbooi on their horses cantering towards me, the spoils of the hunt draped across the saddles before them.

Poppie was shaking me awake. Meisie has been, she said happily, tugging me to my feet. The child is born.

I raced to the dwelling, burst into the room and there was mother: sitting up and smiling in the dim light. In her arms was a closely wrapped parcel, far smaller than a newborn lamb.

It is a boy, Em, she said softly. Your brother.

I embraced mother. Her eyes were lambent with joy; in the thick, fermented air of the birthing room, she smelt milky. I gazed curiously at the squashed squirrel face of my brother. His blue eyelids shone and his dot of a mouth drew in and out as if he were sucking. His head was oddly flattened on one side, with a brush of black hair on top, like the tip of a giraffe's tail.

Tam and Meisie were cleaning up. I saw two buckets, one full of red cloths and the other containing the afterbirth and umbilical cord, meaty and sinewy; but mother's hair had been neatly brushed and her nightgown was fresh and spotless. Brimming with gratitude, I smiled at Tam and she smiled back, pride and relief in the uninhibited display of two broken incisors and spotted brownish gums.

Is he not beautiful, Em, said mother, her clean pink face suddenly wet with tears. Meisie came to her and wiped them gently away. Wordless for once, I reached out tentative fingers and touched the soft upward sweep of my brother's feathery quiff. Bending to kiss the top of his dented head, I sniffed the warm sugary cavern of my mother's womb.

John Henry and Me

AFTER HIS LATE RETURN from hunting on the evening of my brother's birth, father was profoundly apologetic, and professed himself relieved and grateful that mother had not only survived the birth, but was doing surprisingly well.

I witnessed my parents' reunion with covert relief. They embraced each other with silent fervour; then father turned to inspect his newborn child. The inspection was brief, and he did not touch his son. I glimpsed his taut grizzled expression and found I was forced to conceal my distress from mother – even though, glowingly engaged with the new arrival, she did not appear to notice anything untoward.

I had seen that expression on father's face before, several times over the years, when a lamb had been stillborn, or when jackals had contrived to sneak past the dogs to snatch a newborn lamb.

Tam, Meisie and Doekie received special gifts from father for their services to mother. With the help of Tam's herbs and potions, she made a rapid recovery and was able and eager to undertake the care of my brother quite soon after the confinement.

Mother named her son with the minimum of ceremony and a few baptismal drops from the well. John Henry was named after his grandfather, John Henry Bolton, mother's father whom she scarcely knew, since he died when she was four years of age. Father put up no names of his own; in contrast to my own naming, he seemed disinterested when it came to the naming of his son.

Everyone was delighted with John Henry, and mother happily absorbed by her maternal duties. It was left to me alone to feel uneasy, perturbed by what I perceived to be father's withdrawal from his family.

John Henry was a tranquil baby who rarely cried. But he did not take well to mother's breast, although she appeared, this time, to have plenty of milk despite her advanced years. When awake, my brother seemed happiest lying quietly on his blanket under a tree and gazing with his narrow dark eyes at the blue sky, as if fascinated by its hue.

Mother, Meisie, Tam and Doekie fussed over him by turn. When he refused to fasten his little bud of a mouth onto mother's oozing nipple, they fed him with a tiny spoon fashioned from a reed. Mother seemed to have little time for anything or anyone else besides John Henry, and at first her inattentiveness – her brief, inadequate replies to my questions and the abstracted look in her eyes – suited me, because it meant she would be far less insistent on lessons or critical of the quality of the work Poppie and I continued, unenthusiastically, to produce.

My brother's flattish features and bumpy head had improved in shape somewhat since the birth. I liked playing with him, but in the early weeks I did not get to spend much time with him as he was usually asleep. Sleeping, I remarked crossly to Poppie, is what John Henry likes to do better than anything else. A newborn lamb is more fun!

I asked mother how long it would be before he would recognise that I was his sister and therefore quite important to him.

Mother laughed. He knows already, Em. He knows who you are.

I knew he did not.

The weeks passed, and John Henry slept them away. He breast-fed poorly, and fussed only when mother and Meisie tried to feed him with the spoon. He rarely woke spontaneously to be fed and scarcely ever cried. Mother was convinced that he was not getting enough nourishment, and she, Tam and Meisie frowned over him often and anxiously.

As for father, he became excessively busy – too busy to spend time with any of us. Especially his son.

Tiny as he was, my baby brother was large enough to consume all mother's attention. While at first I welcomed her lack of interest in our lessons, it soon became a source of irritation. She asked me few questions and seemed not to care a bit about what Poppie and I did in the mornings. While she was bowed over John Henry, who stubbornly refused to thrive, we did whatever we felt like, often wandering away from the farm alone until one day Brandbooi, on his way back from the well, caught us heading out and gave us a fierce dressing-down about the pride of lions waiting to devour us in a clump of reeds in the riverbed below.

Mother, I must speak to you.

Em, I am resting. What is it you want? She glanced up at me unseeingly.

I stamped my foot like a small child.

It is about lessons, mother. Shall *I* devise them? You appear to have run out of ideas. Or perhaps, I added impertinently, John Henry has sapped them.

I did not particularly want lessons; I wanted my mother back. I was desperately bored without her. I realised, to my dismay, how much I had taken her attention for granted.

Oh, Em, murmured mother reproachfully.

She was sitting with her head in her hands at the large oak table, the same indomitable piece of furniture that not only saved our skulls but was one of the few pieces to survive the flood, albeit deeply scored and battered.

Mother raised her head slowly, as if it hurt her to move. She looked up at me with dull eyes. The delicate patina of her face reminded me of a fine old porcelain dish we owned, brought all the way from England and mapped with tiny translucent cracks.

Devising lessons is an excellent idea, Em, she said wearily. It is important that you keep up. I cannot seem to find the time for lessons these days. When John Henry is a little stronger, we will return to our routine.

Her voice, without inflection of any kind, matched her eyes.

For whom would we be keeping up? I retorted. There does not seem much point to lessons without you, mother.

She shrugged and shook her head. Em, my mind is elsewhere. Can we talk about this later?

I quickly changed tack.

What is *wrong* with John Henry, anyway? Why does he not feed properly? Can Tam not heal him with one of her medicaments?

I do not know the answers, Em; I wish I did. I wish that more than anything in life. Tam has tried several of her potions but, sadly, without success.

Slow tears began falling, dropping into fissures in the table.

I ran to embrace her. He will be fine, mother. He is just very young, that is all.

He *will* be fine, Em. I believe that.

But *I* did not. Horrid thoughts had begun seeping into my head; thoughts that felt like wishes. They made me feel guilty, but not guilty enough to prevent them from ambushing my mind at times when it should have been fully engaged with more productive activities, such as thought-provoking lessons to demonstrate to Poppie and to mother.

Even when doing my chores, these fantasies plagued me. As I pulled up weeds and fetched water and washed dishes, my mind was full of my baby brother. In my fantasies he would somehow have disappeared. Mother's eyes would be only for me, and father would be at home more often instead of out hunting and doing whatever he and Brandbooi were doing away from the farm while Kobie, Slang and Uil took care of farm matters. These imaginings seemed independent of me, roaming mischievously at will in my head; they persuaded me that John Henry was demanding and difficult, consumed far too much of his mother's time and energy and made her low in spirits. With him out of the picture, father and mother would have the time to talk to each other with the animation and affection they had shared before mother fell pregnant. And I would be back in mother's thoughts, the sole recipient of her much-missed attentions.

It was not as though I visualised John Henry dead; I did not. My mind focused on the re-establishment of old patterns and the continuation of comfortable routines that his advent and unsettled existence had disrupted or obliterated entirely.

In the end, in spite of the offer to mother, I could not bring myself to plan a single lesson. I wrote less often in my journal and doodled in it instead. I missed the stimulation of mother's intellect far more than I was prepared to admit: though I did not enjoy arithmetic, her insightful teachings in literature, geography and history demonstrated an extensive command of her subject, a dedication to learning and an endless generosity and patience when it came to sharing her knowledge.

On a day when the sun's glare intensified the ache behind my eyes, a distinctive new voice, unambiguous and knowing, made itself heard inside my head.

John Henry is destroying your family.

What, I thought helplessly, is happening to me?

On a guilty impulse, I took myself to where my brother lay on a blanket in the shade of the only large kameeldoring in the vicinity of the dwelling to have survived the flood. It was not far from the back door. Mother often put John Henry down on a blanket to sleep there, with herself or Meisie close by to watch out for harmless lizards and less harmless insects or snakes.

For once, John Henry was wide awake. I sat beside him and prodded his cheek with my forefinger. To my surprise, his mouth popped open in a delighted smile. I could see his tiny pink tongue and his shiny gums. I touched his cheek again, and he grinned wildly, a spasm of baby joy that instantly illuminated a cold little core inside me. I kissed his small flat face, and scrambled to my feet.

Mother was sitting just inside, sewing yet another baby garment.

He is smiling at me, mother! Come and see! He is so beautiful!

He was not beautiful, but he was my brother. Just like that, I knew I loved him. I wanted very much for him to know; I wanted to see in his eyes that he understood that I was his big sister, and that he could trust me to take care of him.

From that day – or so it seemed – not only I, but John Henry too, turned a corner. He began to feed greedily, and slept far less. Mother was overjoyed. One morning, while she was in the kitchen and I was watching him outside, he rolled over from his stomach onto his back. Observing his startled expression, I picked him up and hugged him. He smiled up at me, his slanted eyes recalling the painting of a Chinese boy I had seen in a treasured art book of mother's.

Knowing how eager mother would be to witness his latest accomplishment, I turned to call her, and found father looming behind me, staring down at John Henry in my arms. The bridge of his nose was crinkled and the expression on his face was a blend of perplexity and distaste; as if his son were a curious, rather unpleasant object rather than his own flesh.

I did not know you were back, father, I exclaimed. Where have you been? We have not seen you in three days.

He took a step back. I have missed you, too, Em. We have been hunting, of course. We must put up meat for the winter.

But we have plenty of biltong already, father.

John Henry found my forefinger with his waving hands and held it loosely in his tiny fist.

Watch, father, I will put him down and make him smile for you; he is such a darling! Perhaps he will turn over again. He turned over for the first time, I believe, a few minutes ago. Even mother has not seen him do it yet!

I put my brother down and sat beside him, tickling his cheeks and making baby sounds in an effort to make him smile. As if he knew his father disapproved of him, John Henry would not cooperate.

Does mother know you are back, father?

No. I am off to the kraals. I will see you all later.

Father, do pick up John Henry for a moment before you go! He is adorable: he has put on so much weight and he smells wonderful, like firecakes and soap.

Adorable? Em, you are still a child, but you are not a fool. Can you not see? He looks nothing like us!

I looked down at my brother. His fist grasped a strand of my long hair. The little tug at my scalp translated into a sudden dragging, unwanted wretchedness.

I do not know what you mean, father, I said softly. I see myself clearly in his eyes; I wonder that you cannot. Sometimes I love him so much that my chest hurts.

Father drew in a deep breath. I will see you at supper. Tell mother I am home.

A Thief, a Decision, a Fight

JOHN HENRY WAS BECOMING rather plump, as if mother, who had shed her own extra pounds within a couple of months of his birth, had given them to him. She had become more herself and my own dear mother again: brisk, glowing with health and full of good ideas about lessons. Yet some disturbing changes had infiltrated the re-established tenor of our lives. One of them was that my parents rarely spoke to each other in my company or out of it, as far as I was aware; and a second was that father had moved into one of several small outhouses located a short distance from the back door of the dwelling.

I observed him emerging from an outhouse early one morning and asked in some surprise what he was doing there; he explained that he was sleeping there because John Henry woke at all hours for feeding and in order to do a good day's work he himself needed to be well rested. I enquired if the change was temporary, and he replied curtly: The matter is none of your affair, Em.

A clever thief was preying on the sheep.

From time to time, predators would snatch a lamb. Leopards were the most successful, furtive and cunning, though it was a challenge to get past Kobie and the dogs. After a lamb was taken, the perpetrator was tracked down by father and Brandbooi, and shot. As a result, we had some beautiful leopard skins on our floors, and even a cheetah skin, which upset me more than I can say as cheetahs are gentle, noble creatures and deserve far better treatment. Father was, however, understandably ruthless in this regard: once a cat was successful, there was a good chance the flocks would be regarded as easy meat and the animal could become a serial sheep predator, any farmer's worst nightmare.

After a lamb was stolen, I never once heard father apportion blame, or even reprimand Kobie; he knew how seriously Kobie took his work. In spite of this, the Hottentot seemed to feel an inordinate burden of guilt. This was adroitly exploited by the Bushmen, who chuckled behind his back (and even to his face) about him not being man enough to protect his flocks.

Though relations between Kobie, the only Hottentot, and the Bushmen had always been uneasy and opportunities on both sides to tease unmercifully and to undermine, if possible, were never overlooked, our people worked efficiently as a team when necessary, owing in part to the fact that father was an excellent manager who communicated what he required with great precision. They were also well aware that if the need arose he could himself execute every task he delegated to them. His close but respectful supervision ensured that relations among his people, though frequently disharmonious, did not deteriorate into open hostility.

The real mystery of the new predator lay in the stealth and smoothness of its incursions: during these, it failed to rouse either Kobie or the dogs. A young sheep or a lamb would be taken without a sound, and without the slightest accompanying agitation that even a leopard, as quick as it might be, would generate among the flock. Kobie, whose sleep was habitually shallow owing to the nature of his responsibilities, slept undisturbed through the night and the dogs did not bark.

At first the Bushmen mocked Kobie for his carelessness, but as the weeks passed and the predation continued, this disparagement fell away. A sheep went missing at least once each week; no predator was tracked down, trapped or shot, and father's brow turned thunderous. The Bushmen began muttering about a spirit stealer.

Immediately after the theft was discovered at dawn, father and Brandbooi, the latter with the eyesight of an eagle and an uncanny ability to track anything that moved, would painstakingly inspect the sand for tracks or scat. Even with the sand baked hard, a cat or a hyena would have left spoor of some nature: faeces, disturbed blades of grass or a bush with strands of fur enabled Brandbooi to instantly identify the animal. There was nothing. Father appointed each of the Bushmen in turn to stand guard with Kobie by night, and the dogs were strategically placed in the kraals. In spite of these precautions, once every seven or eight days, in the dead of night – the time of the spirit stealers, said Tam – the phantom thief came among them, silently stole a meal for itself, and left not the faintest imprint of its visit behind.

Mother was breakfasting and reading Jane Eyre yet again when Meisie came. Sitting across from mother, I had forgotten to eat, so deeply immersed was I in an old favourite, Great Expectations. I read with renewed revulsion of the England depicted by Dickens, and also by mother. It seemed as unpleasant a place as I could conceive of in which to live, and I felt very fortunate to be far away from it.

Madam, said Meisie at mother's shoulder, John Henry is too hot.

Well, take the cover off then, Meisie, said mother absently.

The cover is off, madam. It is his skin. It is like touching fire.

Good God, cried mother, pressing John Henry's brow and cheeks, he is melting from heat. Where is Em – oh, there you are – tell Doekie to fetch Tam; she must bring whatever she has to lower the fever. How can such a thing happen so quickly? This dawn he fed well, he was bright and happy. Now look at him! It is scarcely three hours later and he is as hot as the sand at noon.

I slipped away to find father, who was working at the tan-pit with Kobie. On the way I saw Brandbooi running so fast across the sand that he seemed to be flying over it like a bird rather than touching it with his feet. Father and Brandbooi began walking rapidly in the direction of the outermost kraal. Disappointed, I turned back to the dwelling, wondering where they were bound in such a hurry, but far too worried about John Henry to pay much heed.

Anxiety fluttered in my chest as I gazed down at him. It was almost a year since I had been plagued by evil imaginings; still, I felt a twinge of guilt. Was it my fault that the poor perspiring little mite, wrestling feverishly with his own breath as I watched, was suffering so?

As I reached out a finger to caress his damp head, John Henry vomited. The fluid spun in an oddly graceful arc and splashed messily to the floor. It was by no means his first vomit, but it was without question one of the largest.

I picked up a cloth and wiped his mouth, which still leaked fluid; then I wiped mother's hands, covered in vomit. She lifted him up. He wailed feebly. Opening his soiled garment, she placed the tip of her right forefinger in the small hollow between his collar bones, then raised him higher and put her ear to his chest.

I hear gurgling in his lungs. Oh Lord, where is Tam?

I will find father also, I said. He will surely be back by now.

From where I did not know.

I ran to the kraals, to the tan-pit, to the well. Father and Brandbooi were nowhere to be seen. Tam and Doekie walked rapidly past me, without so much as a glance in my direction.

I found Kobie repairing a wall in the middle kraal.

Where is father?

He shrugged. They are gone, he replied cryptically.

Puzzled, I returned to find Tam rubbing John Henry's chest with an ointment, and mother holding a clot of what looked like wet leaves to his nostrils. My brother appeared to be asleep, an alarming blueness to his nose and mouth. When Tam finished rubbing in the ointment, she took a wet cloth and wiped his naked greasy body from head to foot with cool well water. He urinated as she did so, but did not open his eyes.

Mother, her breathing rapid, her cheeks bloodless, was plainly terrified at this recurrence of my brother's fragility. Filled with pity for her, I took her free hand, hanging loosely by her side, knowing instinctively that she would gladly suffer in his stead were it in her power to do so. She had had little experience of nursing since her mother and younger sister had died in England, and though she herself had a tendency to infections of the lung, I was so healthy that I had never even suffered from the common cold. Father, too, was never ill; and our people turned to Tam if they needed advice about their own excellent health.

Tam dried John Henry's every crease with loving care; then began mixing something in a small porcelain dish. At her request, mother opened his mouth with her baby finger, and Tam placed a few dark drops on his tongue.

His eyes remained closed.

Is he sleeping? I asked mother.

She sighed through ashen lips. His breathing seems easier.

With the back of her hand, she brushed the little Bushwoman's cheek. Thank you. You are our healing angel.

Tam did not look at mother. She tapped John Henry's chest gently.

It is a sickness in there. She picked up her medicaments and left the room.

Where is father, Em?

I cannot find him. I saw him leave the farm some time ago. Brandbooi went with him.

Mother chewed her lip, her fingers entwined.

He is gone from us, Em.

I am sure he will be back soon, mother; I will wait for him at the kraals and tell him he is needed.

Though I pretended not to, I understood her meaning. I sucked air into my lungs with difficulty, as if I were John Henry. The hard dry desert air did not fill them.

I sat cross-legged beside a black thorn at the outermost kraal. Kobie was working some distance away; Poppie and Doekie had gone to fetch more water from the well. Mother wanted a lot of water heated for use later that afternoon, when she and Meisie planned to give John Henry a kind of steam bath in the hope of alleviating the congestion in his lungs.

By the time I saw them coming, the sun was low in a marbled sky. I blinked sleepily, thinking it was a trick of the rapidly diminishing light; but when I opened my eyes properly, they had not deceived me. *Three* figures were coming towards me: father, Brandbooi, and a diminutive third figure so close to Brandbooi that were it not for the stick-like legs, he would have seemed an extension of him.

I shouted for Kobie. Before the little group reached us, I was surrounded by everybody on the farm except for mother and John Henry.

He was so small that I thought him far younger than I, but Brandbooi estimated him to be about sixteen years of age. Clad in a strip of hide that covered his loins and nothing else, terror at his predicament appeared to have shrivelled the young Bushman's tongue, for no matter how much Brandbooi clicked away at him, he did not respond. Despite this, Brandbooi assured father that the boy understood every word.

Father agreed. A thief with the power to turn into a spirit, he said with grim irony, cannot be lacking in intelligence.

Where did you find him, I asked father, staring in dismay at the trembling boy.

He was hiding in deep scrub. He had left absolutely no tracks. May was with us, and she did not sniff him out. It was Brandbooi who smelt sheep's fat. The odd thing was that even that dog, with her well-nigh infallible nose, smelt nothing at all!

Brandbooi was swiftly binding the boy's hands and feet with thick rope. He tied him to a sturdy pole at the corner of the kraal.

Not so tight, I begged Brandbooi. I appealed to father: He deserves punishment for stealing, but surely he was forced to steal in order to survive?

The young Bushman lacked even a bow and arrows with which to kill an animal. I wondered if he had buried them, for his scrawny arms appeared to lack the strength to kill a lizard, let alone a lamb, and he looked too small to carry the carcass. Perhaps he had used a large piece of chalk stone to kill the animal once he had separated it from the rest of the flock and enticed it from the kraal. But the riddle that preoccupied me revolved around the sheep: why had they not become agitated by his presence among them? Why had the dogs not barked? They were still not barking; May and the other dogs were sitting up and eyeing the proceedings, but displaying no special interest in the boy.

Father spoke up thoughtfully, as if in response to my unvoiced questions.

Bushmen have a way with animals. That is the only explanation; there can be no other. Where is his clan? Where did he learn his skill? Where are his bow and arrows?

Brandbooi shrugged. He used a stone, baas. He ate every scrap of your animals and then he buried the skin and bones somewhere so as not to attract hyenas.

And even you cannot find where he buried them! And look at him: he is skin and bones himself. You would think he had not eaten in weeks, yet he is full of about eight of my sheep!

Father sighed. Now the problem is what to do with him.

Kobie, standing behind me, grunted in disgust.

He is a thief, like a lion or a hyena. Baas must shoot him with the rifle.

I turned around, shocked. Kobie! How can you say such a thing? He is a human being. Like you and me. You cannot shoot him like an animal.

He *is* animal, mumbled Kobie sulkily. He is not like me.

I heard muttering from the others. I realised with a shiver that Kobie and the Bushmen, for once, were in accord. Not even Poppie demurred. Looking at the uniformly grave faces around me, their judgement seemed clear: severe and unusual punishment must be meted out to the young Bushman.

I remembered then how our own Bushmen had materialised like ghosts on our farm, battered and starving, and how they had been taken in by my parents. I found myself pondering the quality of Bushman mercy: the boy, though clearly not of their clan, was a Bushman: one of their people. Were their memories so short that they had already forgotten that before the boy was flushed out they had been convinced that the successful thief was a spirit of some kind?

Perhaps, I reflected, they were afraid he was an evil spirit, which must be sacrificed in exchange for the future well-being of the flocks. Or did they want him punished simply because he had stolen from father, who they loved?

Brandbooi squatted at the boy's feet and began speaking rapidly in the Bushman tongue. The boy, his small shaking body almost orange in the fading sunlight, seemed not to be listening. His eyes were slits, caked with dust, his mouth slightly open, lips like the desiccated husks of dead millipedes.

Water.

Father, I cried, he is dying of thirst! I will fetch water from the kitchen.

As I walked away, a long thin cry came from the direction of the dwelling. I broke into a run. I heard father curse.

Then he was beside me.

Mother stood at the door, John Henry limp in her arms. His eyes were wide, staring at nothing.

Get Tam, said father; but Tam was behind us.

She took the baby from mother, turned him upside down and banged his back none too gently. John Henry coughed and choked. She held him away from her, stuck her baby finger in his mouth, pulled out his tongue and cleared his throat. My brother coughed again. Tam put him against her chest and gently patted his back with her small wrinkled hand.

Too much in his lungs, madam. I will give him more of my medicine.

She shook her head. But the sickness is very strong.

John Henry appeared to have fallen asleep in her arms, his breathing soft and regular.

Mother took him gently from Tam and pressed her lips to his forehead. She addressed father.

I will leave with him in the morning for Upington. I will take Em and Meisie with me. I wanted Tam to come with us, but she says she is too old to leave the farm.

Father seemed to hear only what he chose.

You cannot take Meisie, he replied tersely. She is doing your work now as well as her own. I cannot spare her.

Then Em and I will manage the wagon, said mother. She is old enough.

She knows nothing of driving an ox-wagon; neither do you. And the child will require both of you to care for him. Kobie will drive you, but he must return after he leaves you in Upington. I need him with the flocks.

Mother bit her lip. I cannot promise that he will return immediately; it will depend how it goes with my son.

My son?

Father looked taken aback, but when he spoke I realised he had not noticed. Or perhaps he did not care. When the child is well, Deirdre, I will send Kobie back to Upington for you.

I asked if Poppie could come with us, but mother shook her head. She is needed on the farm.

But what of her education, mother, she will miss months, I implored, strangely unmoved at the thought of a visit to the town – my first since I was born there.

Father spoke to me, but his eyes, dulled by a weary displeasure, were on mother.

I am not certain what your mother is educating her for, Em. It does not take a great deal of education to become the serving maid of a white woman.

I filled the tumbler over and over, yet still the little Bushman drank, huddled against the post, his hand on the tumbler like the crabbed thorax of a scorpion.

I helped Kobie and Meisie pack the wagon until it was full dark; then I returned to the captive to find Brandbooi, a flare planted nearby, tightening the rope which bound the boy to the post. Since it was already very tight, I protested. Brandbooi's brow seemed to drop to his eyebrows.

I knew he was displeased.

At table that night, I asked father if I could take the captive a portion of my own supper.

You may not. You must eat everything on your plate. Tomorrow you travel to Upington and you will need all your strength to assist your mother and Kobie.

I appealed to mother. He is just a boy. He must eat.

It is for your father to decide, Em.

Boy or not, he has eaten my sheep, said father grimly. They are enough for many suppers.

I opened my mouth to object, but mother stretched across the table and put her finger to my lips.

Go straight to bed when you have finishing eating, Em, she said in the voice that brooked no objections.

That night, before I slept, I listened hard, longing for the familiar, comforting murmur of my parents' conversation before I fell asleep. A separation of what might amount to many months faced them, yet I heard nothing. In desperation, I realised I would even settle for voices raised in argument.

None came. I heard only mother and Tam and once, a cry from John Henry.

Before I fell asleep, the back door closed with a decisive click.

At dawn, the young Bushman was gone. The thick rope lay in tatters at the bottom of the pole, as if chewed to bits by the hungry jaws of a hyena. I looked away from Kobie's stooped shame – he had been asleep in the nearest shelter – and Brandbooi's averted gaze, and wondered if the latter believed the young boy had shape-shifted to a hawk and taken to the skies, as he had once done when he too was young and sad.

I chose to believe differently: that the boy's spirit was not that of a hawk, but of an African wildcat, which had chewed through the rope and, scentless, soundless, melted into the night.

For father, both the advent and the disappearance of the young Bushman were inexplicable – enigmas which, after venting his ire on both Kobie and Brandbooi, he chose to probe no further.

But the young Bushman's disappearance filled me with hope, even elation. I was well into my thirteenth year and should perhaps have known better; but I could not find an explanation for his magic more plausible than that of a transmogrified spirit. From my heart, I wished the wildcat Bushman safety and freedom on his spirit journey.

John Henry had slept through most of the night, and seemed better.

An hour after dawn, when we were almost ready to set out on our long journey, Brandbooi came loping up to father and spoke softly. Inquisitively, I strained to hear, but could not. Father cursed, left off harnessing the oxen and strode in the direction of the kraals. I hurried after him, wondering if, after all, the young Bushman had been found.

I saw blood, a crimson splash that had not yet seeped away into the sand. Kobie, his face distorted with rage and hatred, his fists clenched, stood visibly shaking above a figure stretched out on the ground.

It was old Slang.

Apparently Slang had blamed Kobie for the captive's escape, and viciously mocked him for a watch so inept that even a young boy could slip through it. Nearby, Brandbooi, steeped in thoughts about the tattered rope and the possibility of spirit intervention, had ignored the altercation.

Kobie, outraged, picked up the nearest chunk of chalk stone and brought it down on Slang's head. By good fortune the blow, though bloody, was a glancing one. Slightly concussed, Slang was tended by Tam, and sent to his shelter to recover.

Father then herded Kobie into his hut. I can only guess what ensued.

Within an hour of the drama, the wagon, fully provisioned and carefully packed, was ready for departure. Mother tried once more to lure Tam to accompany us, but she shook her bristly head and gave last-minute instructions in the ministering of her drops and advice in the event of untoward medical emergencies. Since we would be away months rather than years, the reason she gave for her refusal puzzled me: she said she wished to be buried in the heart of her birth country. Meisie, Doekie and Uil came to say farewell, and to report that Slang was already feeling better and sent his good wishes for the journey.

Poppie, beside me, eyed the wagon longingly. She had been my shadow ever since she had heard that mother, John Henry and I were travelling to Upington to consult a doctor.

I have never seen a town, she said.

Hmm, I replied. Neither have I – or not that I recall.

I hugged her; her bones were as light as the quills of a porcupine. Distressed at the separation that loomed, I felt a prick of conscience that she was forced to remain behind, and sad that I would miss her fifteenth birthday in June, which mother had designated her birth month, as Meisie, who had assisted in her delivery, said it had taken place on a cold night in midwinter.

Kobie, very low after his tongue lashing, was only too happy to take leave of the farm for a while.

Father embraced me, and instructed me to look after mother. No mention was made of John Henry; father scarcely spared his son a glance. His eyes were on mother, and I thought I read in them a certain appeal. What mother read I was not privy to, but I heard her sigh. Eddies of sand rose in the wintry air, as if in sympathy.

They did not embrace in farewell.

The Diagnosis

AT NIGHT, LYING IN THE wagon on one side of John Henry with mother on the other, the cold was so intense that my bones felt brittle, as if the slightest movement could fracture one of them. I was concerned that even the smallest quiver might disturb John Henry and trigger his breathing difficulties, and was forced to master shivers which threatened to infect the confined space in which we slept. If he woke and cried, struggling to fill his lungs with air, mother held him against her to calm him while I applied Tam's ointment to his chest and back. Between us, we would warm and quiet him until his laboured breathing settled and he fell asleep.

But I could not do the same; and I knew mother, too, lay awake on the other side of his small body, filled with fear which communicated itself to me and lingered in the icy air we breathed.

Mother said it was important to keep John Henry warm at night, since catching a cold on top of his already troubled breathing would be extremely hazardous. So he lay between our bodies and despite my barely suppressed restlessness, seemed for the most part to be comfortable, for he slept through some nights without waking.

Sleep was a problem for me for an entirely different reason, which had nothing to do with the cold. Just when I was on the verge of tumbling into oblivion, Kobie's snores would rise in a dreadful clamour, which seemed to jostle the wagon like a prisoner the bars of his cage. He himself slept like a dead man across the covered opening; it was far too cold to sleep beneath. The snores reverberated in the frigid desert silence; I was convinced they would rouse every living creature huddled in their hidden lairs and burrows. Fortunately, this incessant nightly din did not disturb John Henry in the least, though mother's sighs of exasperation were clearly audible.

The early mornings were so dry and chilly that until I had drunk my first sip of water I could hardly swallow, my throat as gritty as if coated with sand. But as the day advanced it grew warm, sometimes hot. At noon, we would outspan and rest for a while, John Henry on a blanket on the sand, gazing in wonder at the flinty sapphire sky. Some days, I spotted a bird atop a skeletal tree: a pale chanting goshawk, a lilac-breasted roller, or a tiny yellow weaver flitting through the scrub.

John Henry appeared to follow my pointing finger, for he grinned and bobbed in my lap as if in imitation, and, unlike mother and me, enjoyed the raucous cawing of ubiquitous crows, which followed the wagon in numbers to scavenge whatever they could when we stopped. I noticed he moved very little, and while his fingers were often in his mouth, sometimes they waved about erratically, like moths. His head had grown much larger, his face was round, his nose small; his close-set, solemn dark eyes, which mother described as almond shaped, reminded me of the narrow pods of a desert shrub. The space between his nose and rosy dribbling mouth that never seemed to close was inordinately broad.

I would study him closely in the hope of tempting him to further advances. On a blanket on the sand, I manoeuvred him to a sitting position and hoped he would sustain it. And there were moments when he sat effortlessly, but they were few. Mostly, he lolled lopsidedly against my hand and collapsed when I removed it.

At times I was astounded by the love I felt for him. As if grateful for it, he would sit by himself for a few seconds, smiling at me in pride and delight. Mother watched with enjoyment as she mended a garment or prepared the mixture for the firecakes Kobie would cook on the small fire he lighted daily. I knew next to nothing of babies, but it seemed curious to me that John Henry would not crawl, let alone get onto his feet, although he had grown a lot in size and weight, and was quite heavy to lift.

I decided to broach the subject.

John Henry is eighteen months old, mother. Why is he not walking – or at least crawling?

Mother shrugged. Children develop at their own pace, Em. His is a slow pace.

When will he begin to talk? He has not spoken a word of sense yet, though I talk to him so much I wonder he is not deaf. I do not believe he is deaf, though, for he looks at me happily when I speak; and when his breathing is regular he gurgles and mumbles to me.

I hesitated. At what age did I say my first words?

Quite young, said mother shortly. You were not yet a year old.

And when did I take my first step?

Mother stood up. I do not recall exactly. Take the mix to Kobie, it is ready; and by the looks of it, so is the fire.

The town of Upington bore as much resemblance to mother's descriptions of the city of London as a locust does to a lion. It was not merely the vast geographic and climatic distance between the two places, nor was it only that I had had no prior experiences upon which to base comparisons.

Perhaps it was the striking contrast between a great city and a growing town. Though I had known, of course, not to expect a sprawling damp giant such as London, Upington was something of a disappointment. My head had been filled from a young age with images of cobbled, grimy, crowded streets filled with horses and carriages, and lined with dense rows of dark, dripping houses and candlelit shops where scurrying people, shrouded in cloaks, were so preoccupied with sloshing through puddles and dodging filth and offal that they rarely spared one another a glance.

Upington had no cobbles, carriages, candles or puddles; nor were there visible mounds of filth; most dispiriting, there was a marked lack of scurrying people. The main track, broad and dusty, was dominated by a tall church steeple that pierced the bleary eye of the sky. To me, the steeple appeared to be pointing an admonishing fingernail at that sky, or perhaps at God. The houses were rectangular, whitewashed, some built in the Dutch style I had seen in picture books, and standing well apart from one another. They had proper roofs of corrugated iron, and smoke belched from chimneys made of brick. I had never seen brick before. Most of the homes had pretty green gardens, since the irrigation canals ensured a good supply of water from the Orange River. The wide, windswept main track made its listless way past the imposing church – Dutch Reformed, said mother, the church from Holland – and the buildings of the mission and several shops; subsidiary tracks branched off from the main one, some petering out into the brush. Deep gullies on either side of the tracks served as gutters.

Mother exclaimed in surprise as we travelled slowly along the track, observing significant growth and change since she had come there from the farm all those years ago to give birth to me.

At last, in the main thoroughfare, there were people to be seen. Though a far cry from the numbers purportedly seething through the streets of London, there were certainly far more men and women than I had ever laid eyes on at one time. They were all colours, white, brown, yellow, and black as the wagon full of coal that ground past us. I saw a few men bound on urgent business judging by their mien, and perhaps fifteen or twenty women, some with young children, all dressed in long dark garments that swept the dust, and wearing wide-brimmed bonnets against the sun. Some carried parasols.

The dark-skinned people, mostly barefooted, were scrawny and clad in rags, with little to shield them from the fierce sunlight. They walked at the outer edges of the track, giving the white people a wide berth, backs stooped and heads drooping. The only sign that we had been observed was a sidewise squint, quickly averted.

Most intriguing to me were the children: of all ages and colours, they gazed back at me with the identical curiosity I levelled at them.

We outspanned at the homestead of a woman named Elise van Heerden. She had assisted the midwife who delivered me, though she was only sixteen at the time, an orphan in training to become a professional midwife herself. Her teacher had retired some years afterwards and gone to live with her daughter in Kimberley. Elise – by then married to her husband Dawid van Heerden, and long since fully competent – took on the role of midwife to many of the townswomen.

She remembered mother well, and seemed delighted to see us; especially me. To my annoyance, she marvelled at my worst feature, my red hair which, according to mother's crack of a mirror, had deepened in hue until it resembled the sickly tint of dried blood. Mother disagreed:

dried blood has no sheen at all, Em, she laughed; and your hair shines brighter than your eyes!

Kobie disappeared as soon as the oxen were watered, though mother had warned him that in accordance with father's instructions he had but three days to rest before he must begin the return journey to the farm.

Elise van Heerden examined John Henry with care shortly after our arrival, trying – but not succeeding, in my opinion – to conceal her shock that a woman as old as my mother had not only given birth to him, but had not bled to death doing so, as had almost happened when she gave birth to me more than thirteen years earlier. Her probing fingers and scrunched-up expression boded ill even to me, and John Henry began to wail.

Soon enough, he was struggling to breathe.

The midwife picked him up and banged him lustily on the back. He only screamed the louder, turning swiftly from red to the ominous blue I had come to dread. Elise hastily handed him to mother while she fetched a vial of an odious-smelling liquid, which she held to his nostrils. I felt my eyes tear from its stinging strength and saw mother's do the same; but in her arms John Henry's wheezing began calming and his colour returned to normal. Somewhat disturbed that the midwife had caused him such distress, whatever was in the vial eased his breathing dramatically, and we were much relieved.

In her heavily accented English, Elise asked mother if she was aware that her son was asthmatic. Mother nodded. I could see by the midwife's expression that she was on the verge of enquiring further, but instead she bit her lip and said no more. Mother told her we had come to town because John Henry had recently developed a high fever as well, and she feared an infection of the lungs, from which she herself had suffered occasionally in the past. Elise said that mother had done the right thing in bringing her son to town, and praised her for her courage in tackling the long journey with only a servant to drive the wagon. I pulled a face at Kobie being thus dismissed, but mother, grateful to be made so welcome, thanked Elise for her kind words and asked her about the hospital in the town.

Fortunately, the doctor who consulted with patients there three days a week was expected back in town the next day, after spending two days visiting the sick on farms scattered throughout the countryside, some of them many miles from Upington. Elise was sure he would be able to make a more definitive diagnosis and advise further treatment.

The next day, before we left for the consultation, our hostess presented us with an orange each; I had tasted this fruit only once before, when a traveller had given us three of them in appreciation of our hospitality. The fruit I now inspected with anticipatory pleasure was lemony in colour. Mother said in England she had eaten oranges from the tropics, which had ranged in hue from deep orange to blood red. The precious segments were wonderfully sweet yet also tangy, and my tongue greedily pursued every drop of juice that escaped.

The hospital was housed in a dusty old building whose whitewash had long since faded to a dreary grey. We mounted seven cracked steps to a bare, ill-polished veranda. The waiting room had a splintered wood floor and a motley collection of uncomfortable-looking wooden chairs against the walls. It was brimful of staring faces, mostly belonging to ill-clad white women clutching babies in their laps with clinging toddlers beside them. There was one boy I thought to be about my age, who stared unremittingly at my hair until he was jogged by his mother's elbow to yield his chair to mother, which he did with some show of reluctance.

Across from where I was standing two girls whispered to each other, and then gaped shamelessly at mother and John Henry. We were strangers in town, but I could not help wondering what it was about us that they found so fascinating. Aside from Poppie, it was the first time in my life that I had been in the company of people close to my own age, and in spite of the blank, unfriendly stares I could not suppress a spurt of excitement at the novelty. But mother had raised me to believe, as Jane Austen had, and probably Charles Dickens too, that staring was impolite, and I tried not to succumb to my pressing curiosity. This hard-won courtesy was not returned by a single occupant of the waiting room.

So we waited, objects of a collective glare so unrelenting that I felt like a specimen being inspected through a magnifying glass. Even the mucus-clogged eyes of small snotty children did not look away. From time to time, a woman with a dirty cap and a creased uniform opened a door, stuck her head around it, and called out a name. When she had done this three times, it dawned on me that she must have some kind of list. The next time she popped her untidy head in, I stood up and addressed her.

Madam, could you please write my brother's name down on your list?

Sy is Engels, said one of the waiting mothers helpfully.

Ja, ek weet, replied the woman irritably. In poor English, she asked for my name.

My brother is the patient, not I, I repeated, and indicated mother and John Henry.

Sy naam, rapped the nurse.

John Henry Johannsen, I replied. As she was scribbling, I came closer and tilted my head to see how far down the list we were.

She clicked her tongue and slammed the door in my face.

John Henry's name was finally called, and I accompanied mother into the doctor's room, mainly because I had wearied of the fresh crop of vacantly staring faces, and did not relish the idea of being left on my own to look past them. To be fair, despite my good intentions, in the end I probably did a good bit of glowering myself; I thought this understandable, though, as I had never seen so many unfamiliar white faces in one place together.

The doctor was tall and spare, with strands of fair hair scraped over a speckled scalp and a scraggy moustache whose pale ginger colour I thought even uglier than the hue of the hair on my head. He frowned constantly and his manner was a little distracted, yet he extended his hand briskly enough to mother, who barely touched it, and introduced himself as Doctor Nel. He gestured to two shabby chairs, and invited us to sit.

Doctor Nel lifted John Henry from mother's arms and placed him gently on the examining table. He opened my brother's mouth and checked his throat, then his ears; he felt his neck, stretched out his limbs, pushed them back. On his chest he used an instrument that was connected to his ear. John Henry, quiescent throughout, gave a small start – perhaps the thing was cold – then gazed serenely at the ceiling, seeming not to mind the doctor's adroit attentions, his little chest rising and falling evenly and lightly.

After he had completed his examination, the doctor sat behind his desk and enquired in excellent, unaccented English if mother was aware that her son had asthma. Mother replied that she was, and repeated what she had told Elise: that it was because he had developed a lung infection with fever that she had brought him from our farm all the way to town.

And where is your farm located, Mrs Johannsen?

Above the Auob River in the Kalahari, replied mother proudly.

Doctor Nel's ginger eyebrows climbed his forehead.

You have come a long way indeed. I was not aware that there are farms deep in the Kalahari itself. He paused, writing something on a notepad on his desk.

At present, ours is the only one that we know of, replied mother.

It is a very isolated situation in which to raise children. He hesitated. I wonder if you are aware that your son's condition makes him vulnerable to respiratory problems; it also diminishes his capacity to resist other diseases.

My spine tingled; it was as if an insect was crawling along its length. Beneath Doctor Nel's grave scrutiny mother's lips began trembling. She turned pale. I stared at her, wondering what she understood from the doctor's words that I did not.

Doctor Nel had not finished. Under the circumstances, madam, I must speak plainly. John Henry's compromised immunity may make it difficult for him to combat common diseases that normal children can easily overcome.

I am not clear as to what condition, other than his asthma, you refer, sir, said mother. To my surprise, she sounded close to tears.

The doctor coughed behind his hand, and I knew he did not believe her.

I refer to his mongolism, Mrs Johannsen. Your son has Down syndrome. Surely you knew that.

I caught mother as she toppled from her chair, but could not prevent the arm from striking her forehead a glancing blow.

Carrying John Henry in my arms, I followed Doctor Nel on trembling legs. He bore mother into an inner sanctum of some kind, perhaps his office, and lowered her onto a couch covered with the fleece of several lambs.

By this time, her eyelids were fluttering. The doctor held a vial to her nose. She started and blinked wildly.

Smelling salts, he said.

Mother's eyes fixed on him. A mottled bump had risen on her forehead, and the faint lines crossing it had deepened and turned an angry pink. Are you absolutely sure, she whispered.

Doctor Nel, applying an ointment he took from a nearby cabinet to mother's forehead, sighed.

Sadly, the diagnosis is irrefutable, madam. His condition is evident in his appearance; and surely the slow pace of his development must have reflected it?

What is Down syndrome, Doctor Nel? I enquired. My voice was filled with foreboding.

It is a form of mental retardation, accompanied by certain physical features which John Henry's appearance typifies, he replied. The condition can vary in severity.

I looked down at mother. I knew there was something wrong, I said softly. He would not sit, he would not crawl, he would not talk.

A thought struck me. Does father know?

I did not know, Em, replied mother, sounding more robust. I do not know what father knows. We did not discuss John Henry.

You did not want to know, mother! Yet poor John Henry and his condition have been part of our family for eighteen months.

Mother's cheeks burned. She rose to a sitting position, assisted by the doctor.

I took a step away from her. I was angrier than I had ever been in my life. My teeth ground against one another, my heart thumped noisily against my ribs.

This is your fault, I cried. He is your fault!

Taking a deep breath, I addressed Doctor Nel.

Is it true that my brother is the way he is because she was too old when she had him?

The doctor shrugged. It is believed to be one of the contributing factors. Not necessarily the only one. We do not know very much about the causes, unfortunately. But the last thing you should do is blame your mother.

Who should I blame then? My father? John Henry? Myself?

Mother looked up at me. Stop, Em; you do not know what you are saying.

Nobody, interjected Doctor Nel gently. Blame nobody. It is your support your mother needs now, not your blame.

He turned to mother. In view of the child's respiratory difficulties, you should probably remain close to medical care until he is at least two years of age, possibly more. Can that be arranged?

Mother rose shakily to her feet. It will be arranged. Thank you, Doctor.

I will see him next week, then. Make the appointment with my nurse.

He smiled at me. What is your name?

Emma.

Well, Emma. Pick up your brother. Your mother is not yet strong enough to carry him.

I bent to lift John Henry. He grinned up at me with vacuous joy.

A Different World

ELISE AND DAWID van Heerden graciously availed us the use of the spare room in their large home for the duration of our stay. The substantial farm holdings had been in Dawid van Heerden's family for several generations. Born with one leg considerably shorter than the other, Dawid, gentle by nature, was as kind to us as his wife was.

In exchange for their hospitality, mother offered to coach their three children in whatever subjects they were weakest. The boy, aged nine, and twin girls, aged seven, attended a school on the outskirts of the town. Elise was delighted, claiming she had always wanted her children to learn good spoken English. Mother, with her beautiful accent, was the perfect teacher for them.

Besides Elise and Dawid, there were few friendly faces in town. At first we were puzzled by the hostile stares from strangers in the streets and in the shops. People turned their backs to us and muttered to one another in what mother haughtily described as 'kitchen Dutch'. I longed to speak better Afrikaans, though, so I could understand their rude slang and retaliate in kind. I asked mother irritably why she had bothered to teach me French when good Afrikaans would have served me so much better, since it seemed to be the most widely spoken tongue in the town.

Mother gave a brief, dismissive shake of her head.

I have heard there are many people in the rest of the country who speak both English and French.

Well, they do not reside in Upington, I replied crossly.

We were enlightened as to the reasons for the townspeople's hostility one bright and sunny winter morning. After buying some oranges and apples from the blessedly cool, high storage sheds behind the shop, mother and I took a walk along the main track. I had become infatuated with fruit: the novel crispness of green apples enticed me almost as much as the juice of the oranges. I was looking forward to biting into a large apple once we got back to the homestead, where Elise was minding John Henry as he slept. Though kept busy by her three children, Elise regarded him as a special child, and never seemed to tire of holding and minding him. John Henry returned her affection, his arms reaching up for her and his round face creasing into smiles when she chucked him under the chin.

Approaching us from the opposite direction were two girls with faded yellow hair hanging to their shoulders in a burred, uncombed tangle. About fifteen or sixteen years of age, barefooted and poorly dressed in long torn skirts, they inspected mother and me from head to foot, eyes fierce and mouths tight.

As they passed us, the taller of the two girls spat on the ground.

Verdomde Engelsmense, she said.

Mother and I stared at the spittle in the dust, shocked. Ants were already scuttling towards the foamy globule. I looked up, and saw a boy about the same age as the girls standing nearby with his hands in his pockets. He bobbed his head at me and addressed us in Afrikaans, apologising for the girls' behaviour.

Disie oorlog; hulle dink elke Engelsprekende mens is die vyand, ook vroumense.

He must have observed mother's blank expression, for he spoke again, this time in precise but hesitant English, strongly accented.

They are foolish. They think all English are enemies, even women.

After this incident, mother no longer tried to persuade me to attend the local school, and our lessons continued whenever she found the time.

A few days later, mother described to Dawid what had taken place on the street.

In hosting us, the generous, tactful Van Heerdens must have themselves been on the receiving end of the disparagement and resentment of the townspeople. Mother tried to apologise for the trouble our presence in their home was causing them, but they denied any embarrassment on their part.

Those girls were young, she said to Dawid thoughtfully, but I think they were merely expressing the sentiments of the local people, however crudely: incomers are deeply resented.

Dawid, who had learned English at school in Cape Town, shook his head.

The reason for their inexcusably disrespectful behaviour is the war, of course.

What war? I asked.

Do you not know that the Boers and the British are at war?

We did not know, replied mother, astonished.

Dawid was mildly reproachful.

Then you are ignorant of a significant historical event that is rocking our country. You dwell so far from the society of others that I suppose it is not surprising that you are completely out of touch with what the rest of the world reads in their newspapers as we speak.

He hesitated. Your husband does not know that the country is at war. Should he not be told?

Mother shook her head. He cannot leave the farm. When Kobie returns home he will take the local paper with him, which I confess I myself have not yet seen. I am afraid my mind has been far too occupied with my own troubles.

I wondered why Dawid thought father should be told; I too could not imagine him leaving the farm to join in the war on either side. Perhaps our host simply believed that nobody should be ignorant of history, as he put it, in the making.

Heavy fighting is taking place less than two hundred miles away, he continued. Near Kimberley and Bloemfontein. Many men of all ages from the area of Upington and the farms roundabout have joined the Boer forces, leaving the women, the old people, the servants and labourers to do the farm work. I have not enlisted because of my disability: I could not have kept up with the kind of guerrilla warfare at which my people have become masters. The Boers are few compared with the legion ranks of the British, but they are excellent shots, and they know the terrain in which they are fighting as if the koppies and rivers were their own flesh and blood.

You are proud of your people, mother remarked.

Dawid nodded. I am. It must be said, though, that your people have regrettably little to be proud of. There is word that they are herding Boer women and children into camps in the Bloemfontein area like sheep into kraals. We have heard that the conditions there are terrible.

I am sorry to hear such news! exclaimed mother, shocked. Why are the British doing such a terrible thing?

A bell rang; Elise was calling them to dinner.

Dawid's voice was sombre. They accuse the women of spying for their men.

Doctor Nel was examining John Henry – whose chest he declared clear, to our relief – when he brought up the subject of the spitting incident.

I know what happened because the boy who apologised to you is my son Danie, he said, smiling.

Your son is a gentleman, Doctor Nel. Please tell him that, and thank him for his kindness to us, mother replied.

The doctor assured her he would, and began demonstrating some of the exercises and massage techniques which might facilitate John Henry's development. He had yet to take his first step.

I do not mean to be inquisitive, Mrs Johannsen, said Doctor Nel, his strong fingers massaging John Henry's limbs, but I confess I find it intriguing that you have chosen to live so far from other people of your kind, not to mention the amenities of a village or a town.

Well, sir, I can understand that such a choice is not for most people; but we have built our farm with our own hands and we take great pride in it. And, strange though this may sound to you, we are content with our own society.

Doctor Nel said no more, his hands working busily with my brother's limbs.

I wonder if you have speculated how a Boer like me comes to speak your tongue, Mrs Johannsen?

Certainly I have noted that you speak English as if born to it, sir.

Doctor Nel nodded, indicating that mother should dress John Henry, who had just urinated all over his clean white coat.

It is because I trained to be a doctor in your country, madam. I spent ten years in England, and attended Oxford University.

Mother looked up in surprise from where she was replacing John Henry's bindings.

The choice of a remote home appears eccentric to you, Doctor; yet you yourself have chosen to practise your excellent skills in a town as distant from Oxford as the moon is from earth.

Doctor Nel smiled. Touché! But the explanation is simple. On my return from England, I practised first in Cape Town, where I met my wife in the house of her aunt, with whom I was boarding. My wife is the daughter of one of the first doctors to practise his profession in these parts, and it was very important to him that his daughter return to live in her hometown.

Mother picked up John Henry and handed him to me. I noticed faint colour in her cheeks and heard animation in her voice for the first time in many days.

You have no plans to fight in this war, then, Doctor?

I think not. I am no soldier, and Kimberley has a surfeit of medical practitioners. It is here that I am needed.

And you have been content here these many years.

It was not a question, but Doctor Nel interpreted it as such.

As you see, madam. This is my world. And I have hopes that my boy will follow in my footsteps.

A fine young man, murmured mother.

Thank you. Please practise the massage techniques I have shown you. I will see John Henry next week. He seems well and happy, but I would not advise haste. It would be best to travel home after the worst of the winter is behind us.

His words were prophetic. Less than a week after our visit, mother woke in the middle of the night. She saw by the position of a lopsided moon that it was very late. Since she was awake, she decided to visit the outhouse. She climbed out of bed and, as she always did when she woke during the night, touched John Henry, who slept between us in an old cot that had belonged to Elise's children. Her cry woke me instantly.

I sat bolt upright, dread creeping back like an unforgiving enemy.

I waited at the front door, trembling with cold and anxiety, for Elise's driver to arrive with the mule cart. Mother and Elise had lighted a lamp in the kitchen and were trying to cool John Henry's scalding little body. He had made no sound since mother lifted him from his cot. Shaking as if taken with fever myself, I vowed to forswear whatever in life was most desirable to me if only he would make the tiniest peep.

The tall stooped figure of Dawid, who had gone to rouse the driver, limped from the shadows towards me.

He is harnessing the mules, Emma, he said reassuringly, his voice resonant in the cold night. He will be here shortly. And I have sent a messenger ahead to the doctor's house.

I heard the clattering of hooves and hurried to the kitchen.

The cart is here. I will go with you to the hospital. The doctor is sure to be there by the time we arrive.

No, Em. Go to sleep. I will go alone. You have done enough.

But mother –

Alone, Em.

I recognised that voice and did not argue. Elise asked mother if she could accompany her instead of me. Mother, helped onto the cart by Dawid, shook her head. She took John Henry from Elise.

I will see you in the morning, she said softly. Pray God, with my babe restored to health.

I got little rest that night. I stared for what seemed like hours through the window, slightly ajar in spite of the temperature. The air was an icy balm on my wet cheeks, the night a black sheet stippled with countless tiny glistening birds. It occurred to me that if my brother died, I might lose my dearly loved mother as well.

The next morning Elise woke me with a cup of tea. Though it was far later than my usual rising, she insisted I breakfast before we set off for the hospital. I felt drained and exhausted from lack of sleep and would have preferred to avoid the unblinking curiosity of her son and twin daughters. The two smiling retrievers repeatedly pawed at my lap to shake hands, and the one-eyed cat licked her chops with every mouthful of porridge I simply could not swallow. The slow hard pulsing in my head was like a clock that ticked away my brother's life. Elise brushed my cheek with her lips in sympathy, and hustled out children and dogs. She instructed me to wait by the gate, and emerged a few minutes later. We walked together to the hospital.

The building was still shuttered, the door bolted. Elise knocked, but nobody came. A rider on a splendid bay horse with a creamy mane cantered towards us. The boy who had apologised for the spitting girl swung gracefully off the burnished animal. He greeted us in Afrikaans from the bottom of the steps, then spoke, I presumed for my sake, in English.

My father is inside, Mevrouw; he is occupied with an emergency. The nurse will be here soon to open the door.

I stared at my feet. He is with my brother, I said glumly.

I remembered his name: Danie.

Danie climbed the steps and joined us at the door, pounding on it with a fist that was almost as large as his father's. I heard footsteps on the floorboards, and then the sound of bolts being drawn back. The door opened and Doctor Nel peered out.

Come in. You must excuse me. I heard the knocking, but I was in the bathroom and Mrs Johannsen is still asleep.

He smelt faintly of citrus. I noticed his hair was combed over his baldness and he was freshly shaved. He smiled down at me, and my empty lungs suddenly filled with oxygen.

John Henry is much better, my dear. The crisis is past; his fever is down.

My mother? Is she all right?

She is well, but exhausted from the anxiety. She would not rest until he was over the worst. Now she is sleeping peacefully.

Softness transformed his face. There was something almost intimate, secretive, in his expression. I was oddly jolted to be reminded of father's eyes when mother smiled at him in a certain way or said something that pleased him. I had not seen that look for a long time.

Aware of Elise and the lanky figure of Danie behind me, I smiled at Doctor Nel.

Thank you, Doctor.

I turned to Danie. Thank you for your assistance again. You are very kind. Now I must go to my brother.

I peeked in at mother first. She was lying on the fleecy couch, covered by a white hospital sheet and a heavy brown blanket. A strand of dark hair blew across her face each time she breathed out. Her mouth was relaxed, her cheeks pink.

I watched her for a moment, thinking how much I loved her.

Closing the door quietly, I followed Doctor Nel to the cot where my brother, too, lay sleeping, his chest rising and falling, his little mouth in a sweet half smile.

Will John Henry be well, Doctor?

He is well now, Emma, as you can see.

Elise went home to her children and her chores, and I walked idly along the main track, kicking a round black river stone that seemed out of place in the arid little town. The sun was already hot, but the heat on my back was like a warm hand. The rest – shabby, unmannerly Boer girls, the bleak faces of older women who turned away as if I was unclean, the ragged black and brown people with sad empty eyes – felt alien and wrong.

I wanted to go home. I missed father; I missed Poppie, Meisie, Doekie and Brandbooi. I longed for the farm with its broad uncluttered horizons, free of the disturbing faces of strangers. I even missed my chores. I looked about me at dusty tracks and bushes, at dull hot buildings, and wondered how a boy like Danie could possibly think of spending his life in such a place.

I passed the largest store, which had a bar in a side shack that Dawid said was popular at night with the farmers when they were not away fighting a war. A heap of glass bottles glistened in the bushes beside the shack. I noticed a bare foot protruding next to a mound of glass. Curious, I went closer.

In the scrappy shade of an ugly, leafless tree, Kobie was fast asleep. His skinny chest was bare, his arms thrown above his head, his legs, in torn trousers, wide apart.

I knelt and shook him lightly. His shoulder was clammy. His bare calloused foot twitched, but even when I shook him a second time, he did not wake. I looked beyond Kobie and saw the others: limp forms in deep, unprepossessing slumber, the snoring making the cawing of crows seem musical.

Kobie has found his old enemy again, I thought gloomily.

His face was turned up to the sun. The glare was ferocious. I tried to move him slightly so that his face would be in shade, but he grunted and turned on his side.

Kobie! I pleaded despairingly. Wake up! It is me, Emma.

Not even a grunt this time. But nearby, somebody else spoke.

I turned in the direction of the voice. Behind a bush, a woman lay against a broken box, her legs straight out in front of her like two knobbled branches. She wore a faded doekie that had once been red, and her face was so squashed and seamed and swollen that it looked as if it had been run over.

He is sleeping, miesies. He will sleep all day.

To my surprise, she spoke good English.

Yes. I see that.

I cleared my throat. Do you know where he is staying? He works for my father, and in a few days he must travel a long way to get back to the farm.

The woman snorted; I realised she was laughing.

That one? I never seen anybody drink like him. He will not go anywhere for a long time. She grinned, displaying naked pink gums. Silvery needles of light glowed in the depths of her crusted eyes.

Miesies, give me a penny and I tell him you came to visit him in the lounge of his home.

She rubbed her fingers together as if I had already placed a coin between them and cackled, sounding like Elise's chickens. I tried to smile, but could not. I turned and walked away.

Journeys

TWO WEEKS AFTER I stumbled on Kobie under that tree, he sobered up and came looking for us. Upon seeing his bedraggled and downcast appearance, mother refrained from giving him too much of a dressing-down. One week later, still sober, he left, well-provisioned, for home.

On the advice of Doctor Nel, mother instructed him to return in three months to fetch us and to bring Tam with him, in the event John Henry might require her skills on the homeward journey. It would be the end of winter, but not yet too hot and thus a good time to travel the long distance. And John Henry would be a little older; hopefully his asthma would be improved.

Though I often felt dreary and bored in Upington, I made my first new friend since Poppie (whom I missed sorely) and poor Imp: Danie Nel. Mother, too, found friendship in the person of his father, Doctor Nel, the only inhabitant of the town who spoke good English, and with whom she seemed to find much in common.

Dinners at the family's pleasant home were lively, but at times somewhat stilted and awkward, largely because Mrs Nel declined to participate in any way in the wide-ranging discussions. These might be about many things, but most frequently were about the progress of the war, and events inside and outside the country that influenced it. Sometimes, when Doctor Nel was feeling expansive after imbibing a glass of what he described as excellent Cape brandy, he would provide moving descriptions of the beauty of the Cape Peninsula with its mountains and oceans. His nostalgia was almost palpable, and it made me wonder how he could bear to live in a barren, scurrilous town like Upington.

Mother's favourite topic for discussion was, of course, whatever book she was reading. Fortunately for us, Doctor Nel shared our love of books and owned many of them, which he gladly lent to mother and me. She would read them with extraordinary speed, as if afraid they would be taken away, before passing them on to me. I was introduced to several new authors, and found the Russians particularly passionate and tragic, spending many wakeful hours pondering the sad fate of Anna Karenina.

Some evenings, the conversation at the Nels' home would become so animated that there was no room for awkwardness: it was as if mother and Doctor Nel, both compelling debaters, were on a stage, with Danie and me cast in the roles of fascinated spectators, our heads swivelling from one speaker to the other. Mrs Nel did not participate: she spoke not a word of English, or purported not to, though it occurred to me that her understanding of the language, if not her speech, was far better than she let on, for her small eyes seemed to follow her husband's conversation, in particular, rather closely.

Besides the Nels and Elise and Dawid, we had little to do with the other townspeople. The Van Heerden children were picking up English rapidly and spoke it, amusingly, with mother's crisp British accent. John Henry grew and flourished in the company of the children, becoming even rounder and plumper; his face often crinkled into smiles, but his tongue uttered not a word of sense.

At the age of twenty-one months, on one of the coldest days we had experienced that winter, John Henry took his first steps.

They were to me. I was playing a game with Elise's twin daughters, and something about it attracted John Henry's attention. I did not see him scramble to his feet, but the sound he made, a chirp of joy that I knew well, drew my eye. To my delight, he had pulled himself up on the leg of a nearby chair. When he saw me watching, he took a step towards me, and then another, and landed in a heap on my lap.

Within days, he was taking ten steps at a time. Mother was transformed.

In the afternoons, Danie and I sometimes took long walks to the river. He would question me about our farm, and I gave him vivid descriptions of the desert and of our people. He said he would love to visit one day. He was intrigued that my only friends were Bushmen, pointing out that white people of his acquaintance had no relations with black people other than that of master and servant. Bushmen were regarded by many farmers as thieves and rascals that were barely human; he had even heard them described as baboons or monkeys. I repeated some of the conversations I had shared with Poppie and Imp, and he was surprised when I informed him that Poppie's English was better than his.

Truth to tell, Danie's English was improving daily, as was my Afrikaans; he told me that was a good thing, as Afrikaans would one day be an official language of the country in place of Dutch.

We had one conversation that for me sealed our friendship. I was relating to him how Poppie, Imp and the Bushmen had come to live with us, and some of the things Brandbooi had told father about their previous employer, the Boer who had been a vicious slaver and rapist.

Danie, horrified yet fascinated, asked the name of the Boer. When I told him, he exclaimed that the family had been patients of his father's. On one occasion, his mother invited the Boer and his wife to dinner at their home. His mother found the man handsome and charming, but his father thought he spoke too much and his wife too little. Silent, subdued, she barely looked up from her plate and consumed little of what was on it.

Encouraged, my tongue flowed even more freely: I told Danie about the police who had come looking for Brandbooi, and of the investigation that was turned on its head by their own witness, who turned out to be the daughter of the murdered couple.

You have so many stories, he said admiringly. You will surely be a writer one day.

I wondered if I should tell him that many of my stories were recorded in a journal, but decided I would save that confidence for another day, when I knew him better; though already I felt as if I had known him for years rather than months, and found that I trusted him as if he were a member of my family rather than a new friend. I never tired of reciting to him the wonders of the Kalahari, and I could see that he was moved by my love for it. Few people in the area, he said, had bothered to explore the desert. I told him that was like kicking aside a jewel in your path as a mere pebble, simply because you were blind to its beauty.

I confided that Poppie and Imp were half-sisters, the seed of the Boer who had lain with their mothers; that Poppie was a graceful combination of her white and Bushman antecedents, with the Bushman's lithe figure and small facial features, but taller than most Bushmen, with skin, where the sun had not darkened it, the colour of thick cream. The loss of Imp was like an old bruise, and I found it difficult to speak of her, even to Danie. Since her death, I had realised with guilt and remorse that she was the loser in our friendship because of the greater affection I had always felt for Poppie; I wondered if she had known and been hurt by the knowledge. So I spoke instead of Imp's art, her rare gift of bringing an animal to life on the page within seconds.

Danie was perplexed that mother was so insistent that Poppie should sit in on my lessons and learn whatever I was taught.

What will she do with all that learning, Em? She may be a white Bushman, but she is still a Bushman; in the towns she will suffer the scorn of both black and white, because she belongs with neither. Rather than the good you intended, you may have done her harm. She will surely be safer if she remains on the farm, where she has a good home and is among friends.

I shook my head in disagreement: mother had converted me to her belief that learning could never go amiss in life.

I believe Poppie's life will only be the better for her learning, wherever she chooses to spend the rest of her days.

Well, said Danie, you have had a taste of living in a small town; and you and your mother, white-skinned, better educated than most, have experienced unpleasant prejudice from the people here, partly because they regard you as different from them.

That is not the reason! It is because there is a war on, and they think we are on the British side because of the language we speak. If there were no war, we would find acceptance if we sought it.

Danie raised an eyebrow, but chose to say no more.

That night, thinking about Poppie with her joyous green eyes and her gentle ways in this uncongenial place, a shiver of trepidation slid down my spine. Had mother and I, full of good intentions, inadvertently done her harm, as Danie seemed to believe? Had we been thinking of ourselves or of her when we insisted she join in the lessons? I remembered father's bitter words about her, and wondered if he was right: had we educated Poppie to become a permanent misfit?

Not long before Kobie was expected back, John Henry caught a cold, which turned into an infection of the lungs. This time, Doctor Nel was there well before the crisis in his breathing came, and though John Henry and mother spent two nights in hospital with Doctor Nel, his recovery after that was gratifyingly swift.

By the time the wagon rumbled into town, my brother was toddling about, knocking into everything and everybody, his breathing as even and easy as my own.

I recognised the wagon when walking with Danie in the main street, ignoring the grimaces, whispers and disdain of several passing girls, and, less stinging, the teasing of boys who were his friends.

I ran to greet Kobie and Tam. Kobie, driving the wagon, stopped and smiled down at me. I climbed up, waving to Danie. The wagon moved off in the direction of the Van Heerden home.

Is Tam in the back?

I was longing to see her crumpled little tsamma melon face.

Kobie shook his head, hawked up phlegm, and spat it onto the track.

Where is she? I cried. When he told me, I jumped off the wagon.

I saw mother at the gate, holding John Henry in her arms and welcoming Kobie, who stood in front of her, looking down and fidgeting with the hat in his hands. She asked if all was well back at the farm. Kobie grunted in reply, as discursive as ever.

Mother repeated my question.

Is Tam in the back?

Kobie again shook his head. She dance her last dance. She bleed from the nose, and then she die.

Oh God, said mother, biting her lip. Her eyes filled with tears. And I need her more than ever. I need her with us on the return journey.

I watched Kobie watering the oxen and thought that Tam must have known that her last dance was already beckoning when we left the farm. She knew she would not see us again in this life. I hoped her death had been quick, and took comfort that she had breathed her last in the arms of the beloved dunes of her birth.

Nearly six months after we had arrived in Upington, Kobie drove the fully provisioned wagon out of town on the track to the Kalahari.

Leaving Elise, Dawid and the children had been more difficult than I had anticipated: the children cried, and I felt tears pricking at the sight of theirs. John Henry was in such fine fettle that illness seemed remote, a thing of the past. The children clung to him and he laughed merrily, utterly oblivious that this was a parting which might extend, in all likelihood, into years.

Elise and Dawid were worried that we were travelling alone with only one servant, as they described Kobie; the fact that we had arrived in the same way did not dispel their anxiety. However, they bade us farewell with a good grace and many good wishes, and a substantial quantity of Elise's excellent cooking, including boxes of her buttermilk rusks and jars of the preserved fruits and jams that I adored.

I had purchased gifts for everybody at the farm with the few coins I had saved from birthdays, and felt very excited at the thought of the pleasure they would bring to the familiar faces I loved. Most of all I longed to see father, to whom I had whispered a private goodnight every night of our stay before I fell asleep. I missed him with an ache that had become part of me, yet had not ceased to hurt.

Danie and I had said our farewells the evening before we left.

He promised that he would prevail on his father to visit us when he could find another doctor to fill in for a few weeks, and school was closed for the holidays. He bent down – I was tall for my age, but he was much taller – and gently kissed my cheek, which grew exceedingly hot. Then he touched my blazing hair.

Sometimes your hair makes me think of the embers in a fire that is almost out, and other times it is the scarlet and orange colour of the sky before the sun dips below the horizon.

I wondered if he were jesting.

Danie, I hate my hair! It is the ugliest thing about me!

There we disagree, Em. It is uncommon; like you. It becomes you very well.

The jolting of the wagon rocked John Henry to sleep in mother's arms. Kobie stopped so that we could climb into the back, and mother put him down in his makeshift crib. Then she and I sat, legs swinging over the edge of the wagon, looking back at the town.

Will you miss young Danie, Em? The two of you seem to have become good friends.

That place would have been a desert without him.

Mother chuckled at my choice of words.

It is true; I have nothing in common with those Boers.

He is a Boer and you do not appear to mind. The Van Heerdens too, of course.

They are a wonderful family, and I love them. Danie is different from most people. I will miss him very much.

I chewed pensively on a hank of hair. What of Doctor Nel, mother? Will you miss him? You and he had much in common.

Yes, that is true. I enjoyed his company. Did I mention that he insisted on giving me his first edition of The Brothers Karamazov? He would not take no for an answer. It is a wonderful gift.

Silence, but for the wheels grinding noisily on the stony track.

Something popped into my mind. How did we pay him for his services, mother?

Mother shifted in her seat. Why should that concern you, Em? I had some money that father gave me. I paid him with that.

Was it enough?

It was not.

Do we *owe* him money?

Em, the matter of payment is really no concern of yours. But since I know to my cost that your curiosity demands satisfaction, Doctor Nel would take no money after the second visit. And do not ask me why he would not, because I have no answer for you. I told him he was embarrassing me, and he replied in that case, on my next visit, I could bring him payment in kind, perhaps some biltong from the farm.

I said no more. I knew the answer for myself: Doctor Nel wanted to give to mother, not take from her. It was mildly discomfiting that the good doctor had such strong feelings for her. Did she know? I thought not. As far as I was aware, they had not even exchanged first names.

I remembered then that he had indeed called her by her first name: when she was most anxious about John Henry, he had said: Deirdre, please do not upset yourself so.

If a name can sound like a caress, Doctor Nel saying it at that time was just that.

I clicked my tongue irritably. Such idle conjecture, I berated myself, can be laid at the feet of too frequent readings of Jane Austen.

It was the last week of September, and the days were not yet unbearably hot. In the early morning, I took John Henry in my arms after he had eaten his breakfast and walked with him, the dry ground crunching underfoot. A fresh breeze lifted his straight dark hair. We stopped to visit the squirrels and mongooses, and I offered them crumbs from my rusk. These were greedily received, the mongooses elbowing the squirrels to one side, pointy noses twitching, yellow eyes pinned on my every move, their clawed front paws extended like hands for more. John Henry's own hands reached out constantly, and I had to take care to keep a safe distance. A bite would quickly become infected.

On the third morning, as we prospected for such treasures as pebbles and pods, John Henry put his dear face to my cheek and said my name for the first time: *Em.* A week short of two years old, it was also the first coherent word he had ever articulated. I whooped with joy, and Kobie stopped the wagon, which had been grinding along a fraction ahead of us.

Mother climbed down from the back of the wagon. What have you found, Em?

Not I, mother; I have found nothing. It is John Henry. He has found his tongue!

I lifted my little brother high in my arms. Say my name for mother, John Henry. Say *Em!* Shout it out loud!

John Henry giggled and raised his arms as if he were about to take to the skies and fly.

That night we outspanned in the shade of two large trees, which grew sparsely in the empty landscape through which we were travelling. In one of the trees, a spotted eagle owl slept with one eye open; in the fork of the other I observed a tiny, exquisite Scops-owl, watching us closely with round unblinking yellow eyes, apparently undaunted by our cumbersome, noisy intrusion.

After a light supper of biltong, and firecakes spread with Elise's delicious peach preserves, we each had an apple and went to bed. Kobie warned that we must make an early start in the morning, as the temperature was beginning to rise, and by mid morning the heat would be oppressive.

He bedded down beneath the wagon, as was his preference when the weather was not cold.

John Henry, covered with a warm quilt, smiled a sweet goodnight from his crib.

I woke very early, as soon as first light pierced the canvas and struck my eyelids. I had slept well and dreamlessly. I lay contentedly, looking up at the roof, feeling the chill of the night melt gradually from my limbs. Through the crack in the opening, the new day slid almost playfully into the wagon.

Mother was still asleep. I rose carefully to a sitting position, seeking out my brother's round face in the still dim interior. The faintest stir from me would alert him, and he would hold out his arms, avid for his first drink of the day.

I bent over the crib, my hair brushing his cheek. I would wake him gently, then rouse Kobie to start the fire, for the instant I touched John Henry he would be clamouring for his breakfast. I reached out light-heartedly and tugged at a lock of hair.

To my surprise, he slept on without a sound. I leaned into his crib and planted a soft kiss on his cheek. It was as cold as stone to my lips. I put out a hand and felt his forehead, his neck, his chest, his hands.

God, such icy cold!

Mother, I whispered, beginning to weep.

She slept on, her head turned to the crib, her breath warm. Was it not warm enough to heat that dreadful rigor?

I again put my palm on John Henry's forehead. Then I placed it gently on mother's cheek. Her flesh burned my palm.

Please, wake up, I sobbed. I cannot wake John Henry.

How did he get so cold?

We tried to hold her between us, Kobie and I. I could barely see the twisted claw of her face for the blinding stream of tears. But I felt the jerking of her limbs through my entire body, and I could not deafen myself to her raving.

Even through my shock, mother was terrifying, her body rigid, her neck stretched, her mouth a yawning howl. Her strength was un-manageable. She shook off both Kobie and me, and snatched up my brother's lifeless body. Clutching him to her chest, she sprang recklessly from the wagon and began shrieking again, one fist pummelling at the ostentatious display of the cruel dawn sky. With inhuman strength, she thrust John Henry upward, again and again, as if to hurl him up to God.

Where are you, God, you monster, you devil? You gave him to me, and then took him back! He deserved to live! You stole him like a thief and I did not know! He is mine, I tell you, mine! Give him back to me!

You cannot, you will not have my darling!

A minute later, she fell with him to the ground, mumbling despairingly.

Only give me back my son, my poor John Henry ...

My brother's name a lamentation of such inconsolable torment that I feared it would stop her heart.

Kobie saved us: Kobie the wordless one; Bushman hater, imbiber of strong spirits. He led me to the fire he had lighted, then took John Henry from mother's limp arms and climbed with him into the wagon. He got down and escorted mother, collapsed in on herself like an empty sack of flour, behind the wagon. Its bulk concealed them, and I do not know what Kobie said to her, for I heard nothing, and it was not in any case in his nature to say much in words. But when they came towards me as I shivered by the small fire, mother was leaning against him as one would against a trusted friend.

Kobie helped her onto the wagon, and I rose shakily to my feet. I would not have known what to administer from the medical kit which Doctor Nel had provided for us, but Kobie found the tiny bottle of laudanum. As I watched from below, she obediently drank a few drops. Her staring eyes closed almost immediately. Kobie laid her down and covered her with a quilt. She clutched her dead son's blanket to her face, as John Henry used to do when ready for sleep.

Kobie removed spare blankets from a box in the corner. He lifted the body of my poor sweet brother from his crib – how painfully small he seemed, as if death, in robbing him of his animating spirit, had also shrunk him – and wrapped him in a worn old quilt he had liked to munch.

Lowering him carefully into the blanket box, Kobie covered him with the blankets and closed the box. I did not see if John Henry's face was covered.

Kobie urged me eat something, but I could not; I noticed he did not either. Without an invitation, I climbed onto the seat beside his at the front of the wagon and waited, tiny tremors rippling through me. I watched him harness the oxen and ready the wagon for departure, and did not move a finger to help.

As the wagon began moving, the sun grew warmer. With some dismay, I observed the direction in which Kobie was driving.

Are we not going back to Upington? To Doctor Nel?

We are going home, replied Kobie softly. *That is madam's wish.*

Home

WE MADE OUR WAY down to the Auob River, and this time, father was not waiting.

My rigid control since my brother's death felt close to breaking. The days had been frightful, the dazzle of late spring horribly at odds with our bitter grief. The nights were the worst, filled with dreams in which my brother's voice was unfamiliar: he cried, danced, reached out his arms to me; he rose from the box in which he lay and hovered like a leprechaun above my bed, imploring me to take him to mother. Sometimes his entreaties would be in mother's crisp, no-nonsense voice of command.

I would sit up in the dark wagon, shaking with horror.

Mother lay day after day on her bed beneath the quilt, no matter how rutted and jarring the track or how hot the noon sun. She could scarcely be persuaded to sip water; and food, even in the form of a thin gruel, made her gag.

Once, I came to offer her a drink and found she had risen and opened the box in which John Henry lay. It had been five days since he died, and in spite of the dry climate, there was an unpleasant odour. I was just in time to catch her as she fell, and we tumbled together to the wagon floor. I left her where she lay and clambered to my feet. I closed the box without looking at my brother's dead face. Then I made mother as comfortable as I could, and sprang from the wagon, inhaling the clear, sharp air until my lungs threatened to burst.

Kobie did most of the work. I would begin to help, but my thoughts would slow my hands. Next thing I would find that everything that needed doing was done while I sat on a rock or on the ground, my mind alive with sounds and images of my brother: his gurgle of laughter, his first steps; his dear face lit with joy as he said my name. I could not reconcile myself to the harsh reality that John Henry was gone from us, and would never return.

There was little I could do for mother; little she would do for herself. I told myself that once we were home, father would be there and he would know how to coax her to eat; he would prevail on her to find the strength to continue her life without her son in it.

On the last night of our travels, I could no longer bear the thought of sleeping inside the wagon. The odour had intensified. Mother appeared to notice nothing or, if she did, did not care. She was drinking more water, though, and rather than lying flat beneath the quilt with her eyes closed, her head was supported by cushions. Her eyes glistened like two blind moons. She was gazing ahead of her at nothing, her breathing rapid and shallow, her face, all bones and hollows, so pale that it seemed to float.

I dismounted from the wagon with a blanket. The night was chilly and clear, the dense sky flashing a multitude of greetings. I squinted up at the stubby moon, and it smiled crookedly back at me. Arranging my blanket close to the embers of the fire, I drank the air like a cool draught. For the first time in days, rather than a dreadful journey potholed with nightmares, sleep wafted over me as a kindly friend.

A requiem of anguish and yearning tore through the veil of sleep. I listened as the dirge rose in a plaintive, broken wail of woe that swelled into berserk mirth, then subsided to a whimpering and yipping that kept every living thing in the vicinity awake.

Jackals. The pointy snouts of the emaciated, lice-ridden scavengers sniffed the fire and padded closer in the hopes of stealing any remains of the supper Kobie and I had shared.

Kobie, who slept through any disturbance that did not portend danger, and woke instantly to any that did, mumbled in his sleep.

I sat up, and the jackals receded into the darkness, taking their bestial choir with them.

A figure stumbled towards me out of the darkness.

Why are you sleeping outside, Em? There may be lions about.

The voice was cracked and enfeebled.

I stood up, astounded that mother had found the strength to climb down alone from the wagon to seek me out. I went to her and put my arm about her.

Did the jackals wake you, mother? I will take you back inside.

Her bones prodded me like dismembered stalks of dune reeds; her suppleness and honey scent were displaced by a bristly resistance and a staleness of unwashed flesh. Though docile enough, she seemed unable to help herself in the slightest, and I could not lift her despite the fact that she seemed to have lost half her body weight. I was obliged to wake Kobie to assist in getting her back into the wagon.

Once she was lying inside, I sat beside her and held her hand. I had to cover my nose with a corner of a blanket to shield myself from the reek of my brother's decaying flesh.

Mother, I said softly, we will be home soon, and then you will feel better.

She did not reply; I thought she may have fallen asleep.

I will never feel better again.

The words lingered in the night like a portent of evil. I did not go back to sleep.

The wagon rumbled along the Auob. At last, almost within sight of the farm, they were there: Meisie, running, followed by Doekie and Brandbooi, father striding behind them. I leaped from the wagon and raced along the riverbed. Meisie and Doekie hugged me and stroked my hair, looking up at me from their diminutive heights and chirping with pleasure about how tall I had grown. Brandbooi stood beside them, bouncing on his heels. I took both his small hard hands in mine, and we beamed at each other.

Father had taken off his hat. He was grinning and shaking his head in astonishment. His beard, sprinkled with grey, almost reached his chest.

I hugged him and would not let go.

I have missed you so much, father!

I have missed you too, Em, very much. He held me away from him and eyed me gravely. In the months we have been parted, you have become a young lady.

I do not think I will ever be that, father.

He chuckled. Now that I look at you I see you are still my Em, thank heaven. We have longed for your return, my child. You are the light of our lives.

He squinted at the approaching wagon.

I see Kobie driving, but where is your mother? And John Henry?

My heart thumping, I held out my hand. Father, I said slowly, there is bad news.

Mother had climbed down from the back of the wagon. Unsteady on her feet, she was supported by Kobie. She observed father and me coming towards her with a cold eye. When father held his arms out to her, she kept him at bay, her palm before her.

John Henry is dead. He is in a box in the wagon, Alf. I am extremely unwell.

Meisie and Doekie heard, and began weeping. Mother had no qualms about their embraces, though she stood stiffly, as if the slightest movement would fell her. Then she began weeping as well, leaning on the two small women, so insubstantial herself that I fancied if I turned away she would vanish into the sand.

Meisie and Doekie began humming a kind of a lament. They each took an arm and half-carried mother up to the dwelling.

I told father that John Henry had likely died from an attack of asthma, and that mother had refused to return to Upington for his burial, though the distance had been a mere three days. I praised Kobie, saying that without his strength and sound good sense we would have been lost.

Father listened, his head bowed.

It is a terrible tragedy, Em. I deeply regret not being present to support you both at such a time. But you, dear girl, have been brave and strong, and I am proud of you.

We laid John Henry to rest at the back of our dwelling beside the big kameeldoring that the flood had not toppled. May was buried nearby. She died at the age of fifteen, collapsing in our absence on a hunt with father and Brandbooi. I missed her, but felt comforted that her remains were close to the grave of my brother who, even as an infant, had loved to gaze at her and have her near him.

Mother sat stony-faced at the graveside between Meisie and Doekie. She was dry-eyed; perhaps there were no more tears left to shed. For me, the proceedings were nothing more than a blur. Father stood beside me, his head bent. The women rocked from side to side and chanted softly. Even Kobie tried to join in.

John Henry was buried in the same blanket box in which he had lain for ten days, in a small, square, deep pit dug by Brandbooi and Uil. Father had declined to open the makeshift coffin. I knew John Henry's soul had long since departed his lamentable remains, and was truly thankful that I would no longer be obliged to inhale the deterioration of his corpse. I had begun to think that I might never shed the appalling miasma of death. The worsening stench during the journey had confirmed for me as nothing else could that what was left of him was comparable to the broken egg of a bird, rotting in the sun with nothing inside it of the unborn fledgling.

The only reading was The Lord is my Shepherd, which I read in a voice from which I could not dislodge the tears. I found little comfort in all those green pastures, since my brother's bones would lie in the sun-scorched desert home where he was born.

Later that day, I sat alone by his graveside and contemplated the people and animals I had loved and lost.

I saw Poppie for the first time at John Henry's graveside. I had sought her eagerly and asked Meisie where she was almost as soon as we arrived. I had received no reply. In low spirits, I did not immediately pursue the matter; but after I had deposited my baggage in my room, I left to walk over to her shelter.

Meisie ran after me.

Poppie has a sore stomach and is resting, Em. She longs to see you again very soon, but she is still too ill.

This surprised me; Poppie had never been ill even a single day in her life.

I will visit her for only a few minutes. I want to give her the gifts I have brought.

Meisie shook her head. Glumly, I returned to my room.

Early the next morning, an invigoratingly cool, fresh morning, I walked to Poppie's shelter. I found Slang stationed outside.

I eyed him impatiently.

What are you doing here?

Poppie! I called. It is me! I cannot wait to see you! Can I come in for a minute?

There was no reply.

I tried to push past Slang, but he barred the way.

No, miesies, she is sick and now she is sleeping.

For heaven's sake, what is going on? She is my best friend, I have not seen her in months and now you will not even let me near her. Poppie? I shouted.

Silence.

Silly old Slang was unyielding. She sleeps. You will see her tomorrow, at the burial of your brother.

She stood a little way back from the rest of us, looking sick and thin, wearing an old shift I had never seen before that was far too big for her. I hugged her, astounded at how skinny she had become. How sick is she, I wondered. And what sickness causes such wasting of her lithe springy frame?

Her embrace was brief and without heart. I told her how much I had missed her and she did not say she had missed me in return. The complete absence of her customary vitality disturbed and puzzled me; but there were other matters that, for the moment, took precedence.

After the burial, mother retired to rest, and everybody came to the dwelling to drink the fine tea we had brought from Upington and to eat Elise's rusks and preserves. Poppie was nowhere to be seen.

In our absence, father had added another room to the dwelling, thinking to please mother. But she closed the door of the bedroom against him, and avoided his company. Shortly after our arrival, he moved into the new room – an improvement, I thought sadly, on sleeping in one of the outhouses.

Mother steadfastly refused to speak to father beyond a few formal words. Resentful that I should be burdened with adult anxieties and responsibilities, I asked myself questions I could not answer. Why was she so resolute in her hostile attitude to father? Did she blame him for John Henry's death? I remembered their quarrels before my brother's birth: I had eavesdropped as he urged her to terminate the pregnancy on the grounds that it could endanger her life.

I realised that I had always thought of my brother as *hers*; never as theirs. But her persecution of father frightened me. My home, for the first time ever, felt unsafe: currents swirled around me that I did not fully comprehend. At times, I felt myself spinning in their grip.

With a sense of foreboding, I spoke to mother shortly after the burial.

She was abed, her face to the wall. But I had had enough. I spoke to her back.

Why will you not speak to father? He is shocked and grieving about John Henry's death, and your avoidance of him is causing him additional pain.

She took a long time to respond. Em, leave me. I cannot discuss these matters with you.

I responded with some heat. I am not a child, mother. And you have made that very clear by the duties you have burdened me with.

I hesitated. John Henry was father's son as much as he was yours.

She turned her face to me at last. It was as blank as a sheet of paper.

Was he? Even you must recall that father did not want John Henry to be born, and when he was, rejected him. Her hazel eyes, bloodshot, bleary, filled with tears.

Your father wished John Henry dead before he was even born.

It was more than she had spoken since John Henry's death.

Father loves you, mother. I believe he loved John Henry, and mourns his loss. You must speak to him. Not to do so would be cruel; not only to him, but to me.

I do not mean to hurt you, Em.

If that is so, mother, I said, close to tears myself, I must remind you that I need both my parents. John Henry has no further need of you. But you have me. I am alive, mother. My brother, alas, is not.

Poppie

MY WORDS MUST HAVE had some effect, for two days after we had spoken, I observed father and mother in the first civilised exchange they had engaged in for longer than I cared to think about. I did not hear what was said, but felt an immediate lightening of my spirits. Perhaps, I thought, they will at last be able to draw comfort from each other.

The days grew longer and the summer hotter. My grief for John Henry had softened, as if the heat was burning it out of me. Mother, too, seemed less wooden; I thought I observed a certain serenity in her expression, and hoped she had turned a corner of some kind.

Two full weeks after we buried John Henry, Poppie finally seemed recovered from her affliction. Though still wan and weak, she consented to walk with me, and enquired without much animation about our stay in Upington. Her physical ailment appeared to have infected her spirits profoundly: she was as different from her good-natured, inquisitive self as I could conceive of. I continued to blame her illness, and wished Tam were still alive; I had no doubt she would have concocted a tonic that would have boosted my friend's low mood.

I told Poppie a little about the war being fought between the Boers and the British, and about the unmannerly Boers of the town of Upington. I described the good people we had stayed with, Elise and Dawid van Heerden, and praised them highly.

Are they not Boer people also, she asked. I said they were, but good and generous nonetheless.

As I spoke I felt a fleeting yearning for the warmth of their household, followed by a chilling thought: in the minds of our friends in Upington, John Henry was still alive and well.

I spoke of Danie Nel, too, describing his blond hair that was the colour of the grass and just as wayward, his teasing grin and harshly accented English that I could not for the life of me imitate.

He actually likes my hair, Poppie, can you believe that?

Poppie turned to study me. The expression on her face was so odd that it resisted interpretation. I noticed her green eyes were cloudy, the whites splashed with tiny crimson stars.

Your hair is beautiful, Em; it is the colour of the dunes after rain. Tell me, is this Danie a full-grown man, or still a boy?

I smiled. He is not yet sixteen.

Boys grow into men, she said slowly.

I detected an antagonism in her voice I had never heard before.

What do you know of boys and men, I scoffed. Next time, you will come with me to Upington.

Poppie blinked twice. Her sudden pallor was alarming.

What is wrong? What have I said?

She shook her head. Nothing. Your Danie sounds like a fine person. I am happy for you that you have found a new friend.

I sensed that I was missing something, but could not think what that thing could be, so I chose to reassure her.

You will always be my best friend, Poppie. Nobody will ever replace you.

She winced.

You are still in pain, poor girl! I am so foolish, chattering on about myself when you are not yet fully recovered. Come, let us go to the kitchen for a drink, and we will sit there together until you feel better.

That evening, as I was about to enter the dining area next to the kitchen, my parents' voices stopped me. I stood in the narrow passageway and listened.

Deirdre, hear me out: I beg you to reconsider your decision. I have missed you sorely these months of your absence – and the many months before that. It has been the most trying period of my life.

I am aware of your feelings, Alf. But I am in mourning, and I am not well either; it is better we are apart for now.

I hoped we could offer each other some comfort, Deirdre. God knows, if I had been able to shield you from this terrible loss, I would have.

Silence.

If I felt that there was some hope, my dear – that with the passing of time we could – be reconciled – I would feel greatly cheered.

It is not for me to cheer you, Alf. I cannot even cheer myself. Perhaps I loved him too well; but how can a mother love her child too well? I know that I do not trust the future. I can barely abide the present.

You have your daughter to think of. And you have me. Em is growing up fast. Plans must be made for her future.

What plans? What future? demanded mother shrilly. In this wilderness that has robbed me of my son? I promise you one thing, Alf: it will not have my daughter too. It will not take my Em from me.

The desert has nothing to do with our son's illness and death, replied father sadly. And his death has nothing to do with Em's future. I think you know that if the choice were Em's, she would spend her life on our farm.

How little you know her! She is changing, Alf. Very quickly. Soon you will not be the most important male figure in her life. Another will occupy that position, perhaps sooner than you think.

Father pushed back his chair. It is premature for us to be having such a discussion. He paused. I will not argue further with you, Deirdre; I would only be your husband.

Mother was unyielding. I do not want a husband. I want my son. Oh God, how much I want him back!

A strangled sound escaped father.

I heard his step, and fled. I longed to comfort him, but I knew it was not my comfort that he sought.

The next day I awoke with a dry throat and a huge thirst. I stumbled from my bed to the kitchen for a tumbler of water. Uil or Slang usually brought up the day's water from the well early, and Doekie and Meisie apportioned

210

it in the kitchen for drinking, washing, and general household use.

Seeing my dishevelled state, Meisie grimaced.

When last was your nightdress laundered, Em?

Since I could not remember, I did not deign to reply.

I took my first sip from the tumbler, and spat violently. My spittle landed not far from where Meisie stood beside Doekie, who was washing pots. They gawked at me in unison.

It tastes foul! I exclaimed, spitting into the tumbler. A rat or a squirrel must have fallen in again. Or one of those awful crows. It is so ghastly it could even be a jackal this time.

Slang fixed the wire only last week, said Doekie, puzzled. I saw it myself. Not even a baby finger could fit in the side.

Well, taste for yourself. I think I am going to be sick.

Go outside then, ordered Meisie hastily. She took a sip from a tumbler, held the water in her mouth until she got to the back door, then spat repeatedly into the dust.

We will have to boil the water for hours now before we can drink it, she exclaimed crossly.

Father and Kobie were with the sheep, and Poppie was still asleep. Mother was in her bedroom; I knew it would be some time before our lesson would begin. I washed gingerly in the spoilt water, dressed myself, and followed Brandbooi down to the well, which was next to a pretty shepherd's tree.

I hoped the drowned animal was a crow rather than a squirrel; crows were my least favourite bird. Once, a thirsty, determined honey badger had clawed through the wire and fallen in. The effect on the water would have been catastrophic had Brandbooi not been coming down to the well at the time. He saw the creature drowning, picked up a dead branch, and held it out. Honey badgers are notoriously vicious and aggressive beasts, but the desperate creature had clambered aboard. Drenched and red-eyed, it had sprung from the branch and raced away; but not, said Brandbooi (who enjoyed teasing me) before baring its needle-sharp teeth in a smile of gratitude.

Knowing a little about honey badgers, I thought it more likely the foolish animal had been menacing its rescuer!

Carrying the large, long-handled fishing net which Kobie had made from grass, reeds and wire, Brandbooi stooped to inspect the cover of the well.

He sat back on his heels, frowning. I squatted beside him; neither of us could spot a gap. Gnawing on a twig, I sat myself down to watch as he pulled the lid aside and dipped the fishing net into the well as far as it would go. He dipped repeatedly, swirling the net powerfully below the surface of the dark water. He had done this many times before, and it did not take him long to fish out the culprit.

He put the net on the ground and began fixing the cover in place.

Inside the net, huddled as if fast asleep, was an animal the size of a small rat. Hairless except for a patch of wet dark hair on its large head, it was a bluish colour, with miniature mottled arms and legs, and fingers and toes not much bigger than the tip of my quill pen. The bruised pods of its eyelids were half closed over two smeared black seeds that were its eyes. What looked like a shredded root, purplish in colour, was suspended from its belly; below this a tiny kernel and a disproportionately large knot of furrowed flesh protruded.

Sunlight slipped between the branches of the tree, and I saw that the tiny creature was covered all over with a fine down.

Spirits

BRANDBOOI SCOOPED THE creature from the net; it fitted into the palm of his hand. There was nothing in which to wrap it. Numbly, I took off my hide shoe, and he placed the thing inside it. We walked in silence up to the dwelling, Brandbooi carrying the shoe.

In the kitchen, Meisie was calling to Doekie.

The rain barrels are nearly empty! Who knows when we will get rain? She peered out. Was it a rat or a crow or what? Will we be able to draw water tomorrow?

She clicked crossly when she saw Brandbooi holding my shoe.

Why do you put it in her shoe? I do not need to see a stinking carcass that has spoilt our water!

She turned back to the kitchen. Give her back the shoe; I will wash it. And throw that thing far from here, where the mongooses and the crows will find it.

Brandbooi put the shoe down without a word. He went into the kitchen and took Meisie by the hand.

What now?

It was not an animal, said Brandbooi.

Meisie craned her neck to look into the shoe. She squealed and dropped the rag she was holding. It fell on the shoe and covered its contents.

I walked dazedly into the dwelling and removed the other shoe. Mother was in her bedroom, asleep on top of her neatly made bed.

I itched to shake her roughly awake. All she ever did, it seemed to me, was sleep.

As if she sensed my presence, her eyes opened. She gazed up at me blindly. I saw it then, I could not miss it: she wished she did not ever have to wake again.

She pushed herself into a sitting position. I noticed a white streak bled through the untidy spill of her dark hair.

What is it, Em? She rubbed her eyes. Is it time for our lesson? I fell asleep. It must be late, I am so sorry, she murmured.

Speech did not come to me, which was fortunate. I was afraid that once I opened my mouth, howls might stream out of it. Instead, I grasped both her hands and pulled her onto her feet.

What are you doing, Em?

I did not reply. I led her by the hand to the small crushed group outside the kitchen. Word had spread; all were assembled there except Kobie and Uil, who were working with father repairing scavenger damage to the outermost kraal, and Poppie. I was relieved; I did not think she was strong enough to view the contents of that shoe. They made way for us. I pointed at the shoe, and mother looked down at it.

Oh, God, she said succinctly, and slumped to the ground.

She opened her eyes a moment later, her head in Meisie's lap. With the help of Brandbooi, Meisie lifted her carefully and propped her up against the wall beside the kitchen door. Her head lolled slightly; she had cut her forehead on a stone or a twig, and a trail of blood trickled down from her eyebrow along the side of her nose to her mouth.

As Meisie dabbed at the cut with a wet cloth, mother looked about her uncertainly. For some reason, father had not returned home to eat an early lunch, as he usually did.

Whose is it, Meisie? asked mother faintly.

I do not know, madam, replied Meisie, looking down – looking anywhere but at mother or the shoe (which I vowed to throw away as soon as possible, together with its partner).

Mother's voice trembled. Well, it is not yours, since you cannot have children, nor is it Doekie's because she is older than I am. So who does that leave?

Poppie, I blurted without thinking. My head began pounding.

You must have known, I accused Meisie wildly. She has been so ill!

Both Meisie and Doekie shook their heads.

I began weeping, overcome with guilt that since our return I had been too self-engrossed to pay any real heed to my best friend's terrible trouble.

Doekie spoke up, sounding bewildered.

For months, Poppie was very quiet. At first we thought she missed Em; she was lonely, there were no young people here for her. When she got sick, she said it was her stomach. We gave her Tam's medicine for stomach problems and she swallowed it. Her stomach swelled and she said the sickness was worse. She took an old sheet and she sewed it like a box and dressed herself in it. I asked her why. She told me that her clothes were tight and hurt her stomach. I did not think about a child; why would I? There are no young men on the farm.

Meisie cut in. I do not think Poppie herself understood that a child grew inside her, although she must have known that her flow had stopped. She hesitated. And that she had lain with a man.

What man, for heaven's sake, asked mother in a stronger voice. She pushed back her hair and pressed the cloth harder against the cut on her forehead.

Doekie tugged at her knuckles, which cracked like shotguns.

How could we know, madam? There is nobody here; they are too old. Kobie was with you in town. And Brandbooi is her father.

And fathers do not do this to their daughters, said mother nastily.

Brandbooi, standing nearby, gazing down into the shoe, took a step back. His eyes were moist and angry.

A spirit made this thing.

A spirit impregnated a child?

I had regained control at last. She is no longer a child, mother, I reminded her. She is almost sixteen years old.

Have there been any visitors to the farm since we left, Brandbooi?

There has been nobody, replied Brandbooi.

Mother staggered to her feet. I could not bring myself to help her, and she shook off Meisie's hand. She walked over to the shoe. With visible effort, she forced herself to inspect its contents. When she stood up she had turned even paler than she already was; but her voice, when it came, was steady.

This child is not nearly full term. He was probably less than six months in the womb.

Meisie, beside her, murmured agreement.

Mother turned to her. Fetch Poppie. Now.

Poppie walked slowly towards us, Meisie just behind her. Like a guard with a prisoner, I thought dejectedly. They stopped some distance away. Poppie was wearing the rumpled shift she had worn to John Henry's burial.

Poppie, called mother in her teacher's voice. Come here to me, please.

My friend, trained to obey, took another awkward step. Meisie put a hand on her arm and drew her towards us.

As they approached, I felt tears begin again. Poppie's eyes were dull, the lids heavy, and her flawless skin had blemishes flaking on cheeks and chin. She was barefooted. For the first time I noticed that her slim ankles had swollen so much that the fine bones were invisible.

Remorse flushed hotly through me: I went to her and put my arm about her. I whispered in her ear.

What are you saying, Em, asked mother sharply.

It is between Poppie and me, mother.

I held her hand, and led her to the shoe. She looked down, then gave a terrible cry and fell to her knees. She would have snatched up the foetus were it not for Brandbooi, who stooped swiftly and, in a single deft movement, swept away the shoe.

She looked up at him in anguished appeal, but he shook his head.

Why, Poppie? Why did you do this? Mother's reproach was tinged with sadness.

Poppie looked up at me instead of mother. Her dry eyes seemed to explode with tears.

You think I killed him.

She sat back in the dust, as if her knees would no longer support her. I sat beside her and took her loose fingers in mine. She spoke into her chest at last. The others moved closer.

216

I woke from sleep late one night with terrible cramping in my lower belly and back. I got up to walk to the outhouse. There was no moon that night; it was very dark. I could not walk properly. I was bent over from holding back the pain in my stomach. It was so bad that I wondered if something inside me was broken. Suddenly a river of water came out of me, flowing down between my legs. I felt between them. The river had thickened into sticky clots, like mud; I thought my stomach was falling out and wondered in terror if I was dying. I held a hand to my face, and smelt blood.

Then something wet and slippery came out of me. I caught it in my hands.

She paused. The only thing I could think was that my monthly courses had come back at last, and the reason the flow was so thick and clotted was because they had been gone for so long.

Poppie's small frame began shaking with sobs. I put my arms about her, feeling her tears on my skin, and the prick of my own horrified tears.

She drew a deep tremulous breath.

The pain, though, had finally gone. I felt for and found the slippery thing on the ground, and then I washed myself with the water in the bucket. I felt weak, but I was happy. Tam's medicine had worked: it had brought on my courses and was drawing the bloody lumps of sickness from my body. When I stood up, I found there was still something between my legs. I tugged. It was painful, but I drew out a second lump. I washed myself once more, bound the lumps together in an old rag, and walked back to the shelter, carrying the little bundle.

I was exhausted. I decided I could get rid of the bundle early the next morning, and I fell asleep.

At first light, I opened the bindings and saw – Her head twitched in the direction of the shoe.

He was dead.

She looked up at mother this time. Their eyes met.

I did kill him, she said to mother dully. But it was in error.

There was tenderness in mother's reply.

You did not kill him, Poppie. He was too young to live outside the womb. I do not think he drew even a single breath: his lungs were not big enough.

She bit her lip. But, my dear, somebody gave you that baby. It was after that – after that happened – that your courses stopped. Is that not true?

Poppie did not appear to hear her. She had not yet finished.

I could not eat properly for a long time before this thing happened. Food made me sick, it made me vomit. I was afraid to tell anybody that Tam's medicine was not helping, that my stomach was swelling and my womb was not releasing my blood. I was worried that the sickness would prevent me from doing my work.

But this is your home, Poppie, I interjected gently. You should have told Meisie or Doekie. They would have helped you.

I could not. I would have told you, Em. But you were not here.

Why did you throw him into the well? asked Doekie, practical after the fact. You know dead things poison the water.

Poppie shrugged. I could think of nowhere else. If I buried him the animals would dig him up, the vultures would find him and tear him to pieces. I could not bear that. I did not have long, because the sun was beginning to rise and you or Meisie would be coming into my shelter to wake me. She turned to Meisie abruptly.

You are like a jackal, she said accusingly. You can smell blood from a long way, it would not matter how much I had washed. I knew I had to get rid of him speedily, but I could not think what to do; my mind was tightly closed, and would not open.

I picked him up – he was light, like a field mouse – and I took the bundle and walked down the rise as fast as I could. I unlocked the well, lifted the cover and threw him – all of it – into it. Then I went back and cleaned my shelter and the outhouse very well, so that not a drop of blood remained in either place. I washed my hands in the little water that was left at the bottom of the bucket.

Throughout, my mind remained closed. Yet I knew that if I stopped breathing after I had finished washing my hands, it would have been right. But that did not happen.

Poppie closed her eyes. Her long lashes were weighted with tears.

Nobody spoke for a moment.

Then mother said quietly, take her to your room, Em. Her body is already mending, but her spirits are very low. We will nurse her together.

She signalled to Brandbooi, who nodded. He strode off in the direction of the riverbed, taking with him my shoe and its pitiful contents.

I helped Poppie into my bed, my hands busy but my heart full of bitterness against the spirits that had failed to protect her against the stray Bushman who must have stolen into her shelter by night, and robbed her of her innocence.

When I left the room, Poppie was asleep. I found mother in the kitchen, standing on a chair, reaching for the large bottle of medicinal spirits from the shelf on which it was stored.

Mother, it is not long since you recovered from a faint.

I am fine now, Em. She climbed down, took a damp cloth and opened the bottle, spilling a few drops of the spirits.

Now that you are here, would you tend my forehead, please, Em?

The cut was small, with ragged edges; as I dabbed at it, blood welled up. I wiped it gently away.

Mother did not flinch; she appeared distracted.

How odd, she said, sniffing. The spirits do not smell. And the cut does not sting.

I sniffed for the familiar odour I associated with both hygiene and infection. She was right: the air, dry and clear, was untainted by the spirits.

Are you sure that is the right bottle?

There is no other. She picked up the bottle, poured a small quantity into a tumbler, raised it to her lips and took a small sip.

This is water! she exclaimed, astounded. No wonder there is no smell.

She called Meisie, who was in the backyard, hanging laundry with Doekie.

What is in this bottle?

Spirits, madam.

You are wrong. This bottle is full of water. But I believe you already know that.

She waited, but Meisie was silent, her eyes lowered.

Who drank the spirits?

The little woman shook her head. To my surprise, she turned her back on mother and walked out of the kitchen.

The Dream Is Lost

WHEN FATHER RETURNED from work, I was alone in the kitchen, waiting for him. I wanted to be the first to tell him the sad news. He went directly to the bucket of rainwater standing by the hearth, dipped in a tumbler and drank; then refilled it and drank again. I knew he would notice immediately: the sweet taste and scent of rainwater stored in the barrels was quite different from our well water, with its brackish undertow of the desert.

Rainwater, he muttered to himself.

He took a jug, poured some sparingly into a second bucket, removed a cloth and a small towel from a nail, and went outside to wash away the grime of a day spent repairing kraal walls.

Why are we using supplies from the rain barrels, he called to me irritably, sloshing water onto his face and neck. Everybody knows it is for emergency use only. What is the emergency?

I took a deep breath, and stepped outside.

Where is your mother?

She is resting. She will join us for supper. We are using water from the rain barrels, father, because something fell into the well.

What? Again? What was it this time, another honey badger? His voice was muffled by the towel with which he was vigorously drying his hair and beard.

Whew, that feels better. It has been too hot for this work today.

It was not a honey badger.

Well, what was it, then, he demanded impatiently. Brandbooi must do something about that cover; animals are getting through too frequently.

It was not an animal, father.

He put the towel around his neck and glared at me.

Enough, Em! Out with it! What was it?

I found to my chagrin that I was not enjoying being the messenger of such horrid news.

It was a baby, father. A human foetus. I saw it.

The towel fell at my feet. I bent to retrieve it.

It was Poppie's. It was Poppie's son in the well, father.

My friend was sound asleep in my bed. I decided I would not disturb her for supper, but take her a plate of food after I had eaten.

That night my own appetite was poor. Gruesome images of Poppie's struggle accompanied every mouthful. I found it painful and pitiful that she had believed herself finally rid of her sickness: in my mind's eye, I pictured her stumbling to the outhouse with a river of blood flowing out of her; then holding in her hands the foetus her womb had expelled. I recalled the expression on her face when she saw what my shoe contained, and I shivered and could not swallow.

Though there had been silent meals around the dining table before we had left for Upington, now they appeared to be the rule. The clatter of dishes, knives and forks, sometimes the slurping of soup, sounded much louder as a result. I had become accustomed to the absence of conversation, and that night, lost in thought, I failed to notice that the silence between my parents was more fraught than usual.

When father spoke at last, I started slightly.

Why is Poppie sharing your bed, Em? Is her own not adequate?

Before I could say a word, mother responded.

It has obviously escaped your notice that she has been indisposed, Alf. I know you have little to do with her, but it is a wonder to me that you did not at any time observe her suffering; or that this was not brought to your attention by Doekie or Meisie.

Father shrugged. They take care of themselves. They do not need my services for the kind of misfortune that Poppie has experienced.

Misfortune? Such indifference was not your habit once, said mother sourly. Do you have no thoughts to offer, then, as to how she became pregnant?

None, said father, chewing. Have you asked her?

She has said nothing. Our people say no stranger has been to the farm for many months. And I cannot imagine an intruder slipping in, ravishing a young girl, and then vanishing. Nor, she added dryly, is Poppie's impregnation the work of an evil spirit.

Father wiped his mouth with a cloth.

Mother leaned across the table. Do you know, Alf, what has become of the contents of the bottle of medicinal alcohol?

Father chewed his mouthful for an inordinately long time.

I have not the least idea. Is the bottle not in its usual place on the shelf?

Mother glowered at him. It is. You know exactly what I am asking.

Father glanced in my direction. Deirdre, I have no wish to discuss these matters in front of Em.

Do not be a hypocrite, said mother brusquely. If she is old enough to place a human foetus in her shoe, she is old enough for this conversation.

What is this conversation about? I interjected anxiously.

Hush, Em. Well, Alf? I am waiting.

I turned to father, nausea rising at the back of my throat. Somebody drank the spirits, father, and replaced them with water.

In order to deceive. A short-sighted tactic, would you not agree, Alf?

Mother, please! Will you stop?

She ignored me for a moment, watching father without blinking, a queer, hard gaze. Her eyes still on him, she addressed me.

There are tricks afoot that I do not fully understand myself, Em. And I do not like mysteries in my own home. One such mystery is the missing alcohol.

She stood up, her lips compressed, a deep line between her brows. The time has come for you to explain yourself, Alf!

Father sprang to his feet, his colour alarmingly high. What is the charge? That I drank my own spirits? You are a bitter and evil-tongued woman, Deirdre. It is you who are guilty, guilty of abandoning your husband for a child who should never have been born. Whose loss – poor retarded boy – has driven you over the edge!

He stalked from the room, but mother's voice pursued him: Will you place the blame with one of your blameless people? Is that what you will do? Accuse an innocent of your crime?

I wondered if I was going to vomit into the plate of food that I could not eat.

What crime, mother? Do you accuse father of drinking the spirits?

Her hands gripping the edge of the table, mother looked down at her own untouched plate. Her wiry hair stood on end; the ruddy hue of her emotions was already fading to a blanched pallor.

She shook her head, lifting a hand to cover her mouth.

Take Poppie her food now, Em, it grows cold, she said tonelessly. I will clear the table.

The next morning, mother was in the kitchen early. I heard her raised voice berating Meisie and Doekie as I closed the door behind me. Poppie had slept almost around the clock, and was still sleeping.

Kobie was not on the farm, Slang and Uil are too old, Brandbooi is innocent; so who was it? A visitor, a traveller, a thief, a spirit?

No reply.

I will have an answer from one of you. I will not leave this kitchen until I get it, said mother icily.

She heard my step and turned. Em! Leave the kitchen! Not one word from you!

I have only come to fetch Poppie's breakfast, I replied sulkily.

What ensued is packed away in a corner of my brain, and will remain there for as long as I am alive. Many times since the events that rapidly unfolded, I unpleated each circumstance as I would a garment; unravelled each stitch of that garment in order to discover the cause, the agent of tragedy. Each time I failed. Even now, I fail to assign reason, principle; a glimmer of certainty. No matter how I ruck, tuck, turn, unfurl – what happened still seems random and inexplicable. God, fate, fortune remain senseless, and we their fools and pawns.

I was walking back from the outhouse when I heard loud sobs. I ran into my room and found mother bent over Poppie, her fists clenched, the tendons of her neck stretched.

I must know. You must tell me. Then I will know what to do.

Poppie, her face crumpled and wet, shrank into a corner of the bed and covered her head with a pillow.

Mother pulled it away. She spoke imperiously in a voice which Poppie had respected and obeyed from when she was a very young child:

You must speak. I need only a yes or a no. That is all. Was it he?

Finally, a haunting exhalation of three words: It was he.

I heard a gasp. I knew it came from me when mother turned away from the bed, her eyes dark punctures, every angle and curve of her face flattened to a uniform blankness.

Already then, I was as insignificant as a grain of sand; I could change nothing. It was written.

The rest has the jumbled quality of a dream. Father returned home for his lunch to find mother, Poppie and me packed and dressed for travel, and the wagon being loaded by Doekie and Meisie, weeping unrestrainedly.

As brutally as Poppie's innocence was torn from her, my family was ruptured.

As if by some violent upheaval of the planet.

My parents did not communicate again. It seemed there were no words for the unspeakable; no forgiveness for what was immutable. Mother took money from under the bed and father did not stop her. In his presence, she informed Kobie that he would be driving us. He looked to father. Father said nothing; he drank some water in the kitchen, and went back to the kraals.

Before the wagon left late that same afternoon, I sought him out. He was hefting stones to fill in a section of wall, his hair and beard unkempt, dripping with perspiration. I stood nearby, watching him for a moment in great torment.

Father, I cannot hate you. Perhaps I should, but I cannot.

He said nothing, continuing to work.

Farewell, father. I will write. And I will come back some day.

A groan escaped him. He covered his face with one hand. With the other, he waved me away.

Mother did not look back at the farm as the wagon moved off. She spoke to the gaudy sunset, and to the shadows on the dunes.

There was an eerie note of triumph in her thin voice.

This cursed place took my son from me, Em. Now it will not get you as well.

PART THREE

But life must be lived

MOTHER SAT IN THE FRONT of the wagon with Kobie for most of the daylight hours. Her hair was teased from its bun by a hot wind and eddies of dust, her still pretty complexion carelessly bared to their ravages. I was not aware of a single word exchanged between herself and Kobie beyond the essentials, but the arrangement appeared to suit them both.

The further we travelled from the farm, the lighter Poppie became. It was a daily wonder: as the rays of the rising sun pierce the lagging shadows of the night, so her hideous trials began lifting from her features.

Mother ate her dinner alone, inside the wagon, and we – Kobie, Poppie and I – ate beside the fire and sat around it afterwards, covered by blankets, inhaling the fresh breath of the desert darkness. By night, the round silvery eye of the moon seemed to illuminate a secret self in Poppie's elfin face.

On the fifth night, Kobie retired early beneath the wagon. Poppie and I lingered beside the fire. Her voice was a faint rustle in the night hush, a sound that might cock the sensitive ear of a hunting fox.

After you and your mother left with John Henry for town, Em, he changed. He liked to talk, even sing, as he worked, but as the days passed we noticed that he spoke less each day and sang not at all, working himself – and us – terribly hard. Once, Uil fell asleep after his lunch and your father punched him with both fists. He had never hit any of us before. After that we were afraid, although we had never feared him, and became very careful not to displease or anger him. But still, nothing we did was right. Some days he shouted that we were stupid Bushmen; he said insulting things that we had never heard from him before.

Brandbooi ordered us to be patient. He told us the baas was lonely and sad without his family; that we were the only family he had left. The time had come for us to pay him back for all the good things he had done for us.

All that your father wanted was hard labour. He sucked up our energy as if he was on fire and we were water; yet with each bucketful he gulped down, the fire in him burned ever higher. Not a day passed without him cursing and barking commands at us like bullets from his rifle.

About three weeks after you left, I woke up one night and heard heavy breathing close by. I thought it was a big animal. The air smelt sour. I sat up on my pallet and saw something weaving about at the entrance. The others were asleep, and I was frightened. I called out: Who is there?

There was no answer. A shape rose in the entrance. I saw your father's hair, his beard, in the moonlight. He staggered, and then fell on top of me. He put his hand across my mouth. I could do nothing to stop him, Em. He had the strength of a lion. Tam would have said he was possessed by an evil spirit.

She paused. But his odour was in my nostrils, and it was of another kind of spirit.

I wept. Poppie put out a finger and brushed the tears from my cheeks. The tears were for her. For father I felt – I knew not what I felt. But that night, in the deepest part of myself, I admitted for the first time to bitter disappointment in mother. Surely she should have known better than to turn away from her husband, as she had, long before he violated my best friend? Emotions warred within me, drenching me with perspiration in the frosty night. How had the love my parents shared haemorrhaged to a wasteland of enmity and despair?

I wept for the injury committed against innocents who had given us their loyalty and trust. More than that, they had given us their hearts.

When it was done, continued Poppie, your father left the shelter. Outside, he stumbled into Meisie, who must have heard something, since she rarely woke during the night. Your father brushed her aside. She entered my shelter without my permission, sniffed the air and asked only if I was all right. My tongue felt as if it had turned to stone, but I said I was. Nevertheless, she insisted on taking me to the outhouse, where she urged me to wash myself repeatedly with the icy water; which I did.

They knew! I cried. Why then did they not suspect that you might be carrying a child?

Poppie shook her head, her eyes on the dying embers. *I did not know that I was with child. I believed I had rinsed that night away with cold water. I think we all wiped it from our minds. I continued working the next day as if nothing had happened. None of us ever spoke of it again.*

She sighed. Our minds could not hold it, so we pushed it out.

Did he come to you again?

He never came again. Meisie found the bottle on the kitchen floor at dawn the next day. It was unbroken, but completely empty.

I had never known my father to touch a drop of spirits.

Drinking the entire contents that night must have driven him crazy, said Poppie. Meisie filled the bottle with water, so that your mother would not notice.

She gave a wry chuckle. But your mother noticed. She overlooks nothing.

Except what is most important, I thought sadly.

I am afraid, Em, said Poppie softly.

It will be all right, I replied, shivering. Let us go to sleep. It is very cold.

But I, too, was afraid.

Elise and Dawid van Heerden were shocked to see us return so soon after we had left, and deeply saddened by the news of John Henry's death. Though they welcomed us and made us comfortable, they were clearly dismayed at my insistence that Poppie share my room when there were adequate quarters for her with the other servants.

Poppie herself had forgotten her fear the instant the wagon rolled down the main street to Elise's home. She was amazed and fascinated, exclaiming at the mission buildings, the church spire and the irrigation channels. It was market day, which made her first sight of the town rather busier than it might have been on an ordinary day. Her chatter as we swung our legs from the back of the wagon lifted my mood, and I was pleased that I was able to answer most of her excited questions.

Unfortunately, she was soon silenced by the ragged procession of gaunt black and brown families on the dusty tracks all about us, seeking to spend their few coins at the crumbling stalls at the far end of the main street. These, unpatronised by the white folk, sold the cheapest cuts of meat, displayed in reeking mounds of bones and organs; chicken feet, boiled up in huge vats, were being chewed hungrily by small children with mucus streaming from their eyes and noses. Brownish produce sprawled like offal onto the track.

Poppie looked away. I leaned across and took her hand, but she gently disengaged herself.

I confess that by now my thoughts were not with her. They were with Danie Nel. He had been in my mind often during the long hours of the journey, and I found myself longing for the uncomplicated comfort of his friendship. As soon as we had unpacked sufficiently for our immediate needs, I left mother and Poppie resting at the Van Heerdens and walked to the home of the Nel family, near the outskirts of the town.

Mrs Nel opened the door to my knock. She appeared none too pleased at the sight of me, alone and travel-stained. Perhaps in her eyes I was disregarding the rules of polite behaviour for a young lady, but I did not care.

To my relief Danie was home. The surprised pleasure in his eyes as he greeted me more than compensated for his mother's disapproval. We walked into the garden and sat on the grass. I told him of John Henry's death. He took my hands in both of his; they were lost in his large square palms. His fingers that gripped mine were tipped with clean pink nails. I thought such hands would surely make him a fine doctor.

What has brought your family back to town so soon after John Henry's death? he asked, frowning slightly. Does your father accompany you this time?

He is not with us, I replied gloomily. It is a long story, and one that must wait a while. But I can tell you this: we will not be returning to the farm for a long time.

He exclaimed in Afrikaans. I understood him perfectly.

You are shocked by this news.

I took my hands away. They felt as cold as a Kalahari midnight.

My friend Poppie is with us, I said brightly. You will like her.

Rising to my feet, I tugged at his hand. Come, let us walk to the Van Heerden home and you can meet her.

On the way there, Danie and I stopped at the hospital to greet his father. The nurse, as abrupt and untidy as ever, hustled us into his office.

Doctor Nel rose to his feet, surprised at the sight of me. His first question was in his eyes before it reached his lips.

Your mother is with you?

She is, Doctor. I hesitated. I have sad news. My brother, John Henry, died of an asthma attack on our homeward journey. We were but three days from Upington when it happened.

Doctor Nel looked shocked. Good God! Yet you continued the journey?

We did, Doctor. Mother wished to bury him on the farm.

How is your mother faring?

She is in great pain.

His death occurred some months ago.

Yes. I paused. Her spirits are still worryingly low.

Is that why you have come back to town? Because your mother requires medical attention?

It is – a delicate matter.

Doctor Nel nodded. I will be happy to visit her at the end of the day.

Perhaps she will tell him what she is thinking, I reflected. For she had not shared a single thought with me.

That evening, Doctor Nel and mother sat together on the porch, engaged in quiet conversation.

Poppie and the Van Heerden children had taken a liking to one another, and she was sharing their supper while Elise and Dawid took the opportunity of visiting Elise's mother, who lived with her sister on a farm some miles from the town.

The window of the formal lounge was open to the porch. It was the perfect opportunity for me to eavesdrop from behind the curtain, and the quickest way to learn something of mother's plans – if she had any.

The first thing I heard was my name on Doctor Nel's lips.

Em is concerned about your health, Deirdre. She says you are very low. Which is to be expected after the loss of a child. It is a dreadful tragedy.

He cleared his throat. But time must, of necessity, accommodate even this. I know it is little consolation, but John Henry's life, had he lived longer, would not have been easy, owing to his general health and the condition with which he was born.

Silence.

Doctor Nel soldiered on.

If this mood of sadness you are experiencing does not improve, it may be a good idea to take a tonic, which I will be happy to prescribe.

Mother spoke up wearily at last. A tonic will have no power to uplift my mood, the causes of which leave little room for confusion, I fear.

Well, if it is not too intrusive a question, may I respectfully enquire as to the reason for your return to town?

Indeed you may. It is because I have decided to return to England.

Shock trickled coldly down my spine.

I will mail on the morrow a letter I have written to an old friend who tutored with me in London. I am certain she will assist us in the beginning, perhaps with lodging but definitely with work. We will wait here until I receive a reply to the letter. But I am confident she will be eager to assist.

I do not understand, said Doctor Nel, sounding dismayed. You do not plan to return to the farm?

We will never return to the farm.

I pinned my ear to the rough weave of the curtain.

This decision cannot be owing to the death of John Henry alone, said Doctor Nel slowly. Something else has happened.

It was not a question. I wondered how much she trusted Doctor Nel.

Not enough, it seemed, to tell him the truth.

Events occurred of which I cannot speak, Jacques; they have changed my life, and Em's life as well.

Deirdre and Jacques.

What about your husband?

A chair scraped the ground. You are a doctor: I will put a question to you in the hopes that your medical expertise might provide insights I am unable to discover for myself. The question is this: What power or influence can transform a clever, contented, warm-hearted person into an angry, self-pitying, deviant one?

For the first time, there was intensity of emotion in mother's voice – a seething rancour and despair.

How can I respond to such a question in a just manner when you will not share the circumstances of which you speak?

I have shared as much as I am able, replied mother morosely. I am sorry. She sighed. However, I do have a favour to ask of you, Jacques.

I am happy to offer my services in any way I can, responded Doctor Nel stiffly.

It is about Em's friend, Poppie. The little Bushwoman. She has been raised on the farm with my daughter. She speaks English as well as I do; her Afrikaans is much better, and she is almost as far in her schooling as Em is.

I have seen her; she opened the door to me. She is a pretty young woman.

She is in need of a good home, said mother shortly. We cannot take her with us to England. Will you find employment here for her?

I am sure a solution can be found. I will discuss it with my wife.

Scraping of chairs again. I slithered from the room, tiresome tears persisting like squally spells of sun and rain.

Upington to Cape Town

I DO NOT WANT TO go to England, mother. You must go alone.

We had risen to clear the breakfast dishes from the table, and I could no longer contain myself. It was the day after mother's conversation with Doctor Nel. Elise was already working in the garden and Poppie, infatuated with the hues and fragrances of the profusion of lovely blooms – almost all of which she had never seen before – was with her.

You have been eavesdropping again, Em, accused mother. It is an unfortunate habit of yours.

She chewed her lip. A habit that, from now on, must change.

You are changing the subject, mother. If the only way I can uncover the truth about decisions which affect my life is by eavesdropping – then so be it.

You are insolent, Em.

Mother, the situation has gone beyond insolence or bad habits. You have kept me in ignorance of your plans; that is as unfair to me as my eavesdropping is to you. But now that I have found out what is in your mind, you should know that I have no wish to leave this place. I repeat: I will not accompany you to England.

Mother laughed. It was not a sound of amusement, but filled with mockery and misery.

What place? This stifling coven of dust and prejudice? There is nothing for us here.

Yet I will not leave.

That is quite enough. You are still a child; there are things you do not understand. It is I, not you, who make the decisions in this family. And where I go, you go.

I understand, I retorted rudely, that your decisions thus far have been disastrous. I will not leave Poppie behind. I will not leave the Kalahari. I will not leave – father.

This last said with defiance and a pinch of trepidation.

Mother pounced.

Father? Your father is sick! I would not have you anywhere near him!

You are not blameless, mother, I muttered sulkily.

And you are not old enough to judge, Em. So do not presume to do so. We await my friend Olivia's reply. The instant it arrives, we leave for Cape Town.

Since to her I was still a child, I responded childishly, in a voice sugary with spite.

It has been many years since you have been in touch, mother. Your friend Olivia may not reply to your letter, and then what will you do? Entreat Jacques for assistance?

I spent the weeks of waiting with Poppie and, of course, with Danie. They took to each other, as I knew they would, but after the three of us dared to walk together along the main track, the talk among the people, white and brown, crackled with disapproval. Some of the white townsfolk were blatantly disgusted.

Danie's mother was one of them. Informed of the company her son kept by a well-known gossipmonger in the town, she was offended and humiliated, and blamed me for her son's unconventional behaviour. I knew she had taken against mother and me from the first. In her mind, as in the minds of the slovenly Boer teenagers, we were British, and therefore enemies. As for dark-skinned people, she regarded them as inferior beings, born to labour for their white betters, and Bushmen the least of all, whether of mixed blood, like Poppie, or not. Danie, shamefaced, told me she viewed them as 'God se fout'. God's mistake.

Cruel, horrid woman! How could she possibly be Danie's mother?

He, like it or not, was ordered to walk with me alone in the town or not at all. His father, who gave the instruction, explained that their living and well-being were dependent on the goodwill of the townsfolk and farmers, while mother and I were temporary residents. Furthermore, he pointed out that Poppie was going to be left behind, and therefore needed to align herself with her own people to gain acceptance; the alternative – ostracism by all the different groups – would make her life unbearable.

But she is my sister, I replied in distress. In some ways she seems more like me than I am! Yet I am abandoning her in a place where she knows nobody!

Doctor Nel nodded. I know you are unwilling to leave her, he said gently, but that is what is going to happen. It is in this town that she will be obliged to make her way in life. I hope it will ease your mind a little if I promise that I will do my best to see that she is safe, and well equipped to take care of herself.

I know it is asking a lot of you. I am not unmindful of that, nor am I ungrateful, I replied glumly.

Danie spoke up. It is as we discussed on your first visit, Em. She is white by upbringing and education; but in town she is a Bushman. That is her reality; the one she must learn to live with. He shrugged. It is a hard thing.

Mrs Nel refused outright to employ Poppie, so Doctor Nel took her on almost immediately as a general factotum at the hospital. Within a few days, he professed himself delighted with his decision. He told mother and me that he found her quick and clever, and that she could read and write far better than his nurse in Afrikaans (father taught us both) and English.

Poppie, anxious to allay my fears, barely voiced her own; but I continued to feel despondent and guilty.

You will be entirely alone in the world, I told her. And it is our fault.

She would have none of it.

I will miss you very much, Em, but I must manage without you. You must help me to stay strong. One day, I will make you proud of me.

I would have cause to remember those brave words.

Had Poppie been white, I reflected bitterly, she could have become a doctor – anything else in the world she chose to be. She sacrificed hundreds of mornings of play to keep abreast of me; now, through no fault of her own, our futures will be worlds apart.

A day later, we were seated in Elise's lounge. Poppie was beside me. I had recruited both Danie and his father in a last-ditch effort to convince mother that we needed more time before making the drastic move to England. Surely an alternative, even a temporary solution (which I hoped would become permanent) could be found?

Unfortunately mother, taken by surprise at the sight of our little gathering, was incensed by my attempt to parley.

I could not live here, if that is what you are suggesting, Em!

Yet you lived for many years in a far more isolated situation, Doctor Nel pointed out calmly (not for the first time). And you were happy for most of those years. You created a productive home in a hostile environment with the work of your own hands and a good mind. Surely living here you could do the same, with far fewer challenges?

He cares for her, I thought. Anyone can see it. Did Danie suspect that his father was not a disinterested party? Did mother?

She replied with a catch in her voice.

The Kalahari Desert is unique. And the farm was a kind of miracle. I apologise if I lack tact, but Upington is ugly in both appearance and spirit; it could never become my home. Here, I am a hated foreigner; not even your friendship, Jacques, can change that.

Well, what of Cape Town, then? It is a charming city, blessed with oceans and mountains, and many English-speakers to boot. You would find work there quite easily.

Mother shook her head. I want to go home. I want to go back to England.

Home? I cried. England is no longer your home! It has not been your home for longer than I have been alive! You hate big cities and cold wet weather, you have told me so all my life. And what of those hordes of people in London, mother? How will you live with them?

I will not, replied mother coolly. We will not be in London. Not even for a day. My friend Olivia has written. She lives now in a town called Ely, in Cambridgeshire. She will be delighted to welcome us. She writes that there is a school nearby which is in need of teachers, and we may board with her for as long as we choose in the home she inherited from her uncle. It is spacious, and she lives there alone except for a housekeeper.

How convenient! I spat. You have known this news, I think, for some days, yet you did not say a word to me!

I glared at her and strode from the room, Poppie and Danie in my wake.

Ten days later, we were picked up by a transport wagon bound for Cape Town. Our fellow travellers were a woman and her two young children, whose father was fighting with the Boer army, journeying to grandparents who lived in Paarl, outside Cape Town; and tiny elderly twin sisters who reminded me of two speckled birds. They were spinsters, being shuttled from one brother, a farmer in the Upington area, to a second brother who was a businessman in Cape Town. The two Griqua drivers, known to Doctor Nel, were experienced, familiar with the route and with the detours furthest from the sounds of gunfire. Though the war continued unabated, they assured us it was unlikely we would encounter either Boer or British troops for much of the way; possibly the latter only in the approaches to Cape Town. And both British and Boer soldiers, said the drivers, would go out of their way not to harm women and children.

The evening before we left, I eavesdropped for what turned out to be one of the last times I would attempt that underhand activity. The conversation I overheard took place between mother and Doctor Nel, again on Elise's porch, and was of such an intense nature that I believe any thought of her daughter was entirely absent from mother's mind.

... You are a good man, Jacques! Your conversation is stimulating and your knowledge broad. Your attentions flatter me beyond my due. But none of this signifies. You are blessed with a wife and a wonderful son. I am a woman with a broken heart and a profoundly damaged spirit, of no use to anyone. My son has gone from me, I have left my husband; I have no home. My life, were it not for my precious daughter, would be worthless.

I listened avidly, shamelessly, as my mother's name on Doctor Nel's lips lingered in the air like a caress.

Deirdre: I must speak. I love you. I know that even were you to stay, my love is useless to you. It is my own burden to bear, and I must learn to live with it.

A drawn-out sigh. Yet the thought that you will be across the seas from me is a hard one indeed. I am aware of the impropriety – of the foolishness – of succumbing to selfish emotions that would deeply wound others dear to me, but the simple truth is this: I would give up everything for you. He paused. Even my own son.

Silence.

Perhaps, said Doctor Nel sadly, it is as well that you will be oceans away from me. If you stayed in Cape Town, who knows what insanity I might be capable of?

Mother murmured something in reply, but I had heard all I needed to, and there was no benefit in it other than an aching throat.

I spent most of my last day with Poppie and Danie in a secluded part of Elise's lush garden, near the servants' quarters where, in exchange for a few hours of daily supervision of the Van Heerdens' three children, Poppie would be housed after we left. We held hands, and I swore a solemn oath that I would return to them one day.

Though we tried hard to be brave, Poppie and I wept; even Danie's eyes were so bright they threatened to overflow.

The wagon was loaded with enough excellent food to feed the entire Boer army: fresh and dried fruits, honey, preserves, rusks, sweetmeats and dried meats of all kinds, including lengths of wors that hung from the rafters of the wagon and would permeate our crowded rest for many nights with a gamy, salty odour of wood smoke and dried blood.

By the time we creaked and rolled our way out of town, the road ahead seemed to offer a respite to troubling thoughts of past and future: parts unknown beckoned, and an enticing valley of peace stretched between gloomy departures from all I held dear to friendless arrivals at foreign destinations. The thought of idle days spent drifting through wide landscapes lifted my spirits.

Not far distant from the town, the silence of the barren land held sway. Eccentric jigsaws of molten rock drew my eye, and koppies, flat-topped and pointed, thrust upwards into the light. Raptors, dark specks in the blinding skies, circled above us, seeking dead animals on the track. At first, every rodent, bird, oddly shaped stone or clump of grass caught my attention as I dangled my legs happily over the edge of the wagon, filling my lungs with the pure cold air and my vision with horizons that had no end. But it did not take long for the jolting, monotonous days and icy nights, the scalding heat, pelting rain and gusting winds to tarnish my mood of optimism. The two drivers, Jan and Piet, the war uppermost in their minds, kept up a gruelling pace on the potholed, sinking suture through the baked ground. If it rained, mud sucked at the wheels, and we were forced to dismount as the drivers laboured to free the wagon. My skin, either sodden or dry as sand, tingled and itched perpetually, and my bones and organs felt as if they were jostling one another for position.

But as the days passed, the real problem was my mind: it deteriorated into an unmanageable jungle of repetitive thoughts. When clouds were thick and heavy in the sky or when a relentless sun made walking unbearable, I spent hours and hours brooding. I dredged up every error I had made, real or imagined, and berated myself miserably for the neglect and stupidity that had caused me to lose my father, my home, my friends.

As bad as it was for me, it was worse for the elderly spinsters and the children, the latter desperate for distraction. At times, boredom and bruises got the better of me: I took to teasing the twittery old twins, who easily became flustered and nervous, and played tricks on the two young children until they wept in frustration and the weary adults begged for mercy. I was often dispatched by mother to sit up front with Jan and Piet, who, ever watchful of their surroundings, bore my company patiently.

To my great disappointment, there was not a single sighting of a soldier, Boer or Brit.

At last, to my delight, we heard the distant stutter of gunfire. That after-noon, I was sitting beside Jan, who was driving, when a dot appeared far along the track. As we drew nearer, it became a mule cart, drawn by four scrawny mules and driven by a weather-scarred brown man and his wife. From time to time, mule carts trotted past, driven by labourers from the surrounding farms. The driver usually stopped and exchanged a few words with Jan and Piet. Sometimes they asked for water, tobacco or dried meat. Later, when certain of our supplies had dwindled, either Jan or Piet climbed on the cart and accompanied the labourers to the farmholdings where they worked. There, they replenished our provisions and topped up our water supplies, and brought them back to the wagon.

This particular cart was very slow, labouring beneath rickety bundles tied on with worn bits of rope and string. Gaunt legs of home-made chairs, a splintered table and unidentifiable animal skins were bunched together, resembling the unruly corpse of a slaughtered beast. An ancient woman – presumably the grandmother of the clan – drooped from the cart like a strip of dried meat, and five young members of the family walked behind it, looking hungry and exhausted.

The laden vehicle came to a stop alongside the wagon, and Jan reined in the oxen. The man and his wife dismounted, greeting the drivers and me. I slipped off the seat and followed as they approached the back of the wagon. They peered inside without expression, their hands cupped. The twins shrank back and began an anxious chirping.

They will not hurt you, I called scornfully; they are hungry, that is all.

Though the interior of the wagon was dim compared with the brightness of the day, I imagined their eyes and hands straining for the thick links of suspended sausage that still remained. Mother reached up, untied a large piece of sausage, and handed it to them. The man thanked us in Afrikaans, and the woman made an odd little curtsey as she took the meat.

Jan came around and spoke to the couple, asking if they had news of the war.

The man replied that they were fleeing from the fighting that was closing in on their home. He mentioned a Boer leader named Smuts, who was conducting tireless raids on British encampments in the area to the north and east of us, near a settlement called Calvinia. The raids generated wild, prolonged bouts of shooting from the British, which caused havoc among the inhabitants of the area, but killed scarcely any Boers.

The next day, as we rolled past a scenic range of mountains, I spotted a scarlet stripe on the green horizon, which got denser and brighter as a marching phalanx of British soldiers, weapons flashing silver in the sun, strode proudly through the empty landscape. I could not begin to speculate what mission brought them to that limitless, unpopulated place, bound, it seemed, for nowhere.

At mid-morning one cloudy day, we began the ascent of a steep, winding track over Van Ryn's Pass, which would take us down into the valley of the Western Cape. Jan and Piet were unable to avoid this pass, because a fire raged unchecked in the region of the easier detour they usually took. The range itself was spectacular, with overhanging rocks, formidable cliffs and ravines, and caverns that brought to mind fierce predators and their lairs. But it was a challenging and punishing traverse, which took all the drivers' skill and attention. Once or twice, the wagon teetered on the rims of precipices, threatening to plummet us hundreds of yards to the valley below. My blood ran as cold as the water sliding down the rockfaces, and the twins set up a thin wailing that made me itch to toss them pell-mell over the edge.

At long last, the wagon wheels rumbled along a deeply rutted section of level track. I had never dreamed to see countryside garbed in such splendour: jade green fields rolled up against mountains so majestic that they dominated the sweep of sky, and the generous early rains of the Cape autumn had spawned verdant flora. Nodding purple, orange, yellow and white blooms greeted us as we passed, their faces smiling up at the great golden head of the rising sun. Even the children, for once, were awestruck.

Piet and Jan guided the wagon safely through the dangerous track across Piekenierskloof, and the mood of both passengers and drivers rose in tandem with the towering heights in the blue distance. Piet, the more taciturn of the two drivers, became positively verbose as the track widened and improved. He praised the people, shops and entertainments in the bustling city of Cape Town, and expressed pleasure at the prospect of staying with his uncle who lived beneath Table Mountain, where they would spend a week. After this, they would pick up passengers bound for Kimberley, and from there return to their homes in Upington.

My aches and annoyances melted away as the world around me changed with each mile. The wagon wended its way past ploughed earth, citrus orchards, fields of cabbages, potatoes and tall green mealies criss-crossed with the stick figures of busy workers; we passed settlements and towns with people everywhere eyeing us with curiosity. Wonderful oranges and other fresh fruits and vegetables were for sale, and we bartered for them eagerly, offering biltong and whatever else we had left of our depleted supplies.

One cool morning, we reached the busy town of Paarl, where the young mother and her two children were welcomed by excited grandparents. They bade us farewell and good fortune, and we continued on the last leg of our journey to Cape Town. Table Mountain reared up ahead of us, a cloud-free, compelling vision on the horizon.

Cape Town to London

THE FLAT TOP OF THE mountain made me think of a line drawn by a skilled but not quite steady hand. I squinted up, feeling as tiny and insignificant as an insect. I thought of the joy and excitement of my parents, who were married in a church at the foot of Table Mountain, and a faint melancholy gripped me.

Mother walked with me for a while alongside the wagon as we entered the city. She looked up at the rugged heights dreamily, and I wondered what she was thinking. For much of the journey, she had been very quiet. She was kind to the old ladies and helpful to the young mother with her two children, but with a distrait, preoccupied air, as if she were already, in her mind and heart, in another place.

Were you not tempted, mother, when you first saw Cape Town and that mountain, to stay and make your life here? I asked quietly.

She answered without any detectable emotion in her voice: Your father filled my vision and fed my dreams, Em. At the time nothing else, including that extraordinary massif, seemed important.

We drove along cobbled streets, which I had never seen before. I quickly found that a big city challenged all my senses. The noise struck me like a blow; it was like nothing I had ever imagined – a clashing, shrieking, buzzing, groaning discordance of sound compounded of wheeled traffic on stony streets, horses and cattle, and people who shouted the louder to be heard above the cacophony of vendors selling fruit, vegetables, flowers, fish, fabric, buttons, hats and everything under the sun.

Accustomed all my life to the gentle rustlings and rumblings of nature, to the rough and tumble of dramatic weather systems, to silences so profound that my own breathing seemed loud, the shock was considerable.

At the foot of that symmetrical mountain was the sea, which I had seen only in picture books. Blue and green, spitting seaweedy foam the colour of tobacco, it was mesmerising. Salty draughts of air bubbled in my lungs, and I could not help but think of father, who had spoken of the sea as one would of an old and trusted friend, long deceased. Why, I wondered, did he not describe the dazzle and drama, the boldness and vigour? I longed to tarry, but Jan and Piet were adroitly manoeuvring the ox-wagon in the density of horse-drawn traffic, driven by the particular urgency which must herald the end of all their journeys.

Not long after our first sighting of the ocean, we arrived at our lodging house in a shady area called Gardens, which boasted lush groves of densely leaved trees, a world away from the subdued hues of a kameeldoring or a witgat. I knew from mother's teachings about the first vegetable garden at the Cape, planted in 1652, and felt gratified to be standing on such historical ground.

Jan and Piet unloaded our baggage. Waving farewell with their crops – even the twins waved – they left us outside the lodging house. I felt unexpectedly forlorn.

We found ourselves at the entrance of a pleasant abode, adorned on both sides by rows of carefully tended flowers. A man was on his knees on the stoep, polishing the red floor to a burnished gleam; his knees, as he sat back on his haunches to allow us to pass, were shiny and scaly. The ammoniac smell of polish vied with the odour of perspiration.

The lodgings had been recommended by Doctor Nel, who had praised

Mrs Bester, the owner, as a reliable and stringently hygienic hostess. As we readied ourselves to knock, a strident voice pierced the heavy wooden door.

Boy, I can see you resting! Get on with your work instead of wasting time staring at your betters! Girl! Come and fetch the baggage!

Mrs Bester, unlike the rest of humanity, saw through wooden doors. A large, black-clad, lipless lady, she took command of all her guests as a general would his army. Her servants, I learned, were 'boy' or 'girl' to her, regardless of their names or age. A hard taskmistress, she abhorred noise, even the clattering of pots and pans in the kitchen, but especially the wheeled traffic that rumbled noisily by in the street outside her door.

She took a dislike to me on sight, and developed a habit, when I was in the vicinity, of lowering her eyes to avoid the sight of me. At breakfast, the day after our arrival, she fixed on me – the only young person in the room – a pinkish glare that reminded me of the screeching gulls, and imparted the rules of the house. I suspect they were trumped up for me alone; it was clear she was unused to the company of a fourteen-year-old girl, and would have chosen, if she had been able, to remain so.

The lodgings, thanks to Mrs Bester's sharp pink eye and the hard labour of her employees, were indeed spotless, but the food left much to be desired, the greasy meals sinking like stones in my stomach. Fortunately, food was of little importance compared with sightseeing and other exciting missions, such as the purchase of a new dress for each of us, and new bonnets. If Mrs Bester's dismay was not sufficient spur to mother's decision to augment our travel-stained and unfashionable dresses, the stares of impolite city folk were. Their rudeness caused mother to lower her eyes, but in childish retaliation, I treated our critical inspectors to some hyena-like grimaces, which made them gape back at me, looking much like hyenas themselves.

I noticed that mother's mood seemed lighter in Cape Town, the lines around her eyes softer and her mouth less grim. We followed Mrs Bester's eager directions to a well-recommended seamstress who sold inexpensive, pretty fabrics. I chose pale blue for my dress – mother said that it flattered my colouring – and she found an emerald green that deepened the colour of her hazel eyes. The seamstress promised us completed garments within three days. From there we walked to a shop that sold hats and bonnets, and mother chose a bonnet for each of us. I enjoyed the shopping expedition very much, but did not take as much pleasure in the results. Mother looked well in her new headdress, but reflected in the shop's candlelit mirror, my irrepressible hair gave the baneful illusion of setting the confection atop it on fire.

After our purchases, we strolled to the harbour to locate a shipping office to reserve our places on board a ship bound for England. It was the first opportunity for a close inspection of the ocean, and I was captivated, even a little intimidated, by its restless activity. At my insistence, we went down to the water's edge, where the waves lapped almost at our skirts. I removed my unsuitable shoes (hartebeest hide, well made by Kobie) and worked my feet into the wet sand. It felt marvellous. I thought fleetingly of the dry, crusty feel of the desert sand between my toes, then wiped my feet on the hem of my skirt, donned my shoes and rejoined mother, who was watching the boats, a smile on her face for the first time in months.

Mother reserved two second-class berths on a mailship of the Union Castle Line with the evocative name of Falcon, due to leave Cape Town in a fortnight's time to sail to London via Walvis Bay – where, in 1884, father's African adventure had begun.

I would have preferred to stay in the city longer. I found the harbour fascinating. Sleek seals sunned themselves on rocks and walls, and seabirds – gulls, gannets, Cape oyster catchers – foraged busily. There were sailing boats and fishing boats, with fisherfolk displaying their glistening wares. Some of the fish, flat-eyed, slightly bloody, with brilliant silver scales, were large and still alive, flopping around on the ground in a frantic search for the watery home from which they had been unceremoniously pulled. I felt pity for them; then, stupidly, pity for myself.

British soldiers were everywhere, in pairs or small groups, lounging against walls or bargaining for goods in the stores. Well-dressed couples, the men in black suits and top hats, the women in fashionable headdresses and colourful, flounced dresses, promenaded against the backdrop of tall buildings with flashing windows.

With a god's eye view of it all was the mountain, cloud-covered or cloud-free, at times dark and forbidding. As the days passed, my ears became more attuned to the din and multilingual jargon of the city, and I learned to shut out those sounds that were more intrusive. I inhaled the briny, sticky breath of the sea and a green sharpness that drifted down on wintry breezes from the mountains; I sniffed the fishiness of the fish traders and their catch, and the ever-present odour of woodsmoke, and filleted out the swill of oil, tar, iron, rust, drains, manure, offal and oniony perspiration: the carrion sweepings of labour, of beasts of burden, commerce and industry.

Mother's anxiety in the first week to please Mrs Bester had disappeared. Perhaps she was feeling more herself; perhaps donning new, smarter clothes went some way to repair her self-regard. Whatever the cause, her manner with our landlady became more distant and formal, yet this frigid politeness seemed only to feed Mrs Bester's burgeoning esteem for her.

Delighted that Mrs Bester had been bested, I, clad in my new dress, was beginning to feel quite the lady; to my chagrin, unlike mother, my newfound composure did not make a marked impression on our hostess.

Mother, however, noticed. I am glad that you are more polite, Em.

I shrugged. We have become quite formal in Cape Town, mother, I remarked. Is it the city, or is it our new clothes?

We are no longer on a farm in the Kalahari, Em, replied mother seriously. We reside in a city, and our future lives will be spent in another. It behoves us to behave as city people do.

That only confirms what I have always known, mother. I am not a city person.

Her face darkened. Withhold your judgement, for once, Em. Have patience. We are on the brink of new lives, and must adjust accordingly.

After two weeks, I did not believe that I would ever adjust to a new life if it was to be in a city. I admired the natural beauty of Cape Town, but there was much about the place that dismayed and distressed me as well. I had ample opportunity to note that there were different categories of city people, and that the benefits of city life were much reduced when it came to dark-skinned people. Humble and hard-working, they performed all the hard labour of city life, cleaning, laundry, cooking, gardening, building, road and harbour maintenance, and seemed little appreciated and frequently abused. Beggary was rife, even among children who should have been in school: beggars ranged from tiny mites to gangling, hungry-eyed youths and crabbed, crippled adults whose hands were always extended, eyes riveted on any object about our persons that might be worth a few pennies.

I had seen poverty in Upington, but this was far worse: here the poor swarmed like fleas snatching a bite now and then from the peacock wealth around them, displayed in rich clothing, gold chains and flashing gemstones, and flamboyant buggies pulled by splendid, high-headed horses.

When I pointed out these inequalities to mother, she shook her head. It is not right, but these things are a part of city life, Em.

Why is that, mother? I asked, genuinely curious. Why should hard-working people be maltreated – as Mrs Bester maltreats Betsy and John? Why is poverty a part of city life?

It is the way of the world, Em, replied mother inadequately. It is time to dress for dinner. Mrs Bester dislikes it if we are late.

I did not like the way of the world. Or perhaps it was the way the world worked in towns and cities.

England

I WAS PERVERSELY pleased on the day we left Cape Town: mist and rain obscured Table Mountain, Lion's Head and most of the city, and I could not behold their beauty fading away into the distance. This diminished the sense of loss that was becoming almost familiar, a sensation not unlike an empty stomach, and the effect similarly weakening. Mother and I stood, well-wrapped, on the second-class deck among a crowd of others deprived of a last glimpse of the scenery which, all agreed, was magnificent. The deck shook under my feet, and a mildewy fog subdued the metallic odours of anchors and chains. The railing was wet, but I clutched it, suddenly awash with misery: I was leaving Africa, my Kalahari, our beloved farm. I was leaving my father.

Tears dropped onto the railing. I felt mother's arm around my shoulders. It will be all right, my darling.

My hands shook on the railing. I knew it would not.

Yet I took to the sea as if I had known it all my life. As the daughter of a sailor, perhaps this was not surprising. Even our cramped quarters, which had almost no light and little air, and were separated from the quarters of others by only a flimsy partition, did not inconvenience me in the least. Mother, however, was disgruntled by the lack of privacy. She took the only bunk, and I slept happily in a hammock strung from the ceiling, imagining myself in a boat at sea, braving the waves. I had never slept better.

I spent every possible waking hour on deck, savouring the brisk breezes, and alert for sightings of schools of dolphins or whales. Mother was unwell from the first, the vigorous waves slapping against the hull causing her to suffer severe seasickness. I kept her supplied with fresh water, and if she would take it, a little soup, and regularly cleaned out an extra bucket I begged off an elderly sailor who took pity on her indisposition.

When not tending mother, or gazing out at stormy seas (which inspired no fear in me at all, though they did in many others) I played cards with various older women, and two brothers returning to school in England, the only people of my age in second class. We played whist, rummy and piquet, though mother, when she could summon up the energy, expressed weary disapproval.

After dinner, I watched the dancing, or sneaked into first class with the amused collusion of a young sailor. There, largely overlooked, I observed people doing what they did less ostentatiously in second class. Over-rouged, overdressed women minced along in silly, stylish shoes, and porcine men in tight collars and starched shirts chewed on cigars and discussed among themselves the politics and economics of war, and the multiplicity of opportunities to make money from it. Judging from their talk and from their bejewelled wives, many among them had already reaped generous benefits from the spilt blood of others.

To my delight, the library on board was quite good, and I got through many of the books on offer. I would wrap myself up warmly and sit on deck for hours at a time, gritting my teeth through War and Peace and Crime and Punishment. I finished Wuthering Heights, weeping over doomed love and yearning to experience for myself a love that would endure beyond the grave. I read until it grew dim and my limbs froze to columns of ice, resentful of the encroaching dark that plucked me rudely from another world. I would blink it away as best I could, creak clumsily to my feet and go down to the cabin to see if mother was in any state to accompany me to dinner.

There was one book I read, The Story of an African Farm, which gave me a sense of common cause with its writer. It offered insights into a different kind of all-consuming love: the attachment to home and the land beneath one's feet. For a long time after I finished reading it, I sat in the dark library and thought about my own homeless feet and the land that had been wrenched from beneath them. That land filled my heart with pain and longing and love, and a kind of dread that I might never see it again. It will forget me, I thought painfully, and those I love will forget me too, because I have abandoned them all.

Early in the voyage, I befriended a middle-aged couple returning home to England from a visit to their son, a soldier stationed in the British army in Cape Town. The lady tripped going down some stairs and were it not for me putting out an arm to break her fall, she would certainly have done herself an injury. When mother was well enough to come to dinner, I introduced her to Mr and Mrs Litton, and we were invited to share their table. They were sympathetic to mother's indisposition, but tactful and unintrusive. I think mother, constantly unwell, was relieved that I was in good hands.

For the first weeks, despite mother's sensitivity to the turbulence, the weather was not extreme and the ship made good progress; but in the fourth week a storm blew up. The sky grew dark, and enormous waves whipped and spun wildly around the ship. I watched from the deck, soaked through, as the ship slid into craters of monstrous size. The entire vessel seemed to stand on end, then plunge downwards, driven by the brute force of the swell. I was cautioned to go below, and gazed through the porthole in the second-class lounge as a wave like the maw of a whale swallowed up the entire ship, which foundered for a breathless moment in its throat, then was vomited up with astounding violence.

Eventually, slightly queasy from the pitching of the ship, I remembered mother and ran below. I saw at once that she was very ill. She was retching helplessly, close to collapse, a stringy spool of spittle hanging from the side of her mouth. I rushed to hold her, but was forced to bend over the bucket myself. I vomited up what felt like every meal I had ever eaten.

After the storm, the ocean was flat and calm. One by one, the passengers drifted onto the deck, wan in recovery, and sat limply in the pale sunlight as the ship floated on gleaming, listless waters. I saw dolphins and, in the distance, the spume of a whale. Mother, thin and white, sat beside me, tucked up in blankets. I carefully fed her spoon after spoon of a chicken soup whose golden globules turned my own still tender stomach. For once, she sipped obediently, appearing not to notice the less than appetising oily film.

At last, she pushed the spoon aside. Her voice, close to my ear, was still scratchy from her sore throat. We will be home soon now, Em.

For once, I did not contradict her.

We left Cape Town with its scenery obscured by mist, and we docked at East India Dock at Blackwall, along the Thames River, in a dense fog. For all that we could see of the river or London, we might as well have been stone blind. I tasted sleet on my tongue, and fog stung my nostrils with a pernicious blend of rust, corrosion, mould and horse droppings. We descended from the ship, and were immediately engulfed in a sour tide of unwashed humanity, bawling in accents that ground in my ears like gravel: 'Over 'ere, nice comftible lodgings, good warm beds, safe transport, over 'ere lydies and gen'lmen'.

The Littons were a godsend. Mr Litton, with one hand supporting mother and the other his wife, called to me in front of him, clutching tightly to a small bag of our documents and essentials.

Hurry along, Em, our Will is sure to be nearby, look to your things, pickpockets are rife as rats and gimlet-eyed!

His experience guided us through customs, and through the maelstrom and clangour that exploded around us, all of it cloaked in a sulphurous fog that made the perpetrators as invisible as a company of raucous phantoms. Advancing blindly, I fell slightly behind, and felt a thrill of fear that I would lose them to the leaden embrace of the fog. I was profoundly grateful to hear, above the squawking accents all about me, Mr Litton's stentorian voice: This way, Em, follow closer now! Then, joyfully, Will, our Will, we are safely home! We have missed you so!

The Littons insisted that we spend what was left of that day and the night in their home before we embarked on the next stage of our journey, which was to catch The Great Eastern Railway train from London Liverpool Street Station to Cambridge, where we would be met by Olivia Parrington.

Mother was too exhausted to argue, and we were driven in a closed buggy drawn by two spindly horses to the Littons' home which, we were told, was close to the city centre.

Nothing of London could be seen. The great city remained submerged in a spongy yellowish soup – the viscous 'London special' – which grew ever thicker. I admired Will's skill in negotiating street after street in which the vehicle ahead could scarcely be seen until we were almost on top of it. I would have liked to have at least had a sighting of Buckingham Palace and some of the grand buildings and museums of which I had read, but mother seemed feeble and ill, and concern for her overshadowed any disappointment I might have felt.

Though she wanted to leave London as soon as possible, she was in no state to do so. Once inside the Littons' pleasant firelit home, she lay on the bed in the small spare bedroom with her eyes closed. I consulted with Mrs Litton. Kind, hospitable soul that she was, she felt mother's brow and said she found no fever; that the lethargy was probably owing to prolonged bouts of seasickness and the malnourishment that resulted from them. She suggested that we stay a day or two longer to give mother an opportunity to recover her strength.

Mother, stirring restlessly without opening her eyes, spoke up. I thank you for your kindness, madam, but we must leave on the morrow. My friend Olivia expects us.

She fell asleep. I hovered in the doorway. Her head was moving from side to side on the pillow, and she murmured a word, over and over. It sounded to me like father's name.

The steam engine pawed the ground and hissed, hot to charge to the next station. I would have enjoyed the novel sight of it, and the sights of the bustling, brightly lit Liverpool Street Station, had mother not been so unwell. Despite this, she had prevailed, fending off the Littons' concern, and accepting the offer of their obliging son Will to transport us to the station.

Once there, she perched uncomfortably on the edge of a crowded bench, waiting with the luggage and a porter while I stood in a long queue and purchased the tickets, struggling to understand the babble of conversation taking place around me.

The carriage we finally entered had worn, cracked seats, dark with soot and littered with debris. Mother sank into the nearest seat, leaving me to manage the baggage and tip the porter. The carriage filled up quickly with damp-smelling people, stamping their feet against the cold. Eyeing mother's blue eyelids and bloodless lips, I wondered whether it would not have been wiser to have followed the advice of our hosts, and purchased first class tickets. But mother had been adamant that we could not afford the additional expense, so I had given in and bought the cheaper tickets.

The train whistled and jolted, and our journey began at last. Ramshackle buildings stood in endless rows on the outskirts of town. There were patches of green where vegetables grew, where cows grazed or pigs wallowed, and ponds with ducks and geese. We passed platform after platform, scummy with dirt, scattered about with bedraggled, half-frozen people. Often I saw little: fogbanks or driving rain smothered what outlook there was. Mother slept, snoring lightly, her mouth slightly open; but I was afraid to close my eyes for fear our unguarded baggage might be tampered with.

She was better off asleep, for she might have objected to the rank brew of fried food, vinegar, urine, perspiration and unaired clothing; to snotty noses wiped by hands that had not seen soap in many a long day; to the draughts of stale heat alternating with freezing gusts that flowed in at every station where passengers were disgorged and others embarked, all bulkily clad, glum faces fish-eyed and raw with cold and discomfort.

Though very chilly, the station at Cambridge, clean and free of debris, was a pleasant surprise. Mother, awake at last, said the town boasted one of the best universities in the world, and upkeep was a matter of pride. The porter deposited our baggage at our feet, accepted his tip, and left us. We scanned the rapidly emptying platform with some trepidation: everybody else seemed either to have somebody to meet them, or to know their direction.

A tall fair woman, sporting a smart black hat with a square of charcoal lace obscuring her face, approached us.

Mother started, her palm across her mouth, her eyes wide. Olivia? Is it you?

Indeed it was. Olivia Parrington embraced us with cries of welcome, and told us she had expected us the day before. She herded us to a covered buggy as it began to drizzle. In less than two hours, we were in her two-storeyed home, close to the renowned cathedral in the town of Ely, named for its busy eel-fishing industry. We sat down almost immediately to a marvellous tea: the table was laden with an assortment of sandwiches and fruit-filled cakes, and we were served by a plump, florid lady called Jemima. I devoured the food, and even mother brightened considerably, picking at a sandwich and a slice of cake. Afterwards, the three of us sat in an elegant lounge on comfortably upholstered sofas in front of a roaring fire.

Olivia, glancing anxiously at mother, whose eyelids were already drooping in the unfamiliar warmth, bade me tell her the story of our journey.

Halfway through, I fell fast asleep.

At the reputable church school Olivia recommended highly, the nuns were strict, kind and curious. Most were also good teachers. At first, the girls, too, were inquisitive and asked questions, but I was too bereft and overwhelmed to respond in a manner that pleased them, and they soon left me alone. I found out, at last, what it was like to be learning together with many other girls, and while my parents' tutoring served me well in all subjects, the experience of being in a classroom felt unreal: I was the outsider, the intruder, yet I felt intruded upon, as out of place as a wild animal among a pack of domestic dogs.

In the cold, full classroom, as my breath spiralled in smoky puffs from my lips, I would frequently be overtaken by crippling fits of melancholy and loneliness. My desk mate, a large, pale, pimpled girl, soon tired of my dullness and it was not long before I sat alone at my desk. With the exception of one or two girls, outcasts themselves, the others found me dingy and odd, and in truth I could not blame them. As daily lessons droned about me, I stared out of the window at the rain-heavy sky and the brilliant green of the lawns, and saw instead vast hot open spaces, high rusty dunes, and the beloved face of father. But the thick grey cloud, the dimness and dampness outside the classroom, persisted, clinging to me as if determined to erase the images of home; to blight my inner eye with dreariness and gloom. Still, for long months, I awoke each morning to the expectation of heat and light, only to find my vision narrowed to the point where I longed to close my eyes and dwell quietly with my nightly dreams of the desert.

After father and my dear friends, the greatest loss, a dark hollow in my very soul, was the absence of light – the radiant, enigmatic, beating heart of the Kalahari. It was replaced by the thin mundanity of town life, by order, predictability and a way of life dictated by others; by a society from which I longed to turn my face. At times, the dank English mornings filled me with such rage against mother, that, seated opposite her and Olivia at breakfast, I would lower my eyes in fear that the window would shatter from the hostility that exploded from behind my eyeballs. But when these fits of rage occurred, both mother and Olivia seemed impervious, oblivious; and there was nothing else to do but get on with my day.

After a year, the deprivation of light became, at last, less brutal. I found that my vision had narrowed to accommodate it. With the pressing need to adjust, to move on, to live with new sensations and unaccustomed clutter, the listening soul loses the delicate, precise ear of the desert, and becomes silent and deaf.

At school, the nuns praised me for my academic achievements, and wrote in reports that I had adjusted beautifully and was a model pupil. Two gentle girls, neighbours, became my friends. Too tactful to ask about my absent father, they asked about the Kalahari. I tried to answer as best I could, but found that I had put my home away in a hidden corner of my heart, and could not find the words to do it justice. Thus I fed my friends titbits, and changed the subject. I visited their crowded homes, we played games and we did our homework together. But I kept my home inside me, and shared it with nobody. Gradually, the dreams I had nightly, and the dull disappointment upon waking from them in the dark mornings, began to diminish.

Olivia, Jemima, my two friends, school and town life, took over my thoughts. But none found a place in my heart. In the desert I seldom knew fear. The fear I felt in town was that this small busy world would corrode the vision of my one true home. I knew I must learn to live comfortably with the dictates and constraints of the former if only to preserve my vision of the latter; for society punishes its outcasts cruelly. I could not afford to number among them.

Unlike mother, I wrote my thoughts and feelings down, and found great relief in doing so. I knew mother had no such confidante: Olivia, who tried wistfully to fulfil that role, was gently rebuffed many times.

Mother and I spent little time alone. Olivia was almost always with us. It was not her fault, but perhaps her presence inhibited us from sharing something of what I imagined were our separate burdens. I wrote down a good deal about mother's lingering ill-health, her few words to me, her frequently pained expression that spoke of struggles that surely must have been difficult and lonely. For all that, they were contained within her. The absence of real communication – a wall ever present between us – and the long months that became years of our spiritual separation prevented us from discussing our truncated lives; perhaps I was too self-engrossed with my own alienation to comprehend the desolation she must have felt at having given so much of herself that – in the end – turned out to be not nearly enough.

What did seem clear and unequivocal was that there was no going back. My childhood was over. Would that we had been able, as we sat by the fireside, or in brief moments by her bedside or mine, or on the short walks she sometimes managed, to express something of our hurt, loneliness, rage, grief, whatever the feelings were – it might have gone differently. Once or twice, I did try to speak, but mother turned away, complaining of a headache, and we returned in silence to Olivia's fireside.

At some point, we came to a spiritual parting of the ways that was irreparable. I could not say with certainty when this happened. A coldness grew inside me, and my heart closed towards her. It was not what she had done to me or to others, but what she had done – continued to do – to herself. The past was unalterable, but she made little effort to build a new life. She chose apathy instead, and a growing dependency on Olivia.

One Saturday, when mother was sitting in bed, knitting, I brought her a tray with tea, and she bade me sit for a while.

Will you read me a little of your journal, Em, something from the early days? she asked.

I could not. Instead, I rose to my feet. You will excuse me, mother; I have an exam on Monday and must begin studying. Jemima will fetch your tray when you are finished.

Em, darling, I do not mean to intrude. I only wish to …

I shook my head and left the room.

My dear ones,

I miss you both badly and long to see your faces. Olivia is the kindest of souls and seems happy to have our company in her well-kept home. She employs a busy, cheerful housekeeper, Jemima, whom she treats with consideration and esteem, unlike the disrespect and rudeness accorded servants in South Africa. The household is orderly and well run, and Ely, a bustling market town, is a nice enough place, its gardens and fields as green and lush and full of flowers as a rainy town should be. It has rained, as I have said before, almost every day since we arrived, but hopefully this will change in the coming weeks. Olivia says the region is among the coldest in England and had she not inherited her lovely home (and a generous portfolio of stocks and bonds) from her uncle, she may not have chosen to retire and live out her days here!

There is a brown river with much boating and fishing activity, the latter mainly for eels, thick, slimy, wriggling creatures, rather ugly, whose heads and bodies are summarily chopped up for sale, yet still thrust about as if each part has separately reincarnated itself! A maze of breweries and pubs crowd the waterside, but the smell is strong and unpleasant; I am told that the river regularly claims victims among those who overindulge, lose their direction and fall in. (For some reason, this makes me think of Kobie, who is better off where he is!) The small island of Babylon, opposite the waterside, is more interesting: it has two thriving potteries – Babylon ware pottery – and basket makers there use the osiers and willows to weave their wares. When the rain lets up, I walk in the region of the great cathedral I described in my last letter. On Thursdays, at the Market Place in the town square, rows of stalls sell a variety of produce and other goods, and I often spend time there, strolling about. Once, I saw a cabbage proudly displayed that was almost the girth of two men!

I have discovered verdant fields close to town where cows and sheep graze, and though nothing could have prepared me for the wet, wet countryside, I enjoy the tranquillity of these damp walks.

Mother is not doing well. As Olivia says, it is not only her physical ailments, which are considerable; it is also the lowness of her spirits. There are days when her breath is so short that her lips turn blue, and the doctor is called; other days her breathing is easier and she can sit up in bed and turn her hand to mending, knitting or reading. I fear she may never become strong enough to take up the teaching post obtained for her by Olivia (the headmistress is a friend of hers) and I am uncertain how we will earn our keep. When I broach the subject to Olivia, she becomes quite grim-faced and says she would not take a penny from us whether mother was working or not. I smile at her, but I know father would scoff and say we are nothing more than charity cases!

I enjoy my studies. The school, as I have mentioned, is good, and the nuns kind. I have two friends at last. I like them, but they are quite different from you and will never become best friends. Everything about home seems very far away, and talking of it – and you – is painful; so I do not.

Poppie, my dear, you may not understand this, and I do not blame you for it, but I miss father sorely, though I know that the injury he has done you is unforgivable.

I miss you both very much too, and look forward to your news, no matter how long it takes to get here!
I send a Table Mountain of love to both of you,
Em

I posted the letters to Danie's home, but addressed them to both him and Poppie. Filled with artificial cheer, they took on a monotonous similarity. I wondered if this was the cause of the lengthy gaps between correspondence, theirs lapsing somewhat as mine droned on. I wrote to father every week, trusting that my letters would somehow reach him. In each one I wrote that I loved and missed him, and always would; that I longed to see the farm and the dear faces of Brandbooi, Meisie, Doekie and everybody. I asked him to read parts of my letters to them, so that they would learn something of my life in England.

When mother appeared a little stronger, I suggested we take a slow walk to Ely Cathedral, which she had not yet visited. I had already toured it on my own, and it had left a lasting impression. The cathedral, one of the best examples of Romanesque architecture in England, dominates the town. In the early fourteenth century, the Norman tower collapsed, and Alan of Walsingham designed a central tower that seems to float unsupported above the crossing of the cathedral. This so-called 'lantern tower' is actually formed by a series of massive oak beams, recently restored; much of the glorious stained glass is also quite recent. The cathedral is spacious inside, and gas heated for the most part, so is something of a refuge from the cold. After exploring its many features, notably the Norman and Gothic carvings, one can sit on a bench in quiet contemplation of the remarkable creative energy expended by men in the name of their God.

We enjoyed a brief exploratory stroll, after which mother sat alone on a bench with her eyes closed for some time. I was not convinced that the marvel she had just viewed was in her mind, nor that she was dozing. I held back from disturbing her, hoping she was taking the opportunity to contemplate the workings of her own heart. I could not help wondering, if she was doing so, what she found there.

After her first visit, I accompanied mother to the cathedral whenever she felt well enough to take light exercise. Sometimes I would leave her there, and do some shopping in town. I asked her, once, whether she prayed. She did not reply. I found her attachment to the place ironic, and perhaps she felt the same way: she had always denied that God was more present in a temple of any nature, yet she appeared to find comfort inside one of the most elaborate structures built in His name.

Perhaps she did find succour in the echoing chambers, but I do not believe she found God there. After shopping or walking about, I would return to escort her home, only to find her so removed that she would neither hear my whisper nor respond to the gentle touch on her arm. When I planted myself in front of her, I saw her wide-eyed gaze was not directed outward, but so deeply inward that a fey quality haloed her like a cloudy ghost. Was she meditating, praying, in some kind of trance? On one occasion, immediately after I touched her arm, she turned blindly to me and said, *Meisie.* Did the hushed seclusion of the cathedral enable her to communicate in some way with the people she had loved and left behind?

A year passed, then two. Mother did not teach or tutor. Her health see-sawed. For days she would not stir from her bed; then, abruptly, she would wake in the morning slightly better, her colouring improved. I observed that she talked less and less. Olivia did not seem to mind this; or perhaps, being a talkative person herself, she did not even notice. After I left for school on the days mother was too unwell to leave her bed, Olivia or Jemima would tenderly assist her with her ablutions. Afterwards, Olivia would sit at the bedside and read to her articles from the local newspaper, on subjects ranging from the news of the town to events in the world at large.

I spent many afternoons after school with my new friends, going to shops, the theatre, picnics (when the weather permitted) and doing homework together. I felt comfortable with them, and they confided their exploits to me. I had little to contribute, but they blamed the demands of mother's invalidism for the lack of adventure in my life, and were generous with their sympathy. The truth was that I enjoyed my time with them, but spent many weekends and holidays reading, or in solitary walks among fields of flowers, ankle deep in mud and barely noticing. I was neither happy nor miserable.

I brought home reports of my academic prowess at school, where my teachers described me as gifted, imaginative and disciplined. The marks I received reflected this praise. Olivia's delight far outweighed my own, her response striking me as more maternal than mother's mild, dreamy approval. In a burst of enthusiasm, Olivia invited me to accompany her on a visit to Cambridge University. I confess its noble temples impressed me profoundly, presiding over green pastures as smooth and gleaming as the shaven cheeks of the learned black-cloaked gentlemen who strode along the corridors, bent on who knew what lofty missions within those sacred portals. I spied them at their lecterns, looming above their audiences like marabou storks that had cornered their prey. I noticed few women worshipping at those altars of higher knowledge, and those that I did see appeared harried and driven; it occurred to me that perhaps they were not nearly so assured as their male counterparts of their rightful place in that rarefied atmosphere.

Over lunch in an eating house near the university, Olivia tapped my arm with her spoon.

Cambridge University is your future, Em, she said. Your results will ensure you a place, perhaps even a scholarship.

Her brow furrowed slightly as she spoke. I knew she would have had to be blind not to have noted the minuscule numbers of women scurrying along the corridors.

Sleeping, dreaming, dozing or half awake, there were still nights when Brandbooi's hawk would swoop from behind the moon, bear down on me and transport me back to the Kalahari and to father. As we whirled through the sky, I would be buoyed by rapturous anticipation.

But always, before father could embrace me, my eyes would open. I would glance out of the window into mist, my hawk gone from me and a grey cloud blotting out the moon. A dull pain sat leadenly on my chest until the sky lightened, and the sound of Jemima's voice at the door broke my exhausted slumber.

One morning, in the bathroom, I saw a hairy black spider half the size of my hand in the enormous tub with its clawed feet. Jemima, a pile of fragrant towels in her arms, was shrill with disgust. I coaxed the poor bewildered thing onto a facecloth, opened the window, and gently placed it on the outer sill. I pitied it, as I had the beached fish in Cape Town. Perhaps the spider, too, was an unwilling migrant from warmer climes.

Poppie wrote sporadically; the letters detailed her busy days and did not describe her feelings, but she seemed content. Danie's letters, though few, were more informative; he described the weather, boat trips on the river, his sporting achievements and his plans to study medicine at the University of Cape Town, where a faculty of medicine, the first in the country, was soon to open its doors to students.

Often, after reading their letters, I would have to fight back tears, especially when Danie said he had made enquiries as best he could, but no news of father was forthcoming. He had not once been seen in town since we left.

When we had been with Olivia more than two years, on a frigid winter day when the doctor was called to tend to mother's wheezing, a letter came from Danie: his mother had died suddenly of a massive stroke. I sat down and wrote him a comforting letter, but in truth felt little regret at her passing; my sympathy was for Danie and for his warm-hearted father. I hoped Mrs Nel had gone to a better world, for she had not been fond of the one she had inhabited. Her heaven, I thought meanly, would be a place where there were no dark-skinned 'mistakes'.

The cold settled in my bones and took up permanent residence in mother's lungs, no matter how many fires were lighted and how many visits the doctor made. These visits served to distress mother further: in between fits of coughing, she worried about how they would be paid for, shaking her head at Olivia's repeated assurances that the doctor was a friend of hers and would not accept payment. (A white lie: I saw money changing hands on more than one occasion.)

I would stare despondently at her thin white hands clutching the sheet, unrelaxed even in sleep. She slept most of the afternoons away, yet woke unrested. Watching her, I debated whether her physical ailments, which worsened for days at a time, then abruptly diminished in severity, were an extension of the exertions of her spirit, engaged in a slow and uneven contest with its own extinction.

As tepid summer days were drowned by days of rain, and truncated winter afternoons grew dim and dismal, a kind of darkness seeped into my soul. Olivia would find me seated, neither reading nor studying, in the overwarm room, gazing down at mother's sleeping form. At such times, Olivia's unfailing good cheer seemed the only light in a murky tunnel.

I did not doubt mother's ill-health – her fevers, her infected lungs, her enfeebled breath wrestling with the evil climate – and there were times the old love for her almost choked me; but it did so for the very reason that it was old; and dusty, as if it had been locked away in a cupboard for far too long. As time went by, I understood that the cause of her determination to retain her embattled hold on life was me. I became morbidly persuaded that she had invoked some familial curse that would mould my future into a replica of her past, spent nursing Grandmother Dorothea. The years unravelled bleakly ahead of me, tied to her side in that quaint English town with its monumental cathedral and ubiquitous umbrellas. At the same time, I knew in my heart that her struggles could not continue; that it would not be long before she would succumb and leave me stranded in a country and a town I had grown accustomed to, but had not learned to love.

Thus, selfishly, it was my own losses Olivia found me mourning at mother's bedside. I wanted mother to know that; to acknowledge, in spite of her suffering, how much she had punished me by robbing me of my home. More than that, I wanted her to admit that same loss had robbed her of her health and strength.

One afternoon, Olivia was sitting in the rocking chair beside the fire in mother's bedroom, knitting one of her intricate cardigans, and I was doing homework on the floor. Mother, who was asleep, opened her eyes and spoke: *Personne ne m'aime, et je ne m'en plains pas.*

Olivia looked at her nonplussed – she had been a teacher of arithmetic until her retirement – and asked me to translate.

I had just received the French prize at school. 'Nobody loves me, and I blame nobody for not loving me.'

What nonsense, my dear! cried Olivia, going across to mother and taking her hand. We love you very much! We want nothing more than for you to get well.

I understood Olivia at last. The more enfeebled mother is, the more essential you are, I thought cruelly. She gives you a purpose.

Mother, I said belatedly, Olivia is right. Why do you quote some proud eighteenth-century *grande dame?*

She smiled faintly. I know you love me, Em. It is my illness that you cannot love. And that is how it should be.

I was not brave: as mother became bedridden, more dependent on others as each day passed, she and I skirted each other warily. Rather than growing closer, we became more and more remote, like two ships bound for opposite poles of the planet, mother with her agenda of staying alive for my sake, and I with mounting frustration and despair that I would never find the courage to let her go gently. At the same time, I was filled with foreboding that I would never escape her.

Bent on our separate destinies, we could not – would not – relent.

CODA

One

1914

THE ROAD FROM KIMBERLEY is rutted, dusty, wide and empty. In the heat and stillness, nothing stirs, not even a hawk circles lazily in the sky. The silence is complete, except for the car ploughing its way forward. The sun's rays are like screwdrivers in my eyeballs, the heat a blow to the side of my head. My vision, shrunk to accommodate the gloomy skies and soft colours of England, cringes from the pitiless onslaught. All of it – the heat, the silence, the unforgiving radiance of the skies – is achingly familiar; yet the sense of déjà vu is hollow, oddly flat and disconnected; as if I am looking into a mirror that blinds rather than reflects me.

How much I remember. How much I have forgotten!

But the Kalahari is waiting. I stretch my eyes wide to let in the light.

269

I feel my muscles relaxing, loosening the tightly bound ropes of custom that have long shaped my thoughts and restricted my movements. The old world is behind me now; the desert will welcome me home. Nothing in my life succeeded in expelling it. It will not have forgotten me. No matter how long my absence, my Kalahari will remember me.

Danie's hands on the wheel are confident, and the car responds gracefully, only now and then protesting at a pothole or a deep crack. I have ridden in trams before, but in a motor car never. I long to get out and stride through the barren landscape, drawing the scorching air into my lungs as if they will never rid themselves of the English climate. But the heat is intimidating, and the novelty of the ride is also an opportunity to study Danie's cool adult profile, his clenched concentration.

Well, you are back at last, he says. Does it feel strange to be here?

I look out of the window. In some ways, it does. I am unused to the light. It was almost painful at first, but my eyes are already adjusting. And the hot sun and dry air are something of a shock after the cold and damp of England.

I hesitate. I am grateful for your telegram, but it puzzled me. What possible significance can a farm in the Kalahari have to the course of the war? What does the government want with such an isolated place?

Danie does not turn to look at me, but his profile relaxes slightly.

It seems absurd, I know. Apparently they are drilling a series of boreholes along the Auob River to provide the troops with water in case of a South African invasion of German West Africa along this route – though some say it will be vice versa. There are plans afoot to divide the entire area into farms in the future; there is some Scottish surveyor with the nickname of 'Malkop' – which should tell you something – involved.

He sighs. In town they are saying that your father is German –

Half German. So what?

According to my friend, the troops arrived at the farm –

My God! Of course! I sit up and stare at him. They want the place for the well! That is what it is about!

Danie bites his lip. The entire farm is in ruins, Emma.

(Emma? What happened to Em?)

As if my ears are blocked, the meaning of his words sinks in slowly. *Ruins?* What do you mean, ruins?

Well, replies Danie hesitantly, my friend said there was nobody on the place other than an old man, sitting on a chair among ruins in the full heat of the midday sun. He was dressed in rags, and his beard reached his waist. Nearby, on his haunches, was an ancient Bushman.

The light hurts. I cover my eyes, but tears force their way between my fingers.

Father and Brandbooi.

Danie looks away. The troops asked the man who the owner of the farm was, and he said it was he. They asked him for papers to prove it, but he acted as if he did not understand them. After that, he would say nothing more: when they spoke, he looked through them as if they were not there.

He stirs uncomfortably. I have little more to tell you. The old man spat on the sand, got up and walked off into the desert. The Bushman followed.

The car careens through a deep pothole, and I am jolted from my seat. Danie's hand snakes out; before my head strikes the roof, his hand is on my hair. For an instant, his palm is hot and heavy on the thick braid. Heat spreads to my face and neck. I swipe the back of my hand across my eyes.

Sorry about the bump, he says. This road demands constant vigilance.

There is one more thing: my friend got the impression that your father was ill. He pauses. Or drunk.

My throat opens at last. They invade his land, demand his papers, threaten to steal his farm. That is sufficient to make anybody ill, would you not agree?

Do you know if he has any documentation proving ownership? If he has, he may be able to claim compensation.

I shake my head, gazing out of the window, blinking away shock and dismay.

How would I know? I have not seen him, or the farm, for more than thirteen years.

I know, says Danie gently. It will be all right.

I have heard those words before. It never is.

We stop beside some trees. Danie spreads out a light blanket, and unwraps sandwiches in waxed paper.

These are really good, I say, munching, surprised at how hungry I am.

Father made them. He became rather good with food after mother died, and even better since his illness.

What is wrong with him, Danie?

He had a heart attack some years ago. Since then he has been quite frail, and lately he is working far less.

Why did you not tell me? Why did you not write such news?

He puts his hands behind his head and lies back on the blanket.

It seemed pointless.

Why do you say that?

It was pretty obvious you were never coming home, Em. So why give you bad news?

(Em: at last.)

Because I would have wanted to know. Unlike you, Poppie did not stop writing to me – even though it has been months since her last letter. I too have been remiss, but I have had much to occupy me. Is she well? She loves working for your father; her letters were all about her job. What will happen to her if he sells the practice?

He has sold the practice. To a young doctor from Kimberley, who is marrying a girl from Upington.

That is not good news for Poppie. But with her experience, the new man should grab her.

I smile. I cannot tell you how much I am looking forward to seeing her.

Danie turns onto his stomach. The tips of his ears are pink from sunburn.

You have decided against taking over your father's practice, obviously. Have you made other plans?

I have something to tell you, Em, he says slowly. It is not good.

But I get in first.

Mother died at last, Danie. A year ago last month.

He turns over and sits up swiftly, drawing his knees to his chin. I am very sorry. Now it is my turn: why did you not write such news?

I shake my head.

What was there to say? That her death was a release for both of us? That in spite of being expected, when it finally happened, it caused me to have a kind of breakdown?

His blue eyes appraise me coolly. And why did you not come sooner to find your father? I thought you would come as soon as your mother had passed.

My hair conceals my face. I never heard from him, Danie. Not once in all the years. I wrote almost every week; I have no idea if he received even one of my letters. I wrote to him of mother's death. My last letter was a mere three months ago.

He says nothing.

I help myself to a second sandwich. Poppie is expecting me, of course. I hope she will be pleased to see me.

To my alarm, he buries his face in his arms.

I put down the sandwich, my stomach churning.

Danie's voice is muffled. Poppie is dead, Em. She died seven months ago.

Jacques Nel is a stooped silhouette, waiting at the gate. We are late, but his welcome is warm and gracious. He pretends not to notice the light in the hallway shining on my swollen eyes, as I pretend not to notice the changes in him, his attenuated frame and the white knuckles of his exposed cranium.

Dinner, served to us just before midnight, is cold chicken and roasted vegetables. Though drained from the shock of Danie's news and tired from the long journey, I tell Jacques of my mother's passing.

He nods slowly, but does not look up.

Danie may have told you. She was ill almost from the day we reached England. If it had not been for Olivia Parrington, I do not know what would have become of us.

I was very fond of your mother, he says sadly.

Yes, I know you were. She became an invalid in Ely, and was unable to work. I think the losses she suffered sapped her strength and her will more than she realised. I do not believe she cared about her life. Still, nothing could dislodge the idea that because she had deprived me of my home, she owed it to me not to leave me alone in the land of her birth. Nothing I or Olivia could say reassured her. Her stubbornness kept her alive, struggling for breath every single day.

And her love for you also, he murmurs. I am sorry that she suffered so.

He looks up at me. And that I could offer her nothing.

Smiling faintly, he says, you have become a beautiful woman, Em. I see her in your eyes. It is a comfort to me.

I fall asleep when birds are already beginning to rustle outside my window. My sleep is restless, and I wake four hours later, my mind full of Poppie. The news of Upington is hardly world news, but Danie said her story reached the newspapers of Kimberley, Johannesburg and Cape

273

Town.

As she grew older, Poppie made few friends. As was predicted, both the white and dark-skinned populace of the town avoided her. Fortunately, the Afrikaans nurse who worked for Jacques Nel, Greta Villiers, found her very helpful at work, and took a great liking to her. A mannish, impatient woman, Greta was something of an eccentric: irreligious, solitary by nature, she was indifferent to the censure of the town. The two women were often seen together. This caused something of a scandal: the more virulent of the scandalmongers whispered that the relationship was a 'sick' one – though there was no evidence to suggest anything more than a warm friendship.

After Danie's mother passed, Poppie and Greta were sometimes invited to the Nel home for dinner. Their presence upset the white neighbours. One evening, a prominent leader of the local Dutch Reformed Church knocked on the door of the Nel home. He informed Jacques Nel, who opened the door, that he had been dispatched by the neighbours to warn him of the dire consequences of mixing with black people. By happenstance, Poppie and Greta were in the kitchen, cooking dinner for the four of them. Mischievously, Jacques Nel invited the minister inside, took him into the kitchen, and introduced him to the two chefs. Invited by them to join the dinner party, he refused, clearly affronted by their impertinence and the insult to his dignity.

The relationship began a few weeks after that night. The minister was accustomed to taking a walk before dinner, when it was still light. On one of these walks, presumably lost in thought, he walked further than usual, and passed Poppie's little cottage, where she lived alone in a kind of no-man's-land between the white and black areas. She happened to be in the tiny garden, tending her flower beds – she had learned about flowers from Elise van Heerden – and was startled when the minister addressed her in a friendly manner.

From that evening, he took to coming by regularly, stopping to have a chat if Poppie was in the garden.

Some months after the minister had come to Jacques's home to preach against the complex racial and gender improprieties purported to be tolerated in the Nel home, Greta found Poppie vomiting in the bathroom. Weak and exhausted, Poppie confided that she was having a love affair with the minister. Greta, who thought she knew her friend well, was astounded: not only was the man a white religious leader, he was fifty years old, married to his second wife, father to five children and grandfather to six.

Poppie was pregnant with her lover's child. Greta urged her to tell him about the pregnancy: a solution must be found, and they needed his help. Poppie obeyed. She offered to leave town and, with the minister's support, have the baby in Kimberley. Poppie later told Greta that her lover seemed in great anguish over his sins, but he told Poppie he loved her, and rather than abandon her, was prepared to leave his family. This meant, of course, that he would sacrifice his ministry and his exalted position in the community.

Dumbfounded, she pointed this out, but the minister said that it was too late to concern himself with such earthly matters; he had contravened the laws of God and man with his immoral behaviour, and must pay the price for it in this world.

If you do this, argued Poppie, you will have nothing left. We must find another way.

Her lover was adamant: he had made his choice. Poppie reported his words to her friend: I will have *you,* my darling. We will be together always.

A few nights later, he came to her cottage. After they made love, he boiled water for tea, which they drank from a single mug. They then lay in each other's arms on the bed. (Poppie had told Greta proudly that her lover always insisted on doing this for a few minutes before he left for home.)

Poppie did not turn up for work the next morning. During her tea break, Greta walked rapidly to the cottage, thinking her friend was ill with nausea. The door was unlocked, as it often was. Greta walked into the tiny lounge. She was greeted by silence. And the smell of almonds.

In court, Greta testified that she understood immediately what had happened, and hatred for the minister burnt her throat like acid. She threw open the bedroom door. Poppie and her lover lay on the bed, fully dressed. Her head was on his shoulder, their hands were entwined.

Together always, said Greta bitterly.

Why did she not mention her friendship with Greta Villiers in her letters, I ask Jacques and Danie. She must have been a good friend, but Poppie never said a word about her.

They were the best of friends. I never knew about Poppie and the minister, says Jacques, because Greta thought it was better for me not to know.

If only I had known, perhaps I would understand better, I say forlornly. I feel as if I did not know her at all. She never wrote about herself; only insignificant details about her job, the weather, her flower beds. After I abandoned her as I did, she may have felt her inner life was none of my business.

Did she know what her lover had in mind, Danie?

I do not believe so. According to Greta's testimony, Poppie knew nothing. She thought they would be leaving town together; she told Greta they might even leave the country. The verdict was a murder suicide.

Two

Home

JACQUES WISHES US GODSPEED. Loaded with provisions and camping equipment, we are on our way. Unchaperoned. In spite of my despondency about Poppie, I grin wryly to myself at the thought of what mother would have had to say about that.

I felt bad, says Danie, glancing across at me, that so soon after your arrival I was obliged to give you news that would take your smile away. I am glad it has survived.

The route is somewhat improved owing to the activities of troops in the area, but it is still not much more than a broad track, gloriously illumined by the sun. As we bump along, I am astounded anew at the unbroken blueness of the sky, at the warmth on my bare forearm and my fingers trailing along the creamy skin of the car. The air is sweet and clean, and there seems so much more of it than the small damp crowded breath of England.

Light and space out of time: the sense of anticipation, of freedom, is almost potent enough to displace melancholy. A dust dervish whizzes by and vanishes into the scrub. To the east, in the distance, an isolated storm boils over the lonely land. A knot of purple cloud shoots lightning and a curtain of rain bombards the earth. But the distance is too great to feel its effects.

On a rough patch of track, shortly after our sandwich lunch, the right front tyre bursts. Danie manoeuvres the car with admirable expertise to the roadside, pulling up against a trench of hard sand that is still faintly moist from an earlier thunderstorm. I climb out, pleased to be in the open veld, where I can inspect the earth underfoot for the discreet spoor of small animals and insects. At Danie's request, I hand him tools – the wrong ones – and he waves me away.

After a short stroll and an inspection of the immediate area, which yields nothing of interest, I take the opportunity to admire the rather handsome man Danie has become. His forehead juts a little and the bridge of his nose has narrowed, or perhaps his face has broadened; his lower lip, caught between his teeth, is long and smooth. The veins in the pale skin of his inner forearms stand out as pressure is exerted with the wrench. Of the tall, muscled man at my feet, only his fairness and the extraordinary colour of his eyes recall the boy I once knew.

So, Doctor Nel, I say, wiping my damp forehead with my sleeve, you have not yet answered my question about your future plans.

He smiles, a pleasing upturn of that long lip. You were always persistent. I see that has not changed.

Rising to his feet, he scrubs grease from his fingers with a rag, takes the spanner clutched in my hand and returns the tool kit to the boot. He ushers me into the car, climbs in himself, and turns the key. We drive off, engulfed in dust.

Father wanted me to study in England, but I was concerned about his health and decided Cape Town was much closer if there was a problem. I studied together with two doctors who are starting a general practice in Rondebosch, in Cape Town. They have asked me to join them. The three of us are among the first graduates of the new Faculty of Medicine at the University of Cape Town.

Hmm; interesting. And what of your father?

He swerves to dodge a deep pothole.

Father will be coming with me, of course. His condition requires vigilance and skilled care, and it is better for both of us that we live in a city with a well-equipped hospital.

We cover sections of track so pitted and treacherous that they are almost impassable. After hours of gruelling travel, we reach the Kalahari at last. My bruised limbs and aching back are forgotten: the journey drops from me like a mantle of dust. The glittering bed of my Auob unspools through the wilderness, as dry as the shed skin of a snake, marvellously unchanged. Springbok gaze at us as we pass, and raggedy wildebeest frolic and chase one another. We drive past giraffe, groups of gemsbok, sandgrouse, squirrels, a giant mongoose and a foraging jackal. Within a couple of hours, we are there.

We leave the car in the riverbed, my old hunting ground. It stands heraldic in the sand among the antelope, an alien from another world. We trek together up to the farm. By the time we reach the top of the ridge, we are dripping with perspiration.

A broken chimney lies on its side amid a heap of stones. Beside it, an old iron bedstead that once belonged to my parents stands as if patiently waiting for an occupant, its rusted limbs planted like old bones in the earth. Our dwelling and all the outhouses and shelters have vanished.

The light seems dazzlingly bright. Spangles explode behind my eyes. Heat bounces down from the sky and up from the sand, beating against my head as if bent on murder. I sit on the chimney. Other than the springbok milling in the distance below us, there is not a living thing in sight.

The dream is lost.

So this is it, taunts a voice in my head. The Kalahari has not *forgotten* you: it did not remember you in the first place. It remembered none of you, not even the Bushmen. You were nothing. Mother knew: *Give the desert what you must, but do not expect anything in return.*

I look about me for signposts of our lives; for anything familiar. Nothing draws my eye. The kraal walls have collapsed, become piles of stones that the desert has reclaimed, as it once did the remains of Stone Age people who inhabited the site before us.

Danie guides me into the shade of a kameeldoring that seems much smaller than the one I remember; or perhaps it is because I am no longer the child that knew it so well. We sit for a while in its shade. I lie back on the sand, I do not know for how long, until his voice rouses me.

Let us walk a little, Em.

I trail him, seeing Kobie driving us from our farm for the last time, and hearing my mother's bitter words: *Now the desert will not get you as well, Em.*

A sense of unreality settles over me. The home I loved as much as my own life is a graveyard, reduced to blemishes and bumps, to dust and stones on the desert crust. Near what was once the tan-pit – now occupied by a large termite mound – Danie waits for me. His hand brushes my damp shoulder. I tramp on, comfortless, the sharp chalk stone digging into the soles of my good leather shoes. I sit again – it is that or fall on my knees – on a bit of kraal wall that still stands. I would give anything for a single glimpse of my childhood home restored to its former order. I would give my life for a sight of father. For a sight of all those I love who have abandoned this graveyard.

Danie makes camp as the light begins to fail. I huddle miserably, trying to picture Brandbooi's face, Meisie's smile. But they elude me, as does the mystery of what brought our home to ruin.

Where can they have gone? I mumble. What happened here?

My eye alights on a lone tree a little way off, fast fading into the dusk. I get slowly to my feet. Danie is tending the fire.

I find them not far from John Henry's grave, with its crumbling headstone. The row of lopsided crosses is uneven; the names are carved into wood half eaten by termites. There are no dates. Kobie is first, then Meisie, Doekie, Slang and last of all, the last letter of his name eaten away: *Ui.*

A cry resonates eerily through the darkness, which has dropped like a curtain at the end of a play.

The night is the colour of charcoal. Above us, grey clouds nudge each other, clustering together like a herd of elephants in the sky.

The embers of the fire are dying. Danie gets to his feet.

Where are you going?

He turns. I cannot see his expression in the dark.

To sleep, of course. In the car.

That is silly, I say coolly. It would be most uncomfortable after all that driving. The tent is easily large enough for two.

Em, it is not –

Let us go in, I say wearily. There is nobody to see us, nobody we will offend.

Inside the small tent, a star winks through the flap. Danie's scent is of woodsmoke and the crisp night air.

What killed them, I ask desolately. And when did they die?

Em, we will know more in the morning. There will be clues. Are you warm enough?

Warm? I feel as if I will never be warm again.

He reaches for me then. I turn to him; he feels alive, bursting with life. My icy skin begins to burn in his arms, at the touch of his lips. The tent veils us from the silent darkness outside, quiets the strident voices of custom and caution. His sweet heavy heat is everything, exquisitely unlocking what has been buried for all the long years.

I do not know who said what. I do not care.

Kiss me again
Can I touch you
Touch me here and here and there
Your body warms me like a fire
I am a fire
You are a magician
I have wanted this forever
I feel as if I have not lived
You are fresh water
You are my riverbed
Give me your tongue
You are trembling
Am I hurting you
Your body is beautiful
Your breasts are beautiful
Your thighs are beautiful
You are good to me
I want you
I will never stop wanting you
I will make love to you forever
Hold me. Hold me
You taste like a tsamma melon

You smell hot and spicy
Something is biting me
It is me
It is a mosquito
I have got it
I have got you

The moon casts a beady silver eye into the tent. I rub my thigh to restore the circulation.

Are you awake?

Yes. You do not have to whisper, Danie. There are only ghosts here.

His hand strokes my hair. Do you still hate it so much?

My hair? No. It is too blatant for me to like, but others admire it, so I live with it peacefully these days.

It is magnificent. I always thought so. You are magnificent, Em. More so than in my dreams.

He pauses. I have dreamed of you often: about doing this, making love to you. I have made love to you many times.

I giggle. I wish I had known.

His hand, wonderfully warm in the icy night, moves to my ribs, to my breasts.

I never stopped fantasising about you. Even when –

When what?

He groans softly.

I wait, my breath coming faster.

I am engaged to be married, Em. To one of the two doctors whose practice I am joining. We were students together.

The guy ropes of the tent creak in the grip of a gust of wind.

I cannot find a word to say.

Are you angry?

No. But I wish I had the right to be.

I take a deep breath. Is she pretty as well as clever?

She is. But –

I put my palm across his mouth. His tongue touches it. I quiver like a puppy.

Danie, I have been away a long time; far too long. I am happy for you, truly. You have found somebody you love enough to marry.

He moves away. The cold bites like a swarm of ants.

Is there someone in your life, Em?

I shrug in the dark. Three months before mother died, I told her that the professor of education at the college where I earned my diploma was in love with me. She was happy. It seemed to convince her that she could let go; she was not leaving me alone. I had not seen her happy since before she became pregnant with John Henry. How could I refuse her a serene death?

You do not love this man, then? His voice is slightly hoarse.

He is good to me. I hesitate.

I was shattered when Cambridge turned me down, and he was a great comfort.

You have not told me what happened.

There is not much to tell. The committee – a forbidding brotherhood of ancient men and one hunchbacked crone with Parkinson's – praised my results to the sky, but informed me in my interview that the places in the faculty of law were taken up for the next three years. When the spokesperson gave the bad news in his obsequious Queen's English, the old woman shook so much that she almost overturned the chair she was sitting on. There was nothing I could do about it. To them, scholarships are wasted on females. Olivia was more disappointed than I was; I had already applied for a place at the teachers' training college.

I turn to face him. Funny how things work. I met Ian at my very first lecture.

I wake late. I pull aside the tent flap, and the sun pours in. Danie is nowhere to be seen, but a basin of water sits between two stones. I wash quickly. As I finish dressing, he appears, holding out his hand.

Come with me; I have something to show you.

The cross is intact and much larger than the others, with room for the inscription on the wide planks. I recognise them instantly: they are the remains of a few floor planks my parents brought with them when they first came to the Kalahari. For some reason – perhaps they are made of leadwood? – the termites have rejected them.

I crouch on my haunches.

He came back, I say, wonderingly.

You knew this man?

Solomon Cohen, smous extraordinaire. He came back. And I was long gone. I always hoped I would see him again.

I look up at Danie.

Solomon Cohen was special. He loved children and understood them.

He told us marvellous stories. I thought he was a kind of wizard. He had a small feathered face, like a gentle owl. We knew each other for only a few days, but we had an instant rapport. He was a Jew, from a family of rabbis and scholars, and had fled the pogroms in Eastern Europe. He spent his life in his adopted country as a smous.

I touch the cross, tracing my father's engraving with the tips of my fingers, and read the inscription aloud: *Solomon Cohen, harbinger of joy and death. Died of influenza, May 20th, 1909.*

The grave of a Jew marked with a cross, I say slowly. I hope it has not banished him from the Jewish heaven. Even if it has, from what I recall of him, he would be amused at the irony.

I get to my feet. He must have been sick when he got here. He probably caught influenza at one of the villages or farms he visited. Poor Solomon Cohen. He had seen so much death in his life.

Shivering despite the growing heat, I eye the pitiful crosses thirty yards away: Bushmen and Hottentot side by side, their graves also marked with crosses.

I hope they reached their spirit world, I say doubtfully. I hope the smous never knew what he brought with him. How he would have loathed the role of grim reaper!

Some distance from the graves, in a corner of what was once the outermost kraal, the sun's rays illuminate a shining heap of glass. I walk over and inspect it. I pick out one of the few intact bottles and sniff; not even a whiff of spirits remains.

A piece of dirty paper protrudes from the jagged mass. Tugging at it with care, I recognise my own handwriting. I give the heap a savage kick, and glass clatters in all directions across the stones and sand.

The din brings Danie to me. Scattered among the shards of glass are scores of envelopes. Though they are grainy and stiff with dust and weather, the faded handwriting on them is mostly still legible.

My letters to father.

Not a single envelope had been opened.

Three

What now?

THE STATION AT KIMBERLEY is thronged with people. I am grateful, for once, for the struggle to find a porter, for the jostling and petty annoyances of a train journey.

By the time Danie surfaces, I have located my place in the carriage.

I have seen to the baggage, he says. It will be with you shortly.

Thank you. I lean out of the window. You know how grateful I am for everything you have done for me. You have been the best of friends, and a great deal more. I will miss you very much – more than I can say.

I do not understand you, Em, he says, shaking his head. Or perhaps I am not like you. I want more. Much more. I will say it yet again: there is still time. I want you to stay. Stay with me. Come and live with me in

Cape Town.

Danie, our time together in the Kalahari is precious to me. It always will be. You were there when I needed you more than I have ever needed anyone.

(God, worse and worse.)

His lower lip becomes a stubborn line. Empty words. I have no more words to offer you in return, Em. I have said them all. I will not beg.

You have a good life mapped out for yourself, Danie. You are engaged to be married. Do not let a childhood love get in the way.

I try to smile. Your father tells me your fiancée is charming.

She is. But it is you I love. *The woman*. Not the child. Father knows that.

My baggage arrives. The train lurches. There is a noisy clanking of metal.

We must say goodbye, my dear friend. You have a long way to travel home. Please write. And if you hear anything about father and Brandbooi – anything at all –

Annoyingly, tears come again. I brush them away, but they flow freely. Danie hands me his large handkerchief.

Em, he says, Em, do not go! Marry me. Be my wife.

Stop! I cannot.

Why? Why not? You will be happy with me, you know you will. England is no place for you! The war with Germany will bring suffering to millions of people. It is not safe, as your mother believed. It is dangerous, and will become more so!

He reaches up and grasps my arm. I bite my lip, the pain in my chest radiating to his urgent fingers.

I cannot marry you, Danie, I say softly. I am married already. Do you think that mother would have died content had I not first *married* the professor of education – even though he was closer in age to her than he is to me?

He says nothing, his fingers a frozen band around my arm.

For an insane moment, I am poised for him to insist that we will be together no matter what; to pull me from the train by force and take me home.

Instead, his hand drops and he takes a step back.

I see in his face that it is finally over. My childhood. My one true home.

There is a piercing whistle. The train hisses and begins to move.

Looking down blankly, I find his damp handkerchief balled up in my hand. I scan the faces of bobbing, waving people, desperate for a last glimpse of his dear face.

Danie has gone.

Author's Note

Tsamma Season is a work of fiction and the characters are imaginary. Like many works of fiction, the story is inspired by actual events. A family lived and farmed above the Auob, as did the Johannsens, but well after 1914, when the government of the Union of South Africa drilled a series of boreholes along the Auob River to provide their troops with water in the event of a South African invasion of what was then German West Africa.

I first visited the site of the ruins in the late 1990s. I gazed about me at the immense desolation and the heat-glazed riverbed, and felt the magic that captured the imagination of Alf Johannsen. Some years later, these ruins became the little Auchterlonie Museum, built by the people of Upington to depict the life of the family who farmed there.

The stark unassailable beauty of the Kalahari Desert continued to captivate and intrigue me. On each succeeding visit to what is now the Kgalagadi Transfrontier Park, the story grew, as did my admiration for the Kalahari Bushmen, who, having survived the genocidal intentions of all who came into contact with them in the past, struggle with the increasing challenges of the present. I spoke with a number of Bushmen over seven visits. Patat, old and gnarled as a branch of a camel thorn, insisted that he is Bushman: San, he said, is a white man's name. In my story, I have kept to the terms in use at the time to describe people of colour.

I have juggled with time: the Faculty of Medicine at the University of Cape Town opened its doors in 1912, at least three years after Danie Nel finished his medical studies there; and in March 1900, a year or more before Emma and her mother took a steamship from Cape Town to London, The Union Steamship Company and the Castle Packets Company amalgamated, and Southampton, rather than London, became their destination.

Acknowledgements

Grateful thanks to all at Penguin Books, particularly Claire Heckrath, Alison Lowry and Louise Grantham, and to my editor Pam Thornley. Special thanks to Frank for his wisdom and empathy, and to Sally MacEachern for astute observations and loyal friendship.

Refresh yourself at www.penguinbooks.co.za

Visit penguinbooks.co.za for exclusive information and interviews with bestselling authors, fantastic give-aways and the inside track on all our books, from Penguin Classics to the latest bestsellers.

BE FIRST ▼

first chapters, first editions, first novels

eNEWSLETTER ▼

subscribe to receive our free weekly newsletter

EXCLUSIVES ▼

author chats, video interviews, biographies, special features

BLOG ▼

post your comments, chat with other readers

EVERYONE'S A WINNER ▼

give-aways, competitions, quizzes

BOOK CLUBS ▼

exciting features to support existing groups and create new ones

NEWS ▼

author events, bestsellers, awards, what's new

ABOUT US ▼

advice for writers and company history

Get Closer To Penguin ... www.penguinbooks.co.za